COLIN FORBES

THE

SISTERHOOD

MACMILLAN

First published simultaneously in hardback
and paperback 1998 by Macmillan

an imprint of Macmillan Publishers Ltd
25 Eccleston Place, London SW1W 9NF
and Basingstoke

Associated companies throughout the world

ISBN 0 333 71152 1 Hardback
ISBN 0 333 72114 4 Trade Paperback

1 3 5 7 9 8 6 4 2

A CIP catalogue record for this book is available from
the British Library.

Typeset by SetSystems Ltd, Saffron Walden, Essex
Printed and bound in Great Britain by
Mackays of Chatham plc, Chatham, Kent

Author's Note

All the characters portrayed are creatures of the author's imagination and bear no relationship to any living person.

The same principle of pure invention applies to all residences whether located in Britain or Europe. Equally, the Château d'Avignon is pure invention and non-existent.

For my daughter,
JANET

Prologue

Darkness was her friend – and her enemy.

Paula Grey arrived at the address in Vienna in Annagasse after night had fallen. The side street was deserted. On both sides ancient buildings rose up like the walls of a canyon. The deep silence was unsettling and her rubber-soled shoes made no noise on the cobbles. She opened the small door set into one of two huge wooden gates. In past times the gates had been opened to allow horses to haul large carriages into the spacious courtyard beyond.

Closing the door behind her quietly she paused to gaze round, to listen. More oppressive silence. On three sides of the courtyard apertures in the old grey stone led to staircases giving access to different apartments. Paula looked up and saw lights in Norbert Engel's apartment behind closed curtains. Tweed had sent her to warn the only statesman who could save Germany from chaos in an emergency that his life was in danger.

Paula checked the time by the illuminated hands of her watch as she stood in the shadows. Eleven o'clock. Deliberately she had arrived early for the appointment she had made over the phone. Glancing up again she saw a curtain pulled aside high up. The unmistakable head and shoulders of Engel peered down, then vanished as the curtain closed again. It was as though the German was expecting someone else before she arrived.

That was the moment when she heard the outer door from the street opening. She slipped inside an alcove, waited, then stared in disbelief.

The figure of a woman passed under a lantern. She was clad from head to foot in a black robe, her face and head masked by a black veil. Paula stood stock-still, watching the veiled woman enter the staircase leading to Engel's apartment on the fourth floor, then vanish. Was the widowed Engel keeping a secret assignment with a woman friend? Maybe with a married woman – hence the strange garb she wore. Paula waited, conscious of the creepy silence of the courtyard shut away from the world of bustling Vienna. In June there were many tourists in the city.

Five minutes later the veiled woman reappeared, paused before entering the courtyard, then hurried to the door and vanished into the street beyond. Paula glanced up again at the window of Engel's apartment. The curtain was still closed, the light behind it still on. Why was she filled with a sense of deep anxiety? The veiled woman could have called on another occupant in a different apartment – except that the only light showing was in Engel's window.

She checked her watch, made up her mind. She would still be early for her appointment but she strode across the courtyard, entered the same staircase the veiled woman had used. The stone steps were ancient, worn in the middle where people over the centuries had walked. The silence of the building was nerve-racking – as though Engel was the only person to be in his apartment. But this was the holiday season. The locals would be liable to go away to escape the crowds of tourists visiting the city.

The staircase was circular, winding its way up between old stone walls. She paused on the first landing, heard nothing and continued upwards. The building was lit by dim wall lanterns, giving very little illumination, casting unsettling shadows. She reached the fourth floor.

Earlier in the day Paula had paid a brief visit to locate Engel's apartment, to check on potential hiding places in case she was followed. She stopped suddenly, gazing at the heavily studded wooden door leading to the apartment. The door was ajar.

Opened only a few inches, but wide enough to allow a streak of light to spear across the dark shadows. Instinctively she slipped her hand into the special pocket inside her shoulder bag, the pocket designed to enable her to haul out swiftly her loaded Browning .32 automatic.

Gripping the butt, she moved closer to the partly open door. She had the impression someone had left quickly. Her eyes dropped to a small piece of black material attached to the rough stonework framing the doorway. Using her left hand, she gently detached the cloth, thrust it into her pocket. She listened for any sign of life inside the apartment. Silence.

Again using her left hand, she pushed the door open wider, slowly in case it creaked. Silence again. The hinges were well oiled. She continued pushing the door until she felt it touch the wall behind it. Gazing beyond the doorway she was looking into a large stone-walled living-cum-dining room. A heavy Jacobean table was the centrepiece with six wooden chairs round it. Beyond was a tall round ceramic stove, the source of heating for old Viennese apartments in winter. The stone-flagged floor was partly covered with a Persian rug. She walked softly over the stone flags, reached the rug and eased her way round the table.

In the right-hand wall a single arched wooden door was half open. She paused, listened for the faintest sound of life. There was none. Holding the Browning in front of her, gripped in both hands, she approached the door, alert for any kind of sound. Nothing. As though no one lived here. Arriving at the door, she glanced back, checking to make sure no one was behind her. Then, peering through the open doorway, she froze.

Norbert Engel was seated behind a large antique desk and the bookcase-lined walls suggested this was his office when he visited Vienna. Ice-cold, her nerves under perfect control, Paula looked behind the half-open door to check no one was waiting for her hidden behind the solid slab. No one. She advanced slowly towards the desk, her eyes everywhere, but they kept staring back at the German.

Engel's chair was a leather-covered swivel type. His body was slumped forward over the desk, one large hand close to a Luger, a 7.65 mm pistol. The back of his head was blown off, spattered over the desk, a grisly mix of bone and blood.

Paula walked round the back of him, saw his stocky legs sprawled under the desk because the chair was so close to it. He wore a dark-blue business suit, a white shirt, soiled at the front with more blood. Attached to the muzzle of the Luger was a very modern silencer. Which explained why, waiting in the yard below, she had not heard the shot.

Pointless to check his pulse. Returning her Browning to its pocket in her shoulder bag, she took out a small camera and took four flash shots from different angles. After returning the camera to her shoulder bag she put on a pair of surgical gloves she always carried. Protruding from the top drawer to the right of Engel's slumped body the end of a sheet of paper was just visible. Opening the drawer a short distance, she extracted the sheet. It was headed *Institut de la Défense*. She read a list of names. Seven were crossed out with a single ink line. All had been assassinated. One name startled her, the name Tweed, her boss at SIS headquarters in Park

4

Crescent. She looked for the last time at Engel, touched his left hand with her own gloved hand. Rigor mortis had not yet started. She mouthed the words soundlessly.

'Poor devil. You're number eight. Suicide my foot...'

Before leaving the apartment, the sheet of paper folded, inserted inside her shoulder bag, she used a silk handkerchief to wipe the outer door where she had touched it, removing all trace of her fingerprints. Then she began the nerve-racking descent of the weird staircase.

The building seemed to close round her as she moved from one landing down to the next. Still no sign that anyone else was inside the place. Creepy. Like a mausoleum. She held the Browning in her hand, stopped frequently to listen and heard only the eerie silence of the grave.

Reaching the courtyard, she paused for the last time. Then she headed swiftly for the small door which led into the side street. She had removed her gloves earlier and made no attempt to remove fingerprints from that door – she was too anxious to find herself in a street with people.

The night had become very hot and humid. Annagasse appeared deserted. So why were her nerves beginning to tingle? Halfway to Kärntnerstrasse, the main shopping street, she glanced back – just in time to see a man vanish into the courtyard she had left. Something moved in the shadows. Careful not to break into a run, she walked more swiftly. At the exit to the main street she turned briefly, looked back. A short, heavily built man clad in a windcheater, a beret on his head, was hurrying towards her.

She entered Kärntnerstrasse, breathed a premature sigh of relief. Had she gone straight back to the Hotel Sacher they would have known where she was staying.

Instead she turned right, strode down the middle of the pedestrian street – no traffic allowed. There were far fewer people about than she would have wished for. As she progressed towards the far end she glanced to either side, as though scanning the windows of the expensive shops, many of them illuminated although closed. To her right the stocky man, now minus beret, was talking into a mobile phone, keeping close to the shops. To her left a tall thin man with a hooked nose, a slight stoop, kept pace with her. She was caught in a pincer movement. What were they planning now? The kidnap attempt came at the end of Kärntnerstrasse where traffic flowed.

Paula was distracted by catching sight of a woman walking ahead of her. Her hair was auburn, thick, trimmed just above her shoulders. She wore a sleeveless white cotton blouse, a navy blue short straight skirt, and carried a Chanel carrier bag. She would be in her thirties, Paula estimated. When she glanced back Paula saw she was very beautiful, walking with elegance. But it was the body language which hypnotized Paula. Twice she had seen the veiled woman, who had entered and left the staircase to Engel's apartment. Could it possibly be the same woman?

The more she watched the woman, who had only glanced back once, the more certain she was it *was* the same woman. What had happened to the black robe and the veil? Paula began to think she must be wrong, then she looked again at the Chanel carrier and knew she was right. At that moment the stocky man approached her.

'Excuse me, you ha-a-ve dropped something.'

East European accent. Paula kept walking as she replied, 'Go and pick it up, then . . .'

He sidled away from her, continued his patrol close

6

to the shops. Paula looked ahead. The auburn-haired woman had disappeared. Nowhere to be seen. Her attention had been diverted so Auburn-Hair could vanish. She reached the end of Kärntnerstrasse and a large black stretch limousine had cruised to a stop close to her. The driver leaned over, threw open the rear door. Paula stopped. A sweaty hand closed over her mouth from behind, began to push her into the car.

Paula knew that the only chance of escaping being kidnapped is at the moment when the onslaught begins. Her body twisted like a snake's until she was facing the stocky assaillant. She raised her leg, pressed the sole of her shoe against his shin, scraped it down with all her strength. He grunted with pain. She jerked up her right knee and hit him in the groin. As he doubled over, groaning horribly, she saw the thin man with the hooked nose coming for her with a rope between his hands. She was reaching for her Browning when a third man, a huge apelike figure, appeared to her left. A hand like a vice pinned her gun arm to her side and she knew she was hopelessly outnumbered.

'I wouldn't do that, old chap. No way to treat a lady.'

A familiar upper-crust voice, calm and sardonic. Marler. A close colleague of Paula's at the SIS. An arm covered in a cream-coloured sleeve wrapped itself round the ape's throat, cutting off his windpipe. The ape's eyes bulged, his body sagged away from Paula. The voice spoke again.

'I say, Paula, attend to the driver. Get info.'

As she moved round the car Marler suddenly threw the ape forward, crashing him into the hook-nosed attacker. Paula darted to the driver's window, Browning in her hand. The window was down. She aimed her automatic point-blank at the driver, a weasel-faced thug.

'You've got ten seconds to live,' she snapped. 'Turn off the ignition. That's a good boy. Six seconds to live, then I press the trigger. Who is your boss? I'll know if you lie.'

'Assam,' the driver croaked.

The sound of a patrol's car's siren was approaching rapidly. Marler had used the butt of his Walther to eliminate Ape and Hook-Nose. He heaved the two bodies one by one into the back of the car, slammed the door shut, ran to the front, tore open the door where the weasel-faced thug sat terrified under Paula's gun. Leaning inside, he snatched the ignition key out of the lock, used the other hand to hit the driver across the forehead. The head slumped over the wheel.

'We get moving instanter,' Marler called out to Paula.

They crossed the street with the immense spire of the Dom looming on their right. Marler hustled inside the entrance to Do & Co, a fantastic erection of modern architecture with a curved glass front many storeys high. Before Paula knew what was happening they were inside an elevator, Marler had pressed the button for the top-floor restaurant and they were walking into a modernist restaurant with tables by curved windows looking straight across at the Dom. The giant ancient cathedral sheered far above them.

'This place,' Marler explained, 'is trying the experiment of staying open very late.' He ordered drinks. Then listened with close attention as Paula told him what she had seen and experienced. She showed him the fragment of black gauze she had extracted from the stonework, then the pictures which the camera had automatically developed and printed.

'Something diabolically wrong here,' Marler commented. 'This is murder. We'll call Tweed from the Post Office early tomorrow morning.'

8

1

Tweed, Deputy Director of the SIS, was eating a hearty breakfast at Summer Lodge, an outstanding country hotel in Dorset, on the edge of the village of Evershot. His dining companion was Bob Newman, famous international foreign correspondent, who had long ago been fully vetted and helped Tweed on dangerous missions.

'Do you think Willie could be connected with this series of assassinations of top men in Europe?' Tweed asked in a low voice.

Tweed was a man of uncertain age who wore horn-rimmed glasses, the type of person you could pass in the street without noticing him – a factor which had helped him many times. Of medium height, he radiated an air of calm and iron self-control in any situation. Clean-shaven, the shrewd eyes behind the lenses missed nothing.

'By Willie you mean Captain William Wellesley Carrington,' Newman replied. 'I've checked him out and, as you know, he owns a bit of land near the village of Shrimpton. He's also an arms dealer on an international scale. We know he's an ex-member of the SAS – but he's adopted the captain title to impress people, although he *was* a lower-ranking officer. What I can't find out is where his money comes from – unless it's from arms. Not inherited – that I do know.'

Newman was in his early forties, five feet nine tall, also clean-shaven and had thick flaxen hair. His features were strong and many women found him attractive, although he rarely responded to their overtures. He had high-level contacts all over the world, which Tweed found useful.

'So there is a question mark over Willie,' Tweed mused. 'Otto Kuhlmann in Germany reported Willie was visiting Stuttgart when one of the assassinations took place one week after his visit. Chief Inspector Loriot told me Willie was in Paris just before the assassination of another of Europe's elite – in Paris. Arthur Beck, head of Federal Police in Berne, told me Willie was in that city a week before the assassination there. Once, twice could be coincidence. Three is once too many. In any case I don't believe in coincidence, as you know. And what about Tina Langley, Willie's girlfriend? They talk about her as though most men would give their eye-teeth to know her – she's so attractive.'

'The glamorous Tina has disappeared. Not seen in the usual pubs and bars she haunts for weeks. Just vanished overnight.'

'I find that a trifle sinister. Then there's Amos Lodge, the eccentric strategist who advises governments. Any news about him?'

'Yes. He's in residence in a small thatched cottage he owns just outside Shrimpton.'

'Shrimpton again. I'd like to visit that village after dark.'

'Only if I come with you,' Newman said firmly.

'Morning paper, sir,' a waitress said to Tweed. 'I'm sorry, but they arrived late today.'

'Thank you.'

He opened the folded newspaper and the banner headlines hit him.

NORBERT ENGEL COMMITS SUICIDE
GERMANY STUNNED WITH SHOCK

'Look at this.' Tweed handed Newman the paper. 'We've got to get moving.'

'Suicide?' Newman's expression was grim. 'Don't believe a word of it. The other seven were classed as suicides.'

'But the police everywhere unofficially – at the moment – call them murders.'

Tweed stopped speaking as the waitress reappeared.

'Excuse me, sir. There's a call for you. The lady's name is Monica.'

'I'll take it in my room.' Tweed was already on his feet. He waited until the waitress had gone. 'I'm sure this isn't the sort of place where whoever's on the switchboard listens in. But go and chat to the operator while I take the call . . .'

'Will do.'

Tweed ran upstairs to his tastefully decorated bed-room, which overlooked the hotel's garden and open countryside beyond. He picked up the phone, knowing that by now Newman would be inside the room with the switchboard.

'Tweed here.'

'I've had an urgent call from your friend, Otto Kuhlmann. Wants you to phone him back within one hour. Then he's leaving on stand-by aircraft for the land of Strauss waltzes. Marler is waiting on another line I'm holding. He's in a post office. Kuhlmann first, I suggest.'

'Thanks. I'm going off the line.'

Tweed had detected a note of anxiety in Monica, for many years his competent, trustworthy assistant at Park Crescent. He put down the phone, lifted it again, pressed the numbers of the private phone of Otto Kuhlmann in

Wiesbaden from memory. The German Chief of Criminal Police answered at once in his growly voice. He spoke perfect English.

'Who is this?'

'Tweed. Monica passed on your message.'

'You've heard the news?'

'I just read it in the paper.'

'Suicide? You have to be joking. I'm on my way to Vienna soon as I've finished this call. I know the police chief there – in any case the victim is a German national.'

'Paula and Marler are there.'

'How do I contact them?'

'Both are staying at the Sacher. Otto, don't arrest anyone – just have them followed if you find a suspect.'

'If you say so. Have to fly now. Literally . . .'

The connection was broken. Again Tweed put down the phone, waited a moment, called Monica.

'Marler is still on another line,' she said instantly. 'I'm transferring you to him. Now.'

It was Paula he found himself talking to. He listened while in her concise manner she reported her experiences from the moment she had entered the building on Annagasse. She told him she had extracted the name Assam from the driver. Tweed gripped the phone a little tighter as she described the kidnap attempt.

'Thanks for sending Marler to back me up. I didn't know he was anywhere near this country.'

'You weren't supposed to know. You wouldn't have liked the idea.'

'You're right – I wouldn't. Thank Heaven you did what you did. Bless you.'

'No time for that. I've spoken to Otto. He's flying out there now. I've told him you're both at the Sacher. Both of you wait until he contacts you. That's an order.'

'Which will be obeyed. You have grasped that the

sheet of paper I took away has a *full* list of all members of the *Institut de la Défense*?'

'I know what you mean.'

'Any product where you are now? Or maybe I shouldn't ask.'

'You just did,' he pointed out to her. 'Something weird here. Haven't put my finger on it yet. Must go now. Take care. Stay with Marler.'

'I promise.'

Monica, who had been listening in, which was part of her job, came back on the line.

'Any further instructions?'

'Yes. Phone Loriot, then Arthur. Tell them what you heard. Give them a request from me. Don't arrest any suspects – just have them followed. That's it . . .'

'Don't go, Tweed. Howard wants a word with Bob Newman.'

'Hold the line.'

Puzzled, Tweed left the room, locked his door, hurried down the staircase. Howard was the pompous Director of SIS, a chief he often concealed his movements from, but in a crisis Howard had his feet on the ground. He reached the room where Newman was chatting up the girl handling the switchboard.

'Bob, Howard's on the line. Wants to speak to you. Here's the key to my room.'

As Newman left Tweed began talking to the girl, asking her about her holidays, where she went. Upstairs Newman picked up the phone, identified himself.

'Bob . . .' Howard's plummy voice sounded tense. 'I'm making a very strong request to you. I've read the papers and heard from one of my own personal contacts. Could you, please, be sure not to let Tweed out of your sight. I sense danger. Do that for me, be a good chap.'

'Tweed won't like it.'

'I know. Don't tell him. If necessary be devious. Can I rely on you?'

'That's a question you shouldn't have asked. You've had enough experience of me. Thanks for the warning.'

'I'll sleep easier now. Bye.'

What on earth is going on? Newman wondered as he slowly made his way back downstairs. He had never before known Howard to express such anxiety. Tweed talked to the girl for a few more minutes, then walked out with Newman.

'Bob, let's go for a wander in their garden.' As they walked out into the courtyard leading to the extensive garden he asked the question Newman knew was coming. 'What did Howard want?'

'To make sure I wouldn't be dashing off on some assignment for *Der Spiegel*. He thinks the situation down here calls for at least two of us to cover the ground.'

'I see,' said Tweed, who saw perfectly. 'Now I have a lot to tell you . . .'

He gave Newman all the details of his phone calls. He included every single detail Paula had provided. Newman listened without saying a word, waited until Tweed had finished. They were wandering round the splendid walled garden of Summer Lodge, which was more like a small estate and beautifully laid out. A curving gravel drive led to the distant entrance and no one else was about. Everything was perfect.

'Why did you warn Arthur Beck, Chief of the Swiss Federal Police, as well as Kuhlmann and Loriot, not to arrest suspects – just to track them?'

'Because I feel a phantom network closing round us – look at the attempt to kidnap Paula, the systematic way they followed her down Kärntnerstrasse, the thug with the mobile who had obviously summoned the kidnap car to be waiting. I am now casting out our own

14

network to locate who is behind these sinister actions – involving eight murders.'

'What is this *Institut de la Défense*?'

'A kind of club of the top brains in Europe – men who know not only that something appallingly menacing is facing Europe but are using all their influence for Europe to rebuild a huge defence system. Before it is too late.'

'Who is the enemy?'

'We don't know. It's not Russia – that much we have established.'

'We? I've heard of the outfit but I didn't know you are a member.'

'We try to maintain a low profile. You are probably one of the few people – with your worldwide contacts – who has heard of us. Apart from myself, they are the elite of the continent. None has official positions – as you know Norbert Engel was not, never has been, a member of the German government. But he was making headway, persuading Bonn it should consider expanding its army, to purchase the most advanced powerful weapons in the world. Now I think we had better investigate that village, Shrimpton. Something odd about it. And I'd like a chat with Willie – and with Amos Lodge.'

'I'll drive you there. I wonder what is happening to Paula and Marler? They're in the firing line.'

On the afternoon of the same day Otto Kuhlmann walked inside the world-famous Hotel Sacher in Vienna. A short, barrel-chested man, he was very like the film star Edward G. Robinson. His head was large, his mouth wide and from it protruded his trademark, a large cigar. His appearance intimidated those who did not know him well. Aggressively he marched up to the reception desk, glared at the man behind the counter. He briefly flashed his identity folder.

'Chief Inspector Kuhlmann of Kriminalpolizei,' he growled. 'Show me the card index of guests arrived during the past seven days,' he said in German.

'You're not Austrian police,' the man behind the counter stammered.

'There's a letter from the chief of Vienna police.' Kuhlmann slammed down an envelope stamped with official insignia. 'Authority to operate here. Don't waste my time while you read it. Give me the index. Then waste your own time reading the damned letter if you must.'

Without further question the receptionist produced a card index, pushed it across the counter. Kuhlmann puffed cigar smoke in the man's face as his nimble fingers riffled through the cards. He found Marler's room number, then Paula's. Shoving the index back across the counter he stared at the receptionist.

'I may report your lack of cooperation. Keep your mouth shut. You could be in big trouble . . .'

On which note he headed for the elevator. There was no reply from Marler's room. He headed for Paula's, hammered on the door.

'Who is it?' a cultured voice demanded.

'Otto Kuhlmann.'

Marler, his Walther in his right hand, opened the door, admitted the German, closed, locked it. Kuhlmann looked at the gun, spoke with mock amusement.

'Going to shoot me?'

'Not at the moment.'

Kuhlmann saw Paula sitting on a couch. Slim, with dark hair neatly trimmed just above her shoulders, she had excellent bone structure, was attractive and had very good legs. She wore a cream blouse and a dark-

16

blue skirt, and her only jewellery was a pendant supporting a green stone round her neck. Kuhlmann grinned, went straight over, bent down and kissed her on the cheek.

'Hear you've had a tough time. Vienna is a tough city.'

'So I'm beginning to find out. How do you know? And you got here quickly.'

'I move.' He sat down on the couch beside her, stubbed out his cigar. 'So do you. Tweed gave me a résumé of your visit to Annagasse, the kidnap business. Since I flew in from Wiesbaden I've been to the scene of the crime, to the morgue where they took Engel's body. Someone pretending to be Engel phoned headquarters here, asked for protection, reported a prowler.'

'What time would that be?' Paula asked quietly.

'Midnight.'

'Then "pretended" is the right word. I found him dead at about eleven. Why the fake phone call?'

'Oh, that's easy.' Kuhlmann waved a large hand. 'They – whoever they are – wanted it to hit today's newspapers. I gathered from Tweed you had the wit to take several flash shots of Engel.'

'Here they are.' She produced the prints from inside her shoulder bag. 'I'm not sure why I did that.'

'Glad you did.' Kuhlmann's voice rose, then he got up and switched on the television. 'If this room is bugged that will scramble our conversation.'

'And why may the room be bugged?' Marler enquired.

Kuhlmann looked at Marler who was leaning against a wall and had lit a king-size. He saw a slim man, five feet eight tall, always well-dressed, clean-shaven with light brown hair; a cool man who was the top marksman in Europe. His tone was sardonic and nothing ever ruffled him. He was wearing a linen jacket and razor-edged creased slacks of the same cream colour. Kuhlmann liked, admired him.

'Because you two have been booked here in separate rooms for two days. Plenty of time for the opposition to slip inside while you're out with a master key.'

'And who, may I enquire, is the opposition?'

'Wish to hell I could find that out. No police chief has the faintest idea, neither have the Intelligence people. But my bet is this is the start of something pretty big – eight assassinations so far of the top brains in the world. Someone is laying the groundwork for a catastrophe of historical dimensions. At least that's my opinion. We may not have much time to identify who is behind this campaign.'

'Which is Tweed's opinion,' Paula said quietly.

'Then I'm right.' Kuhlmann took the photos Paula had handed him and spread them over a coffee table. 'You've seen these, of course?' he asked Marler.

'I have.'

'Then take a look at these photographs, both of you.'

He extracted photos from his jacket, spread them out alongside Paula's. She leaned forward and frowned as Marler peered over her shoulder. They showed Engel slumped over his desk – but now his right arm drooped by his side and the Luger lay on the floor.

'He wasn't like that when I saw him,' Paula commented. 'You can see from my pics. I don't understand.'

'I do,' the German said grimly. 'The killer botched this job. If Engel had blown the back of his own head off the Luger wouldn't have landed neatly on the desk. His gun hand would have sagged by his side and he'd have dropped the weapon. So my bet is the man you saw slipping inside the Annagasse building after you'd left went there to check. He saw the mistake, hauled Engel's right arm off the desk, then placed the Luger on the floor. Paula, you were there about eleven at night, Tweed said.'

'I was.'

'These photos were taken by the police photographer when the scene of the crime team arrived in response to the fake phone call from the man saying he was Engel. They got there about midnight. Suicide? Forget it.'

'I thought it was murder,' Paula said in the same quiet voice.

'Like all the previous seven – where again it was made to look like suicide,' Kuhlmann went on grimly. 'I checked the records. We have cases of suicide by the victim shoving the muzzle of a gun into his mouth, by placing it against one side or the other of his head. But how can anyone be sure of killing themselves by placing the muzzle against the back of the his or her head? I've acted it out myself with an unloaded Luger – the position is too damned awkward. No one would even try it. Then there's your sighting of the veiled woman, the weird business of your seeing the woman dressed normally on Kärntnerstrasse later. I can't make head or tail of what is happening. But we need a lead – just one lead. What are you two doing?' he asked suddenly.

'Tweed has ordered me to stay close to Marler, to stay in this part of the world,' Paula replied.

'Like the first part – not so sure about the second,' Kuhlmann responded. 'There's been a violent prison breakout by those men who tried to kidnap you. Haven't told you about that.'

'Then why not tell us?' Marler suggested.

'Last night the police arrested the three men who attempted to hijack Paula. Tried to interrogate them. None of them would say one word. Had no means of identification on any of the three. Locked them up for the night. In three cells next to each other. Not very clever. Dawn comes. A big man they said looked like King Kong—'

'The Ape,' Paula interjected.

'Fits the description I was given. At dawn the Ape starts kicking up hell, complaining he's ill. He was injured, had trouble walking. The night guards let him out. The other two cell doors are thrown open from the inside – must have been an inside job. A small stocky man produces a machine-pistol, guns down three guards. All are dead. The Ape can't move because of a damaged leg. The small man turns the gun on him. They blast their way out. Outside a car is waiting. They dive inside and they're gone.'

'Trifle ruthless, that,' Marler mused. 'Killing one of their own when he can't make it.'

'I don't know how you two managed to knock them out during the kidnap business,' Kuhlmann commented. 'I know you are both good – but you were up against top professionals.'

'We weren't too polite,' Marler told him.

'I said earlier we needed just one lead. We might just have got it. The stocky one had flushed something down his toilet, but what he tried to destroy got stuck. One of the surviving guards found it, had it disinfected. I persuaded my friend, the chief of police here, to give it to me. Brochure of a hotel. Here it is.'

He handed a creased folder to Marler who looked at it. Then he passed it to Paula.

'That might be our lead. Hotel Burgenland, Eisenstadt. As I'm sure you know, Burgenland is the most easterly province of Austria. Borders on Slovakia to the north, on Hungary to the south and east. Wild, remote territory.'

'We'd better pay it a visit,' Paula said calmly.

'I can't recommend such a trip,' Kuhlmann warned.

'And I'm still mystified that the killer of Engel appears to have been a woman.'

'In this age of equality women can be greater villains than men,' Paula told him.

2

The battered Volvo estate car sped across the vast plain well east of Vienna which was Burgenland. The metal body was crumpled, the windows covered with meaningless graffiti which concealed the occupants. At a fork in the deserted landscape it swung north towards a strange mountain rising three hundred feet above the plain. Along the summit of the great barrow-like eminence stood a large long one-storey building.

Behind the hook-nosed driver sat a woman garbed in a long black robe. The black material extended from the top of her head, her face masked by a veil. Her white hands clenched together nervously. She turned to the stocky man beside her, swarthy and unshaven.

'Where are we going?' she demanded.

'Shut your stupid face. You made the mistake,' he snarled, his deep voice mouthing an accent she couldn't identify.

'You're such a nice polite little fellow,' she told him cheekily.

'Always the politeness,' he replied, mistaking her meaning.

'You smell of cordite,' she taunted him. 'Killed a lot of people this morning, have you?'

The unintended accuracy of her remark enraged him. His hairy fists tightened. He would have loved to smash her face in, to spoil her extraordinary beauty for life. He restrained his fury: Hassan would shoot him if he so much as touched her.

'We speak no more,' he snapped through gritted teeth.

'Oh, I like talking to men. Especially to real men.'

She glanced at her companion – guard – and delighted in the confusion her response had caused. She knew she could play the little thug like a fisherman hauling in his catch. Her natural sauciness had overcome her earlier nervousness. The car slowed down as the driver sneaked it across the frontier from Austria into Slovakia by a lonely side road with no checkpoint.

The woman stared ahead through the clear windscreen to check the route it was taking. The road spiralled up the western end of the isolated mountain, reached the summit and she saw the long single-storey house perched above a quarry where she had originally been trained. Now she knew who she was going to meet.

She realized she had messed up at Annagasse but she'd had the feeling someone was watching her. That was confirmed later by Roka, the stocky man at her side. He had questioned her once the car had picked her up from the quiet hotel in Vienna. He had tried to intimidate her, which had amused her.

'What sort of woman follows you down Kärntnerstrasse?'

'I didn't know anyone was following me.'

'You looked back . . .'

'Of course I did. That was to see if you were protecting me. I saw the signal telling me I should disappear off the main pedestrian street. Since I reacted at once what are you waffling on about, you jerk?'

'What is the waffle? The jerk? You insult Roka?'

'As often as possible . . .'

They stopped talking as the car pulled up at the entrance to the strange house with a shallow sloping roof. The house was constructed of plaster walls painted an acid green colour. Only a few small windows were set into the wall and each had a closed, shabby shutter. The moment Roka pressed the button which released the car's door locks she threw open the one nearest to her, stepped out into the blazing sun, holding her black dress to avoid tripping.

Show no fear, she told herself. In any case she wasn't in the least frightened by Hassan. She was simply wary of his childish tricks. She approached the plain heavy wooden door and it opened. Through the veil she stared at the slim man with brownish skin who scared the wits out of his staff.

'Welcome back,' he said.

'I didn't ask to come here,' she rapped back. 'I was escorted here like a prisoner. I don't like that.'

'A thousand apologies,' he said smoothly and bowed from the waist. 'Because of what happened in Annagasse I thought you needed a little more help. A little more training.'

A little more brainwashing, she thought. She was careful not to express her thought in words.

'Please keep on the robe and the veil,' he continued. 'Now be so very kind as to follow me.'

She knew where she was going, knew what she was about to be subjected to. Nothing in her expression gave away her annoyance at this unnecessary waste of time. Hassan took out a key, led the way across a large hall paved with stone flags, unlocked a door, ushered her inside a small room.

Inset into a wall were three powerful strobe lights. They were positioned at eye level and aimed at a high-backed leather chair in the middle of the room. In the wall behind the chair two cine-cameras were attached to the white surface. On each arm of the chair a handcuff was attached with one cuff dangling.

She had endured this previously. Before Hassan could order her she sat down in the chair. The moment she was seated she felt she had made a mistake in showing such confident indifference. She glanced up at Hassan as he bent over her to attach a handcuff to each wrist. His Eurasian face betrayed no surprise – he had assumed she was inwardly quaking, had submitted without protest because she was trembling with fear. He's not all that smart, she said to herself.

'You know what is going to happen,' he whispered in one ear.

'Y-e-s . . .'

She had managed to fake trepidation.

'Then, my dear, I will leave you for a little while.'

She heard the door close behind her, locked. It was now impossible for her to leave the heavy chair screwed to the floor. Weird psychedelic music began blasting from invisible speakers, deafening wild music. The strobe lights began flashing on and off – a blue one, a red light and a green. Strange pictures appeared on the walls, films of men and women cavorting in tempo to the music. A seductive perfume filled her nostrils, very powerful and head-spinning. She crushed a capsule of strong peppermint she had slipped into her mouth when she had left the car. It countered the mind-bending perfume.

Crude brainwashing, she said to herself. An attempt at total disorientation.

Half-closing her eyes, she concentrated on a walk to the sea she had often taken in Devon. She filled her mind with each twist and turn in the path, saw the ocean waves coming in below the cliffs, the freighter she had seen ploughing its way towards the nearest port.

She blotted out the sound of the music by listening to the crash of the waves below the cliffs, neutralized the mad films gyrating on the walls by concentrating on the progress she had seen the freighter making. She ignored the strobe lights which flashed on and off by seeing the picture of the walk in Devon in her mind.

Everything stopped suddenly. The so-called music. The films on the walls. The flashing strobe lights. The peppermint had countered the perfume. She sat very still as she heard the door being unlocked, as Hassan appeared by her side.

Without saying a word he unlocked each handcuff. She made her arms stay limp along the chair. He stroked her cheeks gently to bring her round. She remained like a waxwork figure. He bent down to whisper in her ear.

'You can stand up now.'

She stood up slowly, as though it was a great effort, shook her head, pretending to be dizzy. His strong fingers grasped her arm and she forced herself to hide her revulsion at his touch. Guiding her to another door, he unlocked it and held her still as he spoke in his oily voice.

'Are you all right, my dear?'

Damn his 'my dear' to hell.

'I'm perfectly OK,' she snapped in a normal tone.

'Do not remove the robe or veil. Take this.'

He handed her a Luger. Her fingers clasped the weapon she had practised with for so many hours at the shooting range. She checked the weapon. Fully loaded.

'You made a bad mistake at Annagasse,' he told her in a grim voice. 'Inside this room there is another dummy figure. You have been in there before. Let me see you handle this in the way you should have dealt with Engel.'

She walked quietly into the room which had been carpeted on the previous occasion. No carpet now and the stone flags were exposed. She rested the Luger on a nearby couch, put on a pair of surgical gloves she extracted from a concealed pocket in the black robe. As she did so she stared at the back of a life-like figure sitting in a chair behind an antique desk. They had reproduced the scene she had looked at in Engel's study.

She picked up the Luger, walked one cautious step at a time as she had done in Annagasse, when she had tested the floor for a creak which might have disturbed her target. Pausing, she glanced swiftly behind her – again as she had in the study in Vienna. Checking to make sure no one else was in the room.

Hassan stood with his back to the door he had quietly shut. His arms were folded and there was a sinister smile on his bland face as he watched her. He raised one hand, gestured for her to continue.

The dummy figure at the desk was motionless. It gave her an eerie feeling – Engel, a man noted for his intense powers of concentration, had sat as motionless as this figure, studying a sheet of paper. He had then suddenly slid the sheet of paper into a drawer, ramming the drawer closed. She had moved swiftly, alarmed that he had heard her.

She moved swiftly now. Holding the tip of the muzzle an inch from the head she pulled the trigger. The special silencer attached to the gun muffled the sound of the shot. The top half of the head exploded, scattering shards of bone, hair and blood all over the desk, spilling on to the floor. The figure slumped forward over the desk, both arms outstretched over its surface. Just like Engel.

In a partial state of shock, she still reacted quickly, knowing Hassan was watching. With her gloved hand she lifted the right arm by the sleeve, dropped it so the arm sagged by the side of the body. Bending down, she grasped the right hand, pressed the fingers round the butt of the gun. Then she placed the weapon on the floor, a short distance from the lifeless fingers.

As she stood up, compelling her trembling knees to stiffen, Hassan came forward. He put an arm round her. She turned to face him and he was still smiling.

'Very good, my dear. You have earned your hundred thousand dollars.'

He handed her a fat sealed package. She gripped it tightly, stared through her veil at his smiling face, the smile now tinged with evil satisfaction.

'I've killed another real man,' she said in a steely voice. 'It was a test of nerve. Who was he?'

'No one of importance, my dear. No one will be missed. He was doped, of course – which is why he didn't move.'

'I killed another live man,' she said in a calm voice.

Then she did something which startled even the cold-blooded Hassan. She giggled.

3

At Summer Lodge in Dorset Tweed had taken a decision. He had talked it over with Newman as they took a second walk in the garden of the country house hotel.

'We'll delay our visit to talk to Willie and Amos Lodge at Shrimpton until the early evening.'

'You have a reason for waiting until then?' Newman asked impatiently.

'Yes. First, people are more relaxed at the end of the day, more likely to let something slip. Especially in this glorious sunny warm weather we're enjoying. I'd like to get there when the locals are in the pubs. We might learn something by chatting to a few of them – about the two men we're visiting.'

'Sounds like a good idea. But I sense there's another reason.'

'You do read my mind. I want to be here during the rest of the day where I can be reached.'

'You're worried about something.'

'I'm worried about Paula and Marler. Kuhlmann, as you know, called me from Vienna. He said the two of them are proposing to follow up a lead. They may have a lead, a place called Eisenstadt in Burgenland . . .'

He explained what the German had told him about the hotel brochure one of the kidnap thugs had tried to dispose of before the murderous breakout from prison.

'They sound a pretty tough bunch,' Newman remarked.

'With people like that involved the opposition we seem to be up against sounds highly professional and totally ruthless. I'm trying to stop Paula and Marler going on their own to that wild area. I've called the Hotel Sacher but they were both out. I'm going inside now to phone again.'

Newman followed him inside the hotel and then went to the bar while Tweed ran upstairs to his bed-room. Ordering a double Scotch, Newman sat on a couch close to the bar. As he sipped his drink he mulled over what he knew so far. Some vital element was missing – if only he could put his finger on it.

In his room Tweed had called the Sacher, then he phoned Monica at Park Crescent. She sounded calm but thankful that he was on the line.

'You'll never guess who has just called me. I can get him back on the phone – a safe one . . .'

'Who is it? I don't like guessing games.'

'Sorry. Philip Cardon phoned me! Philip, of all people. I can get him now and switch the line to you.'

'Get him. I'll be out of the room for thirty seconds.'

Laying the receiver on the bedside table, Tweed raced downstairs, then slowed to a normal walk. As he passed the doorway into the switchboard room he glanced inside. He caught a brief snatch of conversation between the girl manning the board and some potential guest.

'I'm sorry, sir. We're pretty fully booked. But since you're a regular I'll juggle with the reservations. It will take me a few minutes. You'll hold on? Good.'

She was absorbed in her task. Tweed ran back upstairs. He picked up the phone and Monica told him Cardon was on the line.

'I'm short of time, Tweed. I'm calling you from Vienna. Couriers are flying from here via Zurich to Heathrow. Each one carries a load of money. In cash. I was urged to report this to you by an unusual character who is known to you. I refer to Emilio Vitorelli. Must go.'

'Thank you.'

Tweed put down the phone, found Newman esconced in the bar with his Scotch. Tweed kept his voice quiet.

'Developments. Another stroll in the garden. Bring your drink with you . . .'

He told Newman what he had learned over the phone. He had a grim expression which Newman noticed as they walked along paths between trim lawns in blazing sunlight.

'Something bothering you?' Newman enquired.

'I called the Hotel Sacher twice to stop Paula and Marler leaving for Burgenland. First time they couldn't be found, as you know. Second time I was told they had both checked out of the hotel. That means they're heading for that weird plain. I wish I was out there with them. I am taking extreme precautions. Butler and Nield are flying out to that part of the world as back-up.'

'They won't get there in five minutes. They have to fly to Zurich, then disembark and take an Austrian Airlines plane to Schwechat Airport outside Vienna. I have visited Burgenland. Weird is the word for that place. There is a feeling of terrible isolation.'

'I admit to a feeling of foreboding,' Tweed replied.

'Amazing that Philip Cardon has come back into our lives. It must be over two years since he left us after he had avenged the torture and murder of his wife. What can he be up to?'

'I predicted he would roam the world. I think he got fed up with that aimless existence, then stumbled on something which just happened to be connected with what we are now investigating.'

'What is this business about couriers flying money to London – large sums in banknotes?'

'Ah, that is something I have told none of you about. It is why we are down here – one reason, anyway. Before Philip told me I knew money was being infiltrated to this part of the world. A Slovene courier was caught at Heathrow flying in from Zurich with an executive case stuffed with banknotes. Luckily, Jim Corcoran, Security Chief at Heathrow and a close friend of mine, as you know, decided to call me first. I asked him to delay the Slovene's departure, then let him go. The courier had documents – forged, no doubt – which made it look like a genuine commercial transaction. Butler followed the Slovene in his car to Dorchester. Then his quarry turned up the road we used to get to Evershot. Unfortunately Butler lost him. He hadn't turned off to Evershot and Butler pressed his foot down.

No sign of the Slovene after Butler passed the turn-off to Shrimpton.'

'And we've found out that the only two men who were in that area who are well off are Amos Lodge and William Wellesley Carrington – both of whom travel to Europe a lot.'

'So far you're right, but I put Keith Kent, the genius at tracing where people get their money, on to the problem. He's reported to me quickly that he can't trace where either of them obtained their wealth.'

'The big fish must be Amos Lodge or Willie,' Newman ruminated.

'Another intriguing problem is where the money is collected from. Remember you reminded me the air route from Vienna passes through Zurich, where you change flights. Maybe it is Vienna, but it could be picked up in Zurich.'

'So why is this mysterious business so momentous?'

'Because Cord Dillon, Deputy Director of the CIA at Langley, called me. American satellites have picked up enormous concentrations of tank manoeuvres in a certain Muslim state. Not Iraq. The tanks are coming in by the horde, supplied by both China and Russia.'

'That does sound menacing,' Newman said quietly.

'Especially when we add the fact that this particular power has built up a huge stock of bacteriological weapons. Plus an advanced type of gas. One whiff of that and opposing troops are paralysed.'

'So our next move is to visit Shrimpton in the early evening. On top of all this Emilio Vitorelli appears to be involved.'

'I'd like to meet Emilio again. He's a riddle.'

Emilio Vitorelli emerged from the Hotel Hassler, strode along in the direction of the Borghese Gardens high above Rome. As in Dorset, the sun was shining out of a clear blue sky. But here, in June, the heat was torrid in the afternoon.

As he walked beautiful women gazed at him with longing. He ignored them. It was not surprising he attracted their attention. Forty years old, a tall man with a lithe gait, his sunglasses were pushed up over his thick black hair. Beneath a well-shaped forehead thick eyebrows were poised over his strong nose, his full-lipped mouth normally twisted in a cynical smile above a firm jaw. Today there was no smile and the women held no interest for a man once notorious for his many and easy conquests.

He wore a smart pale Armani suit and walked with an easy lope, like a panther. A man of many interests, some of them dubious, he had business connections at the highest levels in Milan, New York, London, Paris and Vienna. It was rumoured he had made his wealth in money laundering for the Mafia. Nothing had ever been proved. He had organized the most high-class escort agency in Europe and there were rumours about this – that he profited from blackmail among high society. Again, his enemies had found no proof. The most elegant and aristocratic of women staffed his agency. He met Mario on the Pincio Terrace, above the square of the same name far below.

'You followed the new courier with the money through to the Englishman?' Vitorelli asked in Italian.

'The money went through safely,' Mario replied. 'There was an anxious moment for the courier at London airport when his executive case was opened. He was taken to the Security Chief, but after a while he was released and drove straight to the Dorset village, Shrimpton. Is that the right name?'

'It is.'

Vitorelli was frowning. He pulled down the sunglasses over his eyes, a pair at the height of fashion.

'Let us hope we are on the right track.'

'Yes, we are.' Mario hesitated, unsure whether to bring up the subject, then plunged in. 'You look so sad these days, Emilio. Nothing is going to bring Gina back. You used to be so joyful and brimming with enjoyment of life.'

Behind the dark sunglasses Vitorelli's eyes glazed over. No one except his closest friend, Mario, his most trusted confidant, would have dared to raise the topic of the tragedy. He sensed his friend's discomfort at bringing up the terrible incident. He put an arm round the man's shoulder.

'You are right, Mario. But it takes time to accept what happened. Give me a little more time.'

'Of course. I only wished to show you that I care.'

'I know you care.'

'I had better go. Understandably, I think you prefer your own company these days.'

'Nonsense. Tomorrow you come to my suite at the Hassler and we will get drunk. After the sun goes down.'

'I will look forward to it with great pleasure . . .'

The small fat man, who always reminded Vitorelli of a teddy bear, walked away. Vitorelli placed his slim brown hands on the balustrade, gazing down at the tiny figures of people walking slowly in the heat without seeing them. His mind travelled back to the tragedy of two months before.

He had been on the verge of marrying Gina, an Italian beauty if ever there was one. His whole life as a woman chaser had changed. He had known he could spend the rest of his time on earth with Gina. Then the hated Englishwoman had come into his life.

Arrogant, accustomed always to getting what she wanted, she had wanted Vitorelli. He had treated her with courtesy, had explained the situation, but she would have none of it. Relentlessly, she had pursued him, confident that she would win. He had told Gina of the problem and she had told him to let the woman down lightly. He could remember her musical voice saying it to him.

'You are an attractive man, to say the least. She has a crush on you. Treat her nicely.'

He had followed Gina's advice, had done everything in his power to discourage the Englishwoman. Nothing had worked. There had come a time when the English-woman became convinced that he would never leave Gina. Her hatred at what she considered rejection – something she had never experienced before – welled over.

When Vitorelli was away on a business trip to Zurich she had called at his villa. Gina had opened the door. The Englishwoman had aimed the special phial she was holding, pressed the button which released the jet. Sulphuric acid had splashed all over Gina's face, ruining her beauty for life.

In desperation Vitorelli had taken her to a plastic surgeon. He had assured Gina a great deal could be done to repair some of the damage.

'*Some* of the damage?' Gina had screeched. 'You mean I will still be scarred for life?'

'No, no!' the surgeon had protested. 'I can do a great job for you . . .'

Gina had persisted and, eventually, the surgeon had found himself forced to admit there would always be scars. The acid had bitten so deep. She had left him without making another appointment, her face so band-aged that when she looked in a mirror she felt she was staring at a mask, a quite different woman whose face had been destroyed.

One night when Vitorelli was fast asleep she had slipped out of bed, put on the clothes she had prepared in advance. Calmly she walked to the Pincio Terrace, and without a moment's hesitation climbed over the balustrade and plunged to her death on the square below.

Vitorelli had been distraught, had felt guilty. Earlier that evening he had drunk too much so he could sleep, hoping to escape the nightmare of trying to reassure Gina. Later there had been an incident which converted his grief into cold fury.

He had received a long-distance phone call, doubtless from some other country. The call had been brief, a satisfied, cold, almost detached voice. The Englishwoman had spoken, then slammed down the phone before he could react.

'I warned you, Emilio. If I can't have you no other woman can. Goodbye . . .'

From that moment the idea of revenge had come to him, the iron had entered his soul as the British sometimes said. So far he had not located her whereabouts but his many underground contacts were supplying him with information. He was working on it. Justice would be done one day. He was working on it in the most devious manner, aware that he was swimming in dangerous waters.

4

In his office inside the strange house in Slovakia perched on the edge of a sheer quarry wall which fell three hundred feet, the man who called himself Hassan walked briskly to a corner. His massive steel safe was located in the corner. Operating the combination, he swung open the door, extracted a file, closed the safe.

He took the file to his desk, which had weird

hieroglyphics engraved in the leather top. Settling down in his chair he opened the file. It contained several typed sheets, the one he was looking at listed the members of the Institut de la Défense.

In a similar manner to what Engel had done on his list Hassan had crossed out the names of seven members who had been assassinated. But on this list there were the initials of three different women, all of them attractive but with very different personalities. The Englishman in Dorset had drawn up the list – and so far his insight as to which of the women would appeal to a certain type of man had proved flawless.

Hassan crossed out the name Norbert Engel. Alongside his name were the initials *T. L.*, the woman he had subjected to the ordeal in the training room.

Hassan had a habit of talking to himself as he worked. 'The next target is Pierre Dumont. Most important. The man is a strategic genius. I see our Dorset friend recommends Simone Carnot. Dumont must be interested in tall redheads. He lives in the outskirts of Zurich. I must contact Simone, give her the data on Dumont . . .'

It was early evening when Newman drove Tweed along the country road close to the village of Shrimpton. The sky above the trees lining each side of the road was cloudless, azure blue. Tweed had not spoken since they had left Summer Lodge. Suddenly he sat up straighter.

'Stop the car, Bob.'

Newman reacted immediately. They had seen no other traffic since starting out. Tweed reached over, turned off the ignition, pressed a button to lower the window on his side of the Mercedes.

'Listen to it,' he said.

'To what? I can't hear anything.'

'Precisely. There is an extraordinary silence about this part of Dorset. I noticed it when I went for a walk on my own from our hotel. It's uncanny, almost unnerving.'

'You find it significant?'

'It's an area where anything could be going on and no one would know. We haven't seen a single patrol car since we arrived. It is a district of England hidden away from the world. May seem a bit fanciful, but my sixth sense tells me we've come to the right place. Stop the car again when we reach the outskirts of Shrimpton . . .'

Newman parked in an opening to a field as soon as he saw the first houses. He backed the Mercedes in so they could drive off fast in case of an emergency. Tweed got out, waited while Newman locked the car. The same heavy silence descended on him. They began walking along High Lane, the main street of the village.

Tweed was immediately aware of something very odd about this village. The street was cobbled and on either side huddled together were ancient two-storey houses, joined in terrace fashion. Built of Purbeck stone long ago, each house had a curiously deserted look.

Frayed shabby net curtains were drawn across the windows, making it impossible to see inside. The wooden front doors had not seen a coat of paint in years. But it was the absence of people which disturbed Tweed. There was not a sign of life anywhere. Newman reflected his reaction.

'It must be very dark inside the rooms of these places but I haven't seen a light on inside any house.'

'I had noticed that. Almost as though we are walking through an abandoned village. The atmosphere is quite eerie. There are no TV aerials to be seen either.'

They continued their walk through the brooding silence, which was becoming oppressive, uncomfortable.

There was hardly any street lighting, Tweed noticed, only the odd ancient lantern suspended from a rusty bracket outside one of the houses. They had almost reached the end of the empty street when Newman whistled softly.

'Don't believe it. There's a pub ahead of us, the Dog and Whistle. And it's open – with plenty of lights inside the place.'

'We'll go in,' Tweed decided. 'If any of the locals are in there you do most of the talking while I observe . . .'

As he had expected, the interior of the pub had low-beamed ceilings with large upright oak beams supporting the structure. Between the uprights he caught sight of the wooden counter of the bar, well polished. A large inglenook brick fireplace occupied the right-hand end wall.

He counted eight men in the pub – some leaning against the bar while others sat round small tables in the corners with their glasses of beer. Not a single woman to be seen. Newman led the way to the bar, smiled at the barman, a jolly, red-faced man who greeted him as though he was a regular.

'So what can I do for you two gentleman? Good evening to both of you.'

'I'll have a pint of mild and bitter,' Newman told him.

'The same for me,' said Tweed. He hated the drink, but it was important to merge with the background. 'Seems quiet in the village tonight.'

'Quiet every night,' the barman replied. 'Quiet as the grave.' He corrected himself quickly. 'Shouldn't have said that. You'll think you've arrived at a cemetery. I will have my little joke,' he went on hastily as he served the drinks.

Tweed looked round the pub. The customers were clearly locals – farm workers, probably. Most wore shirts rolled up at the sleeves, corduroy trousers stained with soil marks; they had the weatherbeaten complexions of men who spent their lives working outdoors. Newman turned to an old boy standing next to him.

'I have a couple of friends round here. Haven't seen them for ages. One is Captain Wellesley Carrington. Has he moved? I hope not.'

'The Cap'n.' It was the barman who answered. 'One of the nobs. Don't get me wrong. He comes in here now and then for his pint. Just like the rest of us. Trouble is, he's abroad a lot. You ask Jed there and he'll tell you more than he should.'

Newman turned to the old boy, white-haired and with a stooped back. He ordered him another glass.

'Go on, Jed.' Newman grinned. 'Spill the beans.'

'Bit of a one for the ladies. Seen some real beauties driving in through those gates of his. Classy stuff – at least that be from the ways they dress. Like those pics you see of models in the papers. I wouldn't mind spendin' an hour or two with one of 'em.'

He gave a lecherous wink and the barman, not wishing to be left out of any conversation, intervened. He shook his head at the old boy.

'Face it, Jed – you're long past it. Just pictures in that wicked old mind of yours.'

'You might be surprised,' Jed responded indignantly.

'Still lives in the same place, does he?' Newman enquired casually.

'Dovecote Manor is still his nest for the birds,' Jed said, still glaring at the barman.

'So long ago I've clean forgotten how to get there,' Newman remarked.

'You've got a car? Good. As you goes out of the pub you turn right, follow the road away from the village 'bout 'alf a mile and gates is on your right. In middle of nowhere.'

'I didn't get your name,' the barman said, polishing another glass.

'Dick Archer,' Newman replied quickly. 'I'm in computers.'

'Bet you make a fortune out of them.'

'I earn the odd crust of bread.'

'I have an old friend in this neck of the woods,' Tweed said, speaking for the second time. 'Amos Lodge. Now there's a brain if ever I met one. And as Chief Claims Investigator for an insurance outfit I've met a few. Trouble is I've lost his address.'

He was looking at Jed as he phrased the indirect question. Jed chimed in, ignoring the warning glance the barman gave him.

'He's still at The Minotaur. Used to work for him in the garden. It's a large thatched cottage. Go on past the Cap'n's place, take the first turning to the right. Country lane – only room for one car. The cottage is 'alf a mile down the lane on the left. Can't miss it. No one else lives that way.'

'Amos has been in here once or twice,' the barman interjected, 'and you're right. His mind is so far above mine I can't rightly get what he's saying.'

Tweed realized his tactic had worked. By revealing his fake profession he had reassured the barman. He pressed home the advantage, again staring at Jed as he asked a tricky question.

'Walking down the street to get here we noticed all the houses seemed derelect. No sign that anyone lives in any of them.'

'It's a quiet village . . .' the barman began.

'That tells our friend nothing,' Jed intervened. 'The whole village is owned by a man called Shafto. He rents out the cottages to staff for his place. I live in one of 'em. Can see why you says what you did. Peculiar things go on inside some of those 'ouses.'

'Jed . . .' the barman warned, stopping polishing a glass.

By now Newman had bought Jed another pint, noticing how swiftly he had downed his previous glass. The old boy was well away, but still his mind functioned. He had the eyes of a squirrel as he explained to Tweed.

'Couldn't sleep one night because of the 'eat. Got up, put on clothes to go for a walk and went out into the street. From a cottage lower down I saw an Arab woman come out. She walks off to the end of the village, past the Dog and Whistle. Then I hear a car starting up. Drives off the other way.'

'He has nightmares . . .' the barman began.

'What made you think she was an Arab woman?' Tweed persisted.

'Way she was dressed,' Jed continued. 'Has a black thing on. Covered her from head to toe. And she wore a black veil and that thing on her head Arab women wear. I've seen pictures of them. What was she doing in a place like this? That's what I wondered to meself.'

'That's the only Arab woman you've seen here?' Tweed asked.

'The only one. But it was three in the morning. I'm usually in the land of Nod at that hour.'

'Could have been a woman in fancy dress,' Tweed commented.

Making the effort, he swallowed the rest of his pint, then checked his watch. Newman took the hint.

'Better be on our way,' he said. 'Another pint for Jed.'

Slapping money down on the counter, he followed Tweed out. They chatted as they walked back to the parked car.

'We've come to the right place,' Tweed said grimly.

'Looks like it. Which one first?' Newman asked.

'Willie – also known as Captain William Wellesley Carrington. En route we come to his place and he's the man I want to talk to first. Let's hope he's not on one of his trips abroad.'

The gold-painted wrought-iron gates were open and a curving drive beyond led to Dovecote Manor, a small Georgian gem of a house. Parked on the tarred turn-round close to the entrance to the house was a new red Porsche. Newman moved at a leisurely pace, stopped just behind the Porsche.

'Reeks of money,' he commented. 'Those gates cost a pretty penny. And Heaven knows what he's got concealed behind the closed doors of that double garage by the side of the house. Probably a Roller.'

Tweed said nothing, leaving the car and marching up the flight of stone steps to a terrace and the freshly varnished front door. He pressed the bell, waited. A couple of minutes later the door opened and Wellesley Carrington gazed at Tweed, then smiled with pleasure.

'This is an unexpected delight. Long time no see. Do come in with your friend. I say, isn't he Robert Newman, the famous foreign correspondent?'

'He is,' Newman said without enthusiasm.

Unusually for him, he took an instant dislike to the man framed in the arched doorway. Wearing a navy blue tracksuit, he was about five feet eleven tall, and in his forties, Newman estimated. Well-built, he exuded an arrogant self-confidence verging on the aggressive. His voice was a good public school, his manner said he knew he belonged to the elite and he had a pug nose. His thick hair was a light brown colour with a pencil-thin moustache of the same colour. His eyes were ice-blue and his thick-lipped, sensuous mouth had a beguiling grin above a hard jaw.

A gigolo, Newman said to himself. But a tough one you had to be wary of. A man confident he could dominate anyone, any situation. He gripped Tweed's hand, then shook Newman's. His grip was firm. On the surface he gave the impression he was sociable, glad to have visitors call on him. So why did Newman sense that the timing was bad from his point of view?

'Come in immediately,' he said in an animated tone.

'I hope our arrival isn't inconvenient,' Tweed suggested – which told Newman Tweed also had detected a certain reservation in their host's manner. 'We could always come another time,' Tweed went on, 'but we couldn't get through to you on the phone,' he said smoothly. 'Do say if it's inconvenient, Willie.'

'Damn it! I've just invited both of you in. So come on inside, fellers. We'll have a drink to start with.'

Tweed entered a medium-sized hall with wood-block flooring. In the panelled walls were alcoves with vases of flowers. Closing the door, Willie led them to an open door which led into a drawing room extending from the front to the back of the house.

The room was expensively and tastefully furnished with antiques, a couch as large as a spacious single bed, a scatter of armchairs, a cocktail cabinet with an interior illuminated light, various *objets d'art* on coffee tables which had an Eastern character; the result of his travels, Newman assumed. But what caught his attention was the beautiful brunette lounging on the couch with her legs tucked under her, shapely legs, very much on view. Willie made introductions.

'Gentlemen, this is Celia, my latest girlfriend. Celia, my darling, this is Tweed, and this is Bob Newman.'

'Interesting friends you have, Willie,' Celia commented, staring straight at Newman. 'Such a pity I have to leave now. Another one of those bloody parties I promised to attend in a weak moment. Such a crashing bore but I did accept the invitation.'

She finished the drink in her long-stemmed glass, which Tweed guessed was champagne. Standing up, she straightened her blue, sheathlike dress, which appeared to have been rumpled. She kissed Willie on the cheek, smiled ravishingly at both visitors and with the elegant walk of a model left the room. They heard the Porsche's engine start up and then a scream of tyres as she drove off.

'Girl in a thousand,' Willie commented.

'Bet you always say that,' Newman mocked him.

Willie's expression changed for a millisecond, became venomous, then he replaced the look with his broad smile.

'What's your tipple, both of you?'

'I'll have a double Scotch, please. Neat,' said Newman.

'A glass of white wine for me,' responded Tweed, who rarely drank.

Taking off his glasses, he rubbed them with a clean handkerchief, seated on a corner of the couch Celia had vacated. He put on his glasses and gazed round. A pair of French windows were open at the rear end, looking out onto a large expanse of garden. Inwardly he tensed.

The garden stretched away across a neat lawn and he could see a strange stone arch inscribed with symbols. It had a distinctly Middle Eastern character. Bringing back the drinks on a silver tray, Willie caught the direction of his glance.

'Take you out into the garden later. That arch was shipped to me from Beirut. I take a fancy to things when I'm overseas, try to bring back mementoes. Cheers!'

'Cheers!' said Newman, occupying one of the armchairs. 'I rather liked the look of Celia. What's her second name?'

'Ah!' Willie perched on the arm of the couch at the opposite end from Tweed. 'I can recognize a woman chaser when I meet one. Not going to tell you her surname. She's my friend – for the moment. Drink up – then I'll refresh your glass.'

Tweed was amused. He realized Newman had intended tracing Celia if he could – to get information out of her without any amorous intentions.

'You can't stand the competition,' Newman mocked their host.

He had assessed Willie's character. He steam-rollered people when he could get away with it. He only respected men who stood up to his bluff aggressiveness.

'You think so?' Willie sipped at his Grand Marnier. 'Well, I haven't got where I have without smashing some pretty nasty types into the ground – yourself excluded, of course. The world has become a rough place,' he said genially. 'It comes down to survival. That's the bottom line, survival.'

Newman found he was beginning to like Willie. He was out of the ordinary. A man who went his own way regardless of what more convential types thought of him. He had an engaging smile and Newman could easily see why he was attractive to women. His vitality, the I-don't-give-a-damn attitude, would appeal to the opposite sex. He could also get on with men, provided they were of strong character.

'Tell me again, Willie,' Tweed said suddenly, 'what kind of business you're in.'

'Import-Export. Same as before.'

'Doesn't tell me a thing,' Tweed said. 'So what do you handle?'

'What the West wants from the East, I deliver. What the East wants from the West, I deliver. Crates of Scotch, like Newman is drinking, to Muslim countries. At ten times the price I buy them for over here. There are certain things they'd like I won't touch with a bargepole. I make that very clear to them and they respect my view. Now I'll freshen up our drinks and we can take a walk in the garden . . .'

Newman asked for mineral water, explaining that he was driving. Tweed put his hand over his half-empty wineglass. Willie shrugged, refilled his own glass with Grand Marnier, then led the way out. It was cooler outside than it had been when Tweed and Newman had arrived.

Huge banks of rhododendron bushes flanked both sides of the estate-like garden, masking it from the outside world. They followed Willie along a flagstone path set into the lawn, reached the strange arch. Tweed paused beneath it, stared at the symbols inscribed into the stone. Arabic.

'What do these insignia mean?' he asked.

'No idea,' his host said brusquely.

'But don't you understand Arabic – dealing as you do with the Middle East?'

'I taught myself to speak the lingo,' Willie said in a throwaway manner, 'so as to help with the haggling. But written down I don't understand a word. Contracts are always drawn up in English. Come on, lots more to see.'

Indeed there was. They walked along another path curving round a large lake. In its centre stood an island, and perched on the island was an Eastern statue in stone. A man and a woman were the main feature, with a serpent twined round them. It struck Newman as erotic.

The dead silence of this part of Dorset descended on them as they walked on, turning a corner to see another large lake. This also had an island. Newman stopped and stared. An ancient eight-sided temple-like edifice

46

stood on this island, but what caught his attention were the tall windows, all painted black.

'What on earth is that?' Tweed enquired.

'No idea,' Willie replied. 'But I liked it so I had that shipped over here. There's more to see,' he said quickly and hustled ahead of them.

Curious as to why Willie had attempted to hasten them on, Newman dragged his feet. When he looked back he saw one side was open, the interior illuminated by a huge lantern. Under the lantern stood a large double bed with a Persian rug thrown over it. Willie looked back, saw Newman staring.

'Got a boat to take me over there,' he called out. 'It's an ideal place for me to take a nap, think out a problem without being bothered by the phone or fax messages. Call it my hideaway. At times I need privacy.'

'I'm sure you do,' Newman said cynically.

He was thinking of Celia, of Willie's faint discomfiture when they had arrived, of Celia's swift departure. This is not a normal place, he mused as he started walking after Tweed.

They passed through a narrow closed-in avenue – closed in by seven-foot-high box hedges. Emerging into a wilder, more overgrown area, Willie pointed.

'Another lake. I like water.'

Tweed stood stock still and stared. This large stretch of water was curved in a half-moon shape. Again an island stood near the middle of the lake. This island was shaped like a half-moon, reproducing the shape of the lake. A peculiar squat building occupied half the island. Built of great blocks of misshapen stone, it reminded Tweed of paintings he had seen of the ancient civilization of Assyria. What he found especially odd was a huge stone plaque attached to one rock. It carried the design of the Turkish flag of the present day.

'That's just a bit of fun,' said Willie, now standing alongside his two visitors.

'I have noticed that with each lake you have a landing-stage concealed in the reeds at the water's edge,' Tweed said slowly. 'And each one has a large dinghy with an outboard motor – presumably the way you reach each island.

Willie's manner changed. His face became expressionless. When he spoke his tone was abrupt.

'Time to get back to the house. It's getting chilly.'

Saying which, he hurried back the way they had come, keeping up a rapid pace until they reached the drawing room. He went to the cocktail cabinet, refilled his glass, turned to his guests.

'One for the road?'

'Not for me,' said Newman.

'I'll pass,' Tweed replied. 'Thank you, Willie, for your hospitality. We must keep in touch.'

'Great idea,' Willie said without enthusiasm.

Making their farewells, Tweed and Newman returned to their car. Neither said anything as they proceeded down the drive. They were about to pass through the gates when Tweed spoke.

'Turn right. Keep a lookout for that lane which leads to Amos Lodge's place.' He lowered his window. 'I feel like a breath of fresh air.'

'*Dovecote* Manor,' Newman commented. 'A misnomer if ever I came across one. The house struck me as a front. Once in the garden the place reeked of Roman orgies.'

'That's carrying it a bit far,' Tweed said in a dreamy tone. 'But he knows how to impress visitors from the East. You'll find Amos Lodge a very different proposition.'

5

The same day Butler and Nield received the order from Tweed via Monica to fly to Vienna – to back up Paula and Marler – they boarded a flight for Zurich from Heathrow. In Zurich they were lucky – they just managed to catch an Austrian Airlines plane to Vienna.

'Hope we get there in time to link up with them,' Butler remarked.

'We'll link up. No doubt about it,' replied Nield, who sat alongside his team-mate.

They were very different in appearance and temperament. Harry Butler was heavily built, sturdy and a man who worried. In his mid-forties, he took little trouble with his clothes and wore a windcheater and creased grey slacks. He had put his backpack in the luggage compartment above their heads, next to Nield's. They were travelling as though they were tourists.

Pete Nield was slim with a neat moustache, unlike Butler who was clean-shaven and had a strong jaw. Normally Nield, who was in his late thirties, took a pride in his appearance and had attracted the attention of more than one woman. Now, to fit the part, he was clad in a black Adidas tracksuit with white stripes. He looked by a long way the smarter of the two men.

'I think we ought to hit the Hotel Sacher first before we go out to this Burgenland place,' Butler suggested, always looking ahead.

'I agree,' Nield said. 'My hope is that something has taken them back to the Sacher before they took off into the wild blue yonder. Monica has arranged for a hired car to be standing by for us to collect at Schwechat Airport.'

'Monica never misses a trick.'

'She's the best.'

He checked his watch. Although outwardly cool and in control, as always, he also was worried. The kidnap attempt on Paula, plus the murderous prison breakout of the thugs involved, told him they were up against some pretty ruthless characters.

He wanted the plane to move faster but forced himself to relax. As the machine started its long descent he kept his fingers crossed.

As it happened, chance had kept Paula and Marler in Vienna. After checking out of the hotel, Marler determined to keep Paula close to him. They had locked their luggage inside the trunk of a BMW Marler had hired and parked in a nearby garage.

'We're walking down Kärntnerstrasse,' he told her. 'We only have two handguns. We need more than that – and I know a good man who can supply me – for a price, of course.'

'Do you want an Armalite?'

'It's on my list.'

Reaching the Dom, Marler took Paula inside a crowded department store, told her to wait in the lingerie section. He couldn't take her with him to the arms dealer, who insisted on remaining anonymous.

Checking to make sure he had not been followed, Marler entered an art gallery on Graben, a street of old buildings leading off from the Dom and at right-angles to Kärntnerstrasse. He realized this was the same area where the three thugs had attempted to kidnap Paula before he had intervened, so he was very cautious. He had slipped inside the art gallery doorway suddenly and swiftly.

The owner, Alexander Ziegler, stood with his arms

folded, watching a woman he knew would never buy a picture. He greeted Marler in English, careful not to use his name.

'Welcome back, sir. It has been too long.'

Ziegler was a big man, well dressed in a dark business suit. Very tall, he had a high forehead and hooded eyes.

'I've come to look at that Monet you phoned me about.'

'It is waiting for you in here. Anna,' he called out, 'look after the gallery for a few minutes.'

As he unlocked a door a slim woman with her dark hair tied back to counter the heat appeared. Ziegler ushered Marler inside, closed and relocked the door. On an easel there was a picture which looked like a Monet, but this was pure stage dressing.

'I'm in a hurry,' Marler said.

He gave Ziegler his shopping list and handed over the large canvas satchel slung over his shoulder. The transaction only took a few minutes. With the weapons and ammo packed inside the satchel Ziegler reappeared from the cellar behind a door he had unlocked.

Marler paid for the armoury he had purchased with a large sum in cash. He was out of the shop and hurrying back to the department store in no time. He found Paula waiting for him, fingering some lingerie.

'Pretty sexy,' Marler whispered.

'Not my style. Where to now?'

'Back up Kärntnerstrasse. I'll walk a few paces behind you. We're heading for the garage.'

Paula left him, feeling safe knowing he was watching her. Halfway up the pedestrian street she sensed she was being followed. She glanced across the other side of the street and saw the small stocky thug, one of the men who had tried to bundle her into the stretch limo. She stopped, gazing into a shop window, not knowing that Marler had already spotted the shadow.

51

Roka had been flown back from Slovakia by helicopter with strict instructions from Hassan. He had been alarmed by the ferocity with which Hassan had addressed him.

'You have the description of the woman who followed our contact with Engel. Go back and find her. Bring her here if you value your life.'

Roka had started at the Hotel Sacher, had seen Paula leave the hotel with a slim man dressed in a linen suit. He followed them at a distance. He thought his chance had come when she entered the department store, but going inside he realized the place was too crowded.

Later he followed her back up Kärntnerstrasse, determined to kill her with his flick-knife if he couldn't frighten her into accompanying him to his parked car. Hassan wouldn't be able to interrogate her but would be relieved she was out of the way.

Roka was pleased the man with her had disappeared. He had recognized him as the swine who had successfully prevented their kidnap attempt. He was so intent on watching Paula it never occurred to him to worry about the man she had been with.

Marler had dropped back, had crossed over to Roka's side of the street. Just as Roka had earlier recognized him, Marler had now recognized Roka. With the heavy satchel slung securely over his shoulder, Marler unfastened the flap and extracted a Walther automatic. He continued tracking the thug.

Paula stopped briefly to glance in a shop window – in its reflection she saw Roka, and Marler behind him. She resumed her walk, strolling at a slower pace. How on earth was Marler going to deal with the situation? The street had quite a few people ambling along.

Marler was waiting until Roka reached a certain building. Then he moved. He was alongside the thug in seconds, rammed the muzzle into Roka's side under cover of the satchel. His voice was hard.

'Move inside this place. Slowly. One mistake and you get a bullet in you.'

'This is a church!'

'Get inside, you bastard.'

Roka obeyed, scared by the tone of Marler's voice. The two men went inside the Maltese church. The previous day Marler had explored Kärntnerstrasse, had gone inside the same building, curious that anything connected with Malta should exist in Vienna. The place had been empty.

It was empty now, a vaulted cavern of darkness with a faint light filtering in the gloom. Rows of wooden pews stood on either side of an aisle leading to a distant altar. The babble and hustle of Vienna might have been a million miles away.

Once inside, Marler slipped behind Roka, pressed the Walther against his spine. The thug moved with a slow heavy tread, was urged well down the aisle. Marler then grabbed him by one arm, shoved him into one of the pew spaces.

'Kneel down,' he hissed.

Marler was in a rare rage – controlled but still a rage. He recalled how this thug had treated Paula. Roka, even more frightened by the coldness in Marler's voice, squeezed himself into a kneeling position. The muzzle of the Walther was transferred from Roka's back to his head, just above his thick hairy neck.

'This is how they do it, isn't it? Place the gun an inch from the back of the head and then blow it off.'

'Please, sir. Beg you . . .'

'Begging will get scum like you nowhere. So talk fast and don't stop to think. Where is the headquarters of this outfit?'

'You say what, sir?'

'I don't say anything. I'm asking you a question. And you damn well know I am. Answer the bloody question. Where is the headquarters? Answer now or you'll never speak again, filthy scum.'

'I know not.'

'Take your last breath.'

'Please, please, sir . . .'

'You're a dead man.'

'Slovakia . . .'

'Who is the top man?'

'My knee, sir.'

Roka crumpled forward, his right knee giving way. It was a convincing manoeuvre but Roka had underestimated the man he was dealing with. Forcing himself to swivel round, he held the flick-knife he had extracted from inside his jacket. There was a click, a stiletto-like blade emerged from the carved handle he was holding. He lunged for his opponent's stomach. Marler's movement was so swift a witness would not have seen it. He brought down the barrel of his Walther with ferocious force on the bridge of Roka's fleshy nose.

The thug collapsed, his fall taking him half under the pew. He lay very still. Marler did not wait to check his pulse. This was one of the men who had murdered prison guards in the breakout from an Austrian gaol.

As he walked towards the exit he slipped the Walther inside his satchel, fastened the flap, blinked as he emerged into the blazing sunlight. Paula was shop-window gazing, again using the curved window to watch the Maltese church across the street.

Marler smiled as he crossed the street. He had noticed the expression of anxiety on her face, anxiety for what might have happened to him.

'We walk back up the street to the Sacher,' he told

her. 'I have information for Tweed. It's urgent so maybe we'll try and reclaim our rooms.'

'Why?'

'Because I need a phone to call Tweed. I can code this one. Also I'm not sure now Burgenland is the right place to head for.'

He told her what he had extracted from the thug. She was thoughtful before she replied.

'Shouldn't we get out of Vienna – for your sake? Tell me what happened.'

'I put him out of action.'

'The police may come looking for you.'

'They won't. No one saw us go inside – or observed me coming out. I checked. Let's move it. Got your Browning . . .'

They were able to reclaim their rooms. At Paula's suggestion Marler changed into a polo shirt and a pair of casual slacks, a navy blue and white combination, which transformed his appearance. He went along to Paula's room and she commented on how different he looked. He dumped the heavy satchel behind a chair.

'Goodies,' he explained. 'Here's the Browning and ammo.'

He had just spoken when there was a gentle tapping on the door. Grasping a Walther out of the satchel he went to the door, called out.

'Who is it?'

'Harry Butler, delivering the male. A jerk called Pete Nield.'

Marler let them in, relocked the door. They exchanged the briefest of greetings. There had been so many link-ups like this in the past. Paula felt relieved as each of the new arrivals hugged her. She couldn't rid herself of the feeling that Vienna was a trap.

The Minotaur was exactly as Jed had described to Tweed and Newman. A small gate led to a pebbled pathway between grass and beyond was a large thatched cottage. In the dark purple dusk lights glowed behind the mullion windows. To their right a pebbled drive ran up to a small garage and a Jaguar was parked.

'Willie's place should have been called The Minotaur,' Newman commented. 'And Dovecote would have been more appropriate for this place.'

Tweed pulled the chain which rang a bell inside. There was a pause and the old wooden door swung open. Newman, who had never met Amos Lodge, stared in surprise. He had imagined an aged professorial type.

A six-foot man of large build stood in the doorway with a half-smile on his strong face. Lodge had a squarish head and a short tough nose; his shrewd eyes studied Newman briefly through a pair of steel-rimmed glasses with a double bridge. The lenses were squarish, matching his build. His thick hair was dark and he was clean-shaven. Before he opened his small mouth Newman would have typed him as the boss of a major international corporation.

'Tweed, good to see you. Isn't this Bob Newman? Thought so. Welcome and all that stuff. Come on in.'

None of the effusive greetings they had received from Willie. This was a man who came straight to the point. Newman was impressed by the dynamic energy which radiated from their host.

They entered a neat book-lined hall, passed on through a kitchen-breakfast room with a tiled counter dividing off the kitching from the eating area. Lodge led the way along a short passage into a larger hallway furnished with an oak table, then into a living room with a brick fireplace at one end.

The furniture was comfortable, with a square oak table and four carver chairs round it. Lodge gestured towards the table, asked them what they would drink. Newman opted for a Scotch well watered down. Tweed stayed with a glass of wine. Lodge joined them with his own glass of Scotch as they sat round the table. This was going to be no idle conversation, Newman sensed.

'How much does Newman know?' Lodge demanded, settling himself opposite Tweed.

'He knows about the *Institut de la Défense*,' Tweed replied. 'But maybe you could fill him in on the picture better than I have.'

'Doubt that. But I'll try. Briefly, myself excluded, it's like a club of fifteen men of great talent in their special fields. Men worried, like I am, about the fact that at this time Europe is wide open to attack from the East. Not Russia. We assemble now and again at a mansion near Ouchy on the shores of Lake Geneva, check each other's progress.'

'Progress in what direction?' Newman asked.

'The West is leaderless. We have a bunch of softies at the top: the PM in London, the President in Washington, the Chancellor in Bonn, President of France, and so on. The *Institut* has people with clout, trying to influence our spineless leaders, so-called, to recognize the menace, to do something about it, to rebuild fast the most sophisticated defence systems. So far we're hammering our heads against brick walls. And some organization does fear us – it has wiped out eight members so far. Faking murders as suicides. Eight down and seven to go.'

'Including yourself,' Tweed remarked.

'And including your good self. Then there's the moral issue.'

'Never heard you refer to that before,' Tweed commented.

Their host had refilled his glass with neat Scotch. Tweed had the impression Lodge had knocked back a few before they had arrived. Which surprised him. It was making him more talkative than usual as Lodge explained in his gravelly voice:

'The Roman Empire fell because it became decadent. Every kind of perversion occupied them in the last days. I see the same situation in the West. I believe in equality but women have become the dominant force in the West. They're running the show. The situation shows up in many ways. In fashion you see decadence in the way film stars, society women are dressing – or undressing – in public. "Anything goes" is the motto. Men feel they're a back number. Sure, that's a generalization. I'm not a woman-hater – you know that, Tweed. But the whole fibre of Western civilization is being undermined. In many marriages there is no stability. In the moral behaviour of many people, men and women, all sense of moral values, of decency has collapsed. Our politicians – not all of them – are tarred with the same decadent brush. The same descent into moral chaos applies to America, to Britain, to other key Western countries.'

Amos had spoken with vehemence. Behind the square lenses his eyes glittered with conviction. Tweed asked a question.

'What is your solution to the problem?'

'The assertion of strong leadership in the West. A great deal more discipline, the restoration of stability. No good, I fear, looking to the Church. Few people place any real value in it any more. Take the films people see, the pictures our so-called artists paint. It is a descent into bestiality. Not always, I grant you, but too often, too widespread. As I said earlier, anything goes.'

'Could you be a little more specific?' Newman suggested.

'There is a moral and military vacuum. We are wide open to the imposition of a stronger code of behaviour from the East. I refer to Muslims. Not the Fundamentalists – to more extreme groups who have taken control behind the scenes. They know what they are doing – which is why they are wiping out members of the *Institut de la Défense* one by one. They fear our influence might just reach the top, that the West will rearm. The East is confident it has a moral code it can impose on the West, once we are overwhelmed.'

'Men first, women walking a few paces behind them,' Newman pointed out.

'Exactly. This they believe is the natural order of society. History shows it can be done. Remember Muhammad, the Prophet. His armies started from nothing, swept along the North African shore, crossed the Mediterranean via Gibraltar, which they called Jeb-el-Tarik. They flooded into Spain and then crossed the frontier into France. Only Charles Martel, Charles the Hammer, stopped them at the Battle of Poitiers. That was in mid-France! It will be swifter next time. They have modern weaponry – rockets, tanks, all the equipment for a swift conquest of Europe which, I emphasize, is defenceless under the present pseudo-leadership.'

'Militarily you're thinking of it from a strategic angle,' remarked Tweed. 'That's your forte – strategy.'

'That is correct.' Amos paused, his expression grave. 'Within a few days I am travelling to Zurich to consult Pierre Dumont. He is one of the greatest intellects in the world.'

'He certainly is.' Tweed stood up. 'If you will excuse us I have another appointment.' He smiled. 'Not that we had one with you here – it was very good of you to give us the time you have. I know you never stop working.'

'It is one of my bad habits,' Amos responded amiably. He also stood up as Newman held out his hand. 'And I am glad you have shown the patience to listen to my ramblings, Mr Newman.'

'Hardly ramblings.'

Newman also smiled as they shook hands and he stared hard at their host. Amos's hypnotic eyes were glowing with the intensity of his thoughts.

Tweed remained very still and silent as Newman drove them back towards their hotel. He appeared to be watching the lane ahead, illuminated now night had fallen by the beams of their headlights. Newman was accustomed to these moods of Tweed's when he was mentally wrestling furiously with a major problem. Tweed spoke suddenly.

'When we get back can you pack quickly? I'll be doing the same thing. Also I want to phone Monica. We are returning to London immediately. Park Crescent is our centre of communications and I need to be there urgently.'

'That's easily taken care of. And I'll pay the bill.'

Newman had agreed casually. But he knew that from now on they were facing a grave emergency, that from now on the momentum would build and build until it reached its inevitable climax, whatever that might be.

Hassan put down the phone with a satisfied smile. He had just provided Simone Carnot with the essential data on Pierre Dumont. He was a very well-organized man –

with the list the Englishman had provided him he was able to place the right woman close to her target.

Simone had had a photograph of Dumont in her possession for over a week. Hassan had established her in an apartment in the middle of Zurich off Bahnhofstrasse and now she knew his address, his normal movements. Dumont was a man with a firmly established routine he followed every day.

'He leaves his apartment on Talstrasse at ten o'clock each morning,' Hassan had told Simone. 'He then arrives at ten minutes later at Sprungli, the coffee and cake shop on Bahnhofstrasse. He has a routine like a Swiss watch, being Swiss, I presume. Going to the first floor, he spends precisely thirty minutes eating croissants and drinking coffee. Then he . . .'

He continued, outlining Dumont's day until he went to bed in his apartment. Hassan's watchers were experts – they should be, considering the amount he paid them. Then it was cat's play for the chosen woman to make herself known to the target. And, Hassan reflected, Simone Carnot was a fast worker. The recruiter, the Englishman, had shown great psychological insight in selecting the right women.

6

Simone Carnot wandered through the entrance to the Hotel Baur au Lac in Zurich and paused. Several men stared at her without inhibition. Simone was five feet eight inches tall, slim, a redhead, in her thirties. She ignored the stares as she scanned the terrace to the left of the drive, a place in the open where couples sat drinking.

She recognized Pierre Dumont, who, following his

daily routine, sat at one of the tables which had umbrellas over them. The June evening was hot and she wore a short white sleeveless linen dress which emphasized her figure. A gold-link necklace was clasped round her swanlike neck.

She noticed an empty table next to Dumont's, strolled to it, and down under the yellow umbrella, crossed her long, tanned and well-formed legs. She was half-facing Dumont, who sat writing down his latest conclusions in a leather notebook in a neat script.

A waiter swiftly appeared to serve her. She raised her husky voice slightly as she gave her order.

'You know, I think I'd like a dry Martini.'

Dumont, attracted by the sound of her voice looked up, put down his cigarette. That is a plus point, Simone thought. He also smokes. She casually caught his long glance, her greenish eyes meeting his, then looked away. She knew he had been separated from his wife for over three months, that it was the wife's fault since she had taken a lover and had not been sufficiently discreet. Hassan had supplied a very full report on her prey.

Dumont suddenly found he had lost interest in what he was writing down. This was a very attractive woman and she had no rings on her fingers. He told himself to continue with his work – his speech at the Kongresshaus nearby was less than a week away – but he couldn't concentrate.

Simone timed it after she had received her drink and no other waiter was near. They were all clustered under the yellow awning which splayed out above the serving area. She took out a pack of cigarettes, put one in her mouth, fiddled in her handbag as though searching for a lighter.

Dumont sprang up, walked the few paces which divided his table from her, his gold lighter extended.

She looked up, stared straight at him with the ghost

of a polite smile. She had good bone structure, a chin which expressed determination.

'*Merci, Monsieur.*'

This was another bull point in her favour. She knew that he came from the French-speaking part of Switzerland. He began speaking in French.

'I think the evening is the best part of the day at this time of the year. There is a sensation of peace and serenity you only get now.'

'True. You have a good sense of atmosphere. So many men do not have it. I have been working all day inside my study behind a computer. It is pleasant to be outside, to relax.'

'You prefer to do so by yourself?'

'Not really.'

She tapped the end of her cigarette in an ashtray, which was not really necessary yet. Dumont noticed this, put it down to a slight touch of insecurity.

'Then may I join you, since we are both alone?'

'That would be pleasant. But you were busy with your notebook.'

She had a sophisticated approach. Don't push it, she told herself. Far too early for even a hint of flirtation. He assured her he had had enough of his notebook, fetched his own drink and sat beside her. He pointed to beyond the terrace where the hotel's garden spread away towards the lake, to Zurichsee.

'They have improved the garden enormously in recent years. I can remember when it was neglected. Now it is a park, a park of great beauty. I come here every evening not only for a drink, but so I can watch the shadows spreading over the lawn . . .'

Pierre Dumont was a small tubby man in his mid-fifties. He had a fuzz of brown hair, a plump face, an easy manner. Since his wife had left him he had been very lonely, although nothing in his manner betrayed this to his many friends. His blue-grey eyes had a dreamy look – his mind was so often focused on the world situation and possible solutions. During the three months on his own he had drowned his disappointments in furious work, sitting behind the desk in his apartment as late as 3 a.m. This way he found he could drop into a deep sleep the moment his head hit the pillow. Now he felt the need for some feminine company.

At Summer Lodge Tweed and Newman packed quickly, paid their bill, started their drive back to London through the night. Again Tweed was silent for a long distance and Newman was careful not to interrupt his thought flow.

Frequently, Newman glanced in his rear-view mirror without making any comment. It was Tweed, who had checked his wing mirror without Newman realizing it, who eventually brought the situation out into the open.

'We have been followed ever since we left Evershot. It is still happening.'

'Want me to lose him?' Newman enquired.

'Certainly not. I'm getting the hang of what is going on. Let them go on following. It helps to bring whoever is behind the assassinations out into the open. Then we can confront them.'

'You think it's either Willie or Amos who has set loose the hounds on us?'

'Could be. Who can tell?'

You could, if you wanted to tell me, Newman thought. But he knew Tweed's methods. He played it close to the chest, revealing his hand to no one until he had discovered the identity of the opposition. They were well inside London, approaching Park Crescent, when Tweed spoke again, his voice vibrant with energy despite lack of sleep.

'I called Monica before we left Summer Lodge. She'll be waiting for us when we arrive.'

'Poor Monica. The hours she works.'

'She wouldn't miss it for the world. She realizes we are now getting somewhere.'

'Are we?'

'Yes. I have to stop Paula, Marler and their escorts making a mistake.'

'Then you can get some shut-eye. It's been a long day.'

'Forget sleep. It's going to be a long night.'

Newman bent over Monica when they entered Tweed's office on the first floor. George, the tough guard on the door, had let them in.

'Everyone except you and Monica have gone home,' Tweed had remarked as they had entered.

'Not on your life, sir. Howard is in his office.'

Tweed had groaned. The last person he wanted to see during the night was the pompous Director. Then he remembered that Howard had warned Newman to take care of him when he had spoken to Bob after their arrival at Summer Lodge.

Newman had kissed Monica on one cheek. She had looked up with surprise and pleasure, then teased him.

'Next thing you'll be inviting me out to dinner.'

'It's a date,' Newman joked.

Monica, Tweed's personal assistant for as long as anyone could remember, was a woman of uncertain age, her grey hair tied back in a bun. Tweed sat behind his desk, called out to her.

'Get me Marler at the Sacher in Vienna.'

'I should know where it is now.'

As she spoke she was pressing buttons, recalling the number from her remarkable memory. She warned him as she asked the switchboard operator to put her through to Marler's room.

'Don't forget he'll probably be woken up. Marler? Yes, I know you can always recognize the lilting tones of my voice. Hold on. Someone is calling you.'

'Marler? Good. I'm back at headquarters. This is a direct order to you. It applies to all of you. You are in charge. You stay where you are until you hear from me. No prowling round the streets looking for attractive ladies.'

'Understood.'

Tweed put down the phone, asked Monica to get Pierre Dumont on the line. Then changed his mind, said he'd get the number himself. A woman's voice answered his call.

'Yes? Who is it?'

'Put me on to Pierre Dumont, please.'

'So sorry, he is not available. Who is this calling?'

There was a trace of a French accent in the husky voice which had spoken in English.

'The milkman,' Tweed said, and he slammed down the phone.

He sat thinking for several minutes. He knew Dumont's wife had left him. It was unlike him to seek comfort elsewhere. But it had been three months since Dumont had been left on his own. He had no way of knowing Dumont was taking a shower, that the woman who had answered was Simone Carnot.

Newman was watching him as Tweed sat upright in his swivel chair, gazing into the distance. It was a moonlit night and beyond the heavy net curtains across the windows he could see in the distance the trees of Regent's Park.

'Trouble?' Newman enquired.

'I hope not. In less than two days Pierre Dumont is giving a major speech at the Kongresshaus in Zurich.

He has let it be known that what he says will contain sensational developments in the world situation. What a target – standing up in front of a large audience. CNN is expected to be there with cameras, as well as the world's press and a distinguished audience. I don't like the sound of it. Monica, please get me Arthur Beck.'

Monica phoned, once more from memory, the private number of the Chief of Federal Police in Berne, Switzerland. He was an old friend of Tweed's. Monica nodded a few minutes later, signalling to Tweed that she had him on the line.

'Tweed here . . .'

'Ah, the great man himself,' Beck replied humorously in his perfect English. 'You have a problem? You always have.'

'I'm at HQ in London. Pierre Dumont is giving an important speech at the Kongresshaus in Zurich two days from now.'

'I know. There has been enough publicity about it.'

'I think he could be the target for the next assassination.'

'We've already had one in Geneva. Not another, please.'

'I think he should be heavily guarded. He'd make a star target while he's speaking. I'm guessing.'

'Your guesses worry me. They usually turn out to hit the bull's-eye.' Beck prided himself on his mastery of English. 'I'll call the Police Chief in Zurich, tell him to get cracking. Any clue as to who is behind these murders? And I may have a bit of news for you. One of my brighter types watching Kloten Airport saw Emilio Vitorelli arrive. Tracked him to the Baur au Lac. Booked into a suite indefinitely.'

'Emilio always does that – then no one knows when he plans to leave.'

'When he arrives anywhere it usually means something's afoot.'

'Have him followed. As to who is running the enemy, it could be a man called Assam. I'll spell that . . .'

'It's a state in India. I don't think this concerns India.'

'Neither do I. Keep in touch.'

Tweed began to doodle on a pad. As he did so he repeated out aloud to himself, 'Assam? Assam? Assam?' Could Paula have misheard what the driver of the kidnap car said to her?

He then told Newman about the arrival of Vitorelli in Zurich. Newman pulled a grim face.

'His reputation for dubious dealings runs all the way from Milan to New York. When he turns up something is rotten in the state of Denmark.'

'Which is Beck's opinion.'

Minutes later he took a call from Beck in Berne. He was reassured by what the efficient Chief of Police told him.

'I have alerted Zurich. No one is going to be able to creep up behind Pierre Dumont and shoot him in the back of the head – not in full view of a large audience. Emilio dined at the Baur au Lac, then went straight to bed.'

'Thanks for keeping me so closely informed.'

Beck's remark was to haunt Tweed in the near future.

Mario Parcelli, who posed as a gigolo, had walked past the police watchers at Kloten, Zurich's airport, without being seen. A dapper little man, neatly dressed in a lightweight blue suit made in Savile Row, London, he was actually Vitorelli's chief lieutenant.

He had been careful to disembark from the plane some distance behind his boss.

Ever cautious, he did not take the first waiting taxi, but hung back until he could climb inside the third cab to pull up. Now he knew he was not being followed. He perched his Louis Vuitton case beside him. Crossing his feet encased in navy blue Ferragamo loafers, he looked out of the rear window. He could not resist the instinct to check again.

Turning to face the front, he glanced down at his loafers. His appearance was all part of his image. His main task for Vitorelli was to control the wide-flung network of informants who kept him in touch with what was going on. So often he had enabled Vitorelli to bring off a business coup. Now he had a more difficult task to perform and he reckoned he had come up with pure gold.

'Take me to the Schweizerhof Hotel in Bahn-hofplatz,' he had told the driver.

Arriving at the hotel opposite the main rail station, he had paid off the driver, waited until he had gone. Then he had walked away from the hotel round the corner into the Bahnhofstrasse, bought a ticket from the machine and boarded the first tram.

'You overdo the precautions,' the casual Vitorelli had once remarked.

'I know my job,' Mario had rapped back.

Alighting from the large blue tram near the end of Bahnhofstrasse before it reached the lake, Mario walked into the Baur au Lac, booked himself a room. He looked at the concierge before heading for the lift.

'You have Emilio Vitorelli staying here. I have an urgent message for him. I need his room number.'

'I can deliver the message if anyone of that name is here,' the concierge replied discreetly. 'Excuse me, sir.'

Fuming with impatience, Mario waited. Vitorelli had stayed at this hotel many times before. The concierge returned quickly with a pleasant smile. Having phoned Vitorelli, describing the new arrival, he gave Mario the room number.

Hurrying to the lift while a porter took his case to his own room, Mario stopped at the correct floor. Vitorelli was standing in his doorway, the raised hand in greeting, ushered him inside, relocked the door.

'I could not approach you on the plane,' Mario began, 'even though I had what might be an important discovery.'

'From one of your informants?'

'Yes.

'The name?'

'I cannot reveal that, even to you. Part of the deal. One to one. Someone in the underworld. They told me there is a strong rumour that the organization which is behind the eight assassinations is called The Sisterhood.'

7

Tweed had stayed inside the SIS building – mostly in his own office – for two days. He had hauled out a camp bed from a cupboard, Monica had made up the bed for him, and he had managed a few hours of sleep.

'Action this day?' Monica had suggested on completing her self-imposed task.

'We are at the difficult stage of a loaded pause,' Tweed had replied.

He was not idle. He had got in touch with Keith Kent, based in the City. Kent could locate the mysterious sources of large sums of money more swiftly than anyone. Tweed's instructions over the phone were simple.

'Keith, there are two people I want investigated – where their money comes from. One is Captain William Wellesley Carrington, lives in Dorset at . . .'

He provided as much data as he could and then mentioned the second name.

'Also an apparently less wealthy man living in the same area. Amos Lodge, the well-known expert on world strategy. He lives at . . . Finally, is the village of Shrimpton owned by one man and, if so, who is it? I need the information yesterday.'

'You always do,' Kent's educated voice replied ironically. 'Do either of these men travel abroad?'

'I was coming to that. Willie – that is Carrington – makes frequent trips to the Middle East. Lodge also travels overseas but I don't know where or how often. I have been told by a friend that couriers bring in large sums in cash to someone in the same area. We know one large consignment was delivered recently – but we don't know where in Dorset it went to, or who was the recipient. It could be a matter of life or death to a number of people. Sorry I have no more data to give you.'

'So I'll get working on it now. It will cost you.'

'It always does,' Tweed replied.

Newman had been listening to the conversation. He knew Kent. When Tweed put down the phone he asked his questions.

'You think one of them – Lodge or Willie – is mixed up in these assassinations?'

'I have no idea. It could be a third party we missed down in Dorset.'

'I was waiting for you to ask Willie about what had happened to Tina Langley, his previous girlfriend. You didn't.'

'Deliberately. I didn't want to make him suspicious

71

of me. I noticed her picture was on the grand piano in the living room. The photo of a petite auburn-haired woman in her thirties, standing with her arm through Willie's.'

'I noticed that picture. Tina is a very attractive woman. Had a good figure, an inviting smile on her face. A lot of men would fall for a woman like that.'

'What did you say?' asked Tweed, whose thoughts had wandered.

Newman repeated what he had said. Tweed looked thoughtful, gazing out of the window at the distant morning sun in Regent's Park. It was going to be another heatwave day.

'Did I say something?' Newman pressed.

'You repeated what you had said earlier. Monica, try and get Kuhlmann on the phone. He should have left Vienna now and returned to his base at Wiesbaden in Germany.'

He had just spoken when the phone rang. Monica told him that Paula was on the line.

'What is it, Paula?' Tweed asked.

'If necessary, we'll go on doing it – staying holed up here at the Sacher, I mean. But isn't it an appalling waste of manpower? To say nothing of myself.'

Her voice was grim. Tweed realized she was in one of her rebellious moods. Not because she was impatient but because she sensed an imminent crisis. He had great respect for her judgement, took an instant decision.

'Are you packed and ready to go?'

'As ready as we can be under the circumstances.'

'Then all of you are to catch a flight to Zurich. When you—'

'Could you hold on a moment while I speak to Marler?'

'Of course.'

Marler came on the line very quickly. As always his wording was terse and to the point.

'We don't want to catch a plane. I strongly urge that instead we drive in two hired cars the length of Austria, then cross the border into Switzerland. I have my reasons.'

'I agree,' Tweed said. 'Occupy separate rooms at Baur au Lac and the Gotthard. Rooms will be booked for you.'

Marler turned to the others in his room at the Sacher. He told them about Tweed's order. They had heard his preference for going by car.

'Why by car?' Paula demanded.

'What are you carrying in that special pocket inside your shoulder bag? A .32 Browning. What have I given Harry and Pete?' he said, turning to the two men. 'Each has a Walther and plenty of spare ammo. I have my own Walther – plus my Armalite rifle. We can't fly with them.'

'Dump them in the Danube,' said Paula.

'I know a reliable arms dealer in Geneva.' Marler shook his head. 'The one I know in Zurich is tricky. We don't know what we're walking into when we reach Zurich. Using the two cars I can tape my stuff under my car, plus your Browning and Harry and Pete's weapons. Harry can drive you while Pete comes with me. I know a way we can cross the frontier into Switzerland avoiding any checkpoint.'

'It will take ages to drive across Austria,' Paula protested.

'Tweed has sanctioned the idea.'

'Then that's what we must do,' interjected Butler.

73

'I suppose you're right,' Paula agreed reluctantly. 'But it isn't as though we're going up against a tough mob in Zurich.'

'Don't count on that,' Marler warned.

Newman was present when Tweed took the phone call from Paula. When he had ended the call, Tweed explained what had happened.

'I suppose you can understand them getting a locked-up feeling, being confined to the Sacher,' Newman commented.

'I had to take an instant decision. A sixth sense tells me Zurich could be the next flashpoint. That we'll need plenty of back-up in that city. I'm still worried about Pierre Dumont making that public speech which has been so widely reported in advance.'

'You have warned Beck and he's taking action. I'm going back to my flat – I'm a bit short of sleep. You know you can always get me if anything develops.'

For the rest of the day and late into the evening Tweed worked with Monica on admin, which he hated, but it had to be cleared off his desk. He was just about to take to his camp bed when Howard strolled in. The Director had a habit of intruding at an inconvenient moment. Monica pulled a face behind his back as he settled into an armchair, one leg perched over an arm of the seat.

As usual he was faultlessly dressed in a Chester Barrie suit from Harrods, this time a blue bird's-eye. He adjusted his club tie over a spotless white shirt and looked at Tweed as he spoke in his public school accent.

'Any news from the Dorset front?'

'We met both Willie Carrington and Amos Lodge,'

Tweed began. He had decided to give Howard some news to satisfy him after the way he had taken the trouble to warn him to be careful. 'We didn't really get anything vital out of either of them.'

'So we cross them off the list of suspects about the money you told me a courier was carrying to that part of the world?'

'I didn't say that.'

'I'm worried about the way these top brains are being polished off one by one. I knew Norbert Engel. Nice chap.'

'We're all worried. We just have to wait for something to point us in the right direction.'

'See you're sleeping here. You should go home to your flat.' Howard heaved himself out of the chair. 'That's where I'm going. Keep me in touch . . .'

Five minutes later the phone rang. Monica answered, told Tweed Keith Kent was on the line.

'Any luck, Keith?'

'I've spent many hours checking out both Carrington and Lodge. I've used methods and sources I rarely resort to. It's very odd – I've come up with nothing.'

'Unlike you, Keith.'

'There's something funny about where both men get their income from. I can smell it. But I can't penetrate how they live in style. Thought I'd give you this first report. I'm going on digging. I never give up. I'll come back when I do have something solid.'

'Thanks for phoning me. I'll leave it to you.'

He said good night, gazed at Monica, who had been recording the call.

'What do you make of that, Monica?'

'One or both have a secret source of income and have covered their tracks exceptionally well. People don't do that unless they have a great deal to hide.'

'Could be.'

Tweed had a dreamy look which Monica was familiar with. She posed her question tentatively.

'Where is your mind drifting now?'

'Zurich.'

Earlier Hassan had phoned the Englishman, who was the director of the whole operation. The only man more powerful was the head of an Eastern state, who frequently checked on the group of generals who were preparing the massive onslaught on the West.

'Hassan speaking. I have had reports that a certain person on the list is becoming very active – or rather his cohorts are. There has already been an unfortunate incident in the city of Vienna.'

'Then the right person should visit him next. In case she fails, proceed with the next person below him on the list. You understand me, I trust?'

'Perfectly, sir. I will launch the procedures immediately.'

The man he was talking to had not replied, had merely broken off the call. Hassan, in his fortress-like headquarters on top of the low mountain in Slovakia, shivered. It always worried him, talking to this man. The voice was so cold and menacing. He was unnerved for another reason. *In case she fails . . .*

The Englishman had never before suggested such a possibility. The list he had referred to was the names of all the fifteen members of the Institut de la Défense. Hassan could recite the list in sequence from memory. The next person on the list after Pierre Dumont had only a single name. Tweed.

What, Hassan asked himself, was so special about this man, Tweed? He was the first member the Englishman had showed respect for – even fear of.

He unlocked a drawer to check his memory. Yes, after Dumont there was the name. Tweed. Alongside it were the initials. *K. B.* – Karin Berg, a glamorous blonde Swede noted for her intellect. She had studied psychology and world history at the University of Uppsala, north of Stockholm.

Unlike the others she was not in place. So where to move her to? She had once been a member of the Swedish counter-espionage organization. Hassan picked up the phone, pressed numbers which would put him through to her apartment in Stockholm. He had little hope she would be at home.

'Who is it?' her cool voice enquired in English.

'You know who it is calling,' he replied in his slightly lilting voice.

'I do.'

'Your next appointment is with a man called Tweed.'

'So now you give me an extremely difficult one. I shall need to double the fee.'

Double the fee! Two hundred thousand dollars. Hassan was on the verge of exploding, then he remembered the Englishman's direct order, the fact that the Eastern Head of State had a vast fortune at his disposal. But he had to make a protest.

'That's a lot of money.'

'I have already told you,' she said in her arrogant voice, 'this is an extremely difficult one. That is my fee. Or forget it.'

'I accept,' Hassan said quickly.

She was quite capable of slamming the phone down on him. He had to obey the Englishman.

'Where do I locate myself?'

'I'm not sure yet.'

'I am. Zurich. Dumont, the global expert, is giving a speech in the Kongresshaus. It has been reported in all the papers. Tweed will be there. The nearest de luxe

77

hotel is the Baur au Lac. Book me a suite there. I will be flying from Stockholm to Zurich today. Reserve the suite in my name. Leave the rest to me. Goodbye.'

Taken aback, livid that he should be spoken to in this way, Hassan replaced the receiver. Berg was the only one of his three women who did not treat him with the respect he was sure he deserved. He shrugged his slim shoulders, mopped sweat off his forehead.

He called the Baur au Lac, persuaded them to let him have their last suite in Berg's name. Then he called the arms dealer in Zurich who would supply her with a Luger – to be delivered in a Cartier gift box, well wrapped in polystyrene.

He was still puzzled. Why was this man Tweed so dangerous?

In his own suite at the Baur au Lac, Emilio Vitorelli sat watching his trusted assistant, Mario Parcelli. Mario, who avoided alcohol, had just returned after being away for many hours. He was drinking all of a half-bottle of mineral water.

'This heat,' he complained in Italian, 'we don't get it in Italy.'

'Yes, we do. Have you yet found a clue as to where Tina Langley is?'

'Not really. She disappeared from Dorset in England over four weeks ago. I found a local taxi driver who had taken her – with luggage – to London airport. Then she vanished.'

'You checked the aircraft leaving about the time she got there?'

'Of course. Flights were leaving for New York, Zurich and Geneva soon after Tina arrived at the airport. That I checked out.'

'Interesting.' Vitorelli, clad in a cream open-necked

shirt and trousers of the same colour, stirred his Campari with a swizzle stick, moving round the lumps of ice. 'From here you can easily link up with a flight to Vienna.'

'That's significant?' Mario asked.

'There's been an upsurge of trouble in Vienna. Norbert Engel had the back of his head blown off there. Then they found a dead creep in a Maltese church in Vienna, of all places. A clever German Chief of Criminal Police I have evaded by centimetres on several occasions, Otto Kuhlmann, announced today he's sure the corpse is linked with the Engel murder in some way.'

'I don't see the connection,' Mario commented.

'I'm not sure I do. But an idea is forming at the back of my mind. You have people in Vienna. Tell them to check out the Engel murder – that's what Kuhlmann is calling it. They should concentrate on whether a woman is involved.'

'I'll get moving on it now.'

Marler, Paula, Butler and Nield, in their two cars, were approaching the Swiss frontier in the middle of the night. Marler calculated they should reach Zurich some time during the morning of the coming day.

In the first car, driven by Butler, Paula sat by his side. She had dozed off for a few hours but had now woken up fully alert. She asked Butler to stop the car for a few minutes, then ran back along the road to the other vehicle.

'When do we reach Zurich?' she asked.

Marler told her of his estimation, provided they crossed the border without incident. She nodded, stood thinking.

'That means we'll arrive in time for Dumont's big

speech at the Kongresshaus. I'd like to attend that. It takes place in the evening.'

'Probably be a crashing great bore, but that's up to you. Go back to your wagon and eat while we're on the move. Good job we brought rations with us.'

Everyone was moving in on Zurich. Amos Lodge had driven up from Dorset, caught an early Swissair flight. The big man refused breakfast on the plane and studied a folder stuffed with papers. He drank strong coffee and never once looked out of the window.

When the machine touched down at Kloten he caught a cab to the Baur au Lac, claimed the room he had booked earlier. He made several phone calls, then went downstairs to have something to eat.

Afterwards he walked out of the wide drive, where a Rolls-Royce was parked alongside a Daimler, and headed for the lake. Several women looked at the imposing figure with steel-rimmed glasses but he hardly noticed them. Outside the large modern block on General Guisan Quai which is Kongresshaus he paused. He was staring at a poster advertising Pierre Dumont's speech that evening.

Nothing in his expression betrayed his reaction but he was noted for never giving away what he was thinking. From the lake there was a hooting of a siren as one of the large boats which plied the lake prepared to leave. At the same time a smaller steamer approached the landing stage, carrying commuters who worked in Zurich and had expensive homes well outside the city.

'A lovely day,' Lodge said to himself as he resumed his walk round the glasslike lake with the sun shining out of a clear blue sky. 'A lovely day for Pierre Dumont's speech.'

He resumed his long strides. Amos Lodge was a man who believed in exercise every day.

Hassan picked up the phone when it started ringing. It was the Englishman. Hassan gazed out of his window while he listened. On the side of the long house facing the quarry there was no need to have shutters. Blazing sun scorched the plain which was Austria.

'I thought over the data from Vienna you gave me. You said one of your men had seen the brunette.' He was referring to Paula Grey without realizing it. 'She left with three men in two cars. Your man followed her, then lost them south of Salzburg. They could be heading for Zurich. Isn't that probable?'

'It is, indeed, sir.'

Hassan didn't follow the reasoning but always agreed with anything the Englishman said. He didn't want to be replaced. Permanently.

'I have taken precautions. The Monceau gang is heading for Zurich via Geneva. I have given Monceau instructions – and your phone number. Do anything he says.'

Again the phone had gone dead. When the Englishman came to the end of giving an order he saw no reason for prolonging the conversation. He had an upper-crust British public school accent.

Hassan swore to himself in Arabic. The Monceau gang. By Allah he didn't like this development. Jules Monceau was notorious for his ruthlessness. His gang had robbed banks, killing people in the process. He engaged in blackmail of top people in France. Any activity which made big money.

*　*　*

81

The phone rang in Tweed's office early in the morning. It was Beck, calling from Berne.

'His voice sounds very urgent,' Monica informed her chief. She had her hand over the phone. 'I put him through?'

Tweed nodded. He had just finished taking his shower and shaving. He was now fully dressed with the light meal Monica had prepared in front of him on his desk.

'Arthur, Tweed here.'

'Pierre Dumont has had the back of his head blown off. During the night in his apartment. The local police chief has the approaches to the Kongresshaus swarming with armed men in plain clothes, but omitted to have the apartment watched. I have a witness. He saw a veiled woman in a black robe leaving the apartment . . .'

8

No one is going to be able to creep up behind Pierre Dumont and shoot him in the back of the head . . .

Beck's words came back to Tweed with shocking clarity as he put down the phone. He sat still for several minutes, rather like a Buddha. Monica kept silent while she watched him. He clenched his right hand into a fist twice and she knew he was in a rare mood of controlled fury. Tweed in a state of fury was a formidable opponent.

'You heard,' he said eventually.

'It's dreadful. And Paula said a veiled woman in a black robe left Engel's apartment in Vienna before his murder was discovered.'

'So we have a professional female serial killer on the loose. A very skilled woman with her murderous work.'

82

'It's a horrifying thought.'

She had just spoken when Newman arrived. One look at Tweed's face and he knew there had been a serious development. He listened while Tweed told him the news.

'So we don't sit around here any longer,' Newman suggested.

'No, we don't. Monica, book Bob and me on the first Swissair flight available to Zurich. Then reserve us rooms at the Baur au Lac. Even though it's the season they will find something for us. Give Howard the details after we have left,' he went on, rapping out instructions at top speed, his mind racing. 'Then call Beck, tell him we're coming, the flight data, where we're staying. I've no doubt he's on his way to Zurich now. If so, you can get him at police HQ in Zurich.'

Monica was taking no notes. She had all the instructions in her memory. Tweed looked at Newman.

'Bob, you'd better fetch your packed suitcase from your flat in Beresforde Road.'

'It's already here. Alongside your own case packed for swift departure. I sneaked it in while you were sleeping on that camp bed. I guessed we were close to some real action.'

'Good.' He looked at Monica who was waiting for Heathrow to answer. 'Later, call Amos Lodge. If he answers we'll know he's still in Dorset. Do the same with Willie Carrington.'

'You think one of them is involved?' Newman enquired.

'Somebody in Dorset is – and I think they're in the Shrimpton area. Something about that peculiar village isn't right.'

Ten minutes later, just after Monica had completed a call, the phone rang. She listened, asked the caller to hold on, looked at Tweed.

'It's your friend in Paris, Loriot . . .'

'Tweed,' Loriot began as soon as Tweed had announced he was on the line, 'I have news that might or might not concern your investigation. The Monceau gang, including Jules Monceau himself, has just slipped across the border into Switzerland. In the Geneva area.'

'Inform Beck.'

'I will. He'll pick them up. They always move by car. I'll suggest he watches the airport, too.'

'Thank you.'

Tweed leaned back in his swivel chair, told Newman the news from Loriot. Newman whistled softly.

'We must remember what a tough bunch that lot is – if we have to tangle with them . . .'

'Stop hanging around,' Monica interjected. 'I have seats for you on an early flight. I think you'll miss it.'

The Monceau gang slipped through Beck's grasp. Instead of using cars they arrived at close intervals in taxis. They were deposited at Zurich's rail station, Cornavin.

Separately, they bought tickets for Zurich, boarded the first express, spread through the long train. The express stopped only at Lausanne and Berne and then thundered on to Zurich. On Jules Monceau's instructions they kept well apart as they alighted at the Hauptbahnhof. Each pair knew which small hotel they should put up at, using forged passports.

As soon as he was settled in his own hotel Jules called the number the Englishman had given him. Hassan, nervously, put Jules in the picture.

Tweed and Newman just caught their flight. The waiting hostess ushered them swiftly aboard into their Business

84

Class seats, the main entrance door was closed, secured. Within minutes the plane was airborne.

'Close-run thing,' Newman commented, sitting in the aisle seat.

'I think there are going to be a lot of close-run things,' Tweed replied. 'I'm not confident Beck will be in time to round up Monceau and his cohorts.'

'Then isn't it a good job Marler, Paula, Butler and Nield are approaching Zurich?'

'Yes, sometimes I get it right.'

'You nearly always get it right – in the end.'

'The end of this could be a long way off. We need to locate, identify, this woman assassin before she can strike again. We need to find out who is running this massive operation. We need to track down their head-quarters. We need to do this before it is too late.'

'I'd say that is a tall order,' Newman remarked.

'There is only a minority of members of the *Institut de la Défense* left.'

'And you are one of that minority,' Newman said grimly.

The first person Tweed and Newman met after they had booked in at the Baur au Lac was Paula. Tweed, relieved at seeing her safe and sound, hugged her. She wore a cool white dress with a blue leather belt round her slim waist and he was surprised how fresh she looked. He complimented her on her appearance.

'Well, Marler and I got here three hours ago,' she explained as they settled in his room. 'Monica is an angel – she had booked each of us a room, using your name I suspect. I was pretty tired, but I had a shower before slipping between the sheets and slept for two hours. I snoozed a bit of the way and Marler was in the lead, keeping up a cracking pace. I had a light breakfast after getting dressed and I'm ready for anything.'

'Marler's in his room here?'

'Yes, sleeping, I guess. It was one hell of a drive across Austria. Butler and Nield are staying at the Gotthard. Once again Monica had done her stuff and the rooms were waiting for them.' She lowered her voice. 'We have weapons. I've got a Browning in that shoulder bag and Marler has a .38 Smith & Wesson with hip holster for Bob.'

'Lucky to get them across the frontier.'

'Marler knew an area where we could slip across unobserved. He would—'

She broke off as the phone rang and Tweed picked it up. It was Beck and he was downstairs. Tweed asked him to come up.

Arthur Beck was a man in his late forties, slim, tall, erect as a British Guardsman. His thick hair was greying round the temples and beneath his strong nose was a trim grey moustache above a firm mouth and jaw. His grey eyes had a steely glint with the hint of a sense of humour. He smiled easily.

He stooped over Paula, grasped her by the shoulders and kissed her on both cheeks. Tweed knew he was very fond of Paula without a touch of amorousness. He refused a drink when Tweed offered him one, sat down in a hard-backed chair, facing them both, seated on a large couch.

'No time for that now. The newspapers are printing new editions, reporting the assassination of Pierre Dumont. It will be hitting the world's media now. Dumont had friends in high places. Monica phoned me that you would be here – I called the concierge to inform me immediately of your arrival. We botched this one up badly.'

'Difficult to foresee,' Tweed said sympathetically.

'Someone moves very quickly, is very dangerous. You said you had a witness?'

Tweed explained briefly to Paula the gist of Beck's urgent phone call which had brought him hurrying with Newman to Zurich. She listened intently.

'I have the witness downstairs guarded by two plain-clothes men,' Beck told them. 'He is a bank teller.' He looked at Paula. 'From what you saw it sounds like the same woman assassin who killed Norbert Engel.'

'Reliable witness?' Tweed asked.

'Yes. He worked late at his bank, and left a late-night bar and was walking up Talstrasse when he felt so exhausted he sat down on some shadowed steps – which happened to be opposite the entrance to Dumont's apartment. That's when he saw the veiled woman leave. His description sounds like the woman Paula saw entering and leaving Engel's place in Vienna when he was murdered.'

'Could I talk to him?' Paula asked suddenly.

'Of course. I'll have him brought up now. He's a bit nervous but quite intelligent. Excuse me . . .'

He went to the phone, spoke for a couple of minutes, then resumed his seat. Again he looked at Paula.

'You have an idea?'

'No, I haven't. I just wanted to hear what this witness saw. It will probably correspond with what I saw in Vienna.'

'One witness meeting another,' Beck said with an attempt at cheerfulness.

There was a tapping on the door. Beck jumped up, went to the door, unlocked it, let in a pale-faced man in his thirties, dressed in a dark business suit despite the heat which was already building up. Outside the closing door Paula saw two men in suits, obviously the plain-clothes guards.

Beck cleverly led the witness to an armchair facing

Tweed and Paula, a chair where he would be comfortable, relaxed. He introduced the bank teller.

'This is Alfred Horn. He spent a year in London with a bank to broaden his experience. He speaks good English. Alfred, this lady and this gentleman want to ask you a few questions about what you saw early this morning in Talstrasse. You can answer them as freely as you did with me. I repeat, we know you had nothing to do with the unfortunate incident.'

Paula leaned forward, her blue-grey eyes studying Horn as she smiled. The pale face suggested hours spent indoors away from the burning sun. His dark hair was neatly combed and his eyes were held by hers, his hands were tensely clasped together in his lap.

'Mr Horn,' she began quietly, 'I would like you to describe what you saw when you were resting on the steps in Talstrasse.'

'I have already told Chief Inspector Beck everything I know.'

'Mr Horn, you saw a woman leave in the middle of the night. I am a woman and I might just spot something in your story a man wouldn't appreciate. Please, I am a good listener.'

She was still smiling and she noticed the clenched hands loosen their grip on each other. Horn did not even glance at Tweed, who was lolling back at the other end of the couch as though this hardly concerned him.

'I heard no sound of a shot, although I understand poor Mr Dumont was killed with a gun. What I did see was this woman, dressed from head to foot in a black robe, leaving. She had a kind of black cap on her head and this veil which reminded me of how Arab women dress.'

'This is promising, Mr Horn. How tall would you say the woman was?'

88

'About five feet nine. Something like that. Quite tall and slim.'

Paula concealed her sense of shock. She continued smiling as she went on with her questions.

'We know that, as we all do at times, you had had a certain amount to drink. Could that have dulled your observation?'

'No. By then my mind was perfectly clear. I only stayed seated on the steps a little longer to get the strength back into my legs.'

'The street would be dark,' Paula persisted gently, 'which would not give you a good view of her.'

'It was moonlit. But as she passed under a street lamp the breeze blew her veil away from her face. She quickly held the veil back over her face but she was a redhead.' Horn was speaking more rapidly as what he had seen came back to him vividly. 'Her hair was cut very full – like a flame. She was very attractive.'

'The sort of woman you wouldn't mind taking out to dinner?' Paula asked, smiling more broadly.

'Oh, yes, she was very attractive. Oddly enough, I am sure she was a Western woman, with a good background. The sort I have seen walking down Old Bond Street when I was in London.'

'Do you think she saw you?'

'I am certain she didn't. I was sitting in dark shadow. Before she walked away she looked quickly in both directions. Her glance never paused at the alcove where I was sitting well back.'

'Thank you, Mr Horn. May I suggest you do not mention what you saw to anyone – not even to a close friend or relative.'

'Your life could depend on your keeping your mouth shut,' Beck broke in, much to Paula's annoyance.

'It's just a question of being discreet,' Paula added in

her most gentle tone. 'Thank you for being so coopera-
tive and helpful. One more question. Would you recognize this woman if you saw her again?'

'I doubt it. It all happened so quickly before she was
gone.'

'Thank you again,' said Paula.

She waited until Beck had ushered Horn out, handing him over to the waiting detectives. Then his
expression changed to one of unusual grimness.

'That was a brilliant interrogation,' Beck said when
he came back. 'He didn't tell me she was a redhead, that
he had had a glimpse of her face. Is something wrong?'

'Very wrong,' said Paula. 'The woman with a black
garb and a veil I saw later walking down Kärntnerstrasse was no more than five foot three inches tall. She
had auburn hair.'

'A wig?' Beck suggested.

'No. How could a woman alter her height by five or
six inches? This assassin was someone else.' She looked
at Tweed. 'We are dealing with more than one woman
assassin.'

9

Tweed, after a long discussion in his room, had given
certain orders to Paula and Marler, who he had called to
join them. Saying he would like a breath of fresh air, he
had gone to the door by himself. Behind him Newman's
voice issued the warning.

'I've read the list of members of the *Institut de la
Défense* Paula gave me, the one she found sticking out
of a drawer in Norbet Engel's apartment. Below Pierre
Dumont your name is the next on the list. You're now a
top target.'

'I have a spare Walther you could carry,' Marler suggested.

'You know I hardly ever carry a weapon,' Tweed replied, and he left the room.

Stepping out of the elevator on the ground floor, he walked casually to the main entrance, peered out. The uniformed doorman greeted him, Tweed nodded, his eyes scanning the outside. Another very hot day was in the air and already there were people sitting on the open terrace. Nothing seemed out of the ordinary, but it wouldn't when it came.

Turning back, he wandered into the spacious lounge where a few guests at widely separated tables drank coffee, conversed. She was seated by herself at a corner table. He immediately recognized Karin Berg.

The tall, highly attractive Swedish woman, in her thirties, wore a light-weight green trouser suit with a white cotton round-neck blouse. Her psychology was good – she knew Tweed would not have approved of a display of her long legs, of a low-cut blouse. She raised a hand to catch his eye, not knowing he had already seen her.

Tweed remained standing in the doorway, as though uncertain where to sit. He was thinking of the time when, operating in Scandinavia, he had cooperated with Berg, then employed by Swedish counter-espionage. He had heard she had moved on – no one knew where she had gone.

He pretended to see her for the first time, walked over and shook her extended hand, sat down at a chair facing her, which left an empty chair between them.

'It's been quite a while,' Tweed said with a smile.

'Hasn't it. Too long. We always got on well together.'

'That's true,' Tweed agreed.

Berg had blonde hair trimmed close to her head. Her features were well-formed, her full lips a strong red, contrasting with her flawless pale complexion. Her eyes stared straight at his as she watched him over the glass of iced coffee she drank from. Tweed ordered the same from a hovering waiter.

'I heard you had left your job,' he remarked. 'Why? Where did you go to?'

He had observed she wore no rings on the third finger of her left hand. She put down the glass and smiled warmly.

'Is this an interrogation? You were always good at that.'

'Just questions. Obvious ones, since we once worked together.'

'Well . . .' She paused, still looking at him. 'I left the organization because the money wasn't good enough. Also I had an offer of big money from a security outfit belonging to a major corporation. I'm running the organization.'

'Which major corporation?' he asked sharply.

'There you go again. It's part of my contract that I never reveal whom I'm working for. It's a big hitter, international. I like the things money can buy.'

'A lot of women do.' He waited until the waiter had served his drink and gone away. 'You had two pretty bad affairs. Put you off men, did it?'

'That's rather personal.'

'You talked to me about them when I was in Stockholm. Said I was the only person you'd told about the bad time you'd had.'

'You were. You are.'

She stopped speaking as Newman appeared, his hand on the unoccupied chair. He was smiling broadly as he spoke, glancing at both of them.

'May I join you for a few minutes? Unless I'm intruding – in which case I shall vanish in a cloud of blue smoke.'

Tweed made introductions. Karin Berg indicated she would be quite happy with his company. She gazed at him through half-closed eyes, assessing him.

'Robert Newman? The international foreign correspondent? I thought so. You don't write much these days – I used to read your very perceptive articles in *Der Spiegel*. And in different publications.'

'I saved money. And there's nothing much going on in the world to write about these days,' he said easily, placing the drink he had been carrying on the table. 'But I may be writing a big piece on the eight assassinations of prominent men which have taken place. That is,' he went on, watching her, 'the moment I have tracked down the assassin.'

She froze. Only for a millisecond, but Newman caught her reaction before she resumed her interested look.

'Assassinations? I read it was a series of suicides.'

'Don't believe everything you read in the papers.'

Newman grinned. Lifting his glass he swallowed a little more Scotch.

'I recognized you from the photographs which used to appear in the press. You haven't changed a bit. You look, if anything, younger.'

'Flattery will get you somewhere,' Newman assured her.

'I always speak my mind,' she rapped back and the arrogance showed for the first time.

Tweed stroked his right eyebrow with a finger. He was signalling Newman that he would now like to be alone with Berg.

'I'll leave you two to continue your chat,' Newman said getting up. 'Nice meeting you,' he said to Berg before he wandered across the lounge.

'You could call me a career girl for a while,' Berg told Tweed, continuing the conversation where it had left off. 'But what about yourself? It's a long time since your wife ran off with that Greek shipping magnate. Or have you divorced her?'

'No, I haven't. I never hear from her but all the trauma of a divorce seems a waste of time.' He smiled. 'In any case, I'm a career man, as you should know.'

'You ought to relax more. If you like, I'll cook you a meal in my apartment some day.'

'A generous offer. I've got a better one. We'll take a cab to the Ermitage. It's rather a fine restaurant by the lake's edge, outside Zurich, in the Küsnacht district. Say nine tomorrow evening? I'll book a good table. I could pick you up here at eight thirty.'

'I accept with pleasure.'

'Then if you'll excuse me, I'm going out for a walk. I have a problem I want to sort out.'

'I remember this habit of yours . . .'

In case she fails . . .

The warning the Englishman had spoken over the phone when he had ordered Hassan to eliminate Tweed next had panicked him. If Karin Berg did fail in her murderous mission he was sure whose head would be on the block. He decided to take action on his own.

When Jules Monceau phoned him for the second time Hassan was ready with his instructions. Gripping the phone like a man whose life depended on this call, he began speaking to Monceau.

'You have a target in Zurich . . .'

'Which is where I am,' Monceau rasped.

'Excellent! I have had a report – reliable – that the target is staying at the Baur au Lac Hotel. He has to be liquidated. His name is Tweed.'

'Tweed!' Monceau could not keep the surprise and exultation out of his voice. 'Tweed, you said?'

94

'Yes. I will give you his description. We have it on file. It is rather vague—'

'No description needed. Immediate liquidation?'

'Yes. There will be a substantial fee in cash.'

'No fee needed.'

The phone connection was broken off. Hassan was puzzled – could not understand the Frenchman's reaction. He began to bite his nails. Had he done the right thing? He was going strictly against the Englishman's orders, but if Monceau succeeded then surely the Englishman should be pleased – whoever succeeded.

Jules Monceau had made his call early in the morning from a call box in the lobby of the small hotel he was staying in. Tweed! He could not believe his luck. Several years ago, before the Berlin Wall collapsed, Monceau had made the mistake of dabbling in obtaining French military secrets and selling them to the Russians.

It was Tweed, working with French counter-espionage, who had tracked him down. It was Tweed who had interrogated him in a cell at Rue des Saussaies, HQ of French counter-espionage, Tweed who had tripped him into a damaging admission.

During the years Monceau had spent in the Santé prison he had sworn that one day he would kill Tweed. Now the chance for revenge had been handed to him on a platter. Dawn was turning to daylight as he sat on his bed in his tiny bedroom.

Tweed, he knew, liked an early morning walk when he was able to cram it into his day. Within half an hour he had worked out his plan. He phoned three of his men, after returning to the call box in the hall. Two were staying at the same obscure hotel, not half a mile from his own hideaway. The third could get there even more quickly on the motorcycle Monceau had ordered him to buy.

Jules Monceau was a small, portly man, his black hair smoothed greasily above is forehead. His long nose, thick at the nostrils, combined with a wolfish smile had given him the nickname of The Wolf.

When they were all crammed into his room he stood with his back to the wall, smoking a cheroot as he told them what they had to do, the purchases they must make, including a wig, another item Bernard must buy after donning the wig, then the final item.

'Who will detonate it?' Bernard asked anxiously.

He was tall and lean with a sallow skin and thin eyebrows. Once a gymnast, he could move with great agility, altering his body language at will.

'André, of course. He, as you know, is an expert with explosives, with activating a radio-controlled bomb from a distance.'

'Do not worry, Bernard,' André mocked his colleague, his tone sarcastic, speaking in French as the others were doing. 'Worry about the baby, not yourself.'

'Shut your mouths, both of you,' snapped Monceau. 'Yves, you will drive the car as back-up. I will go over the plan once more. As I stand by the tram stop I will signal you when Tweed appears for his morning walk, rubbing my chin like this. I will be wearing a dark business suit like the bankers – even in this weather. I shall wear pince-nez, as I have before, and will be smoking a cigarette. The target associates me with smoking cheroots. The kill takes place this morning if the target appears.'

When his three men had gone Monceau treated himself to a fresh cheroot. He was enjoying that vision of Tweed's corpse being spread all over the road. So he'd follow at a discreet distance.

10

It was several hours later when Tweed strolled out of the Baur au Lac. Reaching Talstrasse, he glanced around. A few tourists trudging about. A portly man standing, smoking a cigarette, wearing a banker's 'uniform' – a dark business suit – and reading a newspaper. Probably checking on stock market figures. The banker type rubbed his chin. Maybe the news wasn't so good.

Tweed continued his stroll down to the lake. Waiting for the brief moment when the lights at a pedestrian crossing were in his favour, he crossed to the promenade alongside the lake. Zurichsee was calm, a brilliant blue. A steamer was coming in to berth as Tweed walked more quickly towards Kongresshaus on the opposite side of the road. Traffic was speeding along General Guisan Quai in both directions.

A woman with dark frizzy hair passed him, going the same way, propelling a push chair with a small doll-like baby swaddled in clothes inside. Tweed admired the pace at which she was moving as she went on into the distance.

Looking out across the large lake he saw at the point where the lake curved round a bend the silhouettes of large mountains backed by a cloudless sky. He caught sight of a mountain he knew well – the volcano-like shape of the Mythen.

One part of his mind took in what was happening around him while another part worried at the deadly problem he was trying to solve. He muttered to himself the strange name the kidnap car driver in Vienna had told Paula.

'Assam? Assam? Assam? Doesn't make sense. I must

ask Paula to explain again what she heard,' he said to himself.

A grey Volvo, moving more slowly than most of the traffic, passed him. The driver wore a peaked, American-style baseball cap and large wrap-around sunglasses. Tweed prepared to throw himself to the ground. The car continued past him. He relaxed, thinking now of the portly banker he had seen near the Baur au Lac. There had been something familiar about the man. Tweed wracked his brains, thought back into different episodes he had been involved in. Just couldn't place him.

Thirty yards or so behind Tweed Monceau kept pace. He was dying for a cheroot but forced himself to take another brief puff at his cigarette. It had to happen soon. His face twisted into a vicious grin as he anticipated the carnage.

Tweed glanced back, as he had done several times, but Monceau had masked himself behind a couple of backpackers. Tweed looked ahead of him. In the distance he saw the frizzy-haired woman with the pushchair coming back towards him. She must have completed her daily walk along the promenade. He recalled how silently the pushchair had moved. Well-oiled wheels.

Out of the lake a steamer approaching the landing stage hooted its siren. Zurich was a beautiful city, Tweed reflected. It had not one but two Altstadts – old quarters, one on either side of the Limmat River which flowed out of the lake under the bridge well to his rear.

He noticed that the woman with the pushchair was walking far more slowly. Tired out by her initial burst of speed, he assumed. Glancing across the street he saw strolling along the far pavement a stoop-shouldered man carrying a golf bag. He wore a check peaked cap, a windcheater and a pair of slacks. He was trailing along as though he had just completed eighteen holes of golf. His eyes were hidden behind sunglasses and he walked staring down at the pavement.

'Assam, Assam,' Tweed repeated to himself.

He could still make no sense of the word. Concentrate on what is going on around you, he reminded himself. Newman would be furious if he had gone off on his own. But he needed the isolation to get his brain fitting the pieces of the jigsaw together.

Looking ahead, he saw the woman with the pushchair dragging her feet. The baby inside the chair must have been asleep when it passed him – it hadn't made a sound. Then he saw the woman stop, brace her arms, hurl the pushchair towards him at top speed. It raced towards him like a projectile. At the same moment he noticed a man behind the woman holding a small box like the instrument used for guiding model planes by radio.

It was too late to avoid the onrushing pushchair. Out of nowhere the grey Volvo driven by the man with the baseball cap appeared on his side of the road. It had found somewhere to turn round. Behind it a motorcycle was screaming towards him with Newman astride the saddle.

The Volvo mounted the pavement, hit the pushchair, sending it hurtling towards a gap in the wall where steps led down to a small landing point. As the pushchair started sliding down the steps with the doll dressed as a baby André pressed the button on his radio-controlled explosive device. The pushchair exploded with a roar, scattered in fragments over the surface of the lake.

The Volvo was still stationary, halfway across the pavement, when a cream BMW raced along the far side of the road towards Tweed, a machine-pistol poked out of the rear window. Newman had already shot the 'woman', who slumped to the ground, the gun 'she' had produced leaving the man's hand, his wig sliding over the edge of the pavement into the street.

Across the street, the man with the golf bag had hauled out an Armalite rifle. Marler, tearing off his sunglasses, aimed the rifle at the driver of the BMW, pressed the trigger. The driver slumped over the wheel. The car slewed across the road, causing an oncoming car to brake to an emergency stop. The BMW hit the lakeside wall, burst into flames. Newman had fired his second shot, killing André, who had operated the radio-control device.

Tweed had now run back, crouched low against the wall, avoiding the fireball which had seconds earlier been a BMW. Marler had thrust the Armalite back inside the golf bag, ran across the front of the stationary traffic, jumped behind Newman on the motorcycle and it raced away towards the bridge over the Limmat.

Tweed stood up, walked rapidly back towards the Baur au Lac. Way ahead of him, Monceau, his face convulsed with manic fury at the fiasco, turned on to the landing stage, bought a ticket, was just in time to board a steamer on the point of departure. He went up to the enclosed top deck, chose a seat at the stern well away from other passengers and fumed.

Another man in Zurich was furious. Beck stormed at Tweed who had returned to his room at the Baur au Lac.

'Why in hell's name did you go out on your own?'

'I wasn't alone,' Tweed said quietly, seated on a couch. 'You know that now.'

'And did you know that?' the Police Chief demanded.

'No,' Tweed admitted. 'But if I'm to destroy the

enemy – whoever that might be – I have to think things out quietly on my own.'

'Well, we know who the enemy was in this case. It was the Monceau gang. The three dead men have been identified – we have the whole gang on file.'

'Monceau isn't the real enemy,' Tweed insisted. 'He must have been brought in as back-up. What we have to concentrate on is the man behind the eight assassinations. And I'm sure you are not sorry to be rid of these three thugs.'

'Monceau has at least seven more men on the loose,' warned Beck. 'He may try again to kill you.'

'Oh, he will. I'm not exactly his best friend. As you know I put him behind bars in France quite a while ago. This was his personal vendetta. Did you find out who wiped out those thugs?'

'I have not found out,' Beck said carefully, 'because it all happened so quickly that no witness can give a description. But I have my suspicions.'

'Good for you, Arthur. I can tell you that the assassins we are looking for – note the plural – are women. Crime has crossed the equality barrier. The one who murdered Dumont is a redhead – Horn told you that.'

'It isn't as though Zurich isn't full of red-haired women,' Beck said ironically. 'But why did you imply there is more than one woman assassin on the streets?'

'Because I know a very different-looking woman killed Norbert Engel. Know it for certain.'

'This is disturbing. Very,' commented Beck, who had quietened down, and stopped pacing round the room. He checked his watch. 'I'd better go – I have to write a discreet report on that mess of corpses on the promenade who are now in the morgue. I want you to promise me something. That you will not go out without at least Newman or Marler by your side.'

'I'll follow that advice when I can.'

101

'Which means that, as usual, you'll go your own damned way.'

Paula, Marler and Newman came into his room shortly after the police chief had left. Paula looked anxiously at Tweed.

'Are you sure you're all right?'

'I've never felt better. We are beginning to smoke out some of the opposition who obviously brought in Monceau and his nice friends to beef up their power. And thank you, Marler, and you Bob, for saving my life. A feeble appreciation. Again, you went into business on your own – when I had asked you to trace the Monceau mob.'

'Oh,' Newman said casually, 'we know you. So we cooked up a careful defence plan in case you were in danger. Which you were. Rather a diabolical mind planned that bomb in the guise of a baby in its pushchair.'

'That has all the hallmarks of Jules Monceau himself. I'm sure he was somewhere about wanting to see my end. Now,' he said briskly, 'Marler, I want you to explain again in detail the mood when you compelled the thug in the Maltese church in Vienna to name his headquarters.'

'Church was empty,' Marler said tersely. 'I had him on his knees inside a pew. My Walther was aimed point-blank and he thought I was going to pull the trigger – unless he spilt the beans.'

'So you must have really frightened him?'

'Only way to make him talk.'

'Did he answer you clearly?' Tweed persisted.

'Gibbering a bit. Then he came for me with the knife.'

'Gibbering?' Tweed repeated the word thoughtfully. 'So you may not have heard exactly what he did say? By which I mean he was incoherent. Slovakia. That was what you heard?'

'Something close to that.'

'Ah, this is interesting. You realize I'm not criticising you – it was an emergency situation, to say the least.'

'You could say that,' Marler drawled.

'Thank you.' Tweed spoke briskly. 'I told all of you earlier that we're dealing with at least two quite different assassins. Both of them women. Paula gave you her description of the one she saw in Vienna. Beck's witness, Horn, has only been able to provide the flimsiest picture of the woman who probably murdered Pierre Dumont. Of course, in the past women have been used by people like the old KGB to entrap men, but this is something quite different. That's the priority – to track them down. The second priority is to round up what remains of the Monceau gang. I think the two problems are interlinked. The whole city has to be trawled for Monceau's people – Beck says there are at least seven more. He's sending photos of them.'

He had just spoken when there was a knock on the door. Newman unlocked it, opened it a few inches, then took a large sealed envelope from a uniformed policeman, addressed to Tweed.

Opening it, Tweed glanced at the seven glossy prints inside. He spread them out over the table for the others to see.

'There they are. The seven gentlemen I just referred to.'

'Not very nice-looking men,' Paula commented.

'As ugly a bunch as I ever saw,' Newman chimed in. 'This one is Jacques Lemont. Expert knife-thrower. Once worked in a circus before Monceau recruited him. I interviewed him once. At that time Monceau was trying to fool people into thinking he was some kind of crusader – robbing the rich to help the poor. It was a load of rubbish but Monceau was in the room, wearing a mask to cover the upper part of his face.

He smoked one cheroot after another, a short tubby man.'

'That was him,' Tweed said suddenly. 'A short tubby man wearing a banker's outfit. Standing near the Baur au Lac when I set out for my walk. Smoking a cigarette with pince-nez perched on his nose. Thought he was familiar but I couldn't place him.'

'Waiting to see you blown into kingdom come,' Marler remarked.

'Earlier you said this is something quite different,' Paula reminded him. 'Are we dealing with terrorists?'

'Something far more sinister,' Tweed told her.

In the Middle East, well beyond the River Euphrates, a vast black cloud, emitted by numerous machines, hung above the desert. Below it a huge array of fast-moving modern tanks emerged from the underground bunkers where they were hidden.

The cloud, invented by scientists who had emigrated from Russia, was composed of harmless chemicals which made the American satellite crossing the area at intervals unable to photograph what was going on below it.

Under the control of several generals, the tank armada was engaged in more training manoeuvres. Each machine carried a long-range gun. Inside each gun was a shell containing a deadly biological material. The crews manning the tanks were all hooded with a certain advanced type of gas mask which made the wearer immune to the lethal gas.

At one stage the guns were fired. The shells travelled an enormous distance, landing in the desert. Several roaming camels suddenly froze as they inhaled the gas. Then they keeled over, instantly dead. The onslaught on the West was in an advanced state of preparation. All they were waiting for was the signal from the Head of State controlling Hassan. The signal which would tell him the West was now without anyone who could stiffen its leadership.

Newman went into the inside lounge after leaving Tweed and gazed swiftly around. He was convinced the danger was near at hand. Simone Carnot looked at him warily, smoothed down her blaze of red hair.

Normally, after leaving Dumont slumped dead on his couch with half his head missing and 'setting the stage' as Hassan always put it (using gloved hands to press the fingers of his lolling hand on the Luger), she would have caught the first flight out of Zurich. Hassan had again acted on his own initiative, was beginning to enjoy taking a hand in the game.

When Simone phoned to report in a coded manner that she had succeeded in her mission, Hassan had an idea. He told her to remain in Zurich for at least a week. He went on to say that the new target was a man called Tweed and spelt out the highly vague description he had. If the media hadn't reported his assassination by the end of the week she was to eliminate him herself.

'That will earn you the usual fee,' he had told her. 'I want you to call me when you have located him . . .'

Another one hundred thousand dollars. Simone had been more than willing to take the risk for more money. She had no idea that both she and Hassan were breaking the Englishman's golden rule. Once an assassination had taken place the woman responsible had to flee the city involved.

In the lounge she dropped her eyes quickly when Newman caught hers. She had recognized who he was from her extensive reading of the papers and the news magazines. He had an unusually striking appearance and she felt she must maintain a low profile. She had no idea who had been ordered to deal with this new target.

Simone Carnot had been running a public relations agency for top fashion models in Paris when she had been recruited on the basis of her looks and her love of money. She also had the advantage, like certain modern women, of regarding men as marauders, to be exploited at every possible opportunity.

When she realized Newman was approaching her she changed her mind. It would draw attention to herself if she pointedly ignored him. There was always the chance that with his vast knowledge of important people he might just know this Tweed, who had to be important to be singled out as a target.

'Excuse me,' Newman began as she looked up at him, 'but I am always direct. I'm bored and need someone to talk to. You certainly don't look boring. What drink can I order you?'

'A Kir royale,' she said immediately.

He ordered her drink from a waiter and a single Scotch for himself. She was very attractive with her glossy, flame-red hair.

His motive in approaching her was anything but what he had told her. True there were other redheads in the world but her appearance fitted the description Horn had given of the woman who had murdered Dumont. Newman had a vivid imagination and it had struck him that the assassin had to be a woman of great nerve. He would have expected her to get the hell out of town by the first available plane or train. But an astute woman might think it safer to stay put for a few days.

'I'm Bob Newman,' he said as they clinked the glasses the waiter had produced swiftly.

'Simone Carnot. What do you do, Mr Newman – when you are not accosting strange ladies?'

Aggressive, he thought – which again would fit his

image of the murderess. Not that it was likely that he had hit on the right woman.

'I investigate people,' he said provocatively.

'Are you investigating me, then? I wonder why?'

Every word she said fitted in with the portrait of a woman cold-blooded enough to shoot the back of a man's head off. It was too long a shot, he thought – that he could have found the assassin so easily. She had crossed her long legs, exposing them through a slit skirt. He glanced at them, knowing that was what she expected.

'No to both your questions.' He paused. It had occurred to him that Tweed would be the next target for a woman assassin. And she was in the same hotel. 'Are you staying here?' he asked her.

'I wonder what is behind that question, Mr Newman?'

'Which means you are staying here.'

'Possibly. Who can tell?'

'You could,' he said quickly.

'You're very direct. More like an American.'

She was smiling, her firm lips holding the smile. But the eyes which continued staring into his were like ice. He raised his eyebrows, took another sip at his drink.

'I don't know that I regard that as a compliment, but we'll let it pass.'

'How considerate of you,' she retorted, goading him. 'And if you are not investigating me, who are you investigating?'

'The killer of Pierre Dumont.'

He had spoken with great emphasis and didn't look at her as he took a further sip. At that moment Tweed walked into the lounge. He was walking past them when Newman called out.

'Do come and join us. Simone – may I call you that? I just did. This is Tweed. Meet Simone Carnot, Tweed.'

11

A little earlier, before Newman had left the bedroom, Tweed had summoned Butler and Nield from the Hotel Gotthard at the other end of Bahnhofstrasse. While waiting for them Paula and the others, seated, had watched Tweed walking slowly round his suite, hands clasped behind his back, a faraway look in his eyes, a determined look on his face.

No one had spoken. They knew from long experience he needed silence, that he was taking a major decision which would affect them all. Suddenly he stopped, perched himself on the arm of Paula's chair, his arms folded.

'It was Butler who was behind the wheel of the Volvo which hurled the pushchair bomb into the lake, wasn't it?'

'Yes,' said Newman. 'Pete Nield was crouched down in the rear with a gun and a stun grenade. We didn't know what was coming but we planned behind your back for various forms of attack on you—'

He broke off as there was a tapping on the door. He let in to the room Harry Butler and Pete Nield. Tweed greeted them with a grim smile.

'Please sit down, make yourselves comfortable. Harry, I have to thank you for saving me from that bomb.'

'All in a day's work,' replied Butler, who used words as though each one cost him money.

'I've decided we can't play it softly, softly any more,' Tweed began. He explained to the newcomers that there were two women assassins prowling Europe. 'I am now the next target,' he went on. 'Knowing this, that is the ace up our sleeve I am going to play. The technique they're employing is now obvious, cold-blooded, diabolically clever.'

'What technique is that?' asked Nield quietly, fingering his neat moustache.

'To put themselves close to their targets these fiendish women have to first make the acquaintance of their targets. Because they're dealing with sophisticated men, top-class intellects, they have to be very attractive, very experienced at handling men. I suspect someone who knows all the members of the *Institut de la Défense* has analysed each one to decide the sort of woman who would attract him. Someone with a deep insight into a man's psychology. And a lot of money is being sent secretly to Dorset.'

'That fingers Amos Lodge or Willie Carrington,' Newman suggested.

'Possibly. Unless there's a third man in that area who has not yet appeared on the scene . . .'

'Excuse me,' Paula interjected, 'but is either man a member of the *Institut*?'

'Amos Lodge is.'

'And he's still alive. Do we have to look further?'

'We do. His name is below mine on that members' list you brought from Vienna. But before the serial assassinations started we held a party at our headquarters inside a mansion on the shores of Lake Geneva, not far from Ouchy. The subject was the Middle East. We invited a number of people who know the area very well to tell us about it. One man invited was Willie Carrington.'

'His name is not on the list,' she persisted.

'We tried to cover ourselves by announcing this was the last meeting, that the *Institut* was being dissolved. Not my idea – didn't sound convincing. It didn't convince someone. I have worked out our strategy.'

'He said softly, softly was out, a few minutes ago,' Newman whispered to Paula as Tweed stood in the middle of the room. 'Sounds like a thunderbolt is coming.'

'I am now the next target,' Tweed repeated. 'So, knowing their technique, some attractive woman has to approach me, try to persuade me to join her in her apartment or somewhere quiet. All the previous victims have had houses or apartments which the killers could use. I'm in a hotel. This gives them a problem. I want to trap her, whichever woman turns up. Then *we* persuade her to tell us who she is working for.'

'I'll handle that problem when we get there,' Paula said, and there was an undertone of cold anger. 'I told you – in this age of equality certain women can be greater villains than men.'

'How can they do it?' Pete Nield asked. 'Creep up behind a man they've got to know, maybe seduced, then blast the back of his head off?'

'Women, in some ways, are different from men,' Paula explained. 'I'm more likely to penetrate their minds than any man. Take a simple fact. A number of women feel more comfortable talking to their own sex. They have women friends in preference to men – partly because they can talk freely about subjects they'd never dream of discussing with men. And a lot of women are guarded when encountering a new man – for obvious reasons.'

'Give me an obvious reason,' Nield had urged.

'I think it goes back through history – to a time when men were the dominant force. To survive, women had to learn how to handle a man, manipulate him, if you like. Now they have huge freedom those methods are no longer necessary – or desirable in my opinion. But they remain steeped in their old wily ways – so we have an unbalanced situation where some women set out to

110

run the whole show. This bewilders some men, does nothing to make for a stable society. We are on the edge of chaos with some relationships, maybe have gone down into chaos already.'

'I still don't get how a woman can blast a man's head off,' Nield insisted.

'I suspect certain women – a small minority – could do that and enjoy it.'

'That's horrible,' Nield protested.

'It certainly is. Another powerful motive is money. They must be paid a big fee for their filthy work. Tweed has said they must be attractive women. It costs a lot of money for a conceited woman to outgun her rivals in appearance. Cosmetics, clothes, hairdos – later they want facelifts and Lord knows what else. That costs a load of money. They're prowling predators, they want to try to be always desirable to men.'

'You're putting me off ever getting married,' Nield said.

'I'm not trying to do anything of the sort,' Paula said with great emphasis. 'The other side of the coin is there are a majority of women who are decent, honest; who will only marry a man they love – and go on loving. If it's a good match – and there are millions of them – they are content to raise a family, to support their husband always in every way, to live in modest circumstances. They make up the bulk of women in the world, in the West. So don't get me wrong, Pete . . .'

It was shortly after this conversation that Newman left, went into the lounge downstairs, and later introduced Tweed to Simone Carnot. He was following Tweed's strategy – the key to which was that the unknown assassin had to get to know Tweed as an opening gambit.

* * *

When his name was mentioned, Simone stretched out a hand to grasp Tweed's as he sat down. In doing so her hand caught her glass of Kir royale, spilling the contents over the table.

'I'm so sorry,' she said quickly, as a waiter came to mop the table, then brought her a fresh drink. 'That was really very clumsy of me.'

'I've done it myself,' Tweed assured her. 'Think nothing of it.'

Without revealing their reactions both Tweed and Newman were thinking a lot about the incident. It had been the mention of Tweed's name which had thrown Simone temporarily off balance. She could hardly believe her luck – the target was sitting opposite her, conjured up out of the blue. Then she recalled that he was staying at the Baur au Lac, that although she had pretended not to recognize Newman, he was an international foreign correspondent, the type of man Tweed, whoever he was, would mix with, since he had to be important.

'I'll have a glass of orange juice,' Tweed asked the waiter who had brought Simone a fresh drink. He looked at Simone, smiling as he asked the question, and he had noticed her slim legs, that she was very attractive.

'What is your role in life, if I may ask? You could be a successful model.'

She liked that. Her manner towards Tweed was entirely different from her defensive attitude with Newman. This is a fish I can hook, she said to herself. Instead she said something else aloud.

'Thank you. I take that as a great compliment. It is a fact that at one time I ran a fashion agency for models in Paris.' The moment she mentioned the French city she knew she had made a mistake. What was it about this man which caused her to let down her guard? 'Now I am getting over a broken marriage.'

112

'I'm sorry to hear that. I can't understand how any man could contemplate leaving you.'

He's laying it on with a trowel, Newman was thinking. But it seems to be going down well. When he put himself out Tweed could be charming because there was something which many women found reassuring about his personality.

'It just didn't work,' Simone explained. 'May I ask, are you married?'

'Yes, I am,' replied Tweed, without going into the real circumstances behind that statement. 'For a long time,' he added.

Better and better, Simone thought cynically. Some married men came to a point where they needed a little variety in their lives. This could be an easy mark. So why did a little warning bell sound at the back of her shrewd mind?

'I'm glad,' she replied. 'It's comforting to know that a marriage can work. I'm sure yours does. No sensible woman would dream of leaving someone like you.'

'We seem to be vying with each other to exchange compliments,' Tweed said drily.

'It's a more civilized conversation than I have had with many men. Perhaps we could have a drink together some time? I am staying at this hotel.'

'I shall look forward to that. Please excuse me now. I have a business appointment.'

He left Newman with her, walked to the revolving door leading to the drive, passed through it on to the drive. Out of sight of the lounge he paused. The last man in the world he had expected to see was seated at a table on the terrace. Amos Lodge.

Tweed walked slowly towards the terrace, his eyes scanning everyone seated at the various tables. Butler, better dressed than usual, was drinking from a cup. Further away he saw Pete Nield reading a newspaper. Tweed had no doubt that Marler was somewhere close at hand, then he saw him seated close to the bar, with a glass of iced coffee in front of him.

He strolled towards Marler's table, appeared to stumble, and his outstretched hand knocked over the glass. It was the earlier Kir royale incident which had given him the idea. He apologized, as though speaking to a stranger, and then lowered his voice.

'Tomorrow I'm taking a woman I once knew called Karin Berg to dinner at the Ermitage on the edge of the lake outside Zurich. Leave here at eight thirty.'

'Don't worry about it, sir,' Marler said in a loud voice. 'The waiter's coming to clear it up.'

Tweed changed direction, appeared to see Amos Lodge for the first time. The big man with the square-rimmed glasses he had last met in Dorset was wearing a panama hat which seemed to emphasize his bulk. He looked up as Tweed reached his table.

'Good Lord! Last person I expected to see out here. Sit down. Join me in a glass of cold lager?'

'Thank you. Think I'd prefer coffee. I was thinking the same about you – last person, et cetera. What brings you here, Amos?'

'I came to listen to Dumont's speech at the Kongres-shaus. A bloody awful thing – I read it in the paper – about him committing suicide. Last thing I'd have expected.'

'You're right. It was murder.'

'My God! Why? Who did it?'

'That, Amos, is what I'm here to find out. I'm getting closer to the murderer by the hour.'

'You are? He had a big life insurance policy, I suppose.'

'Well, I am Chief Claims Investigator for an insurance outfit,' Tweed replied, evading a direct answer. 'But what are you going to do now?'

'Give a speech at the Kongresshaus tomorrow night. Officially a kind of memoriam – in fact I'm going to use the occasion to express my views forcefully. The agency who acted for Dumont has informed the audience who had tickets. Posters are going up. It will be a big audience.'

'Isn't that a bit dangerous? You're a member of the *Institut*. So were all the previous so-called suicides.'

'You think that will stop me?' The eyes behind the glasses stared at Tweed with a steely look. 'You'll be there, I hope? I have an invitation card – in fact a batch so you can bring any friends you have in this part of the world.'

Saying which, Amos produced a fat envelope from the breast pocket of his summer jacket. He laid a small pile in front of Tweed, who pocketed them.

'Thank you. You got them printed fast.'

'A Swiss printer. The Swiss are very efficient and can move fast. Here's your coffee. Wish me luck with my speech.'

'I wish you luck – and safety.'

'Safety? Forget it. Half Dorset seems to be in Zurich. I'm waiting for someone you know well. Willie Carrington.'

'Willie is here?'

'Staying at the Dolder Grand, up on the hill behind the city. I'd mentioned to him on the phone I was coming to listen to Dumont. He said he was in Zurich for the same reason. Here he comes – the lady-killer . . .'

Willie was wearing the most extraordinary outfit. Over his head and draped behind it was a white cloth as worn by Arabs. The rest of his clothes were a straightforward

115

Western suit and he had a pair of wrap-around sun-glasses masking his eyes.

'Speak of the devil – I heard what you said,' he greeted Tweed as he sat down. 'I certainly didn't expect to find you here. You've heard about poor Dumont committing suicide? Can't understand what made the feller do it. Nasty shock. He was a guest at my club recently, back in London.'

Willie made it sound as though suicide wasn't the done thing as Dumont had visited the club. 'A brain-storm, I suppose. Waste of a world-class brain. I'll have a double vodka,' he told a waiter, then turned back to Tweed. 'I need it after that.'

'Why the unusual garb?' Tweed enquired, putting down his cup of coffee and refilling it from the pot. 'People will think you're one of those fabulously rich sheiks.'

'Oh, that.' Willie pulled at his moustache and grinned. 'After listening to Amos's speech tomorrow I'm off to the Middle East. They like you to turn up like this. Think it shows respect and all that.'

'Another business trip?'

'I hope so. Can't tell until I've seen them. They like playing cat and mouse. Hoping to get the price down. It won't succeed. If necessary I'll say I'm on the first plane home. Usually brings them to heel.' His drink had arrived. He raised his glass. 'To the memory of Dumont. Nice chap. Down the flaming hatch. And I've just pulled off a huge deal on the phone in the Middle East. A real coup. Supposed to keep it quiet.' He winked. 'Just among friends.'

Tweed realized Carrington was already half drunk. Then he recognized the symptoms from the word-ing Willie had used. He was power drunk, but still under a strange iron self-control. His eyes gleamed

116

when he stared at Tweed, gleamed with triumph. Why?

Amos had also noticed the phenomenon. Tweed glanced at the big man. The very different eyes gazed at Willie's with a fierce intensity, as though he could read his mind. The atmosphere had become electric.

'You don't give a damn for Dumont,' he began in his gravelly voice. 'All that concerns you is making another pile of money.'

'I say, old chap, that's not a very nice thing to say,' Willie responded in a quiet voice.

'In this world the truth often isn't very nice,' Amos shot back. 'To hell with your deal. What was it? Guns for the Arabs? Missiles?'

Tweed relaxed in his chair, keeping out of it. He studied both men as he sipped his coffee. What most intrigued him was that Willie was not in the least taken aback by Amos's onslaught. If anything, Willie suddenly seemed sober, was watching Amos with calculating eyes. Tweed hadn't realized how strong was Carrington's willpower, how he could handle any situation. The hail-fellow-well-met manner Tweed was accustomed to had been replaced by a man with great force of character. It was a revelation.

'Come off it, Amos,' Willie said coolly, 'Dumont was a close friend of mine. I know the last thing he'd want is a wake, so we'll let bygones be bygones.'

'If you say so,' rasped Amos.

'I do say so. Now I'll leave you two to chat. I feel like a walk in the sun – to recall old times.'

Saying which, he left them. Tweed watched him walking away and Willie's step was firm and steady.

'Never liked him,' Amos said.

'Why?'

117

'Too much bravado. Never trusted him. If you'll excuse me, I must go. See you later . . .'

He had just disappeared when a tall, bronzed man in a tracksuit strolled up to Tweed's table. Emilio Vitorelli sat down, carrying his drink.

'Something you should know . . .'

'I haven't seen you in a while, Emilio,' Tweed said to the Italian. 'At least three beautiful women have you in their sights.'

'Forget them. I suspect you are here to track down the women assassins who have wiped out eight men like swatting flies.'

'You're guessing.'

'Like you, I'm a good guesser.' Vitorelli stroked a hand over his thick fair hair. 'One of them is my meat.'

'You always talked in hints and riddles. Just for once be a little more specific.'

'You know my fiancée had her faced ruined for life by a woman who threw acid into it. Which caused my fiancée to plunge to her death by jumping from the platform in the Borghese Gardens in Rome straight down into the Pincio Square. That's a long drop. The name of the acid thrower, whom I had done my best to evade, is Tina Langley.'

Vitorelli, his handsome face, expressionless, took a long gulp at his drink. He looks so very athletic, Tweed thought – a man who was bound to attract the attention of women.

'Interesting. Very,' said Tweed.

'You always were cautious in your reactions,' Vitorelli remarked, and gave his engaging smile.

'What makes you say that?'

'Because you know very well, I'm sure, that Tina

118

Langley is an ex-girlfriend of Captain William Wellesley Carrington. Willie, as he is known, just left your
table.'

'Is this what I should know?'

'What you should know is that Tina Langley is a
member of the notorious group of women assassins –
The Sisterhood.'

12

Tweed glanced around the terrace while he absorbed
the shock of what Vitorelli had said. Marler, Butler and
Nield had all disappeared, but Tweed had not been left
on his own. Behind him, with her back to the wall, Paula
sat drinking coffee, looking past him at the garden. Her
shoulder bag hung over her shoulder and he guessed
inside the special pocket was her Browning .32, fully
loaded.

'The Sisterhood?' he repeated. 'Who are they?'

'At least three very attractive women used to lure
their targets to destruction, to a place where the assassin
concerned can shoot her victim in the back of the head –
and then make it look like suicide,' Vitorelli replied
grimly.

'Who controls The Sisterhood?' Tweed asked.

'No idea. Probably someone in your county of
Dorset.'

'Hence your message about the courier carrying a
large sum of money to that area.'

'It was all I had at that time.'

'How did you find out more?'

'I shouldn't tell you this, Tweed.' Vitorelli emptied
his glass and grinned. 'I suspect that as Chief Claims
Investigator for some big insurance outfit you have

119

contacts all over the world who supply information on the quiet. I have the same kind of network. The difference, I imagine, is mine operates at a much lower level than yours – deep in the underworld. Money changes hands, nothing is written down, whispers are exchanged. You understand me?'

'So far. But you haven't told me how you found out about the existence of this Sisterhood.'

'By pure chance. I am trying to trace the whereabouts of Tina Langley. The last I heard of her she was in Salzburg recently. Have I touched a nerve?'

Tweed warned himself to be more careful with his expressions. Emilio Vitorelli was clever, a very observant man.

The Italian *had* touched a nerve. Salzburg was not very far from Vienna. Norbert Engel had been murdered in that city – and Paula had caught a glimpse of his assassin.

'No,' he said quickly.

'I was about to depart for Salzburg,' Vitorelli went on. 'I then heard that she had disappeared again. I also heard she was a member of The Sisterhood. As an assassin . . .' he began slowly.

'What did you just say?' Tweed asked.

'As an assassin she fits the role. A woman who could throw acid in another woman's face is capable of anything. She is clever – up to a point – is Tina. She whisks from one place to another. Hence her nickname, The Butterfly.'

'Some butterfly.'

'If you find her, will you promise to let me know?'

'I will do what I can,' replied Tweed evasively.

'Why is it that I supply you with data and get so little in return?'

'The nature of my work.'

As a cover for the HQ of the SIS there was a plate

120

outside the building in Park Crescent. General & Cumbria Assurance. Tweed's pose as a Chief Claims Investigator explained his many trips abroad, his secrecy. The dummy insurance company was supposed to negotiate ransom claims when rich men were kidnapped.

Soon Tweed excused himself and Paula waited a moment, then strolled after him.

As an . . . Those were the words Vitorelli had spoken. Tweed repeated them to himself. *As an* . . . Hassan. Assam. The name of the man controlling The Sisterhood was Hassan, an Arabic name. It fitted perfectly.

'Hassan?' Paula said. 'That's a pretty common name.'

Tweed and Paula had met up inside his room after leaving the terrace. Walking slowly round the furniture, Tweed took his time before replying.

'It's a name,' he said eventually. 'Something we haven't had before.'

'Clever of you to catch on from what Vitorelli happened to say by chance. Assam – Hassan. They sound similar. Understandably, I must have misheard what the car driver said to me after the kidnap attempt.'

'With your gun on him the driver was probably scared stiff and stammering.'

'Marler told me you're having dinner this evening with Karin Berg at some place called the Ermitage. Aren't you taking yet another needless risk?' Paula commented.

'I knew Karin when she was with Swedish counter-espionage. She's no stranger.'

'So what is she doing now?' Paula demanded.

'Said she had a big security job with some international security organization. She's made for the job,' Tweed remarked.

'Which international organization?'

'She couldn't say. Part of her contract is not to reveal the company she's working for.'

'Very convenient,' Paula said vehemently. 'About The Sisterhood Vitorelli told you about. Women who kill cold-bloodedly for money – because you can be sure they get a big fat fee for their dirty work. Why should Karin know anything about them? She's out of the business.'

'She may know something without realizing she knows it. I'm exploring every avenue,' Tweed emphasized.

'Every dangerous avenue.'

'You know a better way?' There was an edge to Tweed's voice. 'I'm listening. Tell me.'

Paula was stumped. Desperately she tried to think of an alternative. Her mind kept coming up against brick walls.

'You're using yourself as bait,' she said eventually.

There was a knock on the door. In a state of tension and anxiety Paula jumped up, the Browning in her right hand. She went to the locked door.

'Who is it?' she called out.

'Message for Mr Tweed.'

'Shove it under the door.'

'I was asked to deliver this personally into his hands.'

'Shove it under the bloody door or I'm calling the Chief of Police.'

There was a pause. Then a white envelope was slid under the door. She picked it up, saw that it was addressed to Tweed, marked Personal. Picking it up she handed it to her chief. He opened it, took out a photograph, looked at it, slid it back inside the envelope.

'Calm down,' Tweed told her. 'Everything is under control.'

'The last time you said that the world nearly blew up in our faces.'

'Which could really happen if we don't neutralize the enemy. I had a phone call. From Beck. He was sending a car with armed guards to pick me up. I went downstairs in double quick time and two of Beck's men I recognized escorted me to an unmarked car. I was driven at top speed down one-way streets the wrong way to police headquarters overlooking the Limmat River. Beck was waiting for me. He'd had an urgent call from Cord Dillon, Deputy Director of the CIA in Langley – to call him on a safe phone. He had alarming news.'

'Alarm me,' she said quietly.

'Dillon reported the presence of a vast black cloud over the Middle Eastern state which is worrying us. The nature of the cloud made it chemically impossible for the sophisticated cameras of the American satellite passing over the desert area to penetrate it. They estimate the dimensions of the cloud were fifteen miles long by twenty miles wide. No wind, so it remained stationary. They suspect huge military manoeuvres were taking place under cover of the cloud. Beyond the edges of the cloud the cameras picked up ten dead camels, lying prostrate on the sand. It makes Washington think bacteriological weapons were being used.'

'Scary.'

'The President has forbidden any action to be taken – says it is a bluff.'

'What do you think?' Paula asked.

'A vast army is preparing to sweep across the Middle East to obliterate Israel. If successful, that would cause several Arab nations to ally themselves with the aggressor – would compel them to take that action. The army would then advance north to pass through Turkey, where Ultra-extremists – far more fanatical than Fundamentalists – are poised to take over the government in Ankara. From Turkey they would move north through the Balkans. First major objective, Vienna. Then on to

Munich. From there a swift advance to the Rhine. Their missiles could annihilate London.'

'You are quite a strategist – like Amos Lodge.'

'Oh, I expect he's worked all this out for himself,' Tweed replied.

'You have alarmed me.'

'Now, do you still think I shouldn't be using all my energy to find out who is behind the prelude – the assassinations?'

'I'll come with you tonight.'

'That would spoil everything. The answer is no,' Tweed told her.

'You expect me to sleep on that?'

'I don't expect you, of all people, to sleep. Now, I think I should show you the photograph which Vitorelli has sent me with a note. Here is the note.'

I have made copies. Here is a photo of Tina Langley.
Yours, E.

Paula stared at the glossy print which had accompanied the note. It was a good colour print and she studied it for two minutes, then looked up at Tweed.

'This is the woman who murdered Norbert Engel.'

'You're sure?'

'She only glanced round once on Kärntnerstrasse but I had a good look at her. I'm quite certain. We have identified one member of The Sisterhood.'

Tina Langley was staying at the Hôtel des Bergues in Geneva. She had registered as Lisa Vane and had been 'sidelined' there by Hassan. She knew the meaning of being 'sidelined' – it was rather like the coaches of a train which had, for the moment, been parked in a siding.

With her thick auburn hair, her well-shaped figure and her seductive smile she had already acquired a temporary Swiss man friend, a banker. This had been an easy capture for Tina, who was a beauty with smoky eyes. Her slow-moving eyes were her chief weapon, combined with a long nose and the full red mouth above a determined chin. She simply had to look at a man with those eyes and she had him in the palm of her hand. Only five foot five inches tall, she wore high heels to enhance her height. Her escort spoke English as they walked along the Rhône promenade.

'What part of England do you come from, Lisa?'

'Kent,' she lied immediately. 'Not a million miles from Dover. Which bank are you a director of?' she enquired casually.

He told her and she smiled inwardly. One of the major banks. It might be amusing to see how much she could take him for. Her real motive in striking up the acquaintance was that an attractive woman with a man was less likely to stand out than a woman by herself. Not that she expected the police to be looking for her in Geneva while she waited for Hassan to give her details of her next 'assignment'. It was a long way from Vienna.

She led him down a side street where there was a top-class jewellery store. Her preference was for diamonds and she gazed at a necklace glittering with the jewels. Anton, her new friend, stirred restlessly and she knew it was too early to try for a fabulously priced piece.

'It's nice,' she said, 'but so expensive.'

'You like it?' Anton asked.

He could immediately have bit off his tongue. The necklace was worth a small fortune. She glanced at him sideways, a long, slow look.

'Any woman who wore that would have to go out with guards. It's asking for trouble.'

She moved further along the window and stared at a string of pearls. Also very expensive but a fraction of the cost of the necklace.

'You fancy that?' he enquired.

'It's just the kind of thing which suits me.'

Anton, a tall, good-looking man in his forties, couldn't wait to get into her room. He took her into the shop and the manager, who had unlocked the door for them, then relocked it, took the pearls out of the window, placed them round her slim neck, fastened the clasp. She spent just the right amount of time gazing at herself in a mirror.

'They are me,' she said eventually.

Anton produced his credit card. While he was attending to the purchase with the manager Tina took a scarf out of her Gucci handbag, wrapped it round her auburn hair, concealing it. There was a strong breeze blowing along the Rhône but her main reason for the action was to change her appearance.

'The wind blows my hair,' she remarked, explaining why she had put it on.

'Such attractive hair.'

She made no reply. This was her first visit to Geneva and she thought the city beautiful. To their left flowed the green Rhône, which had flowed out of the lake under the Pont du Rhône. Now it was dividing and there were islands, linked to the shore by an intricate system of footbridges. On the far shore a line of old office buildings rose several storeys high. Beyond them a massive cliff, sheer and more like a mountain.

'Geneva is a very cosmopolitan city,' Anton told her. 'A lot of wealthy foreigners live here, working for big international companies.'

She pricked up her ears. It sounded as though there could be rich pickings here. What puzzled her was why she had been 'sidelined' to Geneva. Was there some unknown significance about the city? Without realizing it she had put her finger on the key.

'That Swiss mountain must have a marvellous view from the top.'

'It has. They call it Salève. But it is not in Switzerland. It is actually in France.'

When the phone rang in Jules Monceau's tiny bedroom he let it ring before picking up the receiver. It was bad tactics to make anyone think he was just waiting for the call.

'Yes,' he answered eventually.

'You know who is speaking,' began Hassan's smooth, oily voice.

'Of course.'

'I have heard that tonight Tweed will be dining with a woman at a restaurant outside Zurich called Ermitage. Ermitage,' he repeated. 'They will have a lakeside table, will arrive about nine in the evening. The rest is up to you.'

There was an evil smile on Monceau's face as he put down the phone. He reached for a map of the city which included the Zurichsee. A telephone book would give him the location. He had a lot of elaborate planning to do. This time Tweed would be killed. He'd be too absorbed by his companion, too full of wine to realize what was happening. Before it was too late.

13

Tina Langley was not known as The Butterfly without reason. Her mood changes, her dislike of staying in one place for long, were notorious. The strong-minded Willie

Carrington would certainly have agreed. Anton, her banker friend, was experiencing the same reaction.

'I want to go to France,' she suddenly announced in her soft, persuasive voice.

'Go to France?' Anton asked in surprise. 'It's a bit late in the day.'

'How long would it take to go to the top of Salève?' she persisted with a moue. 'You said your car was parked nearby.'

They were sitting in the bar of the Hôtel des Bergues, situated on a side street leading off the promenade road. She had been knocking back glasses of champagne as though they were water. Anton was hoping she would soon consent to inviting him up to her room.

'I'm not sure that's a good idea,' he said slowly.

'If I think it's a good idea then it's a wonderful idea,' she shouted at him. 'And if you're not interested then say so now and I'll leave. Who do you think you are? If I want to do something I do it. Right away. Hear me?' she hissed loudly in his ear.

It was embarrassing. There were other couples in the bar and they were all staring, some amused, some indignant at this outburst. Anton was not only embarrassed – he was fascinated by this sudden wild streak in her nature.

'If we go now,' he said, 'we should be there and back before dark, Lisa.'

Her mood changed again. She turned, gave him a flashing smile and kissed him on the cheek.

At the imposing Dolder Grand Hotel, perched on a hill overlooking Zurich, Willie was enjoying himself. He was chatting to a woman who was expensively dressed in the height of fashion. She would be, Willie said to himself – to afford to stay here.

'Might be able to put you on to an unusual assignment which would bring you in piles of money,' he said jovially.

'Really?'

The Spanish beauty, separated from her husband, her glossy hair black as the dead of night, was thinking: This is a new ploy. But I'll go along with it, up to a point, she decided. She was bored and Willie's personality had an exuberant animation which was fascinatimg to many women.

'Tell you what,' he continued, pulling at his moustache and grinning, 'we could have dinner at the Ermitage. Supposed to be one of the "in" places on the lake shore. Concierge here told me about it. Tomorrow night suit you? I'll suss out the place, make sure it's good enough for a lady of your standing. Do that this evening.'

'You're very thorough,' she observed, amused.

'Have to be, in my job.'

'What is that?' Carmen enquired.

'Selling guns, ammunition to Arab sheiks. They pay a mint because I'm known out there. Dine at palaces and all that nonsense. I imagine I've shocked you.'

'I'm not easy to shock, Willie.'

If he was telling the truth she was impressed. It sounded romantic, reminded her of what she had read about the days of the Spanish *plata* galleons, carrying gold plate, fighting the English raiders.

It was, in fact, just the impression of bravado Willie had attempted to create. He had a shrewd insight into what would impress a woman. Didn't matter whether they believed what tale he spun them as long as they liked it. In this case he had told the truth – which he rarely did.

'Tomorrow evening, then,' he said. 'Meet you here at eight – I'll drive us there. If the place is pukka. If not, I know somewhere else in Zurich.' He stood up. 'Excuse me, Carmen, but I have an appointment. Hope to pull off a big deal. Probably it will fall through.'

Clad in a blue tracksuit – which normally the management would not have approved of, but he spent a lot of money – he gave her a smart salute and was gone.

Physically, Amos Lodge was the least active. He was spending a lot of time in his room, drafting out the details of the speech he would be giving the following evening at the Kongresshaus.

His speech would be as terse and controversial and hard-hitting as when he was talking to individuals. A natural orator, he intended to blow the roof off Kongresshaus. He was annoyed when the phone rang. It was Beck.

'Mr Lodge, I'm calling to tell you that tomorrow night the Kongresshaus will be crawling with my armed men.'

'That would be a big turn-on. Uniformed police all over the place. Don't do it.'

'All my men will be in plain clothes. They will mingle with your audience. I have already bought a large number of tickets. You can't stop me doing it.'

'Plain-clothes men make it a bit better. I think you're wasting your manpower.'

'I don't. You could be a target. I have men inside the Baur au Lac now. You will be discreetly escorted to Kongresshaus. No good arguing with me, Mr Lodge.'

'If you say so,' Lodge growled, and slammed down the phone.

Anton was worried as he drove Tina up the spiralling road at the eastern end of the mountain called Salève.

130

They had passed through the French frontier post and this was a relief for Anton.

'Can't you drive any faster?' Tina demanded in a petulant tone. 'I could drive up here at twice your speed.'

'I'm sure you could.'

Anton relapsed into silence. At the bar in the Hôtel des Bergues he had made the mistake of keeping up with the woman he knew as Lisa Vane. His head was spinning and he refused to increase his speed. Lisa seemed able to consume huge quantities of champagne without it affecting her in the least.

'Travelling like a snail,' she gibed.

Seething inwardly, he maintained his careful pace all the way to the top of the mountain and then began the descent down the other side. He glanced at her several times and she was always staring ahead, expressing her frustration. As they pulled into the drive the Château d'Avignon in the middle of remote countryside her manner changed abruptly.

'Anton, what a beautiful chateau. And I appreciate your driving so safely.'

He realized she was not being sarcastic, that once again her mood had changed. Before getting out of the car she put a hand on his arm, leaned over and planted a brief kiss on his cheek. He was bewildered as she looked at him with distant eyes and gave him the most inviting smile, then jumped out.

The Château d'Avignon was an ancient building which had been carefully renovated. They mounted a flight of steps, walked through a vast hall to a dining room beyond. Two large doors were thrown open on to a terrace where tables were laid and couples sat drinking. Tina gasped at the view.

Below the wide terrace the land fell away in a series of vineyard-like levels. Grassy fields spread out in descending slopes beyond. In the distance a vast panorama of France stretched out with here and there a small range of hills, a brownish colour in the evening light which was casting a luminous glow over the endless landscape. Hamlets were nestled in the valleys between the hills, the houses like toys. To their left a distant lake glittered azure in the setting sun.

'It's like a painting,' Anton remarked.

Tina didn't hear him. She was staring at a handsome tanned man sitting at one of the tables with a woman. He was gazing back at her with considerable interest. Tina felt a thrill – she lived for admiration from good-looking men, and for money.

'The view is pretty marvellous,' the man said. 'Sam West.'

'Nice to meet a fellow countryman,' she purred, soaking up the admiration in his look.

Then West noticed Anton and realized she had an escort. He nodded, averted his gaze from her. The woman with him was amused. She said in a low voice which Anton heard.

'Enjoying yourself, Sam?'

'We're having a great evening,' he assured her with a smile.

There was an empty table next to where West sat. Anton was looking at other empty tables further away. He moved towards one but Tina spoke sharply.

'Anton, let's sit at this table. We get the view to the best advantage.'

'If you prefer it.'

'I do.' She sat down close to West. Waving both arms in the air she called out as the waiter approached. 'We want champagne. Oodles of it.'

Anton groaned inwardly. He asked the waiter to bring a large bottle of sparkling mineral water as well. West had tactfully swivelled his chair so he was not looking at Tina. One bottle of champagne disappeared and Tina asked for another bottle. She had drunk most of the first because Anton was sipping at his glass and drinking a lot of mineral water. I have to drive back, Heaven help me, he was thinking.

Tina changed to another chair, which positioned her so she could face West. Anton leaned forward, whispered to her, making sure his voice didn't carry.

'He has his own girlfriend with him.'

'You don't own me,' she yelled at the top of her voice.

Other couples at their tables turned round to stare at her. It appeared most of them were French and they looked disapproving at the way she had raised her voice. Once again Anton felt embarrassed. Tina was starting on yet another full glass of champagne when Anton spoke to West.

'Excuse me, sir,' he said in his flawless English, 'but do you happen to know who owns this place?'

'It's a bit weird. I understand French and we were here before when the accountant was talking to the manager. I gathered from what I overheard that some company in the Channel Islands bought it. At least it's registered there. But it's really controlled by some Englishman in Dorset.'

Tina choked on her champagne. She spilt some of her glass on the table. Then she gave Anton a warm smile.

'It's the bubbles.'

14

Tweed had found Emilio Vitorelli sunning himself on the terrace. He asked the Italian to come with him to his room. Paula was waiting when they entered.

'You know Emilio,' he said to her.

'We all met quite some time ago in Rome. Good morning, Mr Vitorelli.'

'Emilio, please.'

She didn't reply as Tweed ushered him to a hard-backed seat behind a polished table. Tweed sat down opposite his guest who was eyeing Paula. She stared back with no particular expression, even when he smiled at her with great warmth.

He had always liked Paula on the few occasions they had met. Paula's reaction was not so approving. She regarded him as the typical Latin on the make with women – but she was still astute enough to realize he had a dynamic personality, that he was clever.

'I asked you here to show you something,' Tweed began. 'The photo you were kind enough to send me. This is Tina Langley?'

He produced the glossy print he had concealed on his lap and slid it across the table. Vitorelli stared at it and Paula noticed the change in his expression. It was now grim.

'That is the lady in question,' he replied quietly.

'I can tell you she murdered a man in Vienna. She is the one who killed Norbert Engel. Came up behind him with a Luger, shot him in the back of the head. You could say she's a fully paid-up member of The Sisterhood.'

'I see.'

Vitorelli teetered back in his chair, folded his large hands across his stomach. He glanced at Paula who was once more studying the list of the men belonging to the *Institut de la Défense*.

'For a moment you surprised me,' the Italian commented. 'On thinking about it I imagine a woman capable of hurling acid into another woman's face – as she did to my late fiancée – would not stop at murder if big money were involved.'

'It had to be a very attractive woman to tempt Norbert Engel,' Tweed continued, pursuing his theme relentlessly.

'Tina Langely is an exceptionally attractive woman. She very nearly distracted me from my fiancée with her vibrant personality. But I pulled myself up, knowing my fiancée had so much more to offer – not only in the way of appearance and poise but, very important, in intellect. Had she remained on this earth,' he reflected sombrely, 'we would have been the perfect couple. A very remarkable woman was destroyed by this hideous killer.'

Paula was startled. His voice had changed. He had spoken with terrible venom. His normally laughing eyes had become ice-cold. Tweed tapped the photo.

'Are there other copies of this print, other than the one I am sure you have kept for yourself?'

'Why do you ask?'

'Because I am convinced there are many copies. We both are after the same person.'

'I'm surprised you wish to collaborate with a rogue like me,' Vitorelli replied with a broad smile.

'The position is so serious I would collaborate with the Devil if it came to it.'

'Perhaps you are doing just that. Yes, there are many copies. They are in the hands of my large underground network which is searching Europe for her. No wonder she has been nicknamed The Butterfly. She flits from place to place, never staying anywhere for long. She is a restless creature. Sometimes I think she is a lost soul, seeking some paradise on earth, a paradise she will never find.'

'You paint a vivid picture of her,' Tweed commented.

'Also, my chief lieutenant and confidant is trawling the main cities of Switzerland with a photo, looking for her.'

'Why Switzerland?'

'Because I know how her devious mind works. She was last seen briefly in Salzburg. So she would move on to another country. Now you tell me she was involved in Norbert Engel's murder in Vienna I am even more sure she would pick a neutral state like Switzerland.'

'Also,' Paula spoke for the first time, 'it strikes me it fits in with your description of The Butterfly – temperamentally never able to stay in one place for long.'

'That is clever,' Vitorelli said slowly, looking at Paula with fresh respect. 'It is very good psychology.'

'Merely one woman seeing into the mind of another.'

'Which cities,' Tweed enquired, 'has your deputy visited so far?'

'Zurich, Basle, Lausanne. He is now in Geneva. From scraps of information my network has picked up there is something odd about Geneva, something important.'

'It is the city where the Monceau gang infiltrated Switzerland from France,' Tweed told him. 'Maybe there is a link somewhere.'

'Who knows. I must go now.' The Italian stood up. 'Perhaps we should keep in touch?'

'I think we should,' Tweed agreed.

* * *

Marler arrived soon after Vitorelli had left them. He wore a rather dingy lightweight suit. No creases in his trousers, his clothes crumpled. Paula stared at him.

'What's happened? Normally you're sartorially so elegant and now, if you'll excuse me, you look more like a scarecrow.'

'Not very noticeable?' Marler replied ironically.

'Hardly, to say the least.'

'That's the general idea. I've been snooping round.' He took off the sunglasses, excessively larger than the pair he would normally have chosen. 'I applied for a job as porter at the Dolder Grand. They turned me down. Amazing!'

'Supposing they'd accepted you?'

'I'd have told them the pay wasn't good enough. Then I pulled out a roll of banknotes which made the concierge's eyes pop. Said I was going to the bar. He was so taken aback he didn't try to stop me. Probably thought I was one of those oddball millionaires who don't care how they look, that it was all a practical joke.'

'You found something there?' Tweed enquired.

'I found someone wasn't there. Captain William Wellesley Carrington, who had been staying there, had checked out suddenly. I got on well with the barman.'

'He's disappeared?' Tweed asked.

'Checked out. Next stage of the report. Amos Lodge so far has spent the whole morning locked away in his room. Had his breakfast sent up. Learn anything from that amiable rascal, Emilio Vitorelli?'

Tweed told him everything the Italian had revealed. Marler looked thoughtful. He leant against a wall, lit a king-size.

'So there's something special about Geneva?'

'Possibly,' Tweed said vaguely.

'I'd better trot off, get into some decent tropical gear before the Baur au Lac throws me out.' He paused at the

137

door. 'Oh, by the way, Butler and Nield have also been very active. Won't bore you with the details. And Carrington is staying at the Gotthard at the other end of Bahnhofstrasse.'

'How did you find that out?' Tweed demanded.

'I gave them a description of Carrington. Not easy to miss *him*. Pete Nield saw him booking in with his luggage at the hotel they're staying at. See you.'

When he had gone Paula stood up and restlessly began walking round the spacious room. She was looking out of the window down at the entrance drive when she saw Marler, smartly dressed in a white linen suit, hurrying to the car he had hired. Butler appeared, got into the front passenger seat. Marler drove off. She told Tweed what she had seen.

'Marler is a law unto himself,' Tweed responded. 'He's up to something. Why are you acting like me, pacing round as though you can't keep still? I'm wondering whether to ask you to go to Geneva. You could take this photo with you – I shall certainly recognize Tina Langley if I ever see her.'

'Marler told me to stay here.'

'And I thought I was running this outfit,' Tweed said with a smile.

'You just approved of Marler going his own way. Newman has disappeared too. Why do you think Willie abandoned the Dolder Grand and slipped away to the Gotthard? He could be running scared.'

'Doesn't sound like Willie. He may have another reason.'

'Such as?'

'The Gotthard is closer to both the main rail station and the airport. Just a thought. What I'm wondering is what is Jules Monceau up to?'

* * *

Mario Parcelli, Vitorelli's confidant, was footsore. The sun was blazing down on Geneva out of a clear sky and the temperature went on rising. He had enquired at every major hotel in the city and had drawn a blank. His technique had been carefully thought out. He approached the concierge in each hotel.

'I am trying to contact my sister, Tina Langley. She sent me a fax just before flying out here but the name of the hotel was unreadable. I'm talking about Tina Langley. You might like to see my card.'

He had then produced the visiting card swiftly printed in Zurich and had laid it on the counter.

RUTLAND & WARWICKSHIRE BANK
Mark Langley. Director.

He knew that in Switzerland bank directors ranked high in the social league. He also knew that no concierge of a major hotel would dream of revealing to a stranger the name of a guest staying there. But he had a trump card. Before a concierge could react he then placed the photo of Tina Langley on the counter.

'That is my sister.'

Again he anticipated total discretion on the part of a concierge. But Mario was very observant. The moment a concierge looked down at the glossy print he watched him like a hawk, watched for the brief sign of recognition in an otherwise impassive face. So far he was convinced Tina was not staying at any place he had visited.

He had just left the Hôtel des Bergues. It was Mario's bad luck that the concierge he dealt with was new to the job, was standing in for the permanent concierge. No reaction.

He picked up card and photo, walked out into the heat, turned right, glanced into the Pavillon restaurant attached to des Bergues. The windows fronted on to the promenade. No sign of her. He started walking along the promenade, looked down a small side street running alongside the hotel, saw her.

She was gazing into a shop window as he walked slowly along the opposite side of the street to make sure. He glanced down at the photo in his hand – which was a mistake.

Tina saw the man dressed like a banker look down at something in his hand, guessed it was a photo. She stiffened, then strolled slowly further down the street. The enemy was looking for her – probably the people Roka had saved her from back in Vienna.

She strolled on, forcing herself not to hurry. Ahead she saw a large department store she had investigated earlier. She walked straight inside, relieved to see it was crowded with people escaping from the heat. Her mind was racing. She had in the past had plenty of experience in the art of disappearing from men she had exploited. She looked back and saw the small fat man standing at the entrance. She decided to nickname him Teddy Bear.

He was obviously afraid of losing her so he was staying hanging about at the entrance. In the luggage department she bought a cheap suitcase. She then proceeded from one department to another, buying cheap clothes at random, anything to make the suitcase heavy.

When Tina had finished buying her purchases she strolled back towards the entrance. Teddy Bear was waiting on the opposite side of the street. She paused, saw a patrol car moving slowly down the street. The perfect opportunity. Going outside, she hailed one of the numerous taxis crawling past.

'Please take me to Cornavin, the rail station,' she called out in a loud voice.

As her taxi took off Mario hailed another cab, gave the driver the same instructions. Tina was careful not to look back, but in the rear-view mirror she saw Teddy Bear's taxi following hers. She smiled to herself.

Arriving at the station, she paid off the driver, carried her case into the station. There was a queue at the ticket counter but she knew Teddy Bear was behind her with one woman between them. He had probably been careful not to be too close to her. She raised her voice again when she reached the counter.

'One single ticket to Zurich, please. Thank you. When is the next express leaving?'

'In about five minutes. Check the monitor for the platform.'

She hurried down a ramp, climbed the steps to the *quai* – the platform from which the express was leaving. Checking with a station official, she located where the front of the express would stop and hurried along to the right place. Putting down her bag, she took out an expensive lace-bordered handkerchief, mopped the moisture off her forehead.

Teddy Bear had stopped a distance away, close to where the end of the express would halt. She picked up her case when the gleaming express, many coaches long, glided in. Boarding a coach opposite a pillar on the platform near the front, she rested her suitcase in an empty compartment, picked up a copy of the timetable which showed her exactly when the express would arrive and leave at the few stations it stopped at.

It was one advantage of Swiss trains that they arrived precisely at the scheduled time, left exactly on the scheduled time. She picked up the suitcase, parked it in the corridor near the exit door. Then she watched the

141

hands turning on a huge station clock outside the window.

Once she risked a glance out of the window, looking down the platform. No sign of Teddy Bear among a whole crowd of last-minute passengers who were scrambling aboard. Fifteen seconds before the automatic door would close, she descended back on to the platform with her case, hid herself behind the large pillar.

Promptly, the automatic doors closed, the express glided out of the station. When it was gone she took a last look at the rear of the end coach. She giggled.

Mario, starting from the end of the train, had a difficult job. So many passengers had piled aboard just before the express had departed it was a slow job trudging slowly from compartment to compartment, from coach to coach, checking every passenger.

He was only halfway along the train when it stopped at Lausanne. He poked his head out of a window, thinking Tina might get off. No sign of her. The train started moving again and the next stop, Berne, was a long way north. His feet were killing him. He was wearing smart shoes to go with the image of a banker and they pinched his toes.

He had checked the whole length of the express long before it reached Berne. He sat down in an empty compartment, bought three cartons of coffee and two bottles of mineral water from the food and drinks trolley when it eventually reached him.

Exhausted, he got off the train at Berne. Sinking down on a seat he waited for the next express travelling in the opposite direction. Remembering he only had a single ticket, he forced himself to walk the long distance to the ticket office, bought a single back to Geneva.

The heat inside the huge cavern which is Berne station was near unbearable. Mario, having bought his ticket, parked himself on a seat to wait for the express. His shirt was pasted to his back, his collar was damp and shapeless, he could feel sweat trickling down from under his armpits. He'd have given anything to remove his shoes but he daren't – if he did he would never get his feet inside them again. But Mario Parcelli was a determined man.

He was sure Tina Langley was still in Geneva – and he was going to find her.

When the express arrived it was apparent the heat was affecting other people badly. Normally well-behaved, they pushed people aside to secure a seat on the train. Mario found himself lifted up by the crush, literally forced aboard. He had to shove himself to avoid tripping over the high step into the coach. He chose to stand in a corridor rather than join other passengers crammed into seats.

The first thing he was going to do on arriving in Geneva was to find a shop which sold shoes. Then have a brief meal – before he took up the search for Tina Langley in earnest.

After taking a cold shower, which made her feel much better, Tina put on a fresh set of clothes. Earlier she had taken a taxi back to the Hôtel des Bergues. Instead of going into the hotel she had wandered along the river front. The heat had driven most people indoors. At a quiet spot, she had thrown the unwanted suitcase into the Rhône.

She checked her appearance carefully in the mirror after making herself up. Until Hassan contacted her she had decided to call Anton, at the number he had given her. She would accept the invitation to dinner she knew

143

he would suggest – but at a restaurant, not at his apartment. She rehearsed in her head how she would make her move after the wine had flowed.

'This is embarrassing for me, Anton, but some traveller's cheques which should have come to me by Federal Express have not arrived. It's left me very short. Do you think you could loan me twenty thousand francs? As soon as the cheques arrive I'll bring the money back to your apartment . . .'

She would give him her very special smile. He was crazy about her. Strike while the iron is hot before the fire begins to fade, she thought, mixing her metaphors. The phone rang. She knew it would be Anton. She let it ring for several times, then lifted the receiver.

It was Hassan on the line.

'I have to leave this hotel for somewhere else . . .' she began.

'You will stay where you are. On no account are you to move.'

'I don't like people speaking to me in that way—'

'I have had too much of your impertinence. Don't dare to interrupt. You will just listen. You are a highly paid employee of the company,' he went on, phrasing his words carefully. 'We can always find someone else to take your place,' he said arrogantly.

She sucked in her breath. This was a different Hassan from the man she had known so far. His voice was demanding, brooking no arguments. The smooth, oily manner had vanished. In its place was a hard, ruthless voice.

'You will have another assignment to carry out soon. You will obtain tomorrow any references you need for the job from this man at this address . . . He has your description. That is all.'

References? She knew he had given her details of where she could obtain a Luger and ammunition. She was about to put down the phone when he spoke again.

'In future, for the moment, you can get me at this number . . .'

This time she did put the phone down. Thinking for a few minutes, she called the concierge, asked him which city had the code number Hassan had given her for his new phone number.

'That is Zurich, madame,' the concierge replied immediately.

In his room at the Baur au Lac Tweed had sat in silence for ten minutes. Paula knew this because she had discreetly timed him. He spoke suddenly.

'I'm checking my memory. You have the list of members of the *Institut de la Défense*. I am next on the list, below me is Amos Lodge. Who is below Lodge?'

'Christopher Kane. Why?'

'We have assumed so far the enemy is working his way down the list. We have overlooked the fact that he may jump one or two names. That would eliminate any chance of the target asking for protection.'

'Who is Christopher Kane?'

'The world's greatest expert on biological warfare – and the antidotes to all its forms. He's moved from London to Geneva.'

'Why?'

'I'm not sure. I knew him in London and asked him the same question. He gave me a curious reply. Said he wanted to move closer to the battlefield.'

'What did that mean?'

'I don't know. I asked Chris the same question and he didn't elaborate. Odd the way Geneva keeps cropping up. Mario Parcelli is in that city, looking for Tina

145

Langley. Monceau and his gang slipped through Beck's clutches passing through Geneva. I sense the net is closing on whoever is behind the murders – and on what I'm convinced are preparations for a great catastrophe so far as Europe is concerned.'

'I keep wondering where Monceau is, what he's doing.'

'So do I.

Hassan had been careful to give members of The Sisterhood the impression he was a middleman, the go-between for someone very much higher up and more powerful. In fact, he was the son of the Head of State of the power which had conducted military manoeuvres under the blanket of the black cloud. The Englishman had great influence with his father, an influence Hassan was jealous of. He had argued with his father to no avail.

'The Englishman understands the psychology of the members of the *Institut de la Défense*,' his father had insisted. 'They must all be destroyed before we can launch our great operation. Even one of them might influence his government to take steps to organize a formidable force at short notice. Do as I say.'

Now Hassan's patience had snapped. He was convinced he could achieve what the Englishman was causing to happen himself. At the moment most of the members of the *Institut* were in Switzerland, or visiting it. Which made sense – their headquarters were at Ouchy on the shores of Lake Geneva.

On the verge of leaving the strange house in Slovakia, he had booked a suite at the Hotel Zum Storchen in Zurich which overlooked the Limmat River and was situated in one of the Old Towns. He had used the name Ashley Wingfield.

146

Hassan had once been educated in England, had attended the military establishment at Sandhurst, rising to the rank of lieutenant. He would have no difficulty passing himself off as an Englishman and he had a forged passport in the temporary name he had chosen for himself.

The fact that his skin was brownish didn't worry him at all. He knew that half the people walking round Zurich had a suntan due to the ferocious heat.

He drove himself down the spiralling road at one end of the mountain and it took him little over one hour to reach Schwechat Airport, well outside Vienna. Ashley Wingfield's planning was always precise. He arrived in time to board the flight for Zurich on Austrian Airlines. In a little over two hours he was esconced in a suite in Zum Storchen.

He wore a Savile Row suit and the tie of a well-known British regiment. The heat did not bother him – he was used to far higher temperatures back home. Lighting a Havana cigar, he stared down, at Zurich's second Altstadt – Old Town – across the gently flowing Limmat River.

Now he had arrived there would be fireworks in this citadel of the declining West. He wanted the remaining members of the *Institut* wiped out quickly. Who, he was wondering, would kill Tweed first? Karin Berg or that piece of rubbish, Jules Monceau? Hassan was a cultured man.

15

'Curious,' Paula said, as Tweed sat in a chair in his room, his mind roaming, 'that Willie should suddenly move from the Dolder Grand to the Gotthard.'

'Yes, it is. I'm wondering if he's meeting someone secretly. The Dolder Grand would be a rather public rendezvous.'

'Who do you think he could be meeting?'

'Maybe someone who has just arrived in town and doesn't want to be observed.'

'So who could that be?'

'Maybe the mysterious Hassan.'

Paula stared at him. She knew Tweed had these odd flashes of insight. It came from his ferocious concentration on all aspects of a problem. He made mind-leaps which had astounded her in the past.

'What would he be doing in Zurich?'

'If he's running The Sisterhood, as I suspect he is, he may have arrived to hurry up the elimination of the surviving members of the *Institut*.' Tweed frowned. 'If my theory should be correct – and it's only a theory – the danger to the West is even closer than I had thought.'

'An Arab should not be impossible to track down . . .'

'I prefer the word Easterner. Don't forget that many have been educated in the West, particularly in Britain. So he'll speak perfect English, could pass for an Englishman.'

'The colour of his skin would give him away,' Paula objected.

'Look out of the window. The heatwave has lasted long enough for most of the locals to have a strong tan.'

'But we could ask Marler to check the top hotels,' she persisted. 'To find out if anyone new has arrived today. Marler has a way of persuading concierges to talk. I'd start with the Dolder Grand.'

'Why that particular hotel?'

'Because it's the one Willie suddenly checked out of.'

'I don't follow that.'

'Because if Willie was going to meet someone in

secret he'd be bound to move to another location to meet that person.'

'Not a very logical conclusion.'

'Call it a woman's intuition. I know it doesn't always work – but often it does . . .'

There was a knock on the door. Paula jumped up, Browning in her hand, unlocked the door. As if on cue, it was Marler who walked in.

'Everything is arranged,' he announced. 'Think I'll have a catnap in my room. I came along to see if there have been any developments.'

'Unfortunately for you,' Tweed said with a smile, 'Paula has come up with a development. You started this, Paula, so you can tell him.'

Marler leant against a wall while he listened. Just when she thought he had forgotten Marler took out a king-size and lit it, studying her.

'I can check the expensive hotels, but it's a long shot. So what have we go so far, Tweed?'

'We have a series of cold-blooded murders. By The Sisterhood. Only known member Tina Langley – confirmed by Paula and the photo Emilio Vitorelli gave me. We know the Monceau gang is close – Beck reckons with seven thugs left after the abortive attempt to kill me. We have Geneva, which may or may not be a key city. According to Vitorelli, and I believe him, large sums are sent by courier to someone in Dorset. Two prominent citizens from Dorset, Amos Lodge and Willie, are here. The Americans report a certain Eastern state is preparing an attack on Western Europe. We have Hassan, who runs The Sisterhood, whereabouts unknown. That's it.'

'In other words,' Marler summed up, 'we have damn-all.'

'We do have a little more,' Paula said. 'We have penetrated the technique whereby the murders are carried out. We know now that an attractive woman approaches The Sisterhood's target, gains his confidence, then at her first opportunity shoots him in the back of the head with a Luger, followed by an amateurish attempt to make it look like suicide.'

'Why amateurish?' Marler queried.

'I've cracked that one,' Tweed broke in. 'It's deliberately made to look amateurish. These nice people led by Hassan are out to intimidate and terrorize after they have killed a target. To make every remaining member of the *Institut* look over his shoulder, to turn him into a nervous wreck – then he'll be easier prey for The Sisterhood, will welcome some feminine company, will then let his guard down.'

'That's fiendish,' Paula protested.

'It's a ruthless, cold-blooded system which has been worked out well in advance. I've analysed their psychology and the method fits. What complicates everything is the arrival of the Monceau gang – which makes two enemies to deal with.'

'I have a suggestion,' Paula said. 'Why not deal with one problem at a time? Concentrate on cleaning up Monceau and his thugs. Then we can turn our full attention to wiping out The Sisterhood.'

'Which means using Tweed as bait,' Marler drawled.

'God!' Paula was horrified. 'I'd forgotten that angle.'

'I hadn't,' said Tweed. 'I think your tactics are sound. Monceau will undoubtedly try again to eliminate me. That is when we trap him. Now,' he went on briskly, 'I must warn Beck about another target – Christopher Kane, who has moved to Geneva. I'll ask Beck to have him guarded night and day. As the prime expert in the world on bacteriological warfare he has to be a number one target. I'm calling Beck now . . .'

*   *   *

In his cramped quarters inside his small hotel Jules Monceau had summoned the remaining six members of his gang. On the bed he had spread out a map which he had studied for hours. It was a detailed map which showed the Küsnacht district and the lake beyond. He addressed most of his remarks to Georges Lemont, his explosives expert.

'You've been to the Ermitage?'

'Yes,' Lemont replied in French, the language his chief was using.

Lemont was a tiny figure with a long face tapered to a pointed chin. He was always smiling as though he found life amusing.

'You really know the layout?' Monceau demanded.

'Yes,' replied Lemont, a man of few words.

'You know it thoroughly?'

'Yes.'

Lemont dropped a carefully drawn pencil sketch on the table which indicated a complete plan of the hotel and restaurant. He had even measured the length of its lake frontage by pacing out the distance. His plan showed the jetty projecting out on the Zurich city side of the hotel terrace.

'You have prepared the special weapon?' Monceau went on.

'Yes.'

'Are you sure it will work? This laser-guided rocket from the boat out on the lake?'

'Yes.'

'And you have back-up weaponry in case the rocket does not work? Will you have a fusillade ready to bombard the terrace?'

'Yes.'

'Tweed will arrive there with a woman companion at nine o'clock this evening. You have the timing worked out?'

'Yes.'

Monceau gave up. Georges Lemont was still smiling when he was dismissed from the room with the other five men. Well, he said to himself, you will see tonight what an excellent planner I am. He had no doubt Monceau would be somewhere near but safe – so he could watch the destruction of Tweed.

'Is that you, Tweed?' Beck's cheerful voice enquired over the phone. 'I have news for you. Amos Lodge's speech at the Kongresshaus has been postponed until tomorrow night.'

'Really? Why?'

'We have had an anonymous call warning us a bomb has been placed inside the building. It will take hours to check the whole complex. It may be a hoax, but we can't assume that.'

'How did Amos react to the news?'

'In a storming fury. I told him to arrange for stickers to be printed and plastered across all the posters he's had put up in Zurich. At his own expense, of course.'

'So he's not best pleased?'

'He thundered at me down the phone. I have more news, which you won't like. You asked me to guard Christopher Kane, the bacteriological warfare expert, in Geneva. Kane has refused point-blank to have any protection assigned to him.'

'That sounds like Christopher. He's a very independent and private person.'

'He's going to be even more private if he has the back of his head blown off. All for now. I expect it's enough . . .'

Paula sat very still for several minutes after the phone call which Tweed had told her about. She was staring at her shoes before she expressed her thought.

'I find something sinister about this bomb hoax thing.'

'Really?' Tweed's thoughts were miles away. 'In what way could it be sinister?'

'The trouble is I don't know. Again, call it my woman's intuition, but don't laugh.'

'I'm not laughing. If you'll excuse me it's almost evening and I have to change for my dinner at the Ermitage with Karin Berg.'

Paula's intuition was dangerously correct. Not far from the top of Bahnhofstrasse the Englishman had boarded a tram which took him up to the summit of the Zurichberg, the high forested hill behind the city.

The tram climbed and curved until it had left the suburbs behind and reached its terminus. Even in the sunlight the dark fir forest looked menacing. He found Hassan sitting on a seat at the edge of the forest.

There was no one else about. The heat had kept the locals and the tourists close to the lake. Sitting next to Hassan, the Englishman stared into the distance. He had left a space between them. Anyone observing them from a distance might well assume they were strangers – they were occupying the only seat in sight.

'Tweed is going tonight. For ever,' Hassan said, his lips hardly moving.

'Good show.'

'The killing will take place just outside Zurich. It is important the police force is otherwise occupied.'

'Would help, I suppose.'

'So when you get back to Zurich you make a call to

police headquarters, disguising your voice. You tell them a bomb has been placed in Kongresshaus.'

'What on earth good will that do?'

'My psychology is better than yours. They have a certain number of police guarding Kongresshaus. I visited the place late this afternoon. It is enormous. Imagine how many police it will take to search such a vast place for a bomb. It will take them well away from where the next target will be tonight. You had better go now, my friend. A tram is arriving – it will soon be returning to Zurich. Make the call as soon as you can. So, Tweed goes down tonight.'

Tweed, smartly dressed, arrived in the lounge of the Baur au Lac promptly at 8.30 p.m. Karin Berg, dressed all in black, which contrasted well with her blonde hair, was waiting for him.

'Punctuality always was one of your virtues,' he greeted her.

'Probably my only one,' she replied with a smile.

The limousine Tweed had ordered was waiting for them in the drive. The chauffeur opened the rear door and they settled themselves. It was air-conditioned, which was a relief. The heatwave had gone on so long that even at night it was humid and sticky.

Tweed took out a silver cigarette case, a present from his wife in the days when he smoked. He offered one to Karin, knowing she still smoked. He'd seen her stub out a cigarette in the lounge when he appeared. He lit it for her with an old lighter as the car swung out of the drive, proceeded towards the lake.

'I told you it was my only virtue,' she said, giving him her slow smile.

Tweed appeared to have trouble closing the case. He

tapped it against the window. As he'd thought, it was armoured glass. Who on earth had arranged that?

Earlier Marler had phoned Beck. The conversation was short, to the point.

'Beck, Tweed is dining with an old woman friend at the Ermitage this evening. He's ordered a car from the concierge, which I have cancelled. Can you provide protection?'

'I can and will,' Beck had replied. 'I will send a car with armoured glass and reinforced bodywork. Unfortunately I can do no more. I can't even send an armed plain-clothes man as driver – most of my men are tied up searching for a bomb at Kongresshaus, the rest are helping with a multiple collision on a road outside Zurich. Alternately, persuade Tweed to cancel his dinner.'

'You know Tweed. He wouldn't do it. Thanks for the car . . .'

Soon Tweed noticed they were driving along Seefeldstrasse. The long street lined with office blocks and later with old villas seemed to go on and on. Küsnacht was further out than he had realized.

'Do you mind if I smoke another cigarette?' Karin asked.

'Of course not.'

She was chain-smoking, lighting one cigarette from another. He remembered from their acquaintance years before it had been a habit of hers when she was either concentrating ferociously on some problem or when she was nervous.

'Something wrong?' he enquired.

'Yes, the heat. Remember, I come from Sweden. On occasion it is very hot in Stockholm but only rarely. I have never experienced such heat going on for so long. Thank Heaven the car is air-conditioned. Do you think it will be cooler where we're going?'

'Let us hope so. The Ermitage is by the lake.'

Secretly he doubted whether there would be any relief there. The heatwave had persisted for long enough to make the nights as sultry and oppressive as the days. Perhaps there would be a breeze off the lake.

'You seem cool enough,' she remarked, discreetly mopping her moist forehead.

'I find I can stand the heat, but that doesn't mean I like it.'

It was a fact that Tweed, although dressed in a dark business suit, was able to endure torrid heat without it affecting his alertness.

Normally, in the past, his social conversations with Karin had always been intriguing. She had talked about serious issues, about the world situation. Now she was indulging in trivia. He sensed the triteness of what she was saying was due to a feeling that she ought to be saying something rather than sitting beside him in silence. It could be the heat, of course, so why did he feel so strongly it had nothing to do with the temperature?

The Ermitage was reached when they had passed a number of very expensive-looking old villas. This was a district for the wealthy. The car eventually turned off the endless road and parked in a drive which was crammed with cars. The manager came out to meet them.

'Mr Tweed, sir? Your friend, Beck, phoned and asked us to look after you. We have reserved one of our best tables at the edge of the lake.'

'Good,' Tweed replied, 'that was what I asked for when I made the reservation myself.'

'You may have an even better table, sir, with Mr Beck calling me. This way, please.'

The Ermitage was a large building standing back a little from the lake. Behind it was a wide terrace with scattered tables overlooking the Zurichsee. Tweed's table was at the very edge of the water with a low stone wall dividing terrace from lake.

'This is a lovely place,' Karin commented, looking round at all the lights illuminating the terrace. 'As in the past, your taste is perfect.'

'Thank you.'

Once they were seated Tweed glanced round at the other tables. All of them were full. At one table further back sat a single man, tall and thin with dark hair draped across his forehead in a way which gave him a faint resemblance to Hitler. He also had a small dark moustache. He was studying the menu and summoned a waiter as soon as Tweed and his companion had sat down. Presumably he had got fed up waiting for his guest.

At another table close to some bushes there was the shadow of a man. He also was alone and sat very still, almost like a statue. At other tables couples and groups were having the time of their lives. There was a lot of noise – the babble of the guests' voices, laughter, mingling with the clink of glasses. The atmosphere on the terrace was one of great party celebrating some great event.

'What would you like to drink?' Tweed asked.

'A dry Martini.'

Tweed also ordered one of his rare aperitifs. He was thinking Karin still liked a strong drink. On her left wrist, exposed below the black cuff of her dress, which did not hug her figure too tightly, she wore a diamond-studded wristwatch. She had glanced at it as they sat down. Now she checked it briefly again.

'We have plenty of time,' Tweed assured her with a smile.

'All the time in the world. Cheers!'

They clinked glasses. Karin drank half hers at one

gulp as Tweed sipped his own. A waiter laid menus before them, a wine list in front of Tweed. He told them there was no hurry, that he would be back later. Tweed was looking at the wristwatch.

'A present from some admirer? You must have plenty of them?'

'Wristwatches?' she joked.

'No, admirers,' he said gallantly.

'As a matter of fact it's a present from myself. I don't mix with men much these days.'

'Why not? You used to. And you're still in your thirties.'

'My job takes up most of my time. If I have a few free hours I usually sleep – ready for the next business onslaught. Security at the top, as you know, requires all your energy. What about yourself? Surely you have the odd girlfriend?'

'My job takes up most of my time,' he replied, repeating what she had said about herself. 'Maybe we should study the menu – I hear it is a good one . . .'

As he held the menu he studied the lake shore and what lay out beyond it. The night was still very hot and humid, had the feel of a pea-soup fog although the view was crystal clear. On the far side of Zurichsee the opposite shore was studded with lights, rather like the diamonds on Karin's watch, which she had just surreptitiously checked again.

The night had a romantic aura. A steamer was passing well out, lit up like a floating Christmas tree. During a brief lull in the babble of voices on the terrace Tweed could hear dance music from the steamer drifting across the water, which was as still as the proverbial millpond.

He would have expected Karin to flirt mildly with him, as she had done in the past. Instead, she sat with her eyes lowered to the menu. He studied her. She really

158

was the most attractive woman with her naturally blonde hair, her perfect complexion, her sympathetic voice when she was in a good mood. And she had the added advantage of a first-rate intellect.

Tweed tore his gaze away from her and again gazed out at the lake. A large launch was approaching, about two hundred yards out. It was moving slowly, had a high foredeck and a luxurious-looking cabin. It was still some distance away, showed up clearly in the moonlight despite the fact that it had nowhere any lights showing – except the warning lights to port and starboard.

Further out a large powerboat was skimming round in circles. It occurred to Tweed that perhaps the owner had a girlfriend aboard and had fixed the wheel to continue its circling motion. Tweed imagined that racing full out it would be able to move at phenomenal speed.

'Have you decided,' he asked Karin, 'or would you like a little longer? No hurry.'

'I have decided,' she said and gave him her quirky smile. 'You were right. It is a very good menu. A surfeit of choice.'

The waiter appeared and they gave their orders. Tweed chose a bottle of wine after consulting Karin. He rather went overboard on the price. She raised her eyebrows when the waiter had gone.

'You really are going over the top with the wine. It happens to be my favourite, but I expect you remembered. You do have the most amazing memory.'

Tweed almost remarked on what a romantic night it was and then stopped himself. Despite the jollification going on all round them an alarm signal was buzzing at the back of his brain. He hadn't been able to identify what had triggered it off.

Except where the moon cast a path across the water the lake now looked like black ice. Not a ripple anywhere. The large launch had stopped, still at least two hundred yards out and less than a quarter of a mile away. The big powerboat was continuing to circle.

The babble was louder now on the terrace, the laughter more pronounced as large quantities of alcohol took effect. Tweed glanced over to where the two single men had been seated at separate tables. 'Hitler' was eating his meal rapidly, as though annoyed his escort had not turned up. The shadow man was still almost motionless, holding a glass near his invisible mouth without drinking from it.

They were now on their main course and Karin was eating with relish. She suddenly became very talkative, speaking rapidly.

'You really should get a girlfriend, Tweed.'

'Now you're lecturing me,' he chided amiably.

'I mean it. You'd probably do your job better if you had a bit of feminine fun.'

'Are you putting yourself forward in the role of helping me to do a better job.'

'That's up to you,' she challenged.

'If I did – notice I said "if" – it would probably be with someone like you. I also like someone worth talking to.'

'Well, don't you think I'm worth talking to?'

Was it the wine? He detected nervousness under the surface of her gaiety. She had never gone so far as this before. It really sounded as though she meant it.

'Let me think it over,' he said evasively. 'I do have a lot on my plate.'

'No, you don't. Like me, you've just cleared your plate. I must say this is the most wonderful meal I've had in ages.'

She dabbed at her lips delicately with a napkin. Her glass was empty. She had consumed most of the bottle, which was unusual for her. Tweed said he would order a fresh bottle and she agreed.

160

'Have some dessert,' he suggested.

'Yes, please. You don't mind if I have a smoke and wait a few minutes?'

'The night is young, to coin a cliché.'

'You haven't changed. You've given me your full attention – and a woman likes that. You've admired my clothes, my appearance, but I'd bet money you could still describe every guest seated on the terrace.'

'I'm sorry if I've *not* given you my full attention.'

'I'm not. If you couldn't describe everyone round us I would think you were going downhill. If anything, you seem more formidable than ever, if that's possible.'

'Flattery will get you somewhere, to coin another cliché,' Tweed said with a smile.

'That's what I'm hoping for.'

She was positively glowing, her eyes never leaving his. Her blonde hair, caught in one of the nearby lights, had a smooth sheen. One part of Tweed felt more relaxed than he had for ages, another part of his mind still kept sending out danger signals.

Was he getting over-suspicious? he wondered. He dismissed the thought quickly. That route led to complacency. The very thing he hammered home when interviewing a new recruit. He slowly drank a whole glass of water – to counter any effect the wine might have had on him.

An alcoholic haze was drifting over several tables. One man stood up, stumbled, had to grasp hold of the table to keep himself upright. A girl seated close to him shoved his thigh and he very nearly fell full length. She gave a high-pitched laugh. The party spirit was well under way. The man decided his visit to the toilet could wait, sank bank into his chair and reached for his glass of wine.

At another table the guests started singing a French song and people at nearby tables joined in. It was

161

becoming a carousal as wineglasses were raised and in some cases the wine slopped over the rim.

'They're enjoying themselves,' said Karin, who had twisted round in her chair to watch what was going on.

'I hope they have taxis to take them home,' Tweed observed amiably.

Then he remembered the last risk they had to fear was being stopped by the police. All Beck's men would still be searching Kongresshaus for the bomb – unless they had found it. The rest would probably still be somewhere outside Zurich tending to the multiple car crash victims.

Weird, he thought, so peaceful and full of enjoyment here and not so far away there is tragedy. What a strange mix the world is. Better to be here.

'I'm not sure I could face dessert,' Karin decided. 'That was quite some meal. Maybe strong coffee would be the best answer for me. But you have dessert if you feel like it,' she added suddenly.

Nothing had changed out on the lake. True, there were no more illuminated steamers with dance bands. But the large launch was still stationary in the same position. The same powerboat was still circling. Tweed had never seen a craft keep it up for so long. And the two men who sat alone at their individual tables were still there. Men on their own were not always a happy sight.

Once again Karin took a quick glance at her watch as the waiter came to their table. Tweed ordered coffee for both of them, saying they couldn't face any dessert. As he walked away to fetch them coffee Karin pushed her chair back, looked at Tweed.

'If you'll excuse me for the moment, I'll go to the powder room.'

Tweed sat quietly, his head not moving, his eyes everywhere. He sensed imminent danger. But from which direction? The large launch was now moving slowly towards the Ermitage. The circling powerboat was now still, its powerful engine ticking over, its prow pointed towrds the shore.

Tweed glanced towrds the two single men still seated at the tables at the back of the terrace. They were still there. Quietly, he edged his chair further away from the table. He placed both hands on its edges, lifted it slightly. It was a substantial weight but one he could handle.

Aboard the launch Georges Lemont had positioned his laser-guided rocket launcher on the foredeck below the bridge. He had his eye close to the rubber-enclosed crosswires. He saw Tweed clearly in the magnification. There was hardly any motion, but a slight swell on the lake moved the crosswires up and down slowly. He would wait for exactly the right moment.

On the bridge the man behind the wheel kept the vessel moving slowly on target. He was waiting for Lemont, visible below him because his eyes had become accustomed to the dark, to give him the signal. Lemont would raise his left hand and drop it while his right hand remained on the trigger.

A window on the port side of the bridge was open. Crouched behind it was another man, holding a Heckler & Koch machine-pistol. When they were close enough he could spray the whole terrace with a fusillade of bullets. Monceau, inside his car close to the Ermitage, had insisted on plenty of back-up.

A fourth man was standing behind the bridge, holding a more convential rocket launcher. The shell inside was filled with deadly shrapnel. The first man to act would be Lemont. Seconds after he had fired the others would operate their weapons.

They all knew they had the right target. A man sitting with a blonde woman, dressed in black, her hair cut close to her head like a helmet. She had left the table at precisely the agreed time. Eleven o'clock. Her appearance, her timing leaving the table – both these factors confirmed the target.

It would all be over in less than two minutes. There would be other casualties, a lot of them – innocent diners. This had worried Monceau not at all. It was far more certain that a target would be shot down, annihilated, among a crowd. A similar technique had been used before in a big bank raid in France. Eight civilians had died, but they had walked away with a small fortune in untraceable banknotes.

Aboard the stationary powerboat Paula waited tensely behind the wheel. Normally, in such a situation, she would have been ice-cold – but the realization that Tweed was a sitting duck for the killers made her hands clench the wheel more tightly.

An outstanding car driver, she had now mastered the art of steering a powerboat. Taking it round in wide circles for so long had been Marler's ploy to distract the launch's attention from it. But it had also given Paula excellent practice in handling the craft with skill.

'How much longer?' she whispered to Marler.

'Any moment now,' he answered quietly, standing by the hull.

His loaded Armalite rifle was slung over his shoulder. He was peering with great concentration through night-glasses, seeing every movement aboard the launch. He was paying the greatest attention to Lemont, whom he could see clearly with his rocket launcher.

164

'When I say "full throttle" smash into the side of the launch at top speed.'

On the deck just below the bridge Pete Nield was aiming his own Armalite point-blank at the man aboard the launch gripping an automatic weapon. Before they had left England Marler had treated him like a sergeant major addressing a rookie while Nield practised with the weapon.

Holding the wheel with one hand, Paula used the other to grip the lever which would turn the powerboat into a flying projectile. Marler had even used his engineering knowledge earlier in the day to soup up the engine.

'Not yet,' Marler warned her.

His glasses were now hanging from a strap round his neck and he was holding the Armalite, peering down the sight, which was focused on Lemont. To some extent he had the same problem as Lemont. The powerboat was moving up and down slightly with the faint swell on the lake. It was only a matter of a few inches rise and fall and Marler was not going for a tricky head-shot. He was aiming for Lemont's broad back.

'You're waiting too long,' Paula hissed.

'Patience is a virtue.'

'If we move forward now . . .'

Paula had only started to say they ought to move closer in when Marler uttered the magic words.

'Full throttle!'

As he spoke he pressed the trigger, a fraction of a second before Lemont launched his missile at Tweed. The bullet struck him under the left shoulder blade. He died instantly. But a reflex action tightened his finger on the trigger and the rocket, laden with high explosive, arced into the air.

Because it was the reflex action of a dead man the

165

aim was changed. The rocket soared up, descended, landed on an empty villa next to the Ermitage. At the same moment, hearing Marler's order, Nield had fired at the man holding the Heckler & Koch machine-pistol. Again the dead man, hit in the head, had with a reflex action pulled the trigger. Paula had already pulled the lever and the strong powerboat headed full throttle for the starboard side of the hull of the launch.

On the terrace all hell broke loose. Tweed saw the rocket's shell arcing downwards. He shoved over the table, crouched behind it, using it as a shield. When the rocket shell landed on the empty villa it detonated with a roar, hurling fragments of stonework into the sky. A small piece hit the table top, tore a hole in it, passing over Tweed's shoulder.

'It's good to get lucky,' he said to himself.

Peering through the hole he saw what happened next. Sheer panic among most of the guests. Women were screaming, men were yelling. Everyone was running, colliding into each other, falling down. There was nothing gentlemanly about their behaviour. Men pushed women out of the way as they fled desperately for the exit to the road.

There was a burst of shrapnel from the launch, fired into the air as the thug holding the weapon panicked, then fell dead as the second shot – this time from Nield's Armalite – hit him. Nobody aboard the launch had switched off the engine as Paula, her gloved hands braced for the shock, rammed the launch amidships. It keeled over, less strongly built than the powerboat.

Paula was ice-cold now the action had started. Swiftly, she reversed the powerboat well away from the stricken launch, an instruction which had been ham-

166

mered into her by Marler. He had suspected there would be plenty of ammunition stored aboard the vessel – and he was right.

Fire broke out aboard the launch. It reached the stock of ammunition. Paula had reversed the powerboat a good distance away when the whole launch exploded. There was a gigantic roar which was heard in distant Zurich. The launch vanished in a tower of flames. Above it sections of the craft were hurled high into the air, falling back into the lake with a hiss. There was a sudden eerie silence.

Tweed nimbly extricated himself from between the legs of the table, stood up. He was brushing himself off when he looked to his right. 'Hitler' was advancing towards him, holding Newman's favourite weapon, a Smith & Wesson .38, aimed at him. For once Tweed wished he had carried a gun himself.

The gunman was leering with sadistic satisfaction as he stopped, taking his time over aiming the gun at Tweed's chest. His target stood quite still, knowing that any movement on his part would activate the pressing of the trigger. There was nowhere to hide, nowhere to run to on the terrace which was now a shambles of overturned tables, smashed glasses.

Strangely enough, beside the gunman one table stood upright. Even stranger, a bottle of unopened red wine stood upright on the same table. The heat had never seemed more intense to Tweed. He thought of talking to the killer but that might also cause him to press the trigger. He remained very quiet, very still. It was suddenly very silent. Not a sound anywhere. It reminded Tweed of the silence he had experienced in Dorset.

A shot rang out. Tweed stiffened, waiting for the impact of the bullet which would end his life. The gunman's face showed an expression of disbelief. He collapsed sideways on to the table. Blood from the hole in his back mingled with the redness of the wine bottle his corpse had smashed. The shadow man came into the open. Newman lowered his own Smith & Wesson, grinned at Tweed.

'You do take chances.'

He bent over the body slumped across the table, checked the neck pulse. He glanced up at Tweed.

'Dead as a dodo . . .'

The manager, ashen-faced, came from inside the Ermitage, looked round at the carnage which had been his restaurant on the terrace, at the slumped body.

At that moment Karin Berg emerged from inside the building. She looked dazed as she stumbled towards Tweed. She tripped over debris, was about to fall, when Tweed grasped her round her slim waist. Newman had disappeared.

'What happened?' she gasped out.

'Some gentlemen who don't like me too much were rather active. We'll go to the car, back to the Baur au Lac.'

'What happened?' the manager asked, also looking dazed.

'I think it's probably a matter for the police. Why don't you call Beck?' Tweed suggested, guiding Karin towards the parked car.

16

It was early in the morning of the following day, not long after midnight, when Tweed assembled his team in his room at the Baur au Lac. After thanking Newman for saving his life, an expression of gratitude which Newman brushed aside, he then told the others of his admiration for the way they had protected him by destroying the launch.

'All in a day's work,' Marler replied.

'It must have been a long day's work,' Tweed told him.

'I simply thought like the enemy after surveying the Ermitage,' Marler said off-handedly. 'I used a detailed map, decided the attack would come from the lake. Newman was back-up close to you. Very simple, really.'

'If you say so.' Tweed paused. 'The incident exposed another member of The Sisterhood. Karin Berg.'

'How on earth do you come to that conclusion?' Paula asked.

Tweed described the constant attention Berg had paid to the time by her watch. He described how she had gone to the powder room just before the onslaught had been launched, her nervousness.

'In the car on the way back,' he went on, 'she invited me to her apartment off Pelikanstrasse for a drink. She tried to become amorous, but I said I was tired. I have the exact address on this piece of paper.'

'Let me visit her,' Paula said grimly. 'I'll get the truth out of her.'

'I need you for something else later. I phoned Beck and he has plain-clothes men watching her apartment round the clock. He is going to phone me the moment she attempts to leave the city – probably by air.'

'He should arrest and interrogate her,' Paula broke in.

'No, we'll play a long game. She may lead us to The Sisterhood's headquarters or base. I'm giving this job to Harry Butler and Pete Nield. The two of you should buy clothes in the morning as soon as the shops open – holidaymakers' clothes and equipment, maybe backpacks. I leave it to you. You all have plenty of money for any emergency.'

'I'll go out and buy what we need,' Nield volunteered. 'That will leave Harry here to take any message from Beck.'

'Maybe I ought to draw a sketch so you can identify her,' Tweed suggested.

'Not necessary,' Nield said promptly. 'I saw the blonde you were dining with on the terrace clearly when Marler loaned me his night glasses. That, I presume was Karin Berg.'

'It was, is. Follow her halfway across the world if you need to. Keep in touch with me.'

'Will do,' replied the taciturn Butler.

'Isn't that suspicious in itself?' Paula remarked. 'She has a room at this hotel – and an apartment in Zurich.'

'That had occurred to me,' Tweed agreed. 'Beck also told me that they found no bomb in Kongresshaus. It was a ruse to tie up a large part of the Zurich police so they would be nowhere near the Ermitage. We won't let on to Amos Lodge what happened. He has a quick fuse.'

'Will you go to listen to the speech he's now making this evening at Kongresshaus?' enquired Paula.

'Yes, I'm rather looking forward to it. He's a first-rate orator and won't mince his words.'

'In that case,' Newman said firmly, 'Marler and I will come with you. Don't try to argue.'

'I always do as I'm told. Thank you. By all means come with me. One other thing – Beck has sent out a large force onto the lake to try and identify the bodies of the men aboard that launch. Let's hope there are seven – including Jules Monceau himself. Since he has photos of the gang he may get lucky.'

'What if Karin Berg does a moonlight flit?' Newman asked.

'Beck will warn me. He has installed a fake road

170

gang to use drills all night long outside her apartment. That was a clever notion.'

'What's his idea?' Paula queried.

'To keep her awake all night. To help break down her nerve. Then if she does take flight, she won't be so alert for anyone following her.'

'Should help,' Butler said.

'Another thing I'm going to do, a precaution which must be taken,' Tweed continued, 'is to phone all the surviving members of the *Institut* to warn them of the nature of the danger. I'll start with Christopher Kane in Geneva.'

'You'll wake everybody up at this hour,' Newman commented. 'I'm sure they'll be asleep.'

'Better to be woken up alive rather than dead,' Paula observed.

'Talking of sleep, I think you'd all better get some,' Tweed told them. 'Tomorrow will be a busy day.'

'What's sleep?' enquired Nield before he followed the others out.

Karin Berg had the jitters, an unusual reaction. Even though the double-glazed windows muffled the road-drill bombardment a little the noise preyed on her mind. She decided to call Hassan at the new number he had given her before leaving Slovakia.

'Could I please be put through to Ashley Wingfield?' she requested the night operator at the Hotel Zum Storchen.

He had given her his pseudonym when he had informed her of the phone number. In his room Hassan was studying his list of members of the *Institut*.

'Yes?'

'Karin here. It was a bust. Our objective survived. And now he's very suspicious of me – he has to be under the circumstances. He's no fool. I don't think I can take him. He'll end up taking me – putting me away for a long, long time.'

'Who do you suggest among the Sisters might do the job?'

'Neither of them. But I do have an audacious idea. He has an assistant, trusts her completely, she's always by his side.'

'They're lovers?'

For Hassan it was the obvious explanation. He could imagine no other sort of relationship.

'They are not,' Karin said coldly. 'But if you doubled the fee, I think she might just go for it. God knows she's eliminated several men – in the line of duty. She's a wizard with a gun. And . . .'

'Be careful what you say,' Hassan snapped, aware that whoever was on the hotel switchboard might be listening in. 'No mention of the names of our competitor. What is the name of this person who might pull off the deal?'

'Paula Grey . . .'

Tweed was very busy in the morning and had asked not to be disturbed. The call from Beck was unsettling, complicated his plan of action.

'If my voice is hoarse, Tweed, it's because I've been up all night with my teams scouring the lake off the Ermitage.'

'You came up with anything?'

'Far more than I'd ever hoped for. Not a task to undertake just after eating a heavy meal. We were fishing bits of the Monceau gang out of the lake. A leg here, a foot there, some beheaded torsos.'

'You wouldn't, I assume, be able to identify everyone.'

Actually, we did. Two were reasonably intact. Then, by trawling and dredging endlessly, we fished up five heads in nets. All seven of the Monceau gang were wiped out by someone – I'm not guessing who.' Beck paused and Tweed realized he knew who had been responsible. 'But we found no trace of a certain Jules Monceau. Didn't expect to.'

'Why not?'

'Work it out for yourself. He'd be watching from a safe distance, preparing to enjoying your destruction.'

'So you think he's still at large?'

'I'm sure of it. He's likely to decide to come after you himself. Don't forget he's good at disguises. Nothing crude like a false wig or moustache. In Paris the police call him The Chameleon. He's a master at blending in with his background, altering his whole personality. Rather like a Dr Jekyll and Mr Hyde. Except he's always Mr Hyde.'

'Trying to put the wind up me, Arthur?' Tweed joked.

'Now look here, Tweed' – Beck sounded exasperated – 'I am very serious. You underestimate this man at your peril. The whole French police force have been after him for years – and have not once laid a hand on him.'

'I appreciate your concern.'

'Then for the Lord's sake, watch your step.'

'You should know by now I never underestimate an enemy. And I know Monceau's motive is strictly personal. That's why he agreed to help The Sisterhood organization.'

'Changing the subject, no move yet by Karin Berg. She's still hibernating in her apartment. If she books a flight I'll know within minutes. I have friends high up at the airport.'

'I have two men standing by,' Tweed told him.

'I'd love to bring her in for questioning.'

'Don't do it,' Tweed said urgently. 'She's possibly our one lead to where this insidious organization is operating from.'

'As you wish.' Beck sighed. 'Sometimes I wonder who is running this police force. Guard your back . . .'

He rang off before Tweed could reply.

The mysterious call came through to Paula midmorning. She picked up the phone, expecting it to be Tweed.

'Miss Paula Grey?' a cultured English voice enquired.

'Yes. Who is this?'

'My name is Ashley Wingfield. You have been recommended to me my a mutual friend who must remain anonymous.'

'Mutual friend? Charles Dickens?'

'I told you I couldn't reveal his name.'

It was at this point that Paula's suspicions were aroused. She didn't expect every educated Englishman to have read the novel – but she did expect him to have heard of it. She listened more carefully to the accent as the conversation proceeded.

'What is the point of this call?' she asked sharply.

'Two hundred thousand dollars. For yourself.'

'And how do I earn this sum?'

She had been astute enough not to appear impressed by such a huge amount. And the English was just a little too perfectly enunciated. She had heard literate Arabs speak with this calculated precision.

'My dear lady' – inwardly Paula winced as she listened – 'I can't explain what is involved over the phone. Such a large business deal.'

'Well, when and where can you explain it?' Paula demanded.

'May I suggest we meet at noon at the top of the Zurichberg? You take a tram—'

'I know how to get up there, so don't waste your breath.'

'I will be waiting on a seat midway between the tram stop and the restaurant where you can obtain refreshments. It is very important that you come alone. If I see any sign that you are accompanied by anyone I shall vanish . . .'

'In a cloud of blue smoke.'

'I beg your pardon.'

'Never mind. How shall I know it is you? Anyone might take it into their head to sit on a public seat.'

'I was coming to that, Miss Grey. I shall be wearing a panama hat and dark glasses.'

'And clothes, I hope?'

'But of course. I don't think you should have said that.'

'I don't give a damn. I'll meet you at noon on Zurichberg. Goodbye.'

Paula sat down to think. She checked her watch. 11 a.m. She had plenty of time before she decided whether to accept this weird invitation. Normally she would have consulted Tweed before doing anything, but she knew he was busy and a very strange idea was forming at the back of her mind. She dismissed it as outlandish.

After a few minutes' thought she went into her bathroom and took trouble over changing and tending to her hairstyle. She tied back her hair – a natural way of wearing it in this heat. She also spent more time than usual over her make-up, applying a generous but tasteful amount of lipstick.

Afterwards, she would have been hard to explain why she acted like this. If pressed, she would have said sixth sense. She then put on a pale blue trouser suit. The

175

jacket had a secret pocket in the inside on her left. Then she took out a large pair of sunglasses.

She hid the glasses in her shoulder bag, tucked her Browning inside the special pocket. Then she went to see Marler, hoping he was in his room. He opened the door, ushered her inside.

'You brought in quite an armoury from Vienna,' she recalled. 'I wonder if you have a Beretta?'

'As a matter of fact, I have. But you don't usually carry that automatic.'

'No, I don't, do I?' she said with a smile.

'None of my business?' He smiled back. 'I'll get it and you might need spare ammo. Tweed knows about this?'

'Of course.'

She disliked telling an untruth but it was necessary. Marler opened a cupboard, pulled aside some clothes and brought out the satchel they had concealed. He handed her the automatic and spare ammo. She thanked him and left quickly.

Hassan had had his doubts about Berg's idea of recruiting Paula Grey for this one assignment. He had even hesitated before he phoned her. If he was doubtful after talking to her he'd simply go nowhere near Zurichberg.

Paula's aggressive attitude had changed all his doubts. He had disliked the way she had talked back to him but he'd had the same trouble with the other three members of The Sisterhood. To do the job they had to be tough nuts, hard as nails. Above all they had to have greed for big money.

On all points Paula had scored ten out of ten. She had not even sounded impressed by his mention of two hundred thousand dollars. Yet in a second call to Berg he had been told that Paula must earn a mere pittance compared with such a sum. This, above all else, had convinced Hassan that Berg's idea might work. There was one other factor which weighed heavily in his decision.

If it fails ... The Englishman's warning kept echoing in his mind. He was certain the phrase had been originally uttered by his father, the Head of State, whom he feared. His father had a swift and deadly way of dealing with failure – and his son was worried he would suffer the same fate. After all, he had younger brothers, any of whom could be substituted for himself. And Berg *had* failed. Not that this meant he would not use her again. Her initials were on the list alongside certain remaining members of the *Institut*.

Paula boarded the tram for the Zurichberg, still with mixed feelings. Tweed would go ballistic if he found out what she was doing without back-up. The heat inside the tram was appalling. Other passengers were removing jackets, ties. One woman never stopped mopping the back of her neck with a handkerchief.

When the tram reached its terminus and she left it the temperature had dropped because of the height. She walked a few paces, then stopped. If she was being observed it would be obvious she was alone.

She saw a road curving upwards and realized she was not yet at the top of Zurichberg. The view was spectacular down over the many church spires of Zurich with a hint of the blue lake beyond. Reaching the top of the hill she saw a man sitting by himself on a seat.

He was wearing a panama hat and dark glasses which concealed most of his face. Slimly built, he wore a cream linen suit similar to the one Marler had in his wardrobe. It was an expensive item. So were his hand-made shoes. His skin was brownish, but it could have been tanned by the sun. She sat on the same seat, leaving space between them.

'So far you have obeyed instructions,' he commented.

'Who are you?' she asked aggressively.

'You know who I am from the way I am dressed. From the fact that I am here.'

'I want a name or I'm catching the next tram back to Zurich.'

'Ashley Wingfield. I believe I have the honour of meeting Miss Paula Grey.'

He knew he was. Berg had given him a detailed description of Paula Grey. Only one detail was different.

'You have changed your hairstyle.'

'None of your damned business. It's a hot day.'

'Are you interested in earning two hundred thousand dollars? In cash. Forget the taxman.'

'Depends what I have to do for the money.'

'We are fencing,' he complained.

'Get to the point. I can't sit here all day.'

'Excuse me.'

He moved closer, gently removed her bag from her shoulder. She glared but let him get away with it. She had left her SIS identity card in the hotel safe. Nothing else in the bag showed the organization she belonged to. He found the Browning, raised his thin eyebrows, removed the magazine, hurled it over his shoulder into the undergrowth behind the seat, did the same with the gun.

'You came armed,' he said.

'Of course I did. I didn't know who you were, what you might try to do.'

'You can use firearms?'

'I belong to a shooting club back in England. I'm not popular with the men. I'm the club's crack marksman.'

'Can you use a Luger?'

Inwardly she froze. She had come to the right place.

She stared at the invisible eyes behind the dark glasses. She was wearing her own sunglasses which she had put on as soon as she had boarded the tram.

'I've practised with it. Get to the point, for God's sake.'

'For two hundred thousand dollars could you shoot Tweed?'

She didn't answer at once. First because she sensed it would be a mistake not to appear to think it over. Second, the question was not totally unexpected but spoken in cold blood it enraged her. She stared out at the view, considering her reply. Eventually she replied.

'It will be difficult.'

Inwardly, Hassan's heart sank. She had used almost the same words Karin Berg had used when he had first mentioned Tweed's name. What made this man so important?

'Why will it be difficult?' he asked after a pause.

'Because he is so heavily guarded,' she replied promptly.

'But I understand you have been his personal assistant for a long time. There must be times when you are alone with him.'

Karin Berg, Paula thought. That's the bitch who has given this piece of work the idea of trying to employ me. All this flashed through her mind and again she replied quickly.

'Yes, there are, but a guard is never far away.'

'Use your sex appeal to isolate him.'

'That might just work.'

'So there is no problem.'

'Yes, there is. I want fifty thousand dollars in advance. To be specific – now.'

'You don't want much.'

'Then forget it,' she said, wrenching her shoulder bag from his grasp.

179

'I can give you something . . .'

'Fifty thousand or I'm leaving and you'll never see me again.'

'I have twenty thousand in this envelope.'

She grabbed the envelope, which was very thick, glanced inside it, riffled through a number of hundred-dollar bills, shoved the envelope inside a compartment of her bag, zipped it up. Her hand rested in her lap. She was on the verge of producing the Beretta and escorting him back to Tweed when he said something else.

'You'll have to fly to my headquarters for a brief training exercise. The flight leaves later this afternoon. You'll get the other thirty thousand the moment we arrive. Now, I want to see your eyes. Remove your glasses.'

'And I want to see yours, or the deal is off.'

She had changed her mind. This was a unique opportunity to locate where they were operating from.

'Take your glasses off,' he snapped.

'Take yours off at the same time or I'm leaving. I like to see who I'm dealing with.'

Reluctantly, Hassan removed his glasses as Paula took off hers. They stared at each other. His eyes were pale, without a trace of human feeling. She had no trouble in making her stare hard. She loathed this man.

'You have a tough look,' he said as he put his glasses on again. 'I think you could do the job. We'll stay together until we board the flight. I have a return Business Class ticket in your name in my pocket.'

You're well organized, she was thinking. Which makes you that much more dangerous. Don't give in to this thug on any point.

'I need clothes, certain personal things,' she said. 'I won't travel without them.'

'So we'll go shopping together. Don't go to any ladies' room. You can attend to that on the plane.'

17

Hassan was a good planner. On the off chance that Paula Grey would prove suitable, would take up his offer, he had checked out of the Zum Storchen, had deposited his case in a left-luggage locker at the main station. He was not surprised when Paula eventually accepted his offer – in Hassan's mind all that Western women were interested in was money, the more the better. It was the way his brain worked.

He had arranged for Karin Berg to travel on an earlier flight to Vienna. He hadn't wanted to risk Paula seeing the blonde on the same plane. While she was shopping for clothes and essentials Paula kicked up.

'I can't have you peering over my shoulder while I purchase certain personal items,' she told him savagely.

They were in the beauty shop of a department store and Paula found herself hoping against hope that someone like Newman would see her. No such luck.

'I'll stand back a few yards but you have to remain in view,' Hassan had snapped.

'Get lost.'

As she contemplated the items for sale she was trying to work out some way of leaving a message for Tweed. It proved to be impossible. She bought an expensive suitcase, knowing that Hassan would expect her to start spending the twenty thousand dollars he had given her.

Then she rammed inside the case the carriers containing the expensive clothes she had bought. Not her usual method of packing, but it would have to do. All the time she looked for a phone she could use, but Hassan was always at her heels.

Later, he escorted her to the Hauptbahnhof, collected

his own case and hailed a taxi outside. He gave Paula her air ticket. She examined it. Destination: Vienna. She had her passport inside her shoulder bag which gave her profession as Business Consultant.

'The airport,' Hassan told the driver.

Earlier, Tweed had received an urgent phone call from Beck. The policeman's tone had been grim.

'I've heard from the airport that Karin Berg is catching the next flight to Vienna. Now what is it to be? I have a strong urge to arrest her, detain her and interrogate her. She marked you out at the Ermitage. We can lay our hands on a member of The Sisterhood at last – I'm convinced that's what she is.'

'Let her go. I'll warn two of my men. They are ready to leave for the airport now. I've booked seats for them on all flights to Vienna. Business Class. Is that how Berg is travelling?'

'Of course.'

'Then I'd better get off the line. How long have they got to reach Kloten in time to make that flight?'

'Three-quarters of an hour.'

'Call you later . . .'

Tweed had run to Butler's room where Pete Nield was waiting with him. They had left immediately. Tweed had had a taxi standing by for most of the morning.

Arriving at the airport, they mingled with the other passengers in the final departure lounge. Both of them had spotted Karin Berg. Nield had given her description to Butler earlier. Both men carried backpacks which contained all they needed. In this way they could take their belongings aboard the plane.

It was, of course, impossible to carry weapons. Nield had consulted Marler, who had given him the name and address of the arms dealer in Vienna who had supplied Marler with the armoury he had smuggled over the border.

They were careful to board the Austrian Airlines aircraft after Berg had taken her seat near the front. The machine was barely half-full and they had chosen two seats alongside each other well back from her. Nobody occupied the seats behind them, in front of them or across the aisle. They were able to talk in quiet voices as the plane became airborne.

'I think I ought to send a radio message ahead to book a hire car,' Nield suggested. 'If she has a car waiting for her at Schwechat Airport we'll lose her without transport.'

'Good idea,' agreed Butler.

Nield signalled to one of the stewardesses after writing out the message. He told her the matter was confidential. Taking the message with her, the steward-ess disappeared inside the control cabin. Nield sat back, relieved he had taken action.

'That's that,' he said.

'Just so long as we don't lose her at the airport,' Butler warned.

So far Berg had not even looked back once. She appeared not to suspect that she might have been followed. Sitting with her head turned towards the window, she was watching the scenery below her, a vista of green and brown fields without a town in sight. Occasionally she glanced to her right where, through the starboard windows, she could see the snowless savage peaks of the Austrian Alps. But never a look backwards.

'I don't think she has any idea that she might have been followed,' Nield remarked.

'Why should she?'

'Because she's a professional – an ex-member of the

Swedish counter-espionage, which is how Tweed came to know her.'

'Maybe she's worried about something,' Butler replied with a flash of insight.

He was right. Karin Berg was wondering what was waiting for her when she reached the strange house in Slovakia.

Boarding the later Austrian Airlines flight for Vienna, Paula insisted on occupying the aisle seat. Hassan tried to compel her to take the window seat, which gave him control over the situation. It almost erupted into a public row. A stewardess arrived to find out why the aisle was being blocked by the two passengers.

'My friend is being kind and wants me to sit by the window,' Paula explained with a smile. 'I don't like flying and I do not sit in window seats.'

'The plane is about to depart,' the stewardess said firmly, staring at Hassan.

Reluctantly, he took the window seat. For Paula it was a small victory in two ways. The aisle seat gave her greater access. Also she had outmanoeuvred Hassan, had showed him he couldn't get it all his own way.

The aircraft had few passengers in Business Class. There was no one near them so she felt she could converse in a quiet voice.

'Why is this trip necessary? I'm quite capable of using a Luger.'

'Let us say it is a psychological test you must undergo.'

'Sounds a bloody waste of time to me.'

'Don't talk to me like that,' he said indignantly.

'Why not? I'm not your servant.'

'You are getting two hundred thousand dollars,' he whispered.

'Of which so far I have only seen twenty.'

'We shouldn't be discussing this in a public place.'

'Haven't you realized there is no one near us? That not a soul can hear what we're saying? Do be more observant. I want to know what happens when we reach Vienna – otherwise I'll catch the first flight back to Zurich.'

Hassan was in a dilemma. He didn't want to tell her too much. On the other hand her aggressive attitude confirmed that Berg had chosen the right woman. He was becoming more and more convinced that Grey could do the job.

If she fails . . .

Hassan was still haunted by what the Englishman had said. Tweed had to be killed. Hassan knew that in an emergency the Englishman had a direct line of communication to the Head of State, his father, who had no patience with anyone who let him down – even his own kith and kin. The Eastern penalties for failure were drastic. They included beheading.

'We don't go to Vienna,' Hassan eventually said. 'A limo will be waiting to take us to the training house.'

'Where is that?'

'I don't know,' Hassan lied quickly, foreseeing the question. 'It is moved from one area to another – for security reasons. Only the driver knows where to take us, the driver of the limo.'

Paula decided to give up for the moment. She didn't believe him but she had sensed fear in Hassan's voice. Who was he afraid of?

It was evening, still hot and muggy, when Beck phoned Tweed in his room. He had just phoned Newman in his room enquiring as to the whereabouts of Paula. Newman had said he had no idea, had told Tweed he was coming to his room. Beck called at the moment Tweed let him in.

'You won't like this, Tweed.'

'These days, when you talk to me I usually don't like it,' Tweed joked.

'I'm very serious. Prepare yourself for a shock. One of my men at Kloten checking passengers spotted someone he knew boarding a later flight. The heat had got him so he went to the security chief's office for a drink of water. Then he promptly fell asleep on a couch. He has apologized for the lapse and has just told me.'

'Told you what?'

Tweed was becoming alarmed. It was something so serious that Beck was having trouble coming to the point.

'He saw Paula Grey boarding a later flight to Vienna. In the company of another passenger, now identified as a Mr Ashley Wingfield . . .'

'Stop the plane in mid-flight,' Tweed said urgently. 'Order the pilot to return to Zurich at once.'

'I would have done just that – after consulting you. But it's too late. The plane landed a while ago. All passengers have disembarked.'

'I want to interrogate your man who saw her board the plane.'

'I've already done that myself.'

'Did it appear she had to go aboard under duress? This is my first news that Paula has gone to Vienna.'

'No duress. How could there be? Wingfield would need a gun. You know all passengers go through a metal detector. The odd thing is she appeared to leave of her own free will . . .'

'Check with the Schwechat Airport police.'

'I have already done that too. They couldn't help. Although there weren't many passengers aboard Paula's flight, another plane landed at the same time. You know how passengers mingle when more than one flight comes in. I regret to say she has vanished without trace. I'm very sorry – you sound worried.'

'I am. Thank you, Arthur. I may call you back . . .'

Tweed told Newman what had happened. After listening, Newman said he would take over, that he was going to phone the Sacher, the hotel she had stayed at with Marler, Butler and Nield.

Tweed paced the room, unable to keep still while Newman made the call. After a few minutes he put the phone down, turned to Tweed.

'The Sacher has no booking for a Paula Grey.'

'I see.' Tweed continued pacing, hands clasped behind his back, then he spoke. 'Get Beck for me, please.'

It seemed to take an eternity before Newman handed him the phone, said Beck was on the line.

'Arthur, have you got a description of this Ashley Wingfield?'

'I called the man who saw her board the plane. He was at home, asleep. He describes him as wearing a panama hat and dark glasses, above five feet eight tall, his complexion very brown, clean-shaven, carrying a suitcase. Paula was also carrying a case, a Louis Vuitton.'

'Louis Vuitton? She doesn't go in for expensive items like that. Are you sure?'

'The man I woke up is very reliable, has the eyes of a hawk.'

'Thank you.'

Tweed gave Newman the additional information, began pacing the room once more. Newman sat on a couch and lit a cigarette. He was careful not to say anything. He knew Tweed's mind was racing, despite his deep anxiety. Suddenly Tweed stopped.

'We've both forgotten something. Nield and Butler are heading for the same destination, following Berg. I must find out from Beck—'

He never completed his sentence. The phone started ringing. Tweed darted for it before Newman could pick it up.

'Yes?'

'Pete Nield here. We've just arrived at Schwechat. Our plane had to return to Zurich – engine trouble. Butler is watching the Berg. She seems to be waiting for transport.'

Tweed swiftly told him about Paula. He gave Nield every detail Beck had provided. When he had finished Nield's cool reaction was typical.

'Harry and I will have to do something about that. It is just possible that Paula's destination is the same as Berg's. I find it significant that Paula isn't at the Sacher. That suggests to me she isn't going anywhere near Vienna. We'll keep in touch. Paula is now our top priority . . .'

'So now,' Newman commented after Tweed told him about Nield, 'we have two good men in the area. No point in my going out there. Yet.'

Tweed resumed pacing. He felt he couldn't keep still. Had he done all he could to locate and protect Paula? Should he adopt Newman's suggestion – or send him out to Vienna?

'Why would she do a thing like that?' he asked aloud.

'Perhaps she stumbled on an important lead. Decided to follow it up. May have had no time to contact you.'

'She's gone over the top this time.'

'That's worry speaking. Don't forget that last year you sent her to California on her own,' Newman reminded him.

'That's true,' Tweed admitted. 'Bob, phone Howard and ask him to check with the passport people whether there's a British passport in the name of Ashley Wingfield . . .'

Racked as he was with anxiety, Tweed had not forgotten there were other aspects of the problem. When Newman had made his call he phoned Christopher Kane in Geneva. He was relieved to hear the very upper-crust Scots voice on the line.

'Well, dear boy, what is bothering you? I always know when you call me something is worrying that dynamo you term a brain.'

'I hope you heeded my earlier warning.'

'To be on the lookout for being approached by attractive women.' Kane chuckled. 'I should be so lucky. The technique you described they use is quite ingenious. Rest your active mind. And thank you for calling . . .'

In his apartment in Geneva, Kane put down the phone and was amused. He doubted whether Tweed would have been amused if he had told him of his recent encounter with the glamorous auburn-haired woman Lisa Vane.

He had seen her in the bar of the Richemond, where it was his daily habit to have one drink. She had made eye contact and Kane had responded.

Now they were going to have dinner at Les Armures, a fine restaurant at the top of the Old City on the far side of the Rhône. He had told her he lived in an apartment but had fended off her question for his address.

Christopher Kane was six foot one tall, quite thin, with black hair and a long face tapering to a determined chin. Speaking with a drawl, it was sometimes difficult to catch what he said. His manners were faultless and he had a charm which women of different ages found very attractive. He was still a bachelor although in his early forties. At random intervals he played the field as a contrast to the intense mental concentration his work involved.

Unlike many scientists or boffins, Christopher did not have tunnel vision, nor did he focus on his work to such an extent he was out of touch with the world outside. On the contrary, he was very shrewd.

Taking a taxi, he deliberately arrived late at Les Armures. Tina Langley, still posing as Lisa Vane, had received fresh instructions from Hassan. Since the fee involved was so much larger than what she had managed to extract from her banker friend, Anton, she had left Anton on the shelf. When she needed more spending money she would contact him again.

'You're late,' she snapped as Christopher was shown to the table in the first room off the entrance.

'It happens,' he agreed, refusing to apologize, and let her score a point in the opening round of the game. 'We'll have two Kir royales,' he told the waiter.

'I like to be consulted,' Tina fumed.

'My dear,' said Christopher calmly, leaning over to pat her hand, 'I know this place. They have the best Kir royales in the world. Just leave everything to me.'

'It would be nice if you allowed me to choose from the menu later,' she said, changing her mood, giving him a ravishing smile which would have hypnotized most men.

'No. I'm a gourmet. If you chose you'd miss the best they have to offer. Just relax and you'll have the meal of your life. I repeat, leave everything to Christopher.'

Tina was confused. By now she would have most men eating out of her hand. What was it with this long streak of a Scot? For the first time she felt out of her depth. It will be a pleasure to blow the back of this bastard's head off, she was thinking. Instead she gave him her smile again, leaned forward so he would get a whiff of her perfume.

'We're going to have a wonderful evening. The two of us,' she said.

'I'm enjoying myself now. There are some interesting characters at the other tables.'

What about this table? she said to herself. He hasn't paid me one single compliment – on my appearance, my clothes, on anything. Yet he kept looking her straight in the eye and had a pleasant smile. She had the uncomfortable feeling he could see inside her head. This was very different from her experience with Norbert Engel in Vienna. He had been a pushover. She expected most men interested in women to be pushovers when they were with her.

She let him choose the wine and the the meal. Perhaps his weak point was his vanity, his confidence that he knew everything. Maybe she ought to play on that.

'You have a remarkable brain,' she said, halfway through the main course.

'Other people have said that. Not an original remark.'

'What exactly do you do? I'd love to hear more about you and your work.'

'What work?'

Tina was taken aback. She noticed he had drunk a lot of the wine. She refilled his glass. He ordered a fresh bottle. She began drinking heavily herself – she knew she could outdrink any man. Alcohol could be her main weapon.

'I see you have a large briefcase,' Christopher remarked.

'Papers in connection with my job,' she said quickly.

'And what job is that?'

'Personal assistant to a Swiss banker,' she replied, thinking of Anton, making it up as she went along.

'So you speak fluent French? You'd have to.'

'I get by. Cheers!'

She raised her glass and drank half of it to divert his dangerous questions. He smiled. Christopher smiled a lot.

'You speak fluent French,' he repeated. '*Peut-être?*'

She had no idea what he had said. Her mood changed immediately to throw him off balance. Her warm smile vanished. She glared at him, her eyes like bullets.

'For God's sake, I speak the bloody language all day long. I do it but I'm sick of it. Talk in English or I'll stop speaking to you,' she said at the top of her voice.

It had always worked before. Her swift changes of mood fascinated men. They usually did their best to warm her up again, fearing the night would end there instead of elsewhere.

'I'd talk a little louder if I were you,' Christopher observed. 'Then they'll hear you the other side of the Rhône.'

He drank more wine and she hastened to refill his glass. His reaction had been one of complete indifference. Tina was nonplussed. What did it take to get inside this man?

By the end of the meal Christopher had drunk a great deal of the excellent wine. He passed a hand across his high forehead, blinked. He pulled his chair closer to the table as though for support. She smiled inwardly. When coffee had been served with liqueurs she gave him a certain look.

'Why don't we finish off the fresh bottle of wine in your apartment.'

'Great . . . idea.'

He seemed to have difficulty saying the words.

Paying the bill, he fumbled with the banknotes in his wallet. He gave the waiter such a large tip Tina was convinced he wasn't aware of how much he had left inside the folder with the bill.

Inside the taxi which took them to his apartment she hugged the briefcase with her left hand and rested her right hand on his knee. He responded by putting his arm round her slim waist, leaning against her.

His apartment was in an old building near the river. Tina let him lead the way as he stumbled from step to step, holding on to the wooden rail. He had trouble inserting his key into the lock, so she removed it gently from his fingers and unlocked the door herself. He held out his hand for the key and she dropped it into his palm.

'What a lovely apartment,' she enthused. 'Beautiful furniture. They're antiques, aren't they? Oh, what a grand desk. Now, you sit in your comfortable swivel chair. I've got a map of the city in my briefcase. Can you drive up that mountain on the other side of the river?'

'If . . . you wanna go to . . . France.'

'I'd love to. Perhaps you would take me there sometime.'

'Great . . . idea.'

'Which is the bedroom?'

'Through that . . . door.'

'Maybe you'd show me it.'

'What's map for?'

She had spread out a map of Geneva and the surrounding areas on his desk as he sagged in the chair. On the far wall was a collection of pictures. One frame held a mirror which had a curtain slung at both sides, so it was hardly visible to anyone visiting the apartment for the first time.

Standing behind him with the open briefcase from which she had extracted the map, Tina slipped her hand inside it again. Christopher saw the action in the mirror he had been watching. Swinging round in his swivel chair, he jumped up, was by her side before she realized what was happening. She had her hand on the Luger. His hand grasped her wrist, twisted it with great strength. She yelled, let go of the gun, scraped her foot down his shin. He let go of her and she ran, opened the door, fled down the staircase, dropping the briefcase she was still holding. Christopher, suddenly sober, ran down after her, slipped on the briefcase, fell forward. He would have smashed his skull on the stone steps but he grabbed hold of the rail, saved himself. The entrance door to the block of apartments banged shut. He reached it, flung it open and was just in time to see Tina vanishing down an alleyway. He stepped into the street, closed the apartment door behind him and strode to where his car was parked.

Christopher knew Geneva inside out and he drove a certain route which would take him into the street the alleyway led to. His long legs had enabled him to reach his car quickly and as he swung into the street where the alley emerged he was again just in time to see Tina get into a parked Renault.

He didn't think for a moment she would suspect she was being followed. In this he was right. Tina was suppressing a state of panic. She drove off in the car she had hired in the name of Lisa Vane, using false papers supplied by Hassan. Crossing the Pont du Rhône she drove along the same route Anton, the banker, had taken her.

Night had long since fallen but there was a certain amount of traffic. This enabled Christopher to keep her in view without getting too close. He had once been a racing driver and he soon had the opinion that Lisa Vane was a good driver. He passed the checkpoint into France without being stopped – as had Tina.

Half an hour or so later, having passed the summit of Salève, the mountain overlooking Geneva, Tina pulled in to the parking place in front of the Château d'Avignon. She had just entered the hotel, carrying a suitcase, when Christopher drove slowly past, continued on to drive back to Geneva by the western descent from the mountain.

'Think I'd better call Tweed,' he said to himself. 'He'll be amused by my little experience.'

18

Earlier that evening Tweed had attended the Kongresshaus to hear Amos Lodge's speech. The place was packed as Amos thundered from an elevated platform behind a lectern. Behind Tweed sat Marler while Newman stood near the end of the row of seats, next to one of Beck's men in plain clothes.

'Our Western civilization has become decadent . . .' Amos roared.

'You either lead a decent life or indulge yourself, regardless. There is no middle way.

'The once stable relationships between men and women have broken down. Certain women have adopted the American way. They have become dominant, aggressive, and men allow themselves to be beaten down, shoved aside – in politics, in business.

'Once men no longer have confidence in themselves then society collapses into chaos!

'The Roman Empire fell when it became decadent,

when it spent its energy in orgies. Western society has reached the same low level. Filthy films, filthy telvision, filthy books, filthy behaviour between the sexes . . .

'Absorbed by orgies Rome was overwhelmed by stronger forces from the East, destroyed by its own decadence . . . The West faces the same fate!

'There are more disciplined religions, more disciplined societies, therefore stronger powers in the East today. The West is leaderless, its so-called leaders are pathetic dummies concerned only with hanging on to power.

'They have reduced the West to a defenceless state. There is a power vacuum, morally and militarily.

'Equality between men and women is a sound basis for a stable society. Now we have a mushrooming superiority of certain women. Unless the situation is corrected the West faces total disaster – will be taken over by the East.

'Haul our present mock-leaders down . . . put stronger men with the right moral attitudes in their place!' Amos thundered.

'Powerful and controversial stuff,' Newman commented to Tweed as they left. 'You may not agree with him, but for a strategist he must be one of the world's great orators.'

'The ovation lasted ten minutes,' Tweed observed. 'Look who we have here.'

Willie had appeared at their side. They were swept along with the crowd emerging, which was excited and talking nonstop about what they had heard. Willie, more red-faced than ever, tapped Tweed's arm.

'Amos certainly carries you along with him. The audience was almost in a state of hysteria. Adulation might be a better word.'

'Where did you pop up from?' Tweed enquired. 'Still enjoying yourself in Zurich?'

'I moved from the Dolder Grand to the Gotthard. Needed somewhere less public to meet a client. Pulled off a big deal. Now I'm going back to the Dolder Grand.'

'Staying on in Zurich?' Tweed enquired.

'Never can tell what my next move will be. I'm a globe-trotter. Tell you what, why don't I come to the Baur au Lac tomorrow morning, buy you both a few drinks? At the Pavillon. Noon suit you?'

'Thank you. I'll be there,' said Tweed.

'Me too,' Newman agreed.

'Got to fly, chaps, make a phone call. No peace for the wicked.'

Unlike most of the audience, Willie was dressed in a green tracksuit which looked expensive. Round his neck he wore a silk cravat. Yet his appearance was smart and dressy.

'Well, at least there was no attempt to assassinate Amos,' Newman remarked.

'I was thinking about that,' Tweed replied. 'Reminds me of the Sherlock Holmes story. The dog that didn't bark in the night. Something like that.'

They were approaching Newman's parked car, hired by him in Zurich, when a solid body of men pushed their way through the crowd. Beck was in the lead, looking everywhere. Behind him walked Amos Lodge, an expression of disgust on his squarish face. Men in plain clothes walked alongside him and behind him.

Beck walked forward rapidly. He took Tweed by the arm and his voice was firm.

'Amos Lodge is going back to the Baur au Lac in a special unmarked police car. You will travel with him. Both of you are targets.'

'I can drive back by myself,' Newman said.

'Thank you,' Tweed responded to Beck. 'I'll take advantage of your kind offer.'

He had decided it would be a good opportunity to talk to Amos. Tweed was particularly interested in the fact that Willie was lingering in Zurich. Entering the back of the large limo with Amos, he suspected it was the same car which had transported him to the Ermitage. He tapped the window. Armoured glass.

The plain-clothes driver was separated from them by a glass partition which was closed. Amos settled his bulk in his seat as he made the remark.

'Lot of bloody fuss.'

'Beck is simply taking care of you. Remember what happened to Dumont. Incidentally, Willie is still in Zurich, staying at the Dolder Grand. The best is always good enough for him.'

'You can say that again.' Amos grunted as the car began to move off. 'He's Eastern mad.'

'Naturally, that's where his income comes from.'

'I wasn't thinking of that,' the big man commented. 'You've seen his peculiar Oriental garden outside Shrimpton? He's shown me all over the place. Gives me the creeps. Like transferring an Eastern state to Dorset. Of all places. Funny chap. But we seem to get on.'

'You've been to the East?'

'I've travelled everywhere. I'm a good listener. The Arabs like to talk. Sometimes they give away too much.'

'You're talking about military matters? About strategy?'

'I'm talking about strategy.'

Amos lapsed into silence for the rest of the journey. When they reached the Baur au Lac he said good night and went up to his room. Tweed had deliberately not mentioned to Amos the speech he had made. He knew he wouldn't want to talk about it.

Tweed was not amused when Christopher Kane phoned him and related his experience. Newman, who had joined him in his room, saw his expression become grim.

'You were a damned fool to take such a risk.'

'It turned out all right, dear boy. And climbing back up the staircase I picked up – using a handkerchief, fingerprints, you know – the briefcase the murderous lady had dropped with the Luger still inside. Give me credit – it could be valuable evidence.'

'It could be,' Tweed agreed. 'I'll ask Beck, Chief of Federal Police in Berne, to send a courier to collect it.'

'I know Beck. We've played bridge together. Tell him to call me.'

'Can you describe this girl, Lisa Vane?'

Christopher promptly gave a concise picture of what she looked like, how she spoke, the fact that she didn't speak French, although she pretended to.

'You're the first target to avoid being killed by a member of The Sisterhood,' Tweed warned.

'I'm the first at a lot of things. What is The Sisterhood?'

Tweed explained the meaning of the word in grisly detail. He recalled the murder of Norbert Engel in Vienna, that surviving members of the *Institut* were all at risk.

'So that includes yourself,' Christopher reminded him amiably.

'Yes, it does. But I'm asking you to be more careful from now on.'

'Then I won't meet any more beautiful assassins. I've

a good mind to come to Zurich, find out what all the uproar is about.'

'I can't advise that.'

'Don't recall asking for your advice. Toodle-pip . . .'

Newman listened while Tweed relayed the contents of his conversation. He lit a cigarette, blew smoke rings, watched them disperse before he reacted.

'I think you were a bit hard on Christopher. He can look after himself. He was a very good rugger player. I was at school with him.'

'What's that got to do with it?'

'It means he doesn't miss much, that his reflexes are excellent. What about the description he gave of Lisa Vane?'

'It matches perfectly the description Paula gave us of the woman she saw walking down Kärntnerstrasse in Vienna after Norbert Engel had his head blown off.'

'So Tina Langley gets around. If Christopher does turn up here it might be interesting to show him the photo Vitorelli gave us of her.'

'Agreed. What is more interesting is this Château d'Avignon where Tina took refuge. The fact that it is in France, not far from Geneva. That city keeps cropping up.'

'And what did you and Amos talk about, riding like kings in the limo to get back here?'

Tweed recalled the conversation. He was able, despite being very tired, to remember every word that had been said. Newman was frowning as he finished.

'It sounds as though Willie takes a great interest in Eastern objects. And he called Willie Eastern mad. Intriguing remark.'

'I thought so . . .'

He stopped speaking as the phone rang. It was

Monica, still at SIS headquarters in Park Crescent at that late hour.

'You know that fragment of cloth Paula found at the entrance to Norbert Engel's apartment – the bit you sent me by courier for analysis?'

'Yes. I don't expect they came up with much.'

'But they did – the boffins in the basement. They know a man who is an expert on cloths all over the world. Guess what he said it is.'

'Tell me.'

'It's quite definitely a fragment from the long black dresses or robes worn by Arab women.'

'You're sure?'

'I'm not sure,' she said peevishly. 'The expert is sure. It is obviously used as a disguise, from what you've told me. The interesting thing is the nature of the garment used to disguise The Sisterhood.'

'It suggests to me an extreme sect – far more extreme than the Fundamentalists. They are showing how Western women will be dressed – treated – once they have conquered the West.'

'You think the women who wear this disguise to kill our top intellects are aware of this?'

'I'm sure they aren't. They just think it's an excellent way of concealing themselves. The only thing they think about is money. Thank you, Monica. Keep in touch . . .'

'It is an Arab state, then?' queried Newman.

'Possibly. No word from Paula. No word from Nield and Butler.'

When they had arrived at Schwechat Airport Hassan had flown into a rage. Escorting Paula outside, he had been appalled to find no vehicle waiting for him. Well outside the Austrian capital, the airport was surrounded by flat countryside.

201

Trying to use his mobile, Hassan found he could make no contact. He shook the thing angrily.

'That won't help,' Paula goaded him. 'A tower must be down.'

'Tower? What the hell do you mean?'

'Obviously,' she said with a smile, 'you don't know much about the system. The radio signal is transmitted via the nearest tower. When you can't get through it means the tower which should connect you is down. *Kaput!*'

'I can't wait here all day,' Hassan blazed.

'I can – if you tell me where we're going.'

'I told you I don't know.'

'So you say!'

They went back inside to escape the blazing sun. Even Hassan seemed affected by the humid heat. He took off his glasses to wipe his streaming forehead. Again she looked into pallid, soulless eyes. Nasty piece of work, she said to herself.

'My car is waiting outside,' he said.

'So why don't we use that?'

'Because you have one destination, I have another.'

'Who will be taking me where I'm supposed to be going?'

'Don't you ever run out of questions?' he snapped.

'Not often.' She sensed she was wearing him down. 'Where are you going?'

'To a secret rendezvous.'

'Lots of secrets. You could get into your car now and leave me here to wait.'

'You think I would do that?'

'Why not? I'm hardly likely to run away from two hundred thousand dollars.'

'We have to follow the arrangement.'

'What arrangement?'

'Give your mouth a rest, for God's sake . . .'

* * *

They had to wait so long other flights began to arrive. One was from Zurich.

Harry Butler, disembarking from his delayed flight with Pete Nield, walked alongside his partner, both with their packs on their backs. They wore linen shorts and open-necked shirts, looking like a score of other holidaymakers.

Butler grabbed Nield by the arm as they were about to emerge into the blinding sunlight. He pointed.

Paula was being escorted to a Volvo estate car by a man wearing a panama hat and dark glasses. Nield ran to the car-hire desk, went swiftly through the formalities, was shown by the desk girl to their waiting Ford. In the distance Paula was being driven away while Panama Hat entered another car, an Alfa Romeo.

'Nothing but the top cars for some people,' Nield commented as Butler started the engine, after they had slung the backpacks into the car. 'Don't lose that Volvo. Thank Heaven she was still here. Wonder why?'

'Main thing is she was. I can still see her. This country is as flat as a billiard table.'

'Not Vienna,' Nield remarked, as they turned at a fork away from the city. 'Out into the wild blue yonder.'

He little knew how right he was in his description.

Paula had been escorted into the rear of the Volvo by Hassan. He had left immediately without a word, perhaps fearing more questions. The driver had centrally locked all the doors so she was trapped in the back.

Shortly after leaving the airport an Alfa Romeo flashed by at speed. She didn't recognize the driver as Hassan. He had removed his hat and wore a shaggy grey wig. Soon the swift dart vanished from sight ahead of them.

Her driver was a squat, muscular man with a thick neck and a brutal face like some boxers. He had taken

203

her case and parked it on the seat beside him. Presumably another security precaution.

'What's your name?' she asked after a while.

'Me Valja.'

'Sounds as though you're from what used to be Yugoslavia.'

'Me Valja.'

'Is that your first or second name?' she persisted politely.

'Me Valja. Must drive.'

Which Paula interpreted as 'Shut up.' She decided she was not going to be able to needle him as she had with Hassan. For a short time she looked at the countryside. This soon palled. It was all the same. An endless plain stretching away for ever. Cultivated fields on both sides of a road without fences or borders of any kind.

From the direction of the sun she could tell they were travelling roughly south-east. Heading further and further away from Vienna. She felt pretty sure they were in Burgenland, Austria's most easterly province, bordering on the Slovak Republic – or Slovakia – and Hungary.

It was lonely countryside with only the occasional isolated and small village which Valja passed through at speed. This was not difficult as there seemed to be no other traffic, although the road was well surfaced.

'Where are we going, Valja?' she asked after an endless drive.

'Me Valja.'

Hassan had arranged in advance for his own car which he could drive himself. He wanted to reach the base in Slovakia well ahead of the arrival of Paula Grey.

First, he could check out the situation there. Second, he could arrange to have the training room set up for

Paula. A live target who would be injected with drugs to keep him still before the trial kill.

Racing along in the Alfa he arrived at the remote crossing point from Austria into Slovakia where there was no checkpoint. He had the flat-topped mountain and the long house above him before he turned up the winding road at the western end of the moutain. He had a bad shock as soon as he parked the car in a barn at the far end of the house and returned to the main entrance. The door was opened by his brother, Ahmed, second offspring of the large family.

'What the hell are you doing here?' Hassan demanded.

He brushed past him into the coolness of the house. Behind him Ahmed followed at his heels.

'The Head of State ordered me to come here as your assistant.'

None of the sons ever referred to their begetter as 'Father'. He insisted on being called Head of State. His discipline was unbending and ferocious.

'I don't need an assistant,' Hassan raged over his shoulder.

'We all have to obey the Head of State. I am here to help you.'

'To spy on me,' Hassan said to himself.

His worst fears were confirmed by Ahmed's next remark, spoken with a hint of pleasure and malice.

'The Englishman has phoned the Head of State. You appear to have altered the agreed plan, to have acted on your own.'

'I have to get the job done – and quickly,' Hassan shouted back. 'When the situation changes the plan has to be adapted to the new circumstances.'

'The Head of State will require a full explanation after you have completed your mission. Assuming you do complete your mission.'

'If you don't keep out of my way any failure will be your fault for interfering without understanding what you are doing.'

Hassan felt better having said that. It might give him an excuse for anything which went wrong. The trouble was several things had gone wrong. Tweed was still alive. Tina had called him from the chateau in France with a story as to why Kane was still alive – a story he did not believe.

He entered the training room, slamming the door in Ahmed's face. The innocent peasant who would be the live target for Paula Grey was tied with ropes to the chair in front of the desk, which had been cleared of blood. Hassan went to the cupboard, took out a syringe containing the drug. It would render the victim motion-less, but still very much alive. The peasant had been kidnapped working alone in the fields many miles from the house on top of the mountain, perched on the edge of the abandoned quarry.

Karin Berg was nervous. Arriving on the same flight as Nield and Butler at Schwechat Airport, she had mixed with the few passengers disembarking. Nield and Butler had been following her when Pete had spotted Paula. All thought of tracking Berg had left their minds – Paula's safety was their priority.

Berg had waited near the exit and only when all the other passengers had gone did a swarthy man hold up a piece of cardboard with her name on it. Without a word he took her to a waiting BMW, opened the rear door, shut it, got into the driver's seat and locked all the doors.

As he took off Berg smoothed down her blonde hair and smiled at the driver in the rear-view mirror. All men responded to her smile. The driver simply glared, looked away, concentrated on his driving.

Remembering her previous journey to the training house Berg soon realized again she was being taken on a roundabout route – which would make it difficult for her to identify where they were. Realizing she would get nowhere with the driver, she lit a cigarette and closed her eyes.

Vaguely she had heard a helicopter take off as soon as the car left the airport. Inside the control cabin of the Sikorsky Emilio Vitorelli sat in the co-pilot's seat, holding a powerful pair of field glasses. Occasionally, as they tracked the car from a distance, he focused the glasses. Berg's blonde head came up clearly inside the lenses.

'Keep her in sight. Don't lose her. But don't let the driver think we are following him,' he told the pilot.

'In other words,' the pilot answered in Italian, 'perform a miracle.'

'That's what you are paid to do.'

It had been Tweed who had warned Vitorelli that he suspected Berg was a member of The Sisterhood. It was his way of repaying the favour when the Italian had given him a photo of Tina Langley. Tweed had had no idea of how Vitorelli would handle the information but the Italian had acted quickly.

Obtaining a description of the striking woman, he had posted men to watch for her at the airport, at the main station, in areas overlooking the main road exits from Zurich. A small army of his men normally engaged in activities which were not always strictly legal had been flown in to the Swiss city.

He had taken a shrewd gamble in flying in his Sikorsky to Schwechat – because Tweed had told him about the murder of Norbert Engel and the subsequent attempt to kidnap Paula in a car. Knowing the Austrian capital had an incredible mix of nationalities he suspected the base of The Sisterhood might well be in the deserted hinterland outside Vienna.

Inside the Sikorsky, Vitorelli also began to think the driver was deliberately taking a devious route to his destination, wherever that might be. Naturally volatile, the Italian could exert endless patience once he had made up his mind. So he settled back and waited as they kept away from the tiny car moving through the deserted countryside.

'You have the friends?' Valja suddenly asked.

'What are you talking about?' Paula demanded.

'I see Ford car long way behind.'

'What are you talking about?' Paula repeated.

'You have the friends?'

'I have no friends out here. I don't know where we are. So where are we?'

'Me Valja.'

Paula gave it up. She concentrated on trying to see a signpost but there were very few of them. Surreptitiously she had taken a map of Austria out of her shoulder bag. She spread it out on her lap so Valja could not see it.

They had been travelling for a long time when they passed a signpost. EISENSTADT. She recalled the brochure of a hotel in that town which a policeman in Vienna had scooped out of a toilet in a cell during the prison breakout. What was the name of the hotel? Burgenland. Same name as the province on the eastern borders of Austria.

Paula stopped looking for signposts as she considered what lay ahead of her. Aboard the aircraft when she had needled Hassan into talking he had made a reference to 'the training house'. What kind of hideous

208

ordeal had he planned for her? Then she was distracted from her thoughts by Valja picking up a mobile phone and talking rapidly in a language she couldn't identify. It sounded as though he was giving orders.

Her left hand crept stealthily towards her make-up bag, then she withdrew the hand. Whatever happened she had to find out the location of the base of The Sisterhood.

19

Butler was behind the wheel of the Ford. Beside him Nield was studying a map of Burgenland and surrounding areas he had grabbed from a display holder in the airport. Even travelling a good distance behind her they had kept Paula's Volvo in sight, with no other traffic and the countryside so level.

'Driver of the Volvo slowed down for a few minutes,' Butler reported. 'I wonder why, when you have an open road and no other cars to bother about?'

'Maybe using a mobile phone,' Nield suggested.

'You think he's spotted us?'

'I'd be surprised if he hadn't. For miles there have been two cars going the same way – his and ours.'

'Could mean trouble,' Butler observed calmly.

'My very thought. Keep your eyes peeled.'

They came to a fork and Butler took the left turning. Nield was looking south. In the far distance a helicopter was flying steadily on a course parallel to the road they had just left behind.

'Could be that chopper,' Butler mused.

'Don't think so. He'd have come closer to get a better look at us. And since Charlie used his mobile the chopper hasn't altered its course.'

'Charlie?'

'The driver taking Paula. I've got to call him something.'

'Charlie has speeded up, is moving faster than he has since he left the airport.'

'Could be a danger signal. Something Charlie doesn't want to be near when it happens. To us.'

Paula was very alert. She could hardly believe what she was seeing. Rising up from the level plain was a long hill. Perched on top was a weird long single-storey house. The roof, of wood like the walls, sloped up and then rose vertically. It was a large house and she had never seen anything like it before.

They had now turned on to a track, hidden from the house up above them. She saw where the track spiralled up at the left-hand end of this strange hill. In the rear-view mirror Valja caught her eye, grinned wolfishly.

'We go there.'

He took one hand off the wheel to point up to where the house was perched. His evil grin suggested he was anticipating what was in store for her. She extracted the metal nail file from her make-up bag, then leaned forward and while the car was moving slowly pressed the sharp pointed end into his thick neck.

'Valja. Stop the car – or I'll ram this knife right through you.'

His change of expression in the rear-view mirror was dramatic. The grin disappeared and fear showed as he stared back at the hard look in his passenger's eyes. She pushed the point deeper into his neck.

'Lady, please—'

'I've had enough of your bloody nonsense,' she told him, her teeth gritted. 'Make a U-turn. You can do it driving over the grass.'

She could tell he didn't understand, that he was scared witless. She used her left hand to indicate a U-turn. Now he understood her order. Swinging the wheel slowly, he turned the Volvo round on the arid burnt grass and stopped, facing the way he had come.

'Valja!' She snapped out the name with all the venom she could muster. Her expression was not pleasant. 'Airport. Go back to the airport. Move, you bastard.'

He had slipped back on his seat and this caused the nail file to dig more deeply into his fleshy neck. He began driving back the way they had come at a moderate pace. Paula was worried that someone inside the house would soon notice that the plan was going wrong. They were likely to send cars after her.

'Valja!' she screamed deliberately. 'Speed! Faster! More speed! Or I'll kill you.'

He understood enough of what she had said to press his foot down. Soon they were racing along the open road. She kept the nail file pressed into his neck. A few minutes later, looking back, she saw another car appear behind them in the distance. Someone had reacted quickly.

'Faster!' she shouted.

Valja obeyed. Looking back again for a second she saw that the black car coming up behind was closing the gap.

Butler had increased speed, seeing Paula's Volvo disappearing as it turned a corner, then reappearing. Nield was the first one to notice the giant yellow excavator digging up the road in the distance. He focused a small pair of field glasses he had extracted from his backpack.

The driver of the hulking piece of machinery was elevating an evil-looking scoop with huge metal teeth. The scoop descended, tore up a large piece of the

211

surface of the road, dropped it into the field on the verge. Butler shrugged.

'It's the same even out here. Just like back home. They dig holes in the road, then fill 'em up. Just to keep the workforce in a job.'

'I'm not so sure,' Nield replied. 'Slow down. Crawl.'

'OK. But why?'

'Because the driver inside his cabin keeps swinging the arm supporting that huge scoop out over the road where we'll have to pass it.'

'You think he's going to . . .'

'My bet is he has a mobile phone. Watch it, Harry.'

'I'm watching. My damned hands are slippery on the wheel. It's as hot as Hades out here.'

'And very lonely. They could bury us in one of those fields, using the scoop to dig a hole. Who would ever find us?'

'Archaeologists digging for dinosaur bones a hundred years from now. Trouble is we have no weapons.'

'Remember our training course at that mansion down in Surrey. The instructor said there's always a weapon you can use.'

'Surrey seems a helluva long way from here . . .'

Nield's only expression of tension was to light one of his rare cigarettes. He had taken the pack and lighter from one of his pockets. He smoked without inhaling as they came closer and closer to the excavator, travelling at a slow pace. He was studying the terrain alongside the road. Grass and reeds had grown tall, stretching away across the fields. It must have grown during an earlier rainy season.

Now grass and reeds were brown and dead. The fiery sun, day after day, week after week, had burned the life out of the vegetation. It was tinder dry. Butler was concentrating on approaching the excavator, a truly massive machine on caterpillar tracks.

'I may take off suddenly,' Nield warned. 'You save the car.'

'You seem sure it will need saving.'

'I'm dead certain. Emphasis on dead.'

'Time somebody cracked a joke.'

'Maybe he's digging for gold. Best I can manage just at this moment.'

'Ha-ha,' Butler responded with a mock laugh.

'Here we go . . .'

Butler drove slowly forward, now very close to the excavator on the right-hand side of the road. Automatically, he had tested the car's reactions in different situations soon after leaving the airport. He knew what he could do with it.

'I'm leaving you,' Nield said.

He opened his door on the verge side of the slow-moving car, dived out, slammed the door shut behind him. He walked a short way into the field beyond the verge, grabbing up handfuls of long grass and reeds. The driver in the cab of the excavator had seen Nield get out but was concentrating on the Ford approaching him.

To pass the machine, parked on the right-hand side of the road, Butler had to swing over to the left. Not that this mattered since there was no other traffic as far as the eye could see. As he did so the excavator's driver, inside his glass-walled cabin, elevated the massive arm, hauling the scoop with its murderous, steel-fanged teeth high up in the air. He held it there for a moment, suspended above the cavernous hole he had gouged out of the highway.

Butler continued to drive slowly forward, watching the man inside the cab closely. He saw him suddenly start moving levers just before the Ford passed the machine. The arm supporting the scoop swivelled out over the road, began to descend at great speed.

Butler reversed quickly, backing a distance away from the machine. Where his Ford had been moments before the scoop crashed down. It was operated with such force its dragon's teeth slammed deep into the road. Had Butler not reversed so swiftly the immense weight of the scoop would have smashed through the roof of the car reducing him to a spiked corpse, skewered to his seat.

While this lethal assault was taking place Nield had collected several sheaths of burnt dry grass and reeds, using some of the reeds to wrap round the sheaths. He ran forward to the side of the cabin as the driver, seeing him coming, flung open his door on the verge side.

The man inside the cab was fumbling with a machine-pistol when Nield, using his lighter, set fire to the first sheaf, hurled it inside the glass cab. Setting fire to a second sheaf, he threw the burning brand after the first. Flames enveloped the driver, who dropped his machine-pistol into the road. Darting forward, Nield picked up the weapon, ran back a few paces, waved to Butler to reverse further back. The Ford shot back, Nield lit the third sheaf tucked under his arm, cast it under the excavator beneath the fuel tank. Then he ran like hell back up the road towards where Butler was waiting.

The third sheaf ignited the fuel tank. There was a thunderous roar, like a bomb going off. Nield dropped flat in the road alongside the Ford. The excavator exploded, vanished in a sheet of flame. Huge fragments of its disintegrated metal soared into the sky, crashed down in the fields. One large piece, lethal in size, landed alongside the Ford, on the far side away from where Nield crouched, holding the machine-pistol.

There was a sudden silence after the deafening blast.

214

Nield climbed back into the front passenger seat of the Ford. He brushed dirt off his clothes. Butler was staring beyond where the excavator had once stood.

'A car coming – like a bat out of hell. Another one behind it . . .'

Nield snatched up his field glasses, focused, then lowered them. His tone was grim.

'The first car is the grey Volvo with Paula in the back, a driver in front. The black Mercedes coming up behind her like a bullet from a gun has four men inside it.'

Paula still had the nail file pressed hard against Valja's neck. She no longer had to glance back. She could see the black Mercedes coming in the rear-view mirror.

'They kill me,' Valja gasped.

'I kill you. Keep driving,' Paula rasped.

She had heard the huge explosion, had seen the column of fire, had no idea what it meant. In a supreme emergency she was ice-cold. She threw the question at Valja, banking on his state of terror to answer without thinking.

'Where is the house on the mountain?'

'Slovakia,' Valja croaked.

It was only when they had raced past the flattened wreckage of what remained of the bulldozer that she recognized the figure standing near the rear of the Ford and outside the vehicle. Harry Butler. She nearly cried with relief. But she kept her nerve.

'Stop behind that car,' she yelled at Valja.

He braked suddenly, almost turned the Volvo off the road into the fields. But he obeyed her, parking behind the Ford. Her nail file was still pressed against his neck when she gave her next order.

'Get out! Crouch – get down – behind the Ford!'

215

Valja jumped out, took cover behind the stationary car. She jumped out herself, was grabbed by the arm as Butler forced her to take cover on the verge side of the Ford. He joined her as the black Mercedes arrived, moving slowly now. All its windows were open and the barrels of guns protruded. She waited for the fusillade.

Before any of the four men could open fire a hail of bullets raked the open windows. Lying in the grass of the field near the Ford, Nield was operating the machine-pistol with deadly precision. Only the driver ducked in time, threw his door open and, holding a machine-pistol, started to run into the grass of the field opposite.

Nield, now near the rear of the Ford, peered round, aimed his weapon. He shot the driver in the back who fell into the grass. Valja, who had not moved from the rear of the Ford, lay on the ground, killed by one shot from a thug inside the Mercedes before he slumped out of sight.

20

Tweed and Newman were sitting at a table in the open-air Pavillon attached to the Baur au Lac when they were joined by Willie.

'Hello there, chaps. Another super day. Hope this heatwave goes on for ever. Drinks are on me.'

'I have one,' Tweed said, pointing to his orange juice.

'I'll have another Scotch,' Newman replied.

'We'll make that a double. Waiter! Over here, my good man.'

Willie was dressed in a smart white jacket and white trousers with a razor-edged crease. Round his neck he wore a yellow cravat. Several attractive women had eyed him thoughtfully as he had walked with a springy step to Tweed's table. His face was red as a beetroot. He sat down in a spare chair, crossed his ankles.

'I hope this heatwave breaks tomorrow,' Tweed told him.

'You're not as accustomed to the heat as I am, old boy. I've spent so much time in the Middle East I love it. You'll get used to it if it lasts long enough.'

'I don't wish to get used to it,' Tweed remarked. He paused as the waiter brought the drinks Willie had ordered. 'I was talking with Amos last night. I gathered he admires your Oriental garden at Dovecote Manor.'

'He should. He supplied most of the statuary and so on from the East. Gave it to me since I have the space for the stuff. He has a key to the place and looks after it when I'm absent abroad. Cheers!'

'Cheers!'

Tweed went silent as he absorbed the statement Willie had just made. The two men were telling totally different stories about the weird sculptures.

'Must cost a packet to transport such large items from the Middle East,' he remarked.

'It has to,' Willie agreed. 'More than I'd fork out. I spend my ill-gotten gains on entertaining sheiks.' He grinned. 'To say nothing of entertaining a bevy of attractive ladies.'

He winked, ran a finger over his light brown, pencil-thin moustache. His expression suggested satisfaction at the memory of some interesting interludes with girlfriends. He does like himself, Newman was thinking.

'I don't suppose Amos meets any of your attractive ladies?' Tweed enquired.

'Oh yes, he does. When I'm going off some filly I phone him up, invite him round for a drink. Amos has a way with the ladies. At times he takes them back to his place to show them his cottage. At least that's his story.' He winked again. 'I wouldn't be surprised if they ended up spending the night there.'

'You don't know that,' Newman said mildly. 'Surely that is a guess on your part?'

'Boys will be boys. What's wrong? Amos is a bachelor.'

'Nothing's wrong,' Tweed intervened. 'Incidentally, do you happen to know whether Tina Langley knew Amos?'

'Yes, she did. They got on well together when he met her at my place.'

'Did she later go round to The Minotaur, Amos's cottage?'

'She might have done. Can't be sure. They both left at the same time. That I do recall.'

'Tina Langley has gone missing.'

'Probably sunning herself on some tycoon's yacht in the Med. She was quite a looker. I found her too expensive. There is a limit.'

'Why would she be on a tycoon's yacht in the Mediterranean?'

'Plenty of fun – at someone else's expense – was her way of life. Time we had a refresher. Told you I'd pulled off a big deal.'

'Not for me. Willie, I'm afraid we'll have to go. An urgent appointment.'

Tweed hurried to the lift with Newman. The two men went to Tweed's room. Newman waited on a couch and was relieved when Tweed sat down instead of pacing like a caged tiger.

'What appointment?' he asked.

'With Beck. He'll be here soon. I've got certain jobs I'm hoping he'll take on. We're overstretched. That was a very strange conversation with Willie. I told you last night what Amos said to me in the limo.'

'Doesn't add up.'

'It most certainly doesn't. First, Amos gives me the idea that all the artefacts – weird objects – in Willie's large garden were brought back by Willie from the Middle East. Now Willie tells us it is Amos who imported them, gave them to Willie because he has the space. He also mentions that Amos has a key to Dovecote Manor.'

'One of them is lying.'

'Yes, but which one? And why?'

'Because,' Newman suggested, 'the man who brought them in has a lot of money – sufficient to have them transported all the way from the Middle East to here. And transporting that lot must have cost one of them a small fortune . . .'

There was a knock on the door. Newman jumped up, opened it cautiously. Beck, wearing a grey business suit, stood outside, was ushered in by Newman. Tweed offered him a comfortable chair.

'I'm going to be asked to do you an impossible favour,' Beck said with a smile.

'You are, if you will.'

'Tell me the worst.'

'I'm short of manpower. I want Amos Lodge and Captain Wellesley Carrington watched round the clock. Amos is staying here while Willie is at the Dolder Grand. I need to know if they make any phone calls from public booths, if so the time they make the call, how long they take to make the call, where they return to afterwards.'

'You don't want much. That will tie up Heaven knows how many plain-clothes men to do the job properly. You do require a twenty-four-hour surveillance?' Beck asked ironically.

'Round the clock. Also anyone they meet, how long they are with them and a description.'

'You have yourself, Newman and Marler. To say nothing of the two who flew to Vienna – Butler and Nield . . .'

'They're looking for Paula,' Tweed said grimly. 'You know she has gone missing.'

'I'm as sorry and worried about that as you are, if possible.' Beck stood up. 'I'll arrange the surveillance of those two men within the hour. But what are you planning on doing?'

'Flying to Vienna . . .'

Tweed was packing his bag. Newman had booked seats for three people aboard the next Austrian Airlines flight to Vienna when the call came through.

'Pete Nield here. Paula is safe. I'm calling from the Sacher. The three of us are staying here. Tried to call you yesterday evening, but you were out. Decided not to leave you a message. We don't know who is OK and who isn't in Zurich.'

'Thank you, Pete,' Tweed said in a subdued voice. 'Could I have a word with Paula?'

'She's still fast asleep. We thought it best to let her recover. She's OK, but there was a bit of a bust-up. Nothing to write home about. Paula has discovered the base, if you understand me.'

'I do.'

'I won't name the location. This phone may not be safe.'

'That's all right. Give Paula my congratulations. When you are all back to normal catch the first flight back to Zurich.'

'Paula thinks we ought to stay here.'

'Tell her that's a direct order.'

'What about us?'

'You escort her back here. That's another direct order. Call me with details of the flight when you know them. You'll be met at Kloten.'

'You're the boss.'

'Remind Paula of that . . .'

Putting down the phone, Tweed sagged on to the couch next to Newman, told him the news. His expression was one of great relief.

'Paula is safe,' he repeated. 'Thank the Lord for that.'

'You need a drink,' Newman suggested.

'A double brandy. No water.'

'Are you sure?'

'Do get it brought up here now.'

When the drink arrived Tweed swallowed half of it slowly as Newman watched him. He then drank the rest. Newman expected Tweed, who rarely used alcohol, to show signs of wooziness. Instead, he sat forward, very alert and obviously thinking hard.

'We have to distribute our forces carefully,' he said.

'Why bring back the team already in Vienna?'

'I need to cover every contingency. When they get back we will hold a battle conference.'

Inside his office in the house in Slovakia, Hassan was in a rage. All the guards who looked after his safety kept out of his way. The cause? The day before, when Berg had eventually arrived, a Sikorsky helicopter had flown several times over the house.

Hassan had no way of knowing that Vitorelli was on board the chopper. Using a powerful German camera with a telephoto lens he had recorded the structure of the building from every angle. Earlier, through his glasses, he had seen the blonde Berg get out of the car and disappear inside the front entrance.

'We have dug up pure gold,' he told the pilot, Mario Parcelli.

'Gold?' Mario enquired as he circled the house.

'This has to be the base of The Sisterhood. Observe it well, my friend.'

'It looks most peculiar,' Mario replied in Italian, the language they were conversing in. 'Someone has run out of the house to observe us with field glasses.'

'He won't see much, will he?'

The perspex-enclosed cabin had a faint amber tint which made it impossible to see who was inside. Vitorelli's camera was aimed through a narrow slit he had opened in the window on his side.

It was Hassan who had rushed out with binoculars. Determined to identify the intruder, he wrote down details of the markings on its fuselage. Then, realizing he might be being photographed, he ran back inside, slammed the front door shut.

Hassan had to wait until the following day to phone a friend in the aviation world, a friend who would expect a large payment for his trouble. The later conversation with Hassan had not gone well.

'I cannot identify the helicopter,' he told Hassan on the phone.

'Why not?' screamed Hassan. 'I gave you the markings.'

'It will do you no good to yell at me,' his informant replied indignantly. 'I have checked with the Records Authority for helicopters. They contacted every country in Europe. No one knows the markings you gave me.'

'I am not paying you for no information,' Hassan shouted.

'I can tell you the same helicopter landed at Schwechat Airport where it refuelled and took off again.'

'Bribe someone in the control tower. They must know where the helicopter was going to.'

'I have no contact in the control tower. Any attempt to pay a bribe to one of their staff would get me arrested.'

'All you think of is your own skin.'

'Someone has to think of it,' his informant rapped back.

'You are useless. A piece of nothing.'

'The fee will be a thousand pounds. Sterling.'

'Send me a bill!'

Hassan had slammed the phone down. He couldn't understand what had happened. Who could have been aboard the chopper? It was very worrying.

What he didn't know was that when the refuelled helicopter had landed at Kloten it had asked to be guided to a remote part of the airfield. There Vitorelli had helped Mario to remove the thick sheet with false markings, exposing the machine's real markings.

Mario, whom Vitorelli had ordered back urgently from Geneva, had then taken the film to an apartment his chief rented in Zurich under a different name. Once closeted in the secret hideaway, Mario produced a set of prints of all the shots Vitorelli had taken in Slovakia. He had worked through the night and delivered them to his chief the following morning.

While Tweed was drinking his brandy and talking to Newman, Vitorelli was studying the photos under a high-powered glass in his room. He grunted with satisfaction and eventually placed them back inside the envelope Mario had brought him. He looked at his assistant.

'Well done, Mario. Order drinks to be sent up so we can celebrate. Our next task is to locate Tina Langley.'

Unknown to Vitorelli, Tweed was engaged on the same mission. He had taken out the photo of Tina that

Vitorelli had given him on an earlier occasion. Showing it again to Newman, he asked his question.

'Photos are deceptive. But what is your impression of this lady from a single photo?'

'First, I suspect it is a good one, showing her character – or, rather, her lack of it. I'd say this woman spends her life living off her looks.'

'I'm waiting for Paula to arrive. I want her to look at the photo again. Then I'm going to ask Beck to have a huge number of prints produced from it.'

'What's the idea?'

'You'll hear when Paula has seen the picture . . .'

'I hear an engine revving up.'

'Engine?'

'Your engine, Tweed. You're so relieved Paula is safe your normal dynamic energy has returned. I sense we are going to get cracking soon. I can't wait for the battle conference.'

'We are going to have to take action swiftly. The clock is ticking. I sense we haven't much time left.'

The Englishman phoned Hassan soon after the call which told him the helicopter could not be identified. With an effort Hassan remained calm when he realized who was phoning him. It would be very dangerous to upset the Englishman.

'I am here,' he said, his hand clammy on the receiver.

'You have not carried out any of the recent instructions.'

'We have had bad luck.'

'You have been incompetent. Tweed and Kane are still alive.'

'Neither of them responded to the women you allocated to them.'

'I hear that Karin Berg is with you. Why?'

'With me?' Hassan was stupefied that the English-man had this information. 'We withdrew her because she panicked.'

'*You* withdrew her because *you* panicked. Send her back on the first flight to Zurich. She stays at the Dolder Grand. A room is booked for her. Her target is Christopher Kane.'

'Kane is in Geneva.'

'Kane has arrived in Zurich. Baur au Lac. Send Tina Langley back from Geneva to Zurich. Her target is Tweed. Again at Baur au Lac.'

'Preparation will be necessary.'

'You have three days to complete the assignments. Zurich will be the killing ground. I have another call to make.'

The line went dead. Hassan, sweat streaming off his brow, wondered how long it would be before he was dead. He was most worried by the Englishman's last remark. Was he calling the Head of State? How could he know so much?

Then Hassan remembered that when he had returned to the long house he had been greeted at the entrance by Ahmed, his hated brother and chief rival. Hassan rose slowly from his chair behind the desk, strolled across to the door, locked it.

Only three people knew the combination to the massive safe in a corner – the Head of State, who knew everything, himself and Ahmed. Inside the safe was a book where Hassan noted down all developments in the master plan, however minor, so he could send regular reports to the Head of State, a man who insisted on meticulous records. The book contained all the details of the accomplishments and movements of The Sisterhood.

Bending down, Hassan examined the circular com-bination lock. It was not quite in the same position as he had left it. So Ahmed had checked the records. It was Ahmed who had informed the Englishman about his failures.

A Persian rug covered most of the tiled floor but there was a margin round it where the exotic tiles were exposed. Picking up a valuable Eastern vase, Hassan, his face convulsed with fury, smashed it down on to the tiles where it broke into a score of pieces. He felt better now, ready to deal with Ahmed.

He found his brother in one of the many living rooms overlooking Austria. Ahmed was holding a bottle of whisky as he poured himself a fresh glass. His hand trembled and he kept tapping the bottle against the rim of the glass. He was unaware of Hassan's silent entry.

Alcohol was forbidden by the Head of State. Ahmed enjoyed his visits to the long house. He could indulge his liking for drink – and on secret trips to Vienna his appetite for a certain type of woman.

'I have had an important message from the Head of State,' Hassan informed him smoothly. 'It is so secret I think I had better tell you outside on the terrace.'

As he spoke he opened the door leading to the terrace, a narrow paved area adjoining the house. Beyond it there was an area of arid sandy ground with rocks protruding at intervals.

Hassan led the way on to the terrace. Ahmed, still holding the bottle, staggered after him, almost tripped as he came out. Hassan saved him by gripping one arm. He guided him to the edge of the terrace. Ahmed, a small heavily built man with a fat face lined from his frequent experiences with the bottle and his trips to Vienna, mumbled, 'What's this all about?'

'Have you yet reported your findings to the Head of State?'

'Not yet. You in big trouble, brother.'

'I'm sure you'll help me out of it.'

226

'Tell me – why should I do that, *brother*?'

There was a sneer as he pronounced the last word. Ahmed lifted the bottle, drank, spilling part of the contents down his suit. He staggered again and Hassan grasped his arm again, guiding him off the terrace.

'We are being watched,' Hassan whispered. 'There are people at the bottom of the quarry with listening devices. Right below us. Look for yourself . . .'

Hassan was now a couple of steps behind Ahmed, had let go of his arm. His brother shook his head, as though to clear it. He was only taking in half what his brother had said.

'Spies . . . you mean? Let's kill them . . .'

Hassan clenched both fists, punched Ahmed in the back, shoved him forward a couple of paces. Perched on the edge of the rim Ahmed fell forward over the edge of the sheer drop. He had dropped the bottle a few paces back. He screamed in terror as he plunged down the sheer wall of the quarry. The scream faded as his body hit the ground three hundred feet down.

Hassan felt the ground shifting under his own feet. He jumped back just in time as a huge boulder went over the drop, followed by a cascade of smaller rocks. Sweating all over, Hassan peered over the edge from the stable terrace. The boulders had buried Ahmed, clouds of dry dust rising. Hassan ran back to waken the servants who were taking a siesta in rooms at the cooler front of the house.

21

The timing was unfortunate by five minutes. The Englishman who had made the call to Hassan from Zurich had left the public phone box, had returned to his hotel before the two plain-clothes watchers sent by Beck arrived. Two other men took up positions where they could watch the hotel where the second Englishman was staying.

'Both your suspects are now under twenty-four-hour surveillance and will be relieved in due course by more of my men,' Beck reported to Tweed over the phone.

'Any movement so far?' Tweed asked.

'None at all. The one in your hotel is in his room. Probably having a sleep in this heat.'

'Amos will be working.'

'The other one is in the hotel lounge of his place, chatting up an attractive lady.'

'How attractive?' Tweed wanted to know.

'A stunner is the correct description, I believe,' said Beck, who was proud of his command of colloquial English.

'Thank you, Arthur.'

Tweed told Newman what Beck had said. Newman grinned as he put down his drink of mineral water. The heat seemed, if anything, to be getting worse. He had decided to switch to water to avoid dehydration.

'Don't know how Willie keeps it up. He has the energy of the Devil,' Newman commented.

'Perhaps he is the Devil. Or are you just envious?'

'I must get to the airport. Paula's flight is due soon.'

'I'll come with you. I think she'd appreciate a reception committee. Let's take your car. Then we can talk in privacy on the way back here.' He unlocked a drawer, took out the photo of Tina Langley. 'I want to call in on Beck on the return trip from the airport. He's set up his HQ at the Zurich Police Chief's place overlooking the Limmat and the University across the river. Let's go.'

Paula was the first to appear at the airport, followed closely by Butler and Nield. She flew into the arms of Tweed, who hugged her affectionately.

'Glad to be back?' he asked as he escorted her to Newman's car, carrying her bag.

'You could say that,' she said as she settled herself in the rear between Tweed and Nield. Butler, parking his backpack on his lap, sat next to Newman and the car took off.

'Slovakia,' Paula started, 'that's where The Sisterhood base is. I've marked the exact location on my map.'

'As far east as that,' Tweed mused. 'Yes, it fits in with the other pieces of the jigsaw I'm building up. Now I'll just listen. Unless you don't feel like talking.'

'I'll talk my head off . . .'

Concisely, she related all the events which had taken place since boarding the plane for Schwechat with Ashley Wingfield. To Tweed's relief she sounded very fresh and alert. Later, Nield gave a brief summary of the encounter with the excavator. Then they pulled in at police headquarters.

Beck greeted Paula in his office with a warm hug. He had always had a soft spot for Paula. Tweed then placed the photo of Tina Langley on his desk.

'Could you reproduce at least fifty prints from this at top speed?'

'Yes,' Beck replied. 'Why?'

'I want them distributed to the police forces in all the major Swiss cities – with special emphasis on Geneva. We have to warn them about the lady – if that's the right word – before she kills someone else as she did Norbert Engel. She attempted to shoot the back of the head off Christopher Kane in Geneva, but he was too smart for her.'

'Christopher Kane? The expert on bacteriological warfare? Is that what we may be facing?'

'Yes.'

'I must alert the Army chiefs – they have advanced equipment to protect troops against such an attack.'

229

'I'd do that, if I were you. You can guess which Eastern power is behind all this. I suspect China, which has supplied them with modern equipment, is using them as an advance guard.'

'What makes you think that?'

'China is making too much fuss about overtaking America. I think it's a smokescreen to cover her real objective. Europe.'

'We live in grim times,' Beck said as he escorted them to the door.

'And few in the West realize the terrible menace hanging over us. But it was the same with Rome – as Amos pointed out in his speech. Rome in ancient times had little inkling that the barbarians were coming from the East.'

'Photos of Tina Langley will flood Switzerland,' Beck promised.

On their way back in the car Paula was silent for a while. She is tired, Tweed decided. He was wrong.

'You know what I would do if I was running The Sisterhood?' she said suddenly.

'What would you do?' Tweed asked.

'Bring them all back to Zurich. The targets are here.'

'Kane said he was coming to Zurich from Geneva.'

'There you are.'

'I meant to ask you if you're sure that photo of Tina Langley *is* the woman you saw walking down Kärntner-strasse after Norbert Engel was murdered.'

'I'm not sure – I'm absolutely certain.'

The first person they met as they walked into the Baur au Lac was Christopher Kane. Smartly dressed in a light grey suit and a pink shirt, he looked pleased to see Paula.

'Always a great pleasure to meet this delightful lady. She has looks, personality – and brains. A most unusual combination. To have everything.'

'You really do go over the top,' she teased him.

He kissed her on both cheeks, gripping her shoulders in his strong hands. His eyes met hers and he seemed genuinely pleased to see her. He presented her with a floral bouquet he had laid on a nearby table.

'Thank you so much, Chris.'

'Merely a tribute to a brave, resourceful lady.'

'I think,' Tweed broke in, 'that the brave lady would like to go to her room to freshen up. I'm sure you will see her later.'

'I shall hope and pray,' Christopher replied, still smiling.

Newman escorted her to her room and left when he heard her lock the door. Downstairs Tweed turned his attention to Nield and Butler.

'Your rooms are here now. I cancelled the Gotthard. We are concentrating our resources. Marler is here.'

'I'll pop in and see him first,' Nield decided.

As the two men headed for the lift after being handed folders with their room numbers, Tweed smiled to himself. He guessed they hoped to obtain fresh weapons from Marler. It was a marvel they had coped with the excavator's driver without weapons – until Nield had got hold of the machine-pistol the driver had been holding.

'Let's go into the lounge for a drink,' Tweed suggested, 'unless you'd sooner go to your room first.'

'Had a shower before I left. Slept on the train. A drink is called for. Waiter, service, please. What are you having, Tweed?'

'Mineral water. Non-sparkling.'

'A dry Martini,' Christopher ordered as they sat down in a corner of the deserted lounge.

231

'Why have you come here?' Tweed wanted to know when they were alone.

'Like to be in at the end of the game. In rugger you don't sit around waiting for the other chap to get you – you go after him. Same applies if the aggressor is a woman. Lisa Vane tried to clonk me for good. This seems to be the centre of the action so that's why I'm here.'

'You're a major target,' Tweed warned quietly. 'And there are at least two different women assassins. Lisa Vane and Karin Berg. We think we know who murdered Dumont, but we can't prove it. Berg's slim, tallish, has blonde hair cut short like a helmet, just in case you meet her.'

He stopped talking, aware that someone had come up behind him, had placed a gentle hand on his neck. He looked up. It was Simone Carnot, the desirable redhead he had last met in this very lounge when she was talking to Newman.

'Hello, Mr Tweed,' Simone said with a devastating smile which Christopher appreciated. 'I'm not going to interrupt, but I just wanted you to know I was still around.'

'Please join us for a drink,' Tweed said immediately.

'Are you sure?'

'We're certain,' Christopher said jovially. 'That vacant chair was just waiting for you.'

'How nice to be invited to join two gentlemen with such good manners,' Simone responded with a quirky smile. 'I think I'll have a Kir royale,' she requested, after eyeing Christopher's drink.

'This is Simone Carnot,' Tweed introduced. 'Miss Carnot . . .'

'Simone, please.'

'Simone, this is Christopher Kane.'

'Delighted to meet such a beauty,' Christopher said gallantly. 'And I'm Christopher. My friends call me Chris.'

'I'm glad to meet you, Chris. You look as though your conversation will be interesting.'

As the waiter brought the drink Kane had ordered Simone was thinking: Thank Heaven I stayed on here. I am talking to both targets. I'm looking at two potential corpses who would earn me two hundred thousand dollars.

Hassan had been very direct when he phoned her. He had told her to kill the two men at the first opportunity, not to bother about faking them as suicides, and had given her the name and address of a man in Zurich who could supply her with a Luger and ammunition. Hassan had been in a hurry.

'You live in Zurich, Chris?' Simone enquired.

'No, in Geneva.' He was watching her closely. 'This is not the best Kir royale in the world, although it's very good. To get the best you go to Les Armures in Geneva. Expect you know the place.'

'I'm afraid I don't.'

'You've never been to Geneva?' he asked amiably.

'Not so far.'

Both men noticed the tiny pause before she had replied to the question. Simone was wearing a form-fitting green sheath. It exposed one shapely bare shoulder. Simone worked on the basis of 'show them a little flesh and they'll want to see more'.

'You're from the French-speaking part of Switzerland?'

'No, I'm from France.'

'The best French in the world,' Christopher went on, 'is spoken in Geneva.'

'Parisians would not agree with you.'

233

'So you're from Paris?'

'I didn't say so. You do it well, Chris, but you almost sound like a detective questioning a witness.'

'I'm just interested in you.'

'So I should be interested in you, which I am. What is your profession?'

'I'm the world's expert on bacteriological warfare.'

Christopher was never backward in broadcasting his importance, thought Tweed, who was deliberately keeping silent while he studied Simone. He knew she thought he was taking a more than gentlemanly interest in her from the sidelong glances which occasionally came his way.

'What a horrible thing to be involved in,' Simone protested.

'It's bound to happen sooner or later,' Christopher said cheerfully. 'The thing to do is to be prepared for it when it comes. Anyone working for the Eastern state concerned should be shot. Stone-cold dead.'

Both men saw Simone blink. She recovered her poise almost immediately, sipped the last of her drink, put down her glass. Checking her watch, a Rolex, she stood up.

'I have enjoyed our conversation. Possibly we could continue it over dinner one evening. My treat.'

'You would be my guest,' Tweed insisted. 'We'll fix something up in the near future. You are staying at this hotel?'

'I have a room here, yes. Sometimes I have to travel for a few days.'

'I will find you sooner or later,' Tweed said in an odd tone.

'What do you think, Christopher?' Tweed asked when she had gone.

234

'From the technique you described they use on the phone I'd say we could well have been talking to a third member of The Sisterhood.'

'I agree. They're getting desperate, or their controller is.'

'I'm not saying so positively,' Christopher said carefully. 'In Scotland we have a jury verdict "not proven". That would be my verdict on the very sinuous Simone Carnot.'

'Well, I got in first with my invitation.'

'You certainly did, you old dog. I was about to make the same suggestion to her. What is happening?'

'The enemy is panicking. They're working to a timetable and running out of time. So are we.'

A man in civilian clothes came into the lounge, saw Tweed and presented him with an envelope. 'From Chief Inspector Beck,' he whispered.

'Thank you.'

'Who was that?' Christopher asked.

'A plain-clothes policeman I recognized. Ah, Beck has returned the photo I gave him. Recognize this lady?'

'It's Lisa Vane,' Christopher said.

'Otherwise known as Tina Langley. The woman who murdered Norbert Engel in Vienna – and the woman who nearly killed you in Geneva.'

'Then I've left her behind.'

'I wouldn't bank on that. I think they're all coming here. I think an Englishman from Dorset is controlling the whole operation to wipe out all members of the *Institut*. I mean either Amos Lodge or Willie.'

'That's a trifle fantastic even for you, Tweed. When did you come to that astonishing conclusion?'

'Just now. They've been working their way down the list of members in sequence. Only someone with the list could work that out.'

'Willie isn't a member,' Christopher objected.

'You'll recall he once attended a session we held at the HQ of the *Institut* near Ouchy on Lake Geneva. He gave us a very informative lecture on conditions in the Middle East. While he was there Dumont foolishly showed him a list of the members.'

'You think he'd remember them in exact sequence?'

'He could have done. Willie, I happen to know, has a photographic memory. I once joked with him about it, tested him. I gave him a page of Somerset Maugham's novel *The Painted Veil*. He read the page once, then recited it back to me word for word.'

'So it could be either of them,' Christopher said.

'Exactly. And both of them keep hanging about in Zurich.'

At that moment Newman came into the lounge and Tweed beckoned to him to join them. He then told Newman what he had been discussing with Christopher.

'Makes sense,' Newman agreed. 'And both of them right under our noses. So which one is it?'

'I have no idea,' Tweed replied. 'But I'm certain whoever it is plans on Zurich being the killing ground. Adrian Manders, the specialist on ballistic missiles, is next on that list. He came here for a holiday and to listen to Dumont's speech. When Amos took over Manders was in the audience.'

'Where is he staying?' Newman asked.

'At the Dolder Grand. Both Amos and Willie must have seen him. Manders had a front-row seat, was the first to stand up and leave during the ovation.'

'Zurich is getting more dangerous,' Newman observed.

'That's why we're going to take drastic action, to move on to the offensive. Today.'

22

'Tell me, first, about this chateau you traced Tina Langley to,' Tweed asked Christopher.

'Isn't this a public place for us to talk?' Newman intervened.

'Yes,' said Tweed. 'Chosen deliberately. We are the only ones here. Everyone else is getting a sunbath out on the Pavillon. Also, my room may be bugged – and we haven't the equipment to check it.' He turned to Christopher. 'That chateau?'

'I'll go over it again, even though I told you on the phone, so Bob is in the picture. Called the Château d'Avignon. A few miles further down the road is the very beautiful Château des Avenières, which is pukka. Run by a nice couple who are renovating it. They advertise it – hand you a brochure if you ask for one. *La Missive du Château!*'

'You said pukka,' Tweed said. 'You mean there's something odd about the Château d'Avignon?'

'Very odd. No one knows who owns the place. Went there for a drink once. The waiters were more like guards. Bad when it came to serving – as though they hadn't been trained for the job. Watched me like a hawk all the time I was there. On the way out I caught one of them noting down the registration number of my car. A mysterious place.'

'And that's where Tina Langley walked inside with her case?' Tweed queried.

'Yes.'

'Monceau and his gang came from France – and you said the chateau is in France.'

'It is. Top of Mount Salève,' Christopher confirmed.

'The great cliff facing Geneva which most people think is in Switzerland?'

'That's it. Eleven hundred metres high. Over three thousand feet.'

'We simply mustn't forget Monceau,' Newman emphasized.

'I'm aware he won't forget me,' Tweed agreed. 'And he's good at disguise. I've warned everyone about that. We're all leaving Zurich,' he announced casually.

'Where for?' Newman wanted to know.

'I've tossed up between Vienna and Geneva. Zurich is a death trap because of its size and complexity.'

'So could be Vienna,' Newman warned. 'Look what nearly happened to Paula.'

'I've thought of that.'

'Geneva could be the same,' Christopher commented. 'Remember my interlude with Tina Langley.'

'So I've decided to get us all out of cities.'

'Where the heck are we going?' Newman asked.

'Somewhere to throw the enemy off balance. We go there openly. Then our opponents will see us. We are checking out of here in one hour. Christopher, I need you to come with us. I'll warn Manders to fly back to Britain immediately. Who knows? We may have the company of three attractive ladies. The three members of The Sisterhood.'

'Where are we going?' persisted Newman.

'To the Château des Avenières on Mount Salève. Book rooms on the phone for all of us, Bob. Except for Butler and Nield. They'll stay at this weird Château d'Avignon. They're good at taking care of themselves.'

His decision startled Newman, even though he was hardened by Tweed's sudden decisions in the past.

* * *

In the park opposite a road leading directly from the drive to the Baur au Lac a man in the uniform of a Swiss private soldier waited. His peaked cap was pulled well down over his face and he was wearing contact lenses. Nearby, against a thick hedge, stood a motorcycle.

He was so intent on watching the exit from the hotel he failed to notice there were two other watchers. One, a Swiss pickpocket, sat in his car a few yards up Talstrasse, pretending to study a road map. The third man, Mario Parcelli, was more skilled in his surveillance. He had lifted the bonnet of his parked car and appeared to be having trouble with the engine.

Mario had been positioned by Vitorelli, who had realized Tweed was avoiding him. He wondered why. Could Tweed be on the verge of leaving for a new destination? He might even lead Mario to Tina Langley. Vitorelli had great respect for Tweed and his bloodhound personality.

Several taxis entered the drive to the Baur au Lac at almost the same moment. Tweed and Paula, rearmed with a Browning .32 supplied by Marler, entered the first taxi. Tweed told the driver to wait. In the taxi behind them Newman, carrying a .38 Smith & Wesson, also supplied by Marler, got into the back with Marler. Keeping to Tweed's strict instructions, they waited while Butler and Nield boarded the third taxi. Only then did Tweed's taxi move off, with the other two vehicles close behind him.

It was a deliberately noticeable cavalcade which proceeded from the Baur au Lac. Tweed's audacious plan was for the enemy to see them. As they headed for the Hauptbahnhof Tweed soon saw Mario's grey Fiat following them. He smiled to himself – the plan was working.

What he failed to observe was the soldier on the motorcycle keeping pace behind the Fiat. Nor did he notice for a few minutes the pickpocket trailing after them in a white Renault.

'Anything happening?' whispered Paula.

'A grey Fiat is following us. Also a white Renault, so far as I can tell.'

'We seem to be popular,' she replied. 'Did you expect two of them?'

'No, I didn't. One of them has to belong to The Sisterhood. The second one is anyone's guess. The trouble is I can't see the driver of either vehicle. The sun keeps reflecting off the windscreens. The Sisterhood's organization may be using two cars – in case one of them loses us. Relax.'

'Never felt more relaxed in my life,' she said ironically.

The three taxis pulled up in front of the main rail station one behind the other. Tweed had hardly paid the fare before Newman and Marler were by their sides.

'We're being followed,' Tweed said.

'We know,' Marler replied. 'A grey Fiat and a white Renault. Here they come.'

'Get inside the station. I'll buy the tickets.'

He joined the queue already formed in front of the window. Tucked behind a woman next to Newman, Mario listened carefully. The motorcyclist abandoned his machine at the kerb, joined the queue, was close enough to hear Tweed, who was deliberately speaking in a loud voice.

'Six first-class return tickets to Geneva, please.'

They left the queue and hurried to the platform where an express was waiting for them. Mario got back inside his Fiat, headed for the nearest telephone, which he knew was near Talstrasse. The soldier bought a first-class single for Geneva.

* * *

240

After settling himself in a first-class coach, Tweed took out a book to read. Paula sat alongside him. Marler sat in a corner seat on the other side of the aisle, diagonally opposite to Tweed. Newman sat facing him as Marler closed his eyes, head back against the rest.

Butler chose a seat at one entrance to the coach while Nield sat at the other end. They had all placed their suitcases on the rack above them to give themselves room for manoeuvre, if an emergency arose.

'Wake me up when we're approaching Geneva,' Tweed asked Paula.

'I'll do that. I'm very alert.'

Looking out of the window two minutes before the train was due to leave she saw a Swiss Army soldier hurrying past. He is obviously afraid of missing the train, she thought. Looking across at Marler she saw his eyes open briefly. He wasn't asleep at all and she knew he wouldn't be before they reached Geneva.

As the express began to glide out of the cavern and into the blazing sunlight she wondered why she felt uneasy. It must be those two cars who were following us, she decided. I wonder who was inside them?

'Mario here,' the Italian said inside the phone booth.

'What is it?' asked Vitorelli from his hotel room.

'Tweed and his whole team have just boarded an express for Geneva. It has probably just left . . .'

'Drive to the airport. Get the helicopter ready for instant departure. I'm driving to the airport now. We might arrive before the train does.'

'I doubt it.'

'Get to the bloody airport.'

Vitorelli put down the phone. He called the concierge, told him he was leaving, perhaps for a few days, that he wanted the room kept for his return. Five minutes later he was driving through Zurich, heading for Kloten.

What was the significance of Geneva? he kept asking himself. Why would Tweed be taking his whole team with him? There had to be some important development which had caused him to leave so suddenly. Something, he suspected, to do with The Sisterhood.

The Englishman, who had been informed by the Swiss pickpocket he had hired as a watcher, called Hassan as soon as he heard what was happening. In the long house in Slovakia Hassan had just reported to the Head of State about the 'accident' which had resulted in the death of Ahmed. His nerves were still tingling from the effort he had put into telling a convincing story.

'Yes?' he snapped into the receiver.

'You know who this is. Tweed has just left Zurich for Geneva. Tina is still at the chateau? Good. Tell her to stay there, that her main target is still Tweed. Also tell Karin Berg and Simone Carnot to go to Geneva immediately. One of them must find Tweed. Kill him immediately. Then kill Christopher Kane. Move, man, move . . .'

Hassan was left holding a phone where the line had gone dead. He swore foully, then began to make phone calls.

Tweed was still asleep when the train stopped at Berne. His companions were all alert and watchful. Nothing happened and the express was still nearly empty. They were the only passengers in their first-class coach.

Few passengers boarded the train at Berne. Marler had opened a window, peered out. He saw nothing unusual about those who had come onto the train at the Swiss capital. Paula watched him as he closed the window. She was still feeling nervous and unsuccessfully tried to work out what was worrying her. At least the train was air-conditioned so they had a respite from the fatiguing heat.

She watched Marler, as the train moved away from Berne, using his mobile phone. Probably reporting their progress to Beck, informing him of their new destination. She also wondered whether the strain was telling on Tweed.

The only reason Tweed was sleeping was that he had been up most of the night, pacing round his room. In his mind he had reviewed a whole kaleidoscope of events. The curious experience in Dorset when they had visited Willie's garden with its weird statuary on islands in the lakes. The contradictory versions Amos and Willie had given him in Zurich as to who had purchased the statuary. The fact that Willie had, at one time, known Tina Langley. The mysterious long house in Slovakia, which was on the way to the East.

Christopher Kane had politely declined Tweed's offer to go by train with them to Geneva. He had driven to Zurich in his Porsche, and packing and paying his bill in five minutes, he had driven out of Zurich.

Once a racing driver, Christopher was confident he could beat any express – which had several stops en route – to Cornavin, Geneva's main rail station. As he sped along the motorway, he tried to work out how he could uncover who owned the Château d'Avignon.

No good approaching one of his banker friends – they had mouths like steel traps. He needed someone who knew about property. Then he remembered a friend

243

he had done a favour for and who happened to be a top-class estate agent. He might be the key to unlock the mystery.

He was also keeping an eye on his rear-view mirror. It seemed unlikely he was being followed, but he had grasped from Tweed the octopus-like spread of The Sisterhood. Knowing what he was doing, he began to talk to himself, his lips moving without any sound emerging.

'One blonde, the Swede, Karin Berg. One red-head, Simone Carnot. One auburn-haired lovely – who called herself Lisa Vane, but whose real name is Tina Langley. Well, poppet, I'll know you if we meet again. Come to that, I'll recognize Simone Carnot equally well. The Sisterhood is coming out of its murderous shell.'

Then he saw a blonde coming up behind him at the wheel of a Ferrari. The trouble was she had long flowing hair. As she passed him she made a wave with her hand, a 'Come on, Buster, catch me if you can,' gesture. He let her go. He was determined to beat the express to Cornavin.

'Wake up, we're close to Geneva,' said Paula, giving Tweed a gentle nudge.

'I am awake. Have been for the last half-hour.'

'Then you're a fake. I feel safer now we've left Zurich behind.'

'Nowhere is safe. Don't forget two cars followed us to the main station. Who knows who might be aboard this express.'

'You're trying to make me nervous,' she grumbled.

'I'm trying to make sure you're as on the alert here as you were back in Zurich – or in Vienna, for that matter. We cannot relax anywhere until we have destroyed the enemy – The Sisterhood.'

The express moved into Cornavin station, the automatic doors were opened. Passengers began to alight. One of the first to leave from the front coach was the uniformed soldier. Lifting his pack onto his shoulder, he moved across to the opposite platform, as though waiting for another train.

Marler was first off the train. On the platform he scanned its very long stretch, saw only a handful of passengers trudging away, a Swiss Army soldier waiting on the opposite platform. Paula lowered herself down the long drop, like Marler carrying her case in her left hand. She kept her right hand free in case she had to use her Browning.

Tweed joined them, followed by Newman, Butler and Nield. As he walked towards the exit his team gathered in front, behind and alongside him. He grunted before he made the remark.

'Stop crowding me. I'm not the King of Siam. Or Thailand, as it is these days, and it hasn't got a king.'

'Just for once leave it to us,' Paula reprimanded him. 'You never know when there could be danger – even on this platform.'

'You phoned ahead from the hotel for hired cars?' Tweed asked Newman.

'They will be waiting for us. Marler will deal with the paperwork – that's why he's now going ahead of us.'

Marler walked briskly, glanced at the soldier on the other platform. You saw them all over the place – soldiers returning from manoeuvres, or setting out to take part in them. They had hired two cars and he had the necessary papers inside his pocket.

'This must be the longest station platform in the world,' Tweed commented.

They were approaching the point where the soldier waited and Butler dropped back a few paces behind Tweed, also carrying his case in his left hand. They were all right-handed. As soon as they had left the platform the soldier moved. He followed them at a discreet distance, then paused when he saw them waiting for a moment at the car-hire office.

The moment they moved off he ran to the office, produced his own papers, asked for the Citroën he had hired by phone. Before leaving Zurich he had also called another firm and hired a car to be waiting for him at the airport, not knowing which form of transport might be used.

He was at the wheel of the Citroën, the engine started, when Tweed's two cars left the station.

Prior to entering one of the cars in the front passenger seat, Tweed had been startled to see Christopher Kane, hands on hips, standing by a red Porsche. He came forward with a grin.

'Even Swiss trains are slow, you know. I've driven here from Zurich while your lot was tanking up in the dining car.'

'Not one drink has passed our lips,' Tweed informed him. 'I want to get away from Geneva quickly. We're heading for the Château d'Avignon. Maybe you'll be able to keep up with us . . .'

Paula drove a cream Renault with Tweed next to her. The rear seats were occupied by Newman and Marler. In the blue Ford behind them Butler had the wheel with Nield alongside him. Christopher's Porsche started by following Butler.

Earlier, back in Zurich, Paula had studied a map of the area, and Christopher had marked the position of the chateau just before he dashed off to his Porsche. She had a clear picture of the map in her head. Passing through the checkpoint for Customs and Passport Control into France, she was soon speeding up the lower slopes of Mount Salève.

As she climbed higher Geneva began to spread out below them and they had a glimpse of the famous sixty-foot-high fountain in the lake which is Geneva's trademark. Moving fast, she went on climbing, climbing. Suddenly she was overtaken by the red Porsche. Christopher gave a wave of his hand. She read the wave as a message, 'Come on, girl, catch me if you can.'

'Chris really slams his foot down,' Tweed commented.

'He does have a Porsche.'

'So what? Can't we go any faster? We're crawling.'

Paula stared briefly at Tweed in amazement. She had never known him to make such a statement. His blue-grey eyes glanced back at hers. He appeared to be enjoying a great surge of energy, and then she understood. They were on the move, taking action, performing a manoeuvre which might well totally confuse and alarm the enemy. Imbued with his sense of purpose, she pressed her foot down.

There was no other traffic on the road and the intense heat they had experienced on getting out of the air-conditioned train had been left behind as they moved into a higher elevation. Soon, she saw Christopher's Porsche ahead of them. Choosing a straight stretch, she overtook him, waved her hand.

'Heavens above!' Christopher said to himself. 'She's going like a rocket.'

He made no attempt to pass her, contenting himself with keeping her in sight as the spiralling road climbed ever higher. Behind Christopher, Butler, driving his Ford, had raised his thick eyebrows and maintained an even distance behind the Porsche.

'I don't suppose we have company?' Nield queried. 'There's a blue Citroën which joined us in Geneva and it's still a little way behind us. Can't see the driver.'

'Let's see if he's still with us when we reach the Château d'Avignon,' Butler suggested. Mustn't forget that's where we have rooms booked. The others are going on to the Château des Avenières. Christopher is going to flag us down when we are close to it.'

23

The Butterfly was appalled when Hassan ordered her over the phone to remain at the Château d'Avignon. Tina Langley never liked to stay in one place for long – partly due to her volatile temperament and partly because she felt it was unsafe not to keep moving.

'I want to go back to Switzerland,' she protested.

'What you want is irrelevant,' Hassan had snapped. 'What is relevant is that you wipe off the face of the earth Christopher Kane and Tweed. Do it any way you can. No more stage-setting – kill them on the street if you can. A Luger with ammunition is on the way to you by courier. In a gift-wrapped Cartier box.'

'I don't like it here.'

'But you do like the prospect of earning another one hundred thousand dollars in cash. Maybe two hundred if you manage to get them both.'

'They both know me. At least, Kane does . . .'

'Why should Tweed know you? I have other calls to make.'

'A man in the street in Geneva was watching me – he looked at a photo in his hand, then tried to follow me.' Her voice lifted, had a tone of domineering confidence. 'But I was too smart for him – I lured him onto a train going to Zurich and I was still on the platform when the train departed.'

'Then be smart is what I've told you to do.'

The line went dead while she was still holding the receiver. She heard a click. She froze. Someone had been listening in. She didn't like the Château d'Avignon – the staff were peculiar, the whole atmosphere of the place was peculiar. She simply couldn't put her finger on what was wrong.

When worried she always sat down in front of a dressing table when she could. In her room she did that now. The top was littered with every type of cosmetic to make a woman look her most attractive. She began to apply lipstick.

'You are catching the first flight from Schwechat to Zurich,' Hassan told Karin Berg in his office in the long house. 'I have booked your return ticket, Business Class.'

'I don't want to go back to Zurich.'

'From Zurich you will catch a connecting flight to Geneva. I have booked a room for you at the Hôtel des Bergues. You have two targets. Christopher Kane and Tweed.'

'You're bloody crazy. Tweed knows me well.'

'Shut your arrogant trap. There's two hundred thousand dollars in this for you. Again, in cash. You've always been paid promptly before,' Hassan raved on. 'Don't you want the money? The fact that you know Tweed is a huge advantage.'

'Tweed suspects me.'

'How does he suspect you? Tell me that.'

'Because I took him to the Ermitage. Monceau told me when the attack would take place. I went to the powder room just before they did attack. Tweed is no fool.'

'Can he prove anything?'

'I suppose not . . .'

'Can he be sure you were involved?'

'I suppose not.'

Berg was weighing up the odds. Money meant everything to her. No, they couldn't be sure she was involved, she decided. Hassan was obviously desperate to eliminate both men.

'My fee will be three hundred thousand dollars.'

'Three hundred thousand! That's absurd.'

'Forget it, then.' She stood up. 'I'm flying back to Sweden. If anything happens to me my lawyer in Stockholm has a document he will send to the news-papers and the police.' She gave her quirky smile. 'You could call it my insurance policy.'

'For both men?' Hassan asked after a long pause.

'Yes. Two hundred thousand if I only get one of them. Where are they?'

'They took the train to Geneva today. I had a man on a motorcycle watching Cornavin station in Geneva. He followed them to the French border but was stopped for questioning by the French Customs. He thinks they were heading for Mount Salève.'

'Big help. When do I leave?'

'Now. I told you to keep a case packed.'

'Which I did, to go back to Sweden.'

'You'll be a rich woman. Here are the tickets in this envelope. And your hotel reservation.'

When the car had left, taking her to the airport, Hassan called Simone Carnot at her apartment. He put the same proposition to her. To his surprise she didn't argue, but she had one objection.

'So long as Tweed or the police haven't linked me to the Dumont episode,' she said cold-bloodedly.

'Has anyone questioned you about it?'

'No!'

'Then here are your instructions. You're flying to Geneva . . .'

When he put down the phone Hassan was weary and worried. He was throwing the entire Sisterhood into this operation. No one would be left to deal with the surviving members of the *Institut*.

Hassan had just finished a glass of brandy when the phone rang again. Cursing, he picked it up. He badly needed some sleep. It was the Englishman.

'Have you carried out my instructions?'

'Yes. All three women are on their way to Geneva. How they are going to trace their targets I don't know.'

'I personally chose them because they are resourceful.'

'But it leaves no one to deal with the other members of the *Institut* who are still alive.'

'It doesn't matter. Once those two men are underground we have dealt with the most dangerous ones. And time is running out.'

'You have been in touch with—'

'Yes. He agrees with me.'

Once more the Englishman slammed down the phone. Hassan felt relieved. He had been going to ask whether his caller had been in touch with the Head of State. Obviously he had, so Hassan felt covered. And what was a few hundred thousand dollars? The Head of State had billions under his control.

When the phone rang again Hassan, sprawled out on a couch, wanted to throw it out of the window over the cliff. With a sigh he got up, answered the call.

'Monceau here. I've decided it should be worth something to you when I kill Tweed.'

Hassan immediately named a large sum. The Frenchman accepted the deal immediately. He would need extra money to recruit a fresh gang in France.

'You can really do the job? You know where he is? Where are you?'

'Zurich,' Monceau lied.

'Tweed is in Geneva. Last reported heading for France via Mount Salève.'

'Really? I can get there fast.'

'Wait a minute.'

'I haven't got a minute.'

Hassan had had an idea. If any of The Sisterhood were arrested he was sure they would try to make an arrangement to provide information in return for lenient treatment. This had worried him when the Englishman had given him the original order – but the Englishman was not a man to argue with.

'Monceau, there are three women I'm concerned about. But only if one of them is arrested. It would be best if they were eliminated if that happened. I'm not sure how you could do it once they were in police custody.'

'A large enough bomb left in a car parked outside the police station where they were held. Or where one of them was held.'

'I'll give you names, descriptions and where they are staying.'

'I have two minutes. Give me the details. I'm on a mobile phone.'

Christopher's Porsche cruised past Paula's Renault as they reached the summit. He waved for the following cars to follow him and parked with a few other cars at the viewing point. Getting out of his car he walked with long strides to Tweed's car which had also parked, followed by Butler and Nield's vehicle.

'The panorama from here is rather splendid. As you can see all Geneva is spread out three thousand feet below us.'

'Tweed's not leaving this car,' Newman said grimly.

'Doesn't have to. You can see the view from the window.'

'We've seen it,' Newman said impatiently.

'Humour Christopher,' Tweed said as the tall man walked nearer to the view. 'He may have given us invaluable information concerning this Château d'Avignon. I've had a feeling for some time that Geneva is a key city.'

'Why would it be?'

'Because, as you've just seen, it is so very close to France. Anyone wishing to escape – or avoid – Beck's eagle eye can be in another country, where he has no jurisdiction, within a few minutes.'

Marler had left the car as soon as it stopped. With his jacket hanging loosely, so he could reach his Walther quickly, he strolled around the small plateau. He was checking on everyone who had stopped to admire the view.

At the edge of the plateau Geneva seemed far away. Marler could pick out individual streets of a city he knew well and to the east the famous fountain was hurling its enormous jet towards the cloudless sky. It was late afternoon and in the clear light he could see every detail of the ancient city, spread out like a map.

Nield had left his car, walked to the roadside at the point where cars entered the viewing plateau. He looked back. The road they had come up quickly turned a sharp bend and went out of sight. He walked back to the car.

'Restless?' enquired Butler.

'Just checking. No sign of that blue Citroën – although I couldn't see far because the road bends where it starts to go downhill.'

'Probably turned off further down. Looks as though we're off again.'

Christopher led the way in his Porsche. Paula followed and Butler's car brought up the rear. Driving along the summit of Salève the character of the countryside was very different. Whereas before, the ascending road had provided glimpses of the lake and distant mountains they were now hemmed in on both sides by dense forest, a mix of pines and firs like a palisade. Tweed was staring out of the window with great concentration.

'Something interests you?' Paula enquired.

'The Château d'Avignon intrigues me. There could be trouble up here. I'm studying the terrain.'

'That chopper is somewhere above us,' she observed. 'I first heard it when we were leaving Cornavin station. I thought it was a traffic helicopter. Now I'm not so sure.'

'The world is full of helicopters,' Tweed said off-handedly, more interested in the forest.

With Mario at the controls of the chopper, Vitorelli sat beside him, gazing through his field glasses down at the convoy of cars passing through the forest of Salève.

Before they had taken off from Kloten Mario had phoned the Hauptbahnhof to find out the arrival time of the express to Geneva. Flying across country as direct as possible, they had arrived at Cointrin Airport, Geneva, in time to refuel.

They had then timed their fresh take-off to coincide with the express pulling in to Geneva's rail station.

Through his glasses Vitorelli had seen Tweed and the others entering the hired cars. They tried to keep a discreet distance but had to keep the cars in sight. Which was why Paula had become aware of the chopper's presence.

'It's odd,' Vitorelli commented, 'but that blue Citroën driven by a Swiss soldier appears to be following them. I wonder who he could be?'

'Probably Tweed's rearguard disguised as a soldier. That would be clever.'

'I suppose you could be right,' Vitorelli replied.

The forest was even more dense as they drove along the well-made road. Here and there were gaps to their left. Through them they caught brief views of a vast landscape receding into the distance.

'France is a lovely country,' Tweed commented. 'Incidentally, I took the precaution of phoning Loriot in Paris. He was very interested when I mentioned the name Monceau. He may be flying down to see us. He could provide massive back-up.'

'Exactly why are we coming to this isolated part of the world?' Newman asked.

'As you will have realized, I advertised our departure. Did everything except take out a TV ad. I want to draw the enemy out of dangerous places like complex cities, as I believe I mentioned earlier. Out here we have to see them coming. It is a much more dangerous battleground – for the enemy. We have to destroy our opponents quickly. I sense we have very little time left.'

'That chopper is still high up but overhead,' Paula commented.

'Good. That might mean . . .'

He never finished his sentence as Christopher slowed

to a crawl. Out of his open window he waved his hand up and down. Paula made the same signal to Butler and Nield behind them.

'We must be close to the Château d'Avignon,' she said.

A minute later they crept past the entrance to a chateau with a fantastic number of turrets. An ugly building, it looked old and decrepit with a creeper covering most of the stonework, a creeper which reminded Paula of a green octopus extending its strangling tentacles. By the open gates she saw a uniformed guard. In her rear-view mirror she saw Butler and Nield's car turn in, then stop.

'I wonder what sort of a reception they will get there,' she mused. 'Eerie-looking place.'

24

A few miles further on Christopher waved his hand again out of his window. Paula slowed down and turned slowly off the road to her left, following the Porsche. At the Château des Avenières there were no gates and the building was standing a short distance back from the road. Paula let out a whistle as she parked.

'What a difference. It's quite beautiful. My idea of what a French chateau should look like at its best.'

Tweed got out, holding his case, while Christopher locked his Porsche. There was no uniformed guard here. Instead, as Tweed walked up the steps a handsome woman came out of the open door.

'Mr Tweed?' she said in perfect English. 'Welcome to the Château des Avenières. We are always pleased to welcome new visitors. A porter will take your case.'

She greeted Paula, Newman and Marler with the same warmth and ushered them inside. Tweed immediately felt at home as he gazed round at the splendid decor. It was rich and tasteful without being overdone. Porters had relieved them of their cases when she made a suggestion.

'I know you must be travel weary after your long journey from Zurich. May we offer you a glass of champagne on the terrace?'

'Yes, please,' called out Christopher, who had just arrived.

They crossed a large room which was also furnished with quiet luxury. Beyond it large doors were open to a long wide terrace where several couples sat having a drink at tables. Tweed chose a large table at the edge of the terrace because it was on its own. Sitting down, after pulling out a chair for Paula, he gazed at the view.

'Never seen anything like it,' he said.

Below was an even larger terrace with an oval swimming pool. Beyond that the ground fell away to fields sloping even further down. But it was the distant view which fascinated him. In the luminous evening light was a series of ranges of hills, one behind the other. To his right, a long way off, a blue sheet glittered in the setting sun. Christopher pointed to it.

'That's Lake Annecy. You can just see part of the old town.'

'It's heaven,' said Tweed. 'I could spend a holiday here.'

Paula gazed at him as he sipped his champagne. She had never before heard Tweed refer with longing to a holiday. The place had a magic atmosphere. Like something out of a Turner painting. The couples at other tables were chatting quietly.

'This is peace,' Tweed decided.

257

'I wonder how Nield and Butler are getting on,' Paula remarked.

Arriving at the Château d'Avignon was rather a different experience. Butler, compelled by Tweed to wear a well-cut linen suit, was stopped by the uniformed guard.

'You can't come in here without an advance reservation.'

The guard was six foot tall, heavily built, and his English accent reminded Butler of the less well-patronized part of the East End of London. He wore a leather belt and from it dangled a holster with the butt of a revolver protruding.

'Really?' Butler paused, staring at the guard. 'Is that how they train you to greet a guest who *has* a reservation?'

'Names?'

'Don't you mean,' Nield intervened, '"Could I please have your names?"'

'If you have reservations it's OK.'

'What is this?' Nield continued. 'A hotel or San Quentin? Why do you need that gun? Overrun with rabbits round here, are we?'

'It's very lonely up here,' the guard informed him.

'I had noticed that,' Butler told him. 'Nield and Butler. Rooms reserved from Zurich. Make with the feet. Go inside and check. We'll come with you.'

'And you can carry our bags,' Nield snapped.

Reluctantly, the guard carried a bag in each of his prizefighter's hands. They reached the reception desk. Behind it a weasel-faced man looked up suspiciously.

'Yes, Ben.'

'Big Ben,' Butler said in a loud voice.

'Nield and Butler. Say they have reservations. From Zurich.'

'They do, Ben.' Weasel became oily, smirking as he pushed forward the register for them to fill in. 'Welcome to the best hotel in France,' he went on.

'Heaven help France, then,' Butler snapped.

He scribbled his name illegibly together with all the other details required. Nield followed suit, staring at Weasel as he scrawled, then shoved the register back across the counter.

Weasel had a French accent despite his good English. He took keys from a board behind him, smirked again. Nield had an idea it was his way of being pleasant.

Both had rooms overlooking the drive and the road they had come along. Neither thought it worthwhile to ask for rooms overlooking the view at the back. After a wash they met in the gloomy corridor and went down in search of food.

There were few people in the restaurant, which did have a panoramic view. The head waiter, who looked down his nose at them as though he was doing them a favour to let them in, escorted them to a table behind a pillar. Butler did not sit down.

'We'll have that table over there.'

'I fear it is reserved.'

'Of course it is. Reserved for us.'

Butler, with Nield following, marched over to the table with a view, sat down. The head waiter rushed after them. He was not pleased.

'The people who reserved this table will be upset.'

'From Birmingham, aren't you?' Butler replied. 'Bring us the wine list, two bottles of mineral water. Sparkling – and we'd appreciate some quick service.'

'Our service is always quick. Sir.'

'Prove it.'

259

When the waiter had gone Butler glanced round the almost empty restaurant. Most of the guests appeared to be French. At one corner table sat a very attractive woman with auburn hair. She caught his glance, held his eye, then looked away. She began to slow down drinking her coffee. It struck her the sturdily built man could be a wealthy industrialist.

'Don't look now,' Butler whispered to Nield. 'The siren at the corner window table on the far side of the room. We've found Tina Langley.'

'I know,' Nield agreed. 'I studied her photo – as we all did. Maybe we have come to the right place.

The driver behind the wheel of the blue Citroën had caught up with the convoy just in time to see Butler and Nield turn into the Château d'Avignon. He drove on until he saw the car containing Tweed turn in later to the Château des Avenières. Slowing down, he cruised past, saw Tweed being greeted on the steps by his hostess.

He drove a little further, then executed a U-turn. Driving back at a leisurely pace, he checked his rear-view mirror to make sure no traffic was coming behind him. The road was empty. He swung his wheel over to the right, drove slowly up a track deep into the forest.

He parked the car in a deserted glade, got out. Listening for several minutes he heard nothing, not even birdsong. It took him only a few minutes to erect a tent. Taking a pack containing rations, the soldier in Swiss Army uniform began to eat.

After finishing their dinner – the excellence of the food had surprised them – Butler suggested Nield should come to his room. It was several doors from Nield's bedroom on the first floor.

'I've got something to show you. You were a cat burglar once, weren't you?'

'I was not – and you know it.'

'You're going to be one now.'

Butler unlocked his door, looked up and down the empty corridor, switched the key to the inside of the lock, walked in without switching on the light. Puzzled, Nield followed him. Butler relocked the door, closed a sliding bolt.

'The window,' Butler whispered. 'The moon gives us enough light. Follow me. There's no furniture in the way. You have got a gun, I hope.'

'Of course.'

Butler had left the curtain over the window pulled back and the moon illuminated the interior. As his eyes accustomed themselves to the dark Nield saw it was a very spacious room with a king-size bed. Even larger than his own room.

'Something funny about this place,' Butler whispered.

'I had already got that impression.'

Reaching the mullioned window, Butler opened the casement very quietly, peered out. No sign of the guard. The gates were shut. Grasping Nield by the arm, Butler guided him to look out. Butler bent down, pulled two pairs of strong gloves from under the curtain draped to the floor where he had concealed them. He handed one pair to Nield, who put them on, still mystified by what his partner was doing.

'It was daylight when I looked out,' Butler whispered. 'You know I don't miss much.'

'On occasion.'

'This room is under one of the large turrets at the front we saw when we arrived. Look what's under this.'

261

Leaning out, Butler used his gloved hand to pull a piece of the creeper away from the wall. By his side Nield saw a very thick cable ascending upwards towards the turret. He knew enough about communications to recognize it as a section of fibre-optic cable.

'What have they got above us?' whispered Butler.

'Could be a highly sophisticated communications centre. Why would a hotel need that?'

'I'm climbing up there to see. I've tested the creeper. It is as thick and strong as a rope. We'll have to leave our shoes behind. I can loan you an extra pair of socks to give extra grip . . .'

Nield found that although he had smaller feet the extra pair fitted well over the socks he was already wearing. Checking to make sure his Walther was secure inside his hip holster, he straddled the window ledge.

Butler was already hauling himself up the creeper rapidly, but exercising due care. Before he climbed higher he tested the strength of the creeper above him. Nield looked down, saw there was no sign of life below, began his own climb.

At the training mansion in Surrey they had practised scaling the wall of the large house using ropes. This seemed no different – except if Big Ben emerged and looked up Nield had no doubt he woud use them for target practice. The large man would enjoy that.

When Butler reached the second storey he edged his way round a darkened window, then continued his ascent. The fact that they were wearing socks helped them to keep a good grip. Arriving at the second storey Butler again had to edge his way round another darkened window. He had to perform the same manoeuvre at the third storey. Then, close to the turret which had a light shining from a window, he felt Nield tugging gently at his ankle. He froze, looked down.

Big Ben had appeared, was patrolling the drive below.

Butler pressed himself slowly closer to the wall, then stayed motionless. Below him Nield did not dare reach for his Walther. The slightest movement could attract Big Ben's attention. He watched as the guard lumbered unsteadily towards the gate and Nield realized he was drunk. This was confirmed when Ben stopped, raised a wine bottle he had held by his side, drank from it.

Arriving at the gate, he seemed to check that it was locked. The tricky part would be when he returned to the entrance – so he could easily glance upwards. The fact that he was drunk wouldn't help, Nield was thinking. He had no doubt there were other armed guards Ben would alert.

Staggering, the big man left the gate, made his shambling way back to the entrance. Nield clearly heard the door shut and let out a sigh of relief. He looked up at Butler, gave him a thumbs-up sign. Butler resumed his climb.

He waited by the side of the turret's open window and Nield joined him, choosing the other side. The reason the window was open, Nield assumed, was the heat, which was still uncomfortable even at this altitude. The earth was giving up the heat it had absorbed during the day. Nield peered round the edge of the window.

The cable ran inside the illuminated room which had six sides. He heard a whirring sound, glanced up in time to see an aerial elevating automatically. The aerial, a complicated affair with a spider's web of wires, had emerged from the summit of the peaked turret.

Inside the room Weasel sat in front of a large transmitter with his back to the window. He wore earphones and spoke into a microphone in English.

'Two possible intruders. Harry Butler and Pete Nield. A reservation for each was received from Hotel Baur au Lac, Zurich. Please confirm what action, if any, should be taken. Yes, they could easily disappear for ever out here. You will confirm after checking identities? I await your confirmation, Dove . . .'

Nield signalled Butler to commence his descent. If anything, they took even more care going down than they had coming up. He kept looking up now, praying Weasel would not feel the need for fresh air and peer out of the window. Both men also had to fight the impulse to return to the safety of Butler's room as swiftly as possible. They were close to the open window when a piece of creeper Butler was holding on to came loose.

Nield watched, his pulse rate rising. Coolly, Butler let go of the dangling creeper, grasped another section. He then tucked the section which had broken loose back inside the rest of the creeper. He wanted no evidence left that someone had climbed up to the turret.

Looking up just before he heaved himself inside his room, the turret reminded him of an evil witch with a hat. Nield joined him, relief flooding through him as his feet felt the firm floor under him. Butler closed the window, pulled the curtains across it, felt his way across the room and switched on the light.

Neither man spoke until they had washed the sweat off their hands, foreheads and necks. Leaving the bathroom, Butler opened a bottle of champagne he had brought up to the bedroom.

'Bit of a snarler, that,' he observed.

'The things we do for England,' Nield replied. 'This place is much more than a hotel. We have to let Tweed know as soon as possible about that communications room.'

'Well, we can't tonight. The gate is locked. If we asked to be let out we'd arouse more suspicion. So, drink up. Cheers!'

Nield remained worried. Butler, on the contrary, accepted they would have to wait. The difference in attitudes highlighted the difference in the temperaments of the two men.

Hundreds of miles away to the east an identical advanced aerial had been elevated above the long house in Slovakia. It was Hassan who had received the information the Weasel had transmitted.

The communication had worried him. The Château d'Avignon was one of the three keys to passing information across Europe and then on to the Head of State even further east. Sitting in his office he had the curtains closed – it was a very black night outside and clouds obscured even a glimpse of the moon.

He was still pondering the communication he had received when the phone rang. In a bad mood, he picked up the receiver.

'Who is this?'

'You know who it is from my voice,' the Englishman replied.

'I am glad you have called. I have just heard from the Château they have two intruders.'

'The exact wording of the message?'

'"Two possible intruders."'

'"Possible"! They sound absurdly nervous at the Château. You know they take ordinary guests to make the place look like a normal hotel.'

'That is true . . .'

'You sound absurdly nervous yourself. Is there any news of the killing of Tweed or Kane? Preferably of both.'

'No, not so far.'

'Wake up, for God's sake. That is the top priority. The Sisterhood should have located their targets by now. Time is getting very short!'

The phone went dead. The autocratic Englishman had again slammed down the phone on him. Hassan sat and simmered with frustration.

Tina Langley was frustrated. The sturdily built man whose eye she had caught had left the restaurant with his male companion. She knew she had caught his eye – and Butler had reacted so quickly she didn't realize he had recognized her. From the way he had been dressed and the meal they had ordered she felt sure she smelt money. Normally her instincts in this direction were right.

She had decided to have coffee in the lounge. At the doorway she looked around. No sign of him. A French couple who had noticed she was on her own looked up. The fashionably dressed woman spoke in English.

'Excuse me, but are you on your own? Such a pity. I have been in that position myself.'

'But not any more,' her husband said with a smile as he clasped her hand. 'We would be happy for you to join us. We like Britain. I spent two years in London.'

'That is very kind of you. I am feeling a little lonely.'

She sat down in the chair the Frenchman pulled out for her. Her main motive in accepting the invitation was she had seen the size of the diamond engagement ring on the wife's finger next to her wedding ring. The Frenchman was good-looking, in his forties, was wearing an Armani suit. There was certainly money here.

The fact that she thought she should succeed in luring this married man away from his wife bothered her not at all. Men liked variety. She might even be able to extract blackmail after she had compromised him. They began conversing after coffee had been served.

'I am Louis Marin,' the man introduced himself. 'This is my wife, Yvette.'

'I'm Lisa Vane. This is very kind of you. Do you often stay at this hotel?'

'Do you?' Marin had lowered his voice. 'It is our first visit.'

'It's my first time here too,' she answered with a seductive smile.

'You know the owners?' asked Yvette.

'No. I don't know anyone here.'

'We made a mistake,' Yvette explained. 'The staff here are not what one expects at a five-star hotel. Please excuse my saying this, but some are English and not pleasant types. We know because we stayed at some wonderful hotels in Britain.'

'How did you make a mistake?' enquired Tina, who was curious.

'We got the wrong place. Since arriving we have phoned friends in Paris. They say we should have stayed at the Château des Avenières, a real five-star hotel.'

'It is a mile or two further along the road,' interjected her husband, who was having difficulty taking his eyes off Tina's crossed legs. She tapped him on his knee and he started drinking more coffee.

'When you go out of the drive here,' Yvette continued, 'you turn left. Our friends said the Château des Avenières has a better view, has superb food, wonderful service. It is run by a very pleasant couple, apparently, on extremely professional lines.'

'Are you thinking of moving, then?'

Tina tried to catch Louis Marin's eye but he was

carefully looking across the room. Scared stiff of his wife, thought Tina contemptuously. If I got him on his own I bet he'd be much more uninhibited. Particularly in a bedroom.

She chatted to them for a while, then pretended to suppress a yawn. She glanced at her watch.

'It has been so nice talking to you both.' She made a point of smiling at Yvette. 'I hope you'll excuse me but I have had a long day . . .'

In her room she became very busy. The members of The Sisterhood were normally provided with all the data they needed to find their target. But they were also trained to locate the target. Tina had purchased a guidebook in Geneva which also gave the details of top hotels in the city. She began calling each hotel. Her technique was always the same.

'A serious emergency has arisen in London. Mr Tweed will want to know about it immediately. It's a crisis situation . . .'

In each case she was informed that no one of that name was staying at the hotel. She persisted. She rang every leading hotel in the city. Every time she drew a blank. No one of that name was staying at the hotel she phoned.

She sat in front of her dressing table mirror, brushed her auburn hair, applied various cosmetics. In the past this had often given her an idea. In any case, she might just meet Louis Marin alone in the corridor. Then she remembered their conversation.

Reaching for the directory with hotel numbers in France she pressed buttons for the Château des Aven-ières. Again she gave the same story. Her lips tightened as the night porter replied, 'I think he is still in the lounge. I will get him . . . Hello! Hello . . .!'

The connection had been broken. Perched on her bed, Tina was smiling unpleasantly. A million-to-one shot had come off. Tweed, her target, was within a few miles of her. Hassan had provided a very detailed description of Mr Tweed.

25

Marler would have been interested. The soldier, after eating his meal outside his tent, was practising with his Armalite rifle. Equipped with a telescopic sight, he aimed the weapon at a bird sitting motionless high up in a tree. In the crosshairs the bird came up so close he could see its eyes. The weapon was unloaded but as he pressed the trigger it made a small click. The bird took off.

The soldier smiled and continued taking aim at different 'targets'. A leaf near the top of a tall tree, a withered cone attached to a pine, a very small rock he could see by a shaft of moonlight a distance away.

When he was satisfied that he had not lost his skill, he walked back along the track, turned left and began to route march along the deserted road. Since it would be difficult to conceal the Armalite he had hidden it under a pile of branches.

He continued his route march. One, two, three, four . . . one, two, three, four . . . He had taken off his jacket to consume his rations, but now the chill of night had descended on the silent forest and he was wearing the jacket for warmth.

He was close to the entrance to the Château des Avenières when he heard a car coming in the opposite direction. Before he could react the car's headlights came round a bend and illuminated him. He had stopped route marching and was strolling along as though taking a walk in the fresh night air.

Well after the rest of the team had retired to their rooms at the Château des Avenières, Marler, who was an owl and needed only four hours' sleep, had taken a decision. He would drive back to the Château d'Avignon in the hope that he could make contact with Butler and Nield.

He was driving at a moderate pace, studying the terrain, when he turned a bend and in his headlights saw a uniformed soldier walking along the opposite side of the road towards him. He drove slowly past, trying to recall where he had seen a soldier earlier.

Then he remembered. As they had walked down the long station platform after arriving at Geneva a soldier with a pack had been waiting on the opposite platform. It was probably a coincidence, but Marler recalled that Tweed didn't believe in coincidences. He was driving on slowly when he took a sudden decision. In his rear-view mirror the shadow of the soldier had disappeared round the bend.

Marler extracted the Walther from his hip holster, laid it on the seat beside him. He executed a perfect U-turn, managing it the first time. Slowly, he began driving back the way he had come.

'I think I'll have a word with you, mate,' he said to himself.

The language problem didn't worry Marler. He spoke French fluently enough to pass as a Frenchman. In fact, he had once had to do so. He drove with one hand as he turned round the bend, his right hand gripping the Walther by his side. Beyond the bend was a straight stretch.

Marler turned his headlights full on. The road was empty. No sign of the lone soldier. Was that peculiar?

Then he recalled that one British Army technique to test a man's ability to survive on his own was to drop him off at some isolated location and see if he could find his way to an agreed destination. Perhaps the Swiss Army used a similar method – in this case marooning him in France.

Marler had noticed there were a number of tracks leading into the depths of the forest. The soldier had probably used one of these to cut across country. He performed a fresh U-turn, headed for his original objective.

He was driving very slowly, with his lights dimmed, when he reached the entrance to the Château d'Avignon. The tall wooden gates were closed, barring entry to the drive. Odd, he thought. Since there was no possibility of contacting Butler and Nield he drove back the way he had come, turning into the open drive to des Avenières.

A short distance from the bend in the road the soldier had darted up one of the tracks leading into the forest. He had then settled down to wait behind the trunk of a huge tree. He heard and saw the car return, shortly afterwards driving back along the original route it had been taking.

He was puzzled. Were people in the car looking for him? It did not seem likely. He continued to wait. He had endless patience. When the car returned later, driving back the way it had come, he thought he knew the explanation. Blinded by the glare of the headlights, he had not been able to see originally who was in the car. Now he thought he had solved the mystery.

Some man had his girlfriend with him. They had just had time to do together what the soldier would have done. But first they had returned to make sure the soldier had not sneaked back to watch their amorous activities. He waited for half an hour before resuming his route march along the road.

When he saw lights he knew he had reached the Château des Avenières, where Tweed was spending the night with his bodyguards. He took time checking the trees which faced the exit from the hotel. He found one large fir near the edge of the road. He began to climb from branch to branch.

Not too high up he found the perfect place. He could straddle a heavy branch, resting his back against the trunk. He had a clear view of the exit from the hotel. He raised both arms as though he was holding the Armalite. From here he could kill Tweed when he emerged from the drive inside a car.

Behind him was thick undergrowth, a jungle of bracken and bushes. It would provide an ideal escape route. If anyone came after him he would with ease ambush them. He climbed down the tree swiftly and agilely. Then he began the walk back to his tent. When he reached it he loaded the Armalite before going to sleep.

Before sunset Vitorelli, from his helicopter, had seen Tweed's convoy turn into the chateau. He had smiled. He gave a fresh order to Mario as he watched Tweed enter the hotel through his field glasses.

'Now we know where he is we can return and land at Geneva's airport. In the morning we'll hire a car and drive up Mount Salève so I can have a word with my friend.'

'Why do we do that?'

'Knowing Tweed, I think he is conducting some devious manoeuvre. His departure from Zurich was so very public. I suspect he may know where Tina Langley

272

is hiding. I'm convinced that his strategy is to lure The Sisterhood into the open.'

'He told you there were several of them.'

'We are one jump ahead of Tweed,' Vitorelli said with a grim smile. 'We know their base is that isolated house in Slovakia.'

'How do we know Tina Langley is not hiding there?'

'Because *you* saw her in Geneva. Then she tricks you by not getting on the train you were aboard. Which means she did not want to leave Geneva. Why? Because it is only a half-hour drive to that chateau in France. Which takes her safely – she hopes – out of Switzerland. And there may be another obvious reason.'

'What is that?' Mario asked as he guided the chopper over the top of Salève and headed for Geneva's airport.

'Tweed is her next target.'

In the lounge at the Château des Avenières Tweed was lingering over coffee with Paula and Newman. Despite the day's exertions his brain was alert as he stirred a fresh cup. Paula asked her question with a note of anxiety.

'What has happened to Marler? He slipped away without saying a word.'

'I wouldn't worry about Marler. He can look after himself. He is checking the surrounding countryside in case we experience a firefight here. I hope so, otherwise our stage-managed departure from Zurich has failed.'

'So again you're using yourself as a target,' Paula snapped.

'Let's say I'm a magnet to attract the iron filings – which are the enemy – to an isolated area where there are unlikely to be innocent casualties.'

They were alone in the lounge so able to converse

without fear of being overheard. Tweed paused as the night porter approached them. The porter stopped to speak quietly.

'Excuse me, Mr Tweed, but I had an odd message over the phone. Someone said there was an emergency in London, then the connection was broken. The caller did not come back. They asked specifically for you.'

'How long ago did this happen?'

'A few minutes ago. I waited to see if the caller would ring back before I came to let you know.'

'Was the caller a man or a woman?'

'A woman, sir. She had a soft voice. I would say she was English.'

'Did you detect the slightest trace of a foreign – that is, a non-English accent?'

'No, sir.'

'Thank you. If she calls back I will take the call.' Tweed waited until the night porter had gone. 'Of course, she won't call back. That was Tina Langley, tracking me in a clever way.'

'How do you know it was Tina?' Newman asked.

'Because,' Tweed said grimly, 'I can always catch just a trace of accent with Karin Berg. Even more so with Simone Carnot.'

'You're a sitting duck,' Paula commented vehemently.

'My plan has worked.' Tweed smiled. 'The Sisterhood is emerging from underground. They are walking into my trap. Paula, we can use their own tactics against them. You can obtain the telephone numbers of the top hotels in Geneva?'

'Yes, I can. I know the names of the leading hotels very well.'

'Then phone the concierge at each hotel. Tell them you have to speak urgently to Karin Berg or Simone

Carnot. That there is a grave emergency in Stockholm, a matter of life and death. With a bit of luck a concierge will let slip the fact that one of them is staying at the hotel you are phoning. Then break the connection.'

'You're turning their own guns on them. And it is a matter of life and death. Look how many members of the *Institut* have died.'

'It may not work,' Tweed warned, 'but it worked for Tina.'

'Then I'll make it work for me. I meant to raise another subject. There was a helicopter overhead when we drove across Mount Salève. I think it was following us.'

'Aboard it, I am sure, would be my old partner in crime, Emilio Vitorelli. He is hoping I will lead him to Tina Langley. He is determined to kill her for causing the death of his fiancée, Gina.'

'Yes, but I've never mentioned that when I was being taken to the base of The Sisterhood, that bizarre house in Slovakia, there was a helicopter in the distance. Perhaps it was a coincidence.'

'You know I don't believe in coincidences.' Tweed thought for a moment. 'I wonder how he located that place? Can you make those phone calls before you go to bed.'

'I'll go to my room and start now.'

'We'll wait here and see if you get lucky . . .'

After enjoying a first-rate dinner with Tweed and the others Christopher Kane had excused himself. He had refused Tweed's offer to join them for coffee in the lounge.

'Must get my beauty sleep,' he said to Paula. 'Otherwise I shall find all the attractive ladies ignoring me.'

275

'I rather doubt that,' replied Paula, amused.

'Christopher didn't look tired,' she had commented later when they were first settled in the lounge.

'He isn't,' Tweed had told her. 'He's gone off to work. Like me, he finds he can concentrate in the early hours. He'll be working on some theory he's created to counter bacteriological warfare.'

As soon as he reached his bedroom Christopher locked the door and took off his jacket. He then perched himself on the bed, lifted the phone, pressed numbers for a long-distance call. The person he had hoped to contact answered immediately.

'Christopher here. I need a lot of information which only you can give me. So make yourself comfortable, old boy. This is going to be a long session . . .'

He was on the phone for a quarter of an hour. He asked questions. He made suggestions, gave instructions. He emphasized the extreme urgency of the situation. Christopher was very relieved when the person he had called agreed with him. He thanked the person and again stressed the supreme urgency of what he had requested.

Putting down the receiver, he opened a bottle of champagne he had collected from the bar on his way to his room. Then he opened a notebook and began to work on formulae and calculations. As he did so he voiced his thoughts aloud, his lips hardly moving.

'Tweed would give anything to have listened in but I think he'd understand. He knows I'm a loner. And the fate of the Western world could hinge on that conversation . . .'

When Paula had left them to make her phone calls, Tweed became even more alert, if that were possible.

Newman, who had plenty of stamina, relaxed, sensing Tweed had had an idea.

'I'm going to make a couple of phone calls myself.'

'At this hour? Who to?'

'First to Amos Lodge. I'm going to ask him to fly to Geneva first thing in the morning. If he agrees, we can have a car at the airport waiting to bring him here.'

'You said a couple of calls. Who is the other one to?'

'Willie at the Dolder Grand. I'm going to make the same request to him.'

'You never forget Dorset, do you?'

'It would be a great mistake to forget Dorset. Don't forget that Vitorelli told me he had traced a courier carrying a large sum of money to someone in Dorset.'

'So you're certain the money was for Lodge or Willie?'

'I'm not certain of anything yet. If you like, you can wait here while I go up and make the calls. Then I'll come back and let you know how each man reacted . . .'

Newman had lit a cigarette, was drinking more coffee, when Marler strolled into the lounge. He sat down beside Newman and told him about the incident of the Swiss soldier, about the curious fact that the gates outside the Château d'Avignon had been closed for the night.

'I don't like the sound of that Swiss soldier,' Newman responded. 'There was one waiting on the opposite platform when we got off the train from Zurich.'

'It could be a Swiss Army training exercise,' Marler replied, and outlined his theory.

'In France? I don't believe it. If a French patrol car saw him they'd question him immediately, probably put him inside.'

'Exactly. That would make the exercise more

277

gruelling. Would make him far more alert. I told you how he disappeared into thin air when I went back to look for him.'

'I suppose you could be right. But I don't like the sound of the Château d'Avignon. Butler and Nield could be trapped inside.'

'Have you ever heard of Butler and Nield being trapped by anybody? Look how they handled that experience with the excavator in Austria near the Slovak border. And neither of them were armed – until Nield got hold of the machine-pistol.'

'I suppose you're right. But if they don't turn up in the morning I'm off to march into that chateau.'

'I'll come with you. Has Tweed gone to bed early? Early for him, I mean.'

Newman explained why Tweed had gone to his room. He told Marler about the two men he was phoning, inviting them to the Château des Avenières. Marler frowned.

'What's he up to? He's like a spider attracting all the dangerous – lethal – flies into his web here.'

'Which is exactly what I think he's planning.'

He had just finished speaking when Paula briskly returned to the lounge. She had just sat down when Tweed reappeared. He sat down and Newman poured more coffee from the fresh pot the waiter had recently brought to the table for both of them.

'Ladies first,' Tweed said, then sipped coffee.

'After a lot of phoning it worked. We have both Karin Berg and Simone Carnot on our doorstep, so to speak. Berg is staying at the Hôtel des Bergues overlooking the Rhône. Simone Carnot is at the Richemond. I think you'd better be very careful, Tweed.'

'I'm always careful. Now my bit of news. Paula, after you'd gone I decided to call Amos Lodge and Willie –

inviting both of them to fly to Geneva and then come on here.'

'You don't forget Dorset, do you?'

'Which is what Bob said. No, I don't. Amos said he had a lot to attend to but he would catch a mid-afternoon flight to Geneva. Willie was apologetic, said he couldn't make it – he has a very big deal he hopes to conclude, that a fortune might be involved.'

'Two very different reactions,' Paula observed.

'Which I find very significant.'

He didn't explain what he had found significant.

26

In her room at the Château d'Avignon Tina Langley sat in front of her dressing table, gazing at herself in the mirrors, attending to her make-up. Then she began brushing her thick auburn hair, paying a lot of attention to perfecting the curls. Her complexion was white, which contrasted with her carmine lipstick. She smiled invitingly, the smile which entranced men. And they loved to run their fingers through her hair.

Full-bodied where it counted, she was slim and had kicked off the high-heeled shoes under the dressing table. They helped to enhance her small stature. She was enjoying herself as she thought of Anton, the banker. She had already spent the twenty thousand francs she had 'borrowed' from him.

It satisfied her self-conceit that she now had two men at the end of a string. She was sure that Louis Marin, husband of the couple she had chatted to in the lounge, was more than interested. When she returned to the lounge she had no doubt Marin would have made some excuse to his wife to dally there while his wife went to bed. She needed more money. She always needed more money. Her tastes were extravagant. Only couturier clothes were good enough for Tina. She swore foully when the phone rang.

'You know who is calling,' Hassan's familiar voice said.

'I should by now.'

'It is vital that you cultivate the acquaintance of Tweed and Kane. If you succeed with both the fee is three hundred thousand dollars. Payable in cash, of course. Have you located either of them?'

'I'm working on it.'

'Work harder. You have received the present?'

'Yes. It arrived during dinner.'

'Then what are you waiting for?'

The phone went dead. She swore foully again. Hassan was a pig, had no manners at all. But he had phrased what he meant cleverly. 'Cultivate the acquaintance' meant kill them. Going to a cupboard she had locked, she again took out the Cartier box she had received earlier, delivered by special courier. Hassan had responded quickly to her earlier call informing him where she was staying. The box was full of flowers. Wrapped in tissue beneath them was a Luger with ammunition. She had already loaded the gun.

Next, she unlocked a case, took out a black Arab garb with a veil. She didn't like wearing this garment, but it was a good disguise in case she was seen leaving a building after an assignment. She was trying to decide how to 'handle' Tweed and Kane. Hassan, the bastard, had told her in his earlier conversation that she had competition – that both Karin Berg and Simone Carnot had been given the same task. This had infuriated her, although she had concealed her reaction.

Hassan had organized a race to kill to speed up the outcome.

'I'll go downstairs and see if I can hook Marin,' she decided. 'Then tomorrow I'll visit the Château des Avenières. After all, there is no danger that Tweed will recognize me.'

'Your room is ready, madame,' the concierge at the Hôtel des Bergues informed the elegant blonde woman.

'I'll go straight up to it. I've had a tiring day travelling,' Karin Berg replied.

'Oh, a package from Cartier arrived for you. The porter could take it up for you.'

'I'll take it up myself. Thank you. The porter can deal with my luggage . . .'

Once alone inside her room, Karin took the wrappings off the package. The usual 9 mm Luger was concealed inside tissue, together with a magazine containing eight rounds. She concealed the automatic pistol, unloaded, with the magazine, under the extra pillow on the double bed.

After taking a bath, she looked at herself in a full-length mirror before putting on pyjamas and a dressing gown. She still had a beautiful body which drove men wild, but she was under no illusions.

'This won't last for ever,' she said to herself. 'And despite all the silicon treatments and other nonsense available men go for someone young. I think I've been wise.'

Born of a Swedish father and a Serb mother, Karin had acquired her looks from her father, who had been a very handsome man. It was the way he had experimented with many women so long after his marriage that had influenced her opinion of – and attitude towards – men. She despised them, marvelled at the ease with which she could play with them.

Her serious, almost severe, side, had made her take a very different view of money from Tina. Karin had a good wardrobe of clothes, but she had selected them carefully. The bulk of the large sums she had received from Hassan had been stashed away in different safety deposits.

She had already killed three men – members of the *Institut* – but she had decided this would be her last assignment. Then she would vanish, assume a new identity – something her experience with Swedish counter-espionage had taught her how to do expertly. She would go to Rome and settle there. She spoke fluent Italian. And taxes in Sweden were very high.

Her only hesitation was concerned with her mission to kill Tweed. She knew about his unfortunate marriage, how his wife had left him for a Greek shipping million-aire. Tweed, she knew, never played around with women. He seemed to have dedicated himself to his work.

'I'll have to steel myself,' she said aloud as she slipped into her dressing gown. 'Three hundred thousand dollars is a lot of money. But if he looks me in the eye, as he will, when I point the gun at him, will I be able to pull the trigger?'

Simone Carnot, only having to fly from Zurich to Geneva, had arrived in the city hours earlier than Karin Berg. Simone, who liked to live it up at night, slept a lot during the day. Now in her room at the Hôtel Riche-mond she had just returned from a walk and an early dinner in the fine restaurant.

She checked her main asset, her hair as red as flame, in a wall mirror. During her walk along the banks of the

Rhône several men had eyed her hopefully. Used to this attention, she had ignored them. Businesslike – she had run her agency in Paris so it made a good profit – she concentrated her mind on her difficult new mission. How to locate Tweed and Christopher Kane?

Her life had changed when she had tried to increase the profits of her model agency by evading paying taxes. She was on the verge of being investigated when an Englishman who had visited her agency 'in search of a really attractive woman willing to earn thousands of dollars' had asked her to accompany him to Dorset in England.

This had given her the chance to escape from France. After a while she had been flown to Slovakia. When she realized what she would have to do she had accepted the strange offer at once. Simone needed money – a lot of it. A year before she had become involved with a man she knew was married. The liaison had not bothered her at all.

'After all,' she confided to a girlfriend, 'he is rich, generous and you know men – they like variety.'

It had all gone wrong when, after a few months, her lover had told her it was over, that he was going back to his wife. Simone was livid. Had she thrown him over that would have been different, but one night she spent an evening in a bar. For a long time she drank heavily.

Later, she realized she knew what she was going to do. To cover her red hair she had worn a dark wig before entering the bar which had a dubious reputation. It was rumoured you could buy almost any type of gun from the barman.

Still clear-headed, despite the amount of different wines she had drunk, she waited until the place was almost empty and casually asked the barman, 'I'm in need of protection. Can you supply me with a gun and some ammunition?'

Clutched in her well-shaped hand she held a sheaf of banknotes. The barman continued polishing glasses while he studied her. She stared him straight in the eye, wily enough to say nothing else.

'You need a Beretta,' he replied eventually. 'Perch your hand over the counter and drop the money on my side.'

She walked out with a loaded Beretta which the barman had shown her how to use as they were now alone in the bar. He had chosen a 6.35 mm Beretta because it was the perfect weapon for a woman. Weighing only ten ounces empty, it was only a little over four and a half inches long. It easily slipped into her handbag.

It was late at night when she waited at the bottom of basement steps close to his apartment. Her lover had also borrowed money off her which he had not returned, a great deal of money. When he eventually appeared she saw he was with another woman who was not his wife. Up to this point she had experienced hesitation about what she had planned.

Any doubts disappeared when the couple paused above the steps she was crouched under. The good night embrace was passionate. Her lover's hands were all over the new woman in his life. He hailed a passing taxi, saw the woman inside. Simone waited until the taxi had gone and Paul was climbing the steps to his apartment. She ran up the basement steps.

'Paul,' she had whispered, 'I thought we ought to say goodbye.'

'Goodbye, Simone,' he had answered with a leer.

Her rubber-soled shoes made no sound as she followed him up the steps. He was fumbling with his keys when she pressed the muzzle of the Beretta against the back of his head, pressed the trigger. As he fell against the door she continued to fire, emptying the gun of its bullets, then ran back into the street.

No one was about as she walked away, shoving the gun inside her handbag. Reaching her apartment, she poured herself a drink, then another. What had surprised her was how easy it had been. She felt no reaction except one of satisfaction.

There was never any danger of her being caught. Because of his wife, Paul had met her at discreet cafés in another district where no one knew either of them. They had used his car for amorous activities, after driving out into the countryside. No suspicion was ever attached to her.

She found it equally easy at the training room in the long house in Slovakia. She realized the 'dummy' sitting with his back to her in a chair was alive. She detected slight movement. As instructed, she walked up behind the peasant, aimed the Luger at the back of his head, and blew it off. It had been easy. And it had netted her an advance of twenty thousand dollars.

Before murdering Pierre Dumont in Zurich she had killed one other member of the *Institut*. In neither case had she had any reaction of shock. Both victims had been married, so she reasoned that they deserved to die since they were scum.

She had been surprised on her arrival at the hotel to find that a Cartier package had arrived. Inside she found a Luger with ammunition. She realized Hassan must be in a frantic hurry since he had originally given her the name and address of a dealer in arms in Geneva.

She stayed in her room, using a list of Geneva's top hotels to phone their concierges. Her method of approach was similar to the one used by Tina Langley, but her wording was different.

'I need to speak to Mr Tweed. His wife is dangerously ill back in England. If he's not available his friend, Christopher Kane, will take a message . . .'

In every case she drew a blank. Her next move was

to take out a map of Geneva and the surrounding areas and draw a circle round them. She noticed that included inside the circle was France, with the border very close. She went down to have a quick meal and noted the night concierge had not yet come on duty. She preferred to chat to him since they were usually bored with very little happening.

It was very late in the evening when she emerged from the Pavillon restaurant, which recalled to her the outdoor restaurant at the Baur au Lac. She smiled slowly as she went up to the night concierge's desk.

'I have reserved my room for two nights. A close friend of mine is staying at a hotel in France but I have forgotten the name. He said it wasn't far across the border. It's a five-star hotel. Have you any idea of which hotel he could be staying at?'

'Well, madame, let me show you somthing. Please come with me to the front door.

'You see that mountain rising up in the moonlight? It is called Salève. I have heard good reports of the Château des Avenières. You reach it by driving up the mountain. Then you are in France. You have a car?'

'I do,' Simone replied.

'I will show you on a map how to get there. Remember you are looking for the Château des Avenières. There is another hotel you will drive past first, the Château d'Avignon. That is not quite in the same class.'

With not much hope, when she returned to her room Simone obtained the number of the hotel the concierge had suggested. She had her story ready when she called the Château des Avenières and the night concierge answered.

'I have to speak very urgently to Mr Tweed. His wife is seriously ill in London.'

'Did you call earlier?'

'Yes,' Simone replied with a flash of inspiration.

'You went off the line. Your voice sounds different.'

'I have a cold. Please put me through to Mr Tweed. He is needed desperately urgently.'

'One moment and I will inform him . . .'

Simone put down the phone, hardly able to credit her good luck. Then she poured herself a drink, sat down in a chair and began to think hard.

Both Tweed and Christopher Kane – if he happened to be staying with Tweed – would recognize her. Did it matter? If the police in Zurich had been able to connect her with the murder of Pierre Dumont she would have been arrested. No one had come near her.

She had hired a car immediately on her arrival in Geneva. She was also disturbed that the concierge had mistaken her for another woman. Had another member of The Sisterhood also located Tweed? Simone thought, decided quickly when she had a problem. She would drive to the Château des Avenières through the night – on the off chance that they'd have a room for her.

27

There were other men in the world who were owls, who had succeeded because they worked while the rest of mankind slept. One of these was Captain William Wellesley Carrington. In his room at the Dolder Grand – where he had taken the earlier phone call from Tweed and declined his invitation – the phone rang as he was studying different estimates for the purchase of machine-pistols.

'Yes? Who is it?'

'You should be able to recognize me by now,' said Hassan.

'No names, no pack drill.'

'Pardon?'

'Just an old Army expression, my dear chap. What keeps you up in the early hours?'

'An enormous deal for you. If the price is right – and you can deliver.'

'I'll decide if the price is right and, once agreed, I always deliver. You should know that by now.'

'You have to fly here. My father has loaned me a Gulfstream jet. It will transport you from Kloten at nine o'clock in the morning.'

'No, it won't,' Willie snapped. 'It will transport you here. I will expect you at the Dolder Grand by ten in the morning.'

'You can't talk to me like that,' Hassan raged.

'I thought I just did, my dear chap. Take it or leave it. I'm too busy to leave Zurich. What is the nature of this so-called enormous deal?'

'You will make millions.'

'I can't wait. But I will. Wait for you here. Unless you decide not to bother coming. And I need a clue. I may have to stay up the rest of the night phoning contacts.'

'I cannot tell you over the phone. The size of the consignment is gigantic. And we need instant delivery at the usual destination in the Middle East.'

'Give me a clue or forget it.'

There was a long pause. Over the phone Willie could almost hear Hassan hesitating. To wear him down Willie kept silent, resumed working on calculating the differing prices in the estimates he had in front of him. He heard Hassan take a deep breath.

'Can you hear me?' he whispered.

'Quite clearly.'

'A bacillus,' Hassan whispered.

'Gigantic quantities, you said?'

'Yes.'

'Be here at ten this morning prompt,' Willie said and put down the phone.

Bacillus? Bacteriological warfare. Willie sat twiddling a pen in his fingers. By providing Hassan with a whole variety of services he had made a load of money out of the Middle East. *You will make millions.* Dollars or pounds? Willie wondered.

Tweed seemed fresher than ever as he ordered more coffee in the lounge of the Château des Avenières. Newman stifled a yawn but Marler and Paula seemed as alert as Tweed.

The waiter had just left them to bring a fresh pot of coffee when the night porter appeared. He approached Tweed again and lowered his voice.

'I've had another strange call for you – again from a woman. She said your wife is seriously ill in London.'

'What?'

For a few seconds Tweed was shaken, then his mind functioned. He knew this was not possible – his wife had left him years ago. He had never heard a word from her since. Even if she had been taken ill in London he was the last person she would bother to inform. Also, she'd have had no idea where to find him – Tweed had not yet informed Monica at SIS HQ of his latest movements.

'Did this sound the same woman who called earlier and then the connection was broken?' he asked.

'No, it didn't. I asked if she'd called earlier. She said yes and I commented that her voice sounded different. She said she had a cold. I'm sure it was a different woman.'

'I seem to be popular tonight,' Tweed joked. 'I haven't got a wife. Did she say anything else?'

'She asked to be put through to you and I said I

289

would inform you. Then the connection was broken again.'

'Tell me if she calls again,' Tweed said.

'What's going on?' asked Paula, who had heard every word.

'A second member of The Sisterhood has somehow traced me to this hotel.' He smiled. 'My plan is working better than I expected.'

'And,' Paula pointed out, 'only three people know you are here. Christopher, Amos, and Willie. One of them has to be linked with The Sisterhood.'

'Not Christopher, for Heaven's sake,' Newman protested.

'I don't trust anyone,' said Paula. She stood up. 'I'm going to ask the porter when that second call came through.'

'She's getting paranoid,' Newman commented after Paula had left the lounge. 'She doesn't trust anyone.'

'In this situation safety lies in being paranoid,' Tweed replied. 'I should have asked the porter that question myself.'

'This is interesting,' Paula said when she returned. 'The porter was apologetic. Just after he received the call he had another one from the chief supplier to this hotel. He had to give him a whole list of provisions they require urgently. The call from that woman was made over an hour ago.'

'This is getting interesting,' said Tweed as he stretched out his legs and crossed them at the ankles. 'I think we're in for one of our long nights.'

'Then I'm going to have some more black coffee,' Newman responded.

'I only need four hours' sleep anyway,' announced Marler.

'I'm suddenly alert,' Paula remarked.

Tweed began to review the entire situation. Verbally,

he played with pieces of the jigsaw he was building up, suggesting various positive actions they might take. He was still talking when he looked up as a woman entered the room. She wore a white form-fitting sheath dress with one enticing bare shoulder exposed.

'We have company,' Tweed said with a broad smile. 'What a nice surprise to see you in this part of the world. I'm not sure everyone knows Simone Carnot.'

A few minutes earlier Simone had parked her car in the drive and, carrying a suitcase, had walked into the reception area. She had asked the night porter for a suite and he had accompanied her upstairs.

Once alone, with the door locked, she had opened her case and taken out the Cartier gift box containing the Luger. She placed this on the floor of a wardrobe together with a carrier holding the black dress and veil. Very quick in her movements, she unpacked, using her hanging clothes to conceal carrier and box before locking the wardrobe and dropping the key into her handbag.

She left out the white sheath dress, stripped off the suit she was wearing, spent only a few minutes in the bathroom before putting on the white dress. Then she went downstairs and into the lounge where she had heard Tweed's voice on her arrival.

'Do sit down and join the happy throng,' Tweed invited her.

Simone chose to sit at the opposite end of the couch from Paula, smiling briefly and watching her like a hawk. Paula had shifted her position slightly so her right hand could dive inside her shoulder bag for the Browning.

'Now what would you like to drink?' Tweed asked. 'This is a great hotel. You can stay up all night and still there is the perfect service.'

'If Christopher were here I'd ask for a Kir royale,' Simone said now that Tweed had made introductions.

'A Kir royale for our guest,' Tweed requested from the waiter who had appeared out of nowhere.

'I think I'll have one too,' Marler decided.

Both Newman and Marler were deliberately gazing at Simone's bare shoulder, knowing that was what she would expect. Simone's eyes slowly switched from one man to the other. She felt sure they were avid to stroke her shoulder with one hand while the other strayed.

Paula read her mind. She forced herself to conceal her loathing of the creature. Tweed was playing some game so she joined in the charade. Smiling, she twisted round so she could stare directly at their guest.

'I do like your dress. It's not only fashionable but it suits you.'

'Thank you, Paula,' Simone replied. 'I've had quite a journey so I thought I'd change into something different. It's good for my morale.'

'Did you say morals?' Paula enquired politely.

'No. *Morale.*'

For a brief second her expression changed and she flashed a look of venom at Paula, then changed it into a seductive smile as she returned her attention to Newman and Marler.

'Cheers!' she said and sipped the Kir royale the waiter had already served. 'Aren't you drinking, Mr Newman?'

'Yes. I'm addicted to coffee at this hour. A long journey, you said. Where have you come from today, then?'

'I flew from Zurich to Geneva very late this afternoon. Then I came by car to this hotel a friend had recommended to me. Zurich was getting on my nerves after that horrific murder of Dumont.'

You really are an audacious bitch, Paula was thinking. I can see why you belong to The Sisterhood. If you do, she added to herself. After all, we can't be certain. Simone had sat more erect. In doing so she had opened the slit in her dress, revealing her superb legs.

'I'm surprised you didn't linger to taste the delights of Geneva,' Newman probed.

'I find Geneva such a crashing bore.' She looked at Paula. 'Is that the correct English phrase?'

'Spot on,' Paula assured her.

'It's not really a Swiss city at all,' Simone continued. 'There are so many international companies based there it's swarming with foreigners.' She made a moue. 'Coming from me that must sound odd. I'm French, from Paris.'

She's clever, Tweed thought. She's sticking to the same story about her background. He was deliberately keeping quiet and he noticed her conversation was directed towards anyone but himself. Yes, he mused, she's very clever, this one. She bears watching.

'The world seems to be going crazy,' Simone went on. 'People are getting shot every day. Read the newspapers.'

'Often with a Luger,' Marler said jovially.

'What's a Luger?' Simone enquired innocently.

'It's a German automatic pistol. Nine-millimetre calibre. It has a magazine capacity of eight rounds – bullets. Very effective.'

'Sounds quite horrid. You seem to know a lot about weapons, Mr Marler.'

'Me? I couldn't hit a barn door at a range of ten feet.'

Paula smiled to herself. Simone had no idea she was talking to the top marksman in Western Europe. In one way Paula was fascinated by Simone. She had met a number of daring and extremely confident women but Simone was something else again. And she had walked into the lion's den with coolness and poise.

293

'How long do you expect to stay here?' Marler enquired.

'As long as the place amuses me. Maybe you and I could have a few drinks in the bar tomorrow?'

'Today, you mean,' Marler corrected her with a grin.

'Then we haven't long to wait.'

Paula stiffened inside. There seemed to be no limit to Simone's pursuit of men. Could Amos have recruited her in Dorset? Then again, would Willie be her cup of tea? She couldn't make up her mind – assuming that either of the two men had persuaded her to join The Sisterhood. Assuming she *was* a member of that hideous outfit.

'It has been lovely talking to you all,' Simone said. 'But if you will excuse me I do need my beauty sleep. I'm afraid I have rather left you out of the conversation, Mr Tweed.'

'I've had my enjoyment simply watching you. Really you need not worry about sleep – you already have beauty.'

'How very gallant.' Simone stood up, extended her slim hand to each of them in turn. Paula noticed she had a very strong grip. She gave a little wave and then glided from the room. Marler accompanied her to the door, watched her walking up the staircase. At the top she threw him a kiss. He returned to the lounge, sat down, lowered his voice.

'You know something? I have a plan. It's a bit complex. I will explain it in the morning. I need Pete Nield and Harry Butler to help me carry it out. Especially Nield.'

'Can't you give us a hint?' Paula whispered.

'Dead men tell no tales . . .'

*   *   *

Tweed went to his room but did not go to bed. His mind was too active. He decided it was time to inform Monica where he was in case there had been any developments. When she answered his call she sounded relieved and tense at the same time.

'Thank heavens you called. Yes, I've got your number and where you're staying. Howard is deperately anxious to speak to you. He's been prowling the building like a caged tiger, wanting to talk to you. Oh, here he is now.'

Howard was usually pompous, even speaking on the phone. Tweed knew that when he dropped his normal affected air something very serious had happened.

'Tweed, have you identified our friends?'

Monica had obviously warned him he was speaking on a hotel line which might not be safe. 'Our friends' meant 'our enemies'.

'Not for certain yet, but I'm getting close. Can't say more at the moment. You sound edgy.'

'There is a crisis. Car bombs of enormous destructive power have been exploded near key power stations. All the stations in London and a number in the industrial North and the Thames Valley where there are stations serving our version of Silicon Valley.'

'IRA?'

'Definitely not. One bomb didn't detonate and I've just had a secret report after the Bomb Squad laddies dismantled it. The mechanism was far more advanced than anything available to the IRA. Incredibly sophisticated.'

'You said "near key power stations". Have any stations been put out of action?'

'No, that's the strange factor – I find it alarming. That's why the perpetrators have not been found. They placed the cars just outside the guarded areas. Doesn't make sense – and that I find disturbing. The country is in an uproar, near to panic. It all happened this evening. And it was a highly sophisticated operation – every car bomb detonated at exactly ten o'clock tonight, that is last night. A few hours ago.'

'Has anyone claimed responsibility?'

'No one.'

'Any casualties?'

'Fifty people killed. Mostly men and women coming out from a night club. The Government is close to panic, although trying to hide it.'

'From what you said earlier it was brilliantly organized. All the bombs detonating at the same moment.'

'You're right. The people who planned this are professionals of the highest order. But to what purpose? No car was near enough to any of the power stations to cause any damage. Could this have anything to do with what you are working on, Tweed?'

'Not obviously.'

'What does that mean? For God's sake don't go cryptic on me.'

'I know as much – as little – as you do. I'll keep in touch.'

Tweed ordered two large bottles of mineral water from room service. When they had arrived he had a shower, put on his pyjamas to relax, and slowly paced his room. It was four in the morning when, going back over the whole series of events which had taken place since he had visited Dorset, he remembered a certain incident and understood.

It meant zero hour was even closer than he had feared.

28

Tweed was about to get ready to go to bed when there was a gentle tapping on his door. He recognized Paula's way of telling him who was there but he picked up a glass of brandy room service had sent up at his request. Paula slipped inside when the door opened and sat in a chair as he relocked it.

'Not like you to drink brandy,' she remarked.

'I'm not drinking it. But if you had been the wrong person a glass of brandy in the eyes can be off-putting.'

'I think you ought to take greater precautions. That's why I'm here. With Simone in this hotel – and Tina Langley at the other chateau only two miles away – you're in great danger.'

'I think you exaggerate.'

'Either woman might get hold of a master key while you're sleeping. Marler or Newman could sleep in the other bed.'

'They would disturb my thinking. What really concerns me is a factor we haven't considered. Clearly we are confronted with a professional and skilled organization. They will need more than one major communications centre. Slovakia is a long way east. And they already have teams operating in Britain.'

He told her of his conversation with Howard. He emphasized that the large number of car bombs hadn't been close enough to wipe out, or even damage, a single key power station. Paula frowned.

'Why do you link this up with The Sisterhood outfit?'

'It's a diversion, to distract the security forces at home from some other target. By now every important power station inside Britain will be guarded by our top security forces. They have played this trick before. It's a hoax.'

'When did they do that?'

'When they lured most of Beck's police force to guard the Kongresshaus on the night Dumont was supposed to make his speech. That was to keep them away from the Ermitage out at Küsnacht where I had dinner with Karin Berg.'

'But that was the Monceau gang who attacked you.'

'I haven't forgotten that. But the ingenious, complex planning had all the hallmarks of the Englishman who, I am convinced, is the mastermind behind The Sisterhood.'

'So we're back to Amos and Willie.'

'I always have both men in the forefront of my mind. Remember the courier Vitorelli told us about, the courier who took a large sum of money secretly to someone in Doreset.'

'And Amos arrives here some time later today.'

'I'll be glad to see him. But it's the major communications centre they must have I want to locate.'

At the Château d'Avignon in the morning Butler and Nield had a quick breakfast. Nield, who liked a full English breakfast, made do with six croissants coated with lashings of butter. As they were walking out to their car Big Ben appeared, looming over them with his huge bulk.

'Will you be staying a few days longer?' he demanded.

'We will,' Nield replied genially. 'The food and the service are first-rate at this hotel. We've been working pretty well nonstop – running a courier service in London. We need the rest. And you make us so welcome.'

'You piled it on a bit, didn't you?' Butler suggested as they settled inside the car with Butler behind the wheel.

'Well, he's such a charming fellow, don't you think?'

'No, I don't,' growled Butler as he drove out of the exit now the gates were open, turned left towards the Château des Avenières.

Even in daylight the road was gloomy, almost sinister, hemmed in by the wall of evergreen giants on both sides. Butler checked his rear-view mirror but no one was following them. As he turned into the drive to the hotel Nield glanced to his right.

'That's a monster of a tree overlooking the drive on the opposite side of the road.'

'Looks like a Douglas fir, although I doubt if they have them out here.'

The soldier in Swiss Army uniform had risen very early. After eating some of his rations and drinking from a flask of tepid coffee he had walked the two miles along the deserted road with his dismantled Armalite concealed inside his clothes.

Climbing the giant tree, he had perched himself on the chosen branch, had carefully assembled the Armalite, then had loaded it. He had heard Butler's car approaching and had hidden himself on the far side of the massive trunk. Then he settled down to wait. He doubted whether anyone inside the hotel had started breakfast when he had first arrived.

Before Butler and Nield appeared he had again practised with his weapon. In the crosshairs he caught the driver of a large provisions truck as he turned slowly into the drive. The face of the driver came up so close in his sight that the soldier felt he could reach out and touch him.

He kept the crosshairs positioned on the man's forehead as he continued his turn. He could have shot him dead three times. He smiled unpleasantly as he lowered the weapon.

'Come on, Mr Tweed. Hope you had a good breakfast. It will be your last,' he said to himself.

'I've phoned Paris again,' Tweed told his team as they walked on the terrace. I wanted to speak to Loriot, Chief of the Direction de la Surveillance du Territoire.'

'You think what we're investigating concerns French counter-intelligence, then?' asked Paula.

'I'm sure it does. If I'm right about a planned invasion of Western Europe the key targets will be France, Germany and Britain. My main worry at the moment is to locate the enemy's communications centre, which I'm convinced must exist.'

'Château d'Avignon,' Butler said tersely.

Nield, the more voluble of the two men, explained how they had both climbed up the ivy creeper and what they had seen inside the turret room. Tweed listened but it was Newman who reacted.

'We could destroy it today. We have enough men.'

'No, we won't do that yet,' Tweed replied. 'Discovering where it is gives us a tremendous advantage over our opponents. Let me think about it.'

'And Tina Langley is staying at the Château d'Avignon,' Nield told him.

'We have two members of the hideous Sisterhood on our doorstep,' Paula said grimly.

'Two members?'

Paula described how Simone Carnot had arrived the previous night, how, bold as brass, she had walked into the lounge and talked to them. Butler's reaction was typically blunt.

300

'Then let's grab them both.'

'Not yet,' Tweed warned. 'We can be on our guard but it's the big picture which is important. In due course they may lead us to the headquarters of this fiendish organization.'

'Unless one of them kills you first,' Paula snapped.

'I said we can now be on our guard,' Tweed responded. 'Pieces of a massive jigsaw are falling into our lap. We'll wait for a while longer. But I think I would like to meet Tina Langley and have a chat with her. Some of us could drive over to the Château d'Avignon. Not too many of us.'

'You'll enjoy meeting the staff,' Nield remarked.

He then described the peculiar make-up of the people running the Château d'Avignon. Tweed was particularly interested when he described the tough English types who made up the majority of the staff. Nield also recalled how they had not been made welcome when they arrived. He conjured up vividly the atmosphere of hostility under the surface.

'Paula, you remember what I said about those hoax car bombs which were detonated in Britain last night?'

'Yes, is there a connection?'

Tweed first put Butler and Nield and the others into the picture about the outrages. He again drew a parallel with the incident in Zurich when most of Beck's police force had been diverted away from the Ermitage by the threat of a bomb being placed inside the Kongresshaus.

They were wandering on the terrace while they conversed. Marler seemed restless, keeping away from Tweed, Paula and Newman, who walked with Butler and Nield. The morning was a perfect summer's day. Dazzling sun shone down out of a clear azure sky and everyone except Tweed and Paula wore dark glasses.

Paula kept glancing at the fabulous view of France stretching away towards the glittering Lake Annecy

301

which was like a mirror of mercury. Such a wonderful peaceful morning, she thought – so far away from the horrors of Zurich they had experienced. She realized Marler was keeping watch, his eyes everywhere.

'Paula asked you if there was a connection,' Newman recalled as Tweed became silent.

'I'm sure the car bombs in Britain were planted by British killers. Now we hear from Nield and Butler about the toughs at the Château d'Avignon – and they're British. I've told you before that I'm sure the master-mind behind The Sisterhood has to be English. The grim women involved in the assassinations were recruited there, I'm sure.'

'And Amos Lodge is arriving here this afternoon,' Paula repeated.

'Exactly. But there we have mystery. Willie, appar-ently, has the type of personality which attracts beautiful women. But we also found out that some of them later went off with Amos.'

'So it could be either of them?' Newman suggested.

'It would appear so.'

'What makes you think the car bombs would be planted by British killers? Isn't that a bit of an assump-tion?' Newman probed.

'The mastermind behind The Sisterhood is a perfec-tionist,' Tweed explained. 'Look how successful he's been. He's known the right sort of woman who would attract different members of the *Institut*. He wouldn't make the mistake of using foreigners to plant those car bombs. A foreigner might attract the attention of the police.'

'So we're up against a brilliant opponent,' Newman concluded.

'We are.' Tweed took one last look at the view. 'Now I would like to be driven to the Château d'Avignon. I

302

think a few words with Tina Langley, if she's still there, might be intriguing.'

'We'll all go,' said Marler, who had not missed a word.

'Too many of us would arouse suspicion. I think Nield should drive me – then he can say he wanted to show his friends round the place. Butler, you could travel in the back of my car with Marler.'

'I'm coming too, in the other car,' Paula said firmly. 'Try and stop me.'

'It's not worth the effort, so I give in.'

They walked up the steps, into the hotel, and continued to the drive where the cars were parked. Tweed sat in the front as Nield climbed in next to him behind the wheel.

At the Dolder Grand Willie checked his watch after a phone call had told him Ashley Wingfield had arrived. He wondered just what Hassan was going to ask him to procure this time.

'Can we talk in the garden?' Hassan suggested when Willie met him in the hall. 'What I have to talk about is supremely confidential.'

'It always is, old boy. All right, we'll waffle about in the garden.'

'Waffle?'

'Forget it. You look very smart in your panama hat.'

'Three women – most attractive – have given me the eye since I got here.'

'Better when they give you both eyes.'

'Pardon?'

Hassan always had the uncomfortable feeling that Willie did not give him the respect which was his due. He never caught on that this was a deliberate tactic to strengthen Willie's hand when it came to the haggling over price.

'Forget it. Let's sit here. No one else is about. Now, I have a number of other deals in the pipeline, so what makes this so very special?'

'The nature of the substance, the method of packing it, the size of the order. Look at these.'

Hassan produced a sheaf of typed papers from the leather executive case he carried. Despite the mounting heat he handed them to Willie wearing white gloves. No fingerprints on the sheets. Willie read them rapidly. Nothing in his expression betrayed his amazement at what he was being asked to supply.

'Delivery in one week from now. At the usual destination,' Hassan snapped. 'Immediately the consignments are received twenty million dollars will be deposited in your Cayman Islands bank account.'

'This is enough bacteria to wipe out half Western Europe. I need to know how it will be distributed.'

'Why?'

'Because that will decide the type of containers which will be used.'

'I don't know that I can tell you that.'

'Then take these papers back. I have another appointment.'

'Let me think,' Hassan pleaded.

'Think fast.'

'Twenty million dollars, I said.'

'Heard you the first time.'

'There are other suppliers . . .'

'Go talk to them. You're wasting my time.'

Hassan removed his panama hat, mopped his smooth brown forehead with a silk handkerchief. He was sweating profusely. He carefully replaced the hat on his head.

'The bacteria, which are, of course, lethal, will be inserted into all major reservoirs for drinking water in Britain, France and Germany. At exactly the same moment. We have spent months reconnoitring every key reservoir, with special attention to military installations in those three key countries. No tank's engine will ever start, no war plane will leave the ground.'

'Then your armies roll West.'

'I cannot comment on that. But once you have made delivery I would advise you immediately to board a plane for the Cayman Islands.'

'Delivery in one week, you said. You need containers which will dissolve immediately on contact with water. They exist. So do the contents. You will, of course, wire five million dollars to the Cayman Islands today, as an advance payment.'

'We have to trust you, then.'

'How long have we been doing business? I resent that remark.'

'I withdraw it. Can you do it?'

'Yes, if you get the hell out of Zurich now. Don't forget the five million advance.'

'That can be wired before I leave Zurich.'

'Then why are you still here?'

Tweed was looking forward to meeting Tina Langley. He wanted to see what kind of woman had cold-bloodedly blown off the back of Norbert Engel's head in Vienna. The car began to move forward towards the exit from the Château des Avenières and on to the road leading to the other chateau.

Paula, with the key to the other car she had obtained from Butler, was walking rapidly to her vehicle. The sun, blazing behind her, warmed the back of her neck.

305

She had a feeling it was going to be the hottest day yet
– as hot even as what she had experienced in Valja's car
when he had driven her towards Slovakia.

'There are some strange kind of women about now-
adays,' Tweed remarked. 'They recall to me certain
aspects of Amos's speech.'

Perched on the branch of the large tree opposite the
drive the soldier gripped his Armalite. In the crosshairs
Tweed's face behind the windscreen came up close. The
car was nosing its way out of the drive. Nield looked
both ways along the road – he expected what he saw, a
deserted stretch in both directions. But this was how
accidents happened – you assumed there would be a
clear road and some macho fool could come round a
corner, also assuming he had a clear way ahead.

In the crosshairs Tweed's face came up so close the
soldier could see his eyes behind his horn-rimmed
glasses. The car was still moving slowly, would very
shortly turn. The soldier's finger began to sqeeze the
trigger. He couldn't miss at this range.

Paula reached her car, looked up. She caught the
glint of the sun reflecting off something which had to be
glass. Up a tree? Her left hand dropped the car key, her
right hand had already withdrawn the Browning from
her shoulder bag. She was gripping the gun in both
hands. Her instinct controlled her reflexes which were
so swift there was only a flash of movement.

She fired. Once. Twice. Three times. The shots were
so close that afterwards Marler, an expert, thought he'd
only heard two shots. A body toppled slowly off the
branch, then fell to the ground and lay still, the Armalite
a few feet away from the slumped body.

Tweed was out of the car first. He ran forward. The
soldier's cap was still on his head, crumpled by the fall.
Tweed bent down, carefully lifted the cap from the
head. The body had twisted over on its back as it had

fallen. He checked the neck pulse. Nothing. The soldier was dead. There were three gaping red bullet holes in the forehead. He stared down at the visible face as the others arrived in a rush.

'Jules Monceau,' he said quietly.

A convoy of four cars arrived a few minutes later. Out of the front car jumped a small man, clean-shaven, in his fifties, with dark hair brushed back over his dome-like forehead. He wore a dark blue business suit and rushed towards Tweed, hand extended.

'You've arrived quickly, Loriot,' Tweed greeted his old friend. 'Your timing is remarkable. That body at the foot of a tree over there is Jules Monceau. He was going to assassinate me. Paula here, whom you know, saved me.'

'Good for you, my dear,' Loriot said in his excellent English.

He hugged her, kissed her on both cheeks. She smiled with pleasure at seeing him. Most of the top Intelligence and police chiefs in Europe liked her, Tweed reflected. They appreciated her tact, competence and strong character.

While Loriot went to examine the corpse personally Tweed took her by the arm and led her back on to the terrace of the hotel. She sagged into a chair.

'That was a damned near run thing, as the Duke of Wellington said after Waterloo. Something like that. I caught sight of a glint of sun reflecting off something and reacted automatically.'

'Thank you, which sounds feeble,' Tweed replied as he sat down beside her. 'What would you like to drink? Brandy or coffee.'

'Coffee. Black as sin.'

'Talking about sin,' Tweed said after ordering the

coffee, 'I'm going to postpone my visit to the Château d'Avignon until this afternoon. There will be formalities Loriot will want me to deal with. He must be very happy with you. He's been trying to trap Monceau for years since he escaped from the Santé prison. No one is sure how many people Monceau killed during those two years. Can I help you?' he asked as the concierge appeared.

'There is a call for you, sir. A Mr Carrington.'

'I'll take it in my room.'

Tweed was away for quite some time and Paula had begun to worry when he suddenly reappeared. He waved his hands.

'Willie is always talkative. He wanted to tell me he had to go away to attend to some urgent business. He said another deal had fallen into his lap. I wonder what he's supplying and to whom this time.'

'He didn't give you a clue?' asked Paula.

'He always plays his cards close to his chest. And Christopher has left the hotel. I was handed this note by the concierge. You might like to read it, Paula. If you can read his writing, which is always atrocious.'

Tweed. Something urgent has cropped up. Will be away for two days. See you when I get back.

Christopher.

'Rather mysterious, isn't it?' Paula commented as she gave the note back.

'Christopher lives a life of his own. He's always been like that. He disappears, Heaven knows where, then pops up when you least expect him.'

'Loriot is coming,' she warned.

'Not a word about that communications centre at the Château d'Avignon. And don't say anything about Tina Langley.'

'Christopher isn't the only one who keeps things to himself,' she retorted.

'I have my reasons . . .'

29

Tweed had completed the formalities with Loriot in his room. He had provided a detailed statement of the events leading up to the shooting of Jules Monceau, sparing Paula the ordeal. When the statement was ready he had asked Paula to come to his room to sign the document underneath his own signature.

'You have done France a great service,' Loriot told her, bowing.

'She has done the world a great service,' Tweed commented. He smiled at Paula. 'Now I need to use the communications system Loriot has in his car – that was how I was able to contact him earlier when he was well on his way here from Paris.'

The neat, compact Loriot led the way downstairs and outside to his large car, which stood apart from the other two vehicles. Curious, Paula accompanied Tweed to the front door. She had not forgotten that Simone Carnot was still in the hotel.

Standing at the exit as the two men hurried to the car, she gazed round. At a distance – where they could not possibly hear what was said – stood several plain-clothes men and even more uniformed French police, each man armed with a machine-pistol. She was satisfied that Tweed was well guarded.

Loriot ushered Tweed into the front passenger seat of the empty car. He pointed to a black box attached to the dashboard. It had a number of dials and switches. Loriot leaned across Tweed, pressed a switch. A large aerial automatically elevated from the rear of the vehicle.

'This,' he explained, 'is one of the most sophisticated communication systems in the world. It cannot be intercepted or listened in to.'

'Are conversations recorded?'

Loriot pressed down a switch. 'Not now. I was about to cut out the recorder. You have complete privacy.'

'I may be making several calls which will take some time.'

'You are my guest.'

Paula sat on the terrace staring at the view by herself. She wanted to think. Also she was experiencing a reaction to the killing of Monceau. She felt no regrets. The shock came from realizing how close Tweed had come to being shot dead. It had all hinged on a fraction of a second. She could so easily have missed seeing the sun glinting off the lens of his Armalite.

Tweed was absent for about half an hour. When he joined her at the table she detected a bouncy spring in his step. He sat down and a waiter appeared.

'I think I'll have a Kir royale,' he said.

'More strong coffee for me, please,' Paula ordered. 'You're starting to drink,' she chaffed him.

'Only for the moment. I feel like celebrating. We now at last have a chance of a major reaction from the people who count. If they move in time.'

'May I ask who are the people who count?'

'I had a long talk with the PM. This time he listened to me. And he's going to speak to the President of France and the Chancellor of Germany later.'

'You must have been very persuasive.'

'If only he acts quickly. If only it is not already too late. We could be the key to the outcome. What I plan we do is very dangerous. And I have conducted a devious manoeuvre.'

'I won't ask you what it is.'

'I wouldn't tell you. This afternoon we'll investigate that Château d'Avignon. And some time today Amos Lodge will visit us.'

'Amos is here,' a gravelly voice said behind them.

'Talk of the devil,' Tweed joked.

Vitorelli was enjoying himself behind the wheel of the Alfa Romeo as he drove it up the curving road on Mount Salève. Beside him Mario was clutching both sides of his seat, wanting to close his eyes but not daring to do so. Vitorelli, who had once been a racing driver, loved speed.

'What made you suddenly buy this car?' Mario asked.

'I do many things on a whim, my friend. You should know that by now. You're not nervous, are you?'

'Of course not. I'm enjoying the ride,' Mario lied.

He knew that if he admitted his anxiety Vitorelli would press his foot down further. Not out of cruelty, but because the Italian loved to thrill people, as he imagined he could do. Before meeting his fiancée he had had many successes with beautiful women by taking them for a spin in one of his fleet of expensive cars. He had found it made them extremely amenable.

'I'm not certain why we are going to meet Tweed,' Mario remarked.

'Because I know the old fox. You can bet on it he will be in at the kill. And I want to be there.'

'You're thinking of Tina Langley?'

'I never think of anyone else,' Vitorelli said.

He wore wrap-around dark glasses, which empha-sized his handsome face. He spun round another bend and Mario dug his fingers into the seat, then saw they had reached the summit. Mario felt he needed a break from the ferocious drive.

'They say the view from here is magnificent. You could pull in for a moment.'

'I could, but I'm not going to. You know me. When I get an idea I go for it. I want to find out what Tweed is planning next.'

'He won't tell you,' said the shrewd Mario.

'You've arrived early – to catch me on the wrong foot,' said Tweed as he invited Amos to join them.

'That will be the day,' Amos replied.

Paula watched him as Amos eased his bulk into a chair. He wore a smart cream linen suit, a cream shirt and a wild tie decorated with a riot of large flowers. His squarish head seemed larger than ever and he studied Paula from behind his square-rimmed glasses as though trying to read her mind. Then he smiled and she felt attracted by his dynamism. The powerhouse of a brain she detected in the eyes was hypnotic.

'What are you having to drink?' Tweed asked as a waiter hovered.

'Double Scotch. I saw Newman in the hall and I guess that will be his drink when he joins us. You realize, Tweed, we are all close to annihilation? I refer to the whole of Western Europe.'

'You've made my day,' said Paula who liked Clint Eastwood's later films.

'No good burying our heads in the sand. We're not ostriches.'

'Trust you to cheer up the party on such a beautiful day,' said Newman, who had come up quietly behind them. 'Look at the view.'

'The view?'

Paula realized Amos had not even noticed the magnificent panorama spread out before him. With the exception of Tweed, she had never met a man like Amos, whose concentration on strategy was total from the moment he woke. He probably dreamt it.

'Don't you ever enjoy yourself?' Paula enquired.

'All the time. With my work. Mind you, I have my moments.' He smiled again at her. 'Maybe we could have dinner together when it is convenient to you. Unless Tweed objects.'

'Tweed doesn't object,' Tweed said. 'Why should he?'

'Have you got anywhere?' Amos asked Tweed. 'I mean as to who is behind the assassinations? Don't forget, I am also a target.'

'Then don't go around with any exceptionally attractive women.'

'But I have just invited one to join me for dinner.'

'So you have.'

'Amos,' broke in Newman, who had occupied a fourth chair. 'Just come with me, for Heaven's sake.'

Taking his drink with him, after excusing himself to Paula, Amos walked with Newman to the wall of the terrace a distance away. He was pointing out the different features of the view to Amos.

'Don't mention Tina Langley or any aspect of the Château d'Avignon to Amos,' Tweed whispered. 'The same applies to Willie, if he turns up here.'

'You think Willie will arrive out of the blue? He said he was too busy to come.'

'That's what he said.'

'Does Loriot know any of this?'

'No. He'd have raided the place, closed down the communications centre – which I want left open for the moment. And he'd have arrested Tina Langley, if she's still there. I want to leave the situation fluid.'

'You're playing with fire.'

313

'According to Amos we're playing with an inferno. And I'm certain Amos is right.'

He stopped speaking as Newman returned with his companion. Amos was talking rapidly, continued to do so as he resumed his seat at the table.

'I don't seem able to convince the powers-that-be that with the collapse of morals – and morale – in the West, we are wide open to attack from a certain Eastern power. The whole family fabric of Europe is dissolving into chaos. "I want it, and I want it now" seems to be the attitude of so many people. Often perversity is involved – just as it was in ancient Rome before the barbarians, again from the East, overwhelmed them. Only a stable, self-disciplined society can survive. Now all we hear about are rights. Hardly anyone ever mentions responsibility, the keystone of a strong civilization able to defend itself.'

Sitting facing the entrance to the terrace Newman saw Simone Carnot appear at the top of the steps. She wore a pale green dress which ended above her knees. It had full-length sleeves and a high neck. The colour emphasized the sunset red of her well-coiffured hair. Standing with her right hand clasped against her hip she looked like a dream.

Walking slowly down the steps, she chose a table as far away as possible from Tweed's. She crossed her legs after sitting down, waved to Newman, then beckoned to him to join her.

'Might as well,' he said to himself. 'See what she's up to.'

He wasn't sure whether this really was his motive. She looked so attractive as she folded her hands in her lap and gave him a warm smile as he arrived, sat down opposite her.

'I suppose this was the idea?' he remarked in a neutral tone.

314

'This was the idea,' she agreed. 'I know you're going to ask me what I'd like to drink. I'm going all the way. I'll have a Kir royale. You'll think I'm addicted to champagne, asking for one at this time of day. Well, I am.'

'Anything to please a beautiful lady,' he said with a smile and ordered two Kir royales from the waiter who had appeared.

'Thank you, kind sir,' she said. 'Who is that large man with the square-rimmed glasses? He just stared at me for a few seconds.'

'I don't know. Friend of Tweed's, I suppose.'

'He gets around. I saw him at the Baur au Lac.'

'We all do. You were there.'

'One of the staff told me the police had been here, that a man had been shot dead. How awful. That man with Tweed has just glanced at me again.'

'He has something to stare at. Cheers!' He lifted one of the glasses which the waiter had just placed on the table. 'You drink champagne all day long?'

'Heavens, no! This is an exception.'

'Are you free for dinner tonight? We could make another exception. I'm thinking we could dine here. The food and service are out of this world. Or would you prefer somewhere in Geneva?' he said, testing her.

'No, I think here would be perfect. Would eight thirty suit you? Give me time to get ready.'

'Call it a date.'

Newman's mind was in a whirl. Simone kept looking at him with her magnetic eyes. One part of his brain toyed with what a wonderful experience it might be to have her as a girlfriend. The other part knew she was going all out to bring him under her spell. She was devious, calculating, the most wily woman he had ever met. Her real objective, he was certain, was to use him

315

to get closer to Tweed. A very wily, cold-blooded woman indeed.

He was smiling broadly to conceal his real assessment of her as she stood up after finishing her drink. She gave him a sensuous half-smile as she spoke.

'That was very pleasant, Bob. I look forward to carrying on this evening from where we left off. If you'll excuse me now, I want to write some letters.'

She leaned forward and her lips brushed his cheek, her hand grasped his briefly and then she was walking slowly away towards the exit.

30

They chose the early afternoon to visit the Château d'Avignon. At Tweed's suggestion Butler and Nield had returned earlier to have lunch there. It was important that there should appear to be no connection between the two men and the rest of Tweed's team.

Tweed was behind the wheel of the car with Paula next to him. In the back sat Marler and Newman. With the exception of Tweed they were all armed. Tweed had decided that four people were not too many to arrive at the chateau, not knowing what reception they might receive. He was driving along the deserted road under the tunnel of trees when Newman spoke.

'I'm having dinner with Simone Carnot tonight at des Avenières.'

'Be careful – that woman is very clever. I noticed how she was playing up to you on the terrace this morning.'

'I thought Amos was the only one who took any notice.'

'That was my intention. Simone did not realize I was observing her from a distance.'

'How is the forceful Amos spending his afternoon?' enquired Marler.

'In his room, of course. Studying strategic ideas. He never stops working.'

'Marler, before Nield left he described to you the exact location of their communications room in the turret at the Château d'Avignon. If it had to be destroyed, could one man, namely Butler, do it in due course?'

'It sounded a tough place to reach, but Butler is tough. Yes, I have explosives and timers in my satchel. I could provide him with a time bomb which would blow the turret to pieces – subject to my seeing it this afternoon.'

'Then take a good look at that turret from their terrace while we're there.'

'If they let us in,' Newman pointed out.

'They will let me in.'

Tweed slowed down as they approached the chateau. The huge heavy gates were open as he turned into the courtyard. Paula looked up and thought this chateau seemed even more ugly than when they had passed it the night before. As Tweed parked the car a giant of a man hurried towards them out of the hotel.

'This must be Ding-Dong, Big Ben,' Marler drawled.

'Don't think we 'ave room for you lot,' Big Ben informed them in his semi-civilized English.

'We're just visiting,' Tweed said pleasantly after jumping out of the car. He looked up at the giant. 'Chief Inspector Loriot of French Internal Security wants a holiday in about a couple of months from now. He'd heard this was the ideal place to have a peaceful rest.'

'You're police?'

317

'Me? No. I run a security organization in England. If you're interested I could check your security.'

'It's watertight.'

'Then you won't be worried about floods.'

'Floods?'

Big Ben was clearly taken aback, having no sense of humour. He stared as Paula left the car, his eyes glued to her legs. She smiled at him. He started to lick his lips, then stopped when he realized what he was doing.

'At least we can have a drink in the bar,' Tweed persisted. 'Or maybe on the wonderful terrace we heard you have.'

'Don't suppose there's any 'arm in that.'

'Well, this is listed as a hotel. Who owns it, by the way?'

'I'll show you the way to the bar.'

They were passing the reception counter when a man behind the counter Tweed recognized as the character Nield had nicknamed Weasel stood up. From behind half-moon glasses eyes like those of a turtle studied the new arrivals. Then he gave an oily smile as Big Ben explained.

'This feller is a friend of the boss of French Internal Security.'

'Oh, really, how extremely interesting.' The remark came after a significant pause. 'Very interesting, I am sure.'

'What's'is name . . .'

'Loriot,' Tweed repeated.

'Lawriot is comin' for a bit of peace and quiet about two months from now.'

'We'll be most pleased to welcome such a distinguished guest. I am Frederick Brown. Perhaps you'd be kind enough to ask him to mention my name.'

'We'd like a drink on the terrace,' Tweed said abruptly.

He had noticed through an open doorway Butler and Nield seated at a table on the terrace. Walking through with the others he stepped down and forced himself not to pause. At another table, sitting by herself, was Tina Langley.

Tweed led the way to a table close to the woman whose photo was circulating throughout Switzerland. He realized the photo had been a striking portrait of her. The table was quite a distance from where Butler and Nield were sitting.

'Do you mind if we sit here?' he asked. 'It provides a perfect place to look at the view.'

'I could do with some company. Preferably English. Those two men over there are British and very stand-offish.'

'I'm Tweed.'

He was watching her closely. Her ice-blue eyes blinked. The hand holding her glass of Campari and soda gripped it tightly. She recovered quickly. Her left hand smoothed her thick glossy auburn hair. Her high-coloured face flushed and the eyes switched from Newman to Marler and back again. Paula, whom she had ignored, could almost hear the wheels going round. Which of the two men would be easier to hook?

Tweed made introductions and Paula chose a chair facing her. It was like a direct confrontation. Tweed was thinking she was superficially very attractive. The recruiter of The Sisterhood in Dorset had been very skilled. He had selected very different women, all of them exceptionally desirable – doubtless knowing that men had varying tastes.

'I'm Lisa Vane,' she said in a quiet, seductive voice.

'You're here on your own?' Newman asked with his infectious smile.

'I was until you came along.' She was looking straight at Marler. 'A long-term relationship I had got smashed up. You could say I'm here to drown my sorrows.'

'You've finished your drink,' Newman said. 'Have another.'

'A good strong one.'

Unlike the service at the Château des Avenières, Newman had to go and find a waiter, who reacted sullenly to his request. He had been sitting looking at a girlie magazine.

'Bring them to you soon.'

'Make it now – not soon. I'll be timing you.'

'Didn't realize His Lordship had arrived.'

'Well, he has. I don't want to complain to the manager..'

'Fred doesn't like complaints.'

'Albert, serve the gentleman.' It was Brown, who had overheard the conversation. 'Make with the feet, you lout.'

'You've been here long?' Tweed asked Tina.

'I never stay anywhere long. It gets boring. I enjoyed shopping in Geneva. And doing my job.' She giggled.

'What job is that?' Tweed enquired.

'I'm a model. For high-class TV commercials.'

'They pay well, I hope?'

'They pay very well. If they didn't, I wouldn't do them.'

Tweed had had a mild shock. He suddenly realized that, unlike Karin and Simone, Tina was totally lacking in any kind of intellect. She was, he suspected, a woman with only one object in life – obtaining money by any means and then spending it lavishly. The dark blue outfit she was wearing must have cost a small fortune. At her feet was a Gucci handbag.

She was also concentrating on attracting the attention

of the three men at her table. Every now and again, carefully timed, she gave Tweed a certain look. It promised a very interesting experience. A lot of men, he felt certain, would go crazy over her.

She had a snub nose and was skilfully made up. Paula recognized she must spend hours in front of a dressing table. It would pay good dividends. She was the kind of woman many men would expect to have a lot of fun with, and would not be disappointed – so long as they spent plenty of money on her. She was just the kind Paula despised. And there was no doubt this was the woman she had seen ahead of her in Kärntnerstrasse in Vienna, the woman who had shot Norbert Engel.

'What part of the world do you come from?' Paula asked.

'Hampshire,' Tina said after a brief pause.

'I know it well. From some interesting old village?'

'I hate old villages. They're so boring.'

'You like travel?' Marler interjected.

'I simply love it. I never stay in one place for long,' Tina said, repeating what she had said earlier. 'It's boring.'

The Butterfly, Tweed thought. A perfect name for her. She was easily bored because she had no inner resources. Tina asked for another drink. Her third in five minutes. The alcohol seemed to have no effect on her. When the fresh glass came she drank half the contents.

'What is your aim in life?' Tweed asked jovially.

'Aim?'

'What would you like to achieve? What are your ambitions?'

'To enjoy myself.' She drank the rest of her glass. 'Nothing lasts for ever.'

'Not even human life,' Tweed said casually. 'Not if it's brought to an abrupt end. People get shot.'

'I don't see what you mean.'

'They get murdered in cold blood.'

'Now you're spoiling a beautiful day.'

She had one ability, Tweed was thinking. She responded swiftly. She could probably out-talk most men. From having a great deal of experience in talking to them, in manoeuvring them. She had had enough of Tweed and turned her attention to Newman.

'What job do you do?'

'I'm a foreign correspondent.'

'Really? That must involve a lot of exciting travel.'

'Up to a point.'

Tweed realized she'd never heard of Newman. But he felt sure she never read the type of serious newspapers and international magazines where so many of his articles had appeared. Not her cup of tea. Earlier she had removed from one of the chairs a copy of a magazine which specialized in scandals. He stood up.

'Excuse me, I have a spot of work to do. Soon we shall be departing for Vienna. It has been most interesting meeting you.'

'Vienna?' She had jumped up and followed him as he left the table alone. Taking hold of his arm, she asked her question. 'I was hoping we could be friends. When do you expect to go to Vienna? I hear it's a fascinating city.'

Her determination to be asked to accompany him was obvious. He crossed the terrace, being careful never to glance up at the turret once. Big Ben was watching them from the top of the steps.

'I'm not sure. First I have to go to Ouchy in Switzerland. To attend a meeting of certain of the top brains in the world – that is, the few who are left. I'll probably go there in a couple of days. Now I'm going back to my hotel, two miles down the road.'

'Which hotel is that? I thought this was the only one.'

'The Château des Avenières. Frankly, it's much more luxurious than this place.'

'I'm used to luxury. Maybe I'll move. Could you book me a very nice room? A suite, if possible? I could move today.'

'I'm sure they have accommodation available. I'll tell the proprietor you're coming . . .'

'You must be stark raving mad,' Paula burst out as Tweed drove them back to their hotel. 'Giving all that information to that tart.'

'I gather you don't like her. She's reasonably well-educated, you have to admit.'

'Which makes the way she lives worse. She's a murderous predator. And her education was wasted, considering her level of intelligence – that is, except when it comes to attracting men and looting them.'

'I had a reason for giving her that information. And we shall soon be moving on to Ouchy, where the *Institut* headquarters is located, as you know.'

'Sometimes I can't fathom you.'

'Then other people won't be able to, which encourages me. Marler, did you get a chance to tell Butler and Nield to have dinner tonight at des Avenières?'

'I did. And I can quickly design for Butler a bomb which will sort out that communications centre in the turret. Will he have Nield to help him?'

'I'm afraid not,' said Tweed, driving slowly, checking the forest on either side. 'We're going to need as large a team as we can muster. I'm going to arrange with Butler to fake a twisted ankle – which will be his excuse for staying on there alone.'

'I had the chance of a quick chat with Butler alone in the loo before we left,' Marler continued. 'I put him in

323

the picture. He's asked me to drive him to Geneva this afternoon so he can purchase a motorbike for his getaway when he's done the job.'

'Poor Harry, I don't envy him,' Paula remarked. 'He'll be lucky to survive.'

'So will all of us,' Tweed told her. 'But the job has to be done. Even if we all end up dead.'

31

The decision Tweed announced as he drove Paula, Marler and Newman back to the Château des Avenières astounded them. He spoke quite calmly but they detected in his tone the iron will he was noted for in an emergency.

'We are leaving des Avenières this evening. Butler is hoofing it with Nield up the road somewhere behind us. Marler, you will produce the bomb Harry needs in the shortest possible time – together with the timer device and so on. I will arrange to call him with a code word when the vital moment occurs. You can drive Harry to Geneva to purchase his motorcycle before we leave late in the evening.'

'Where are we going to?' Paula asked.

'We will be driving to Ouchy on the shores of Lake Geneva – to the headquarters of the Institute. I told Tina that's where we are going, before we move on to Vienna. Undoubtedly she will inform the Englishman we are on our way there.'

'Why, for Heaven's sake?' Newman demanded.

'Because it is the next stage of my plan. All I will say is I noticed at the Château d'Avignon there is a large staff of English thugs of the worst kind. It takes me back years ago to when I was with the Homicide Division at Scotland Yard.'

'The youngest superintendent in its history,' Paula recalled.

'Ancient history,' Tweed said dismissively. 'In those days I met some pretty ugly customers. But they were nothing compared with today's villains, who do not hesitate to use knives and guns. So pack your bags . . .'

There was silence inside the car from that moment until Tweed turned into the drive of the Château des Avenières. He made one more remark before hurrying away to his room. With his hand on the door of the stationary car he looked back at Newman.

'Have your dinner with Simone. During the conversation I'd like you to inform her casually that we are bound for Ouchy – and later for Vienna.'

Saying which, he slammed the door shut, and left the others dazed inside the car. Here they could react undisturbed.

'I'd better love you and leave you,' said Marler. 'I have a job to do. See you for dinner – if we're back from Geneva in time.'

Newman and Paula knew what he was in such a hurry for. He had to prepare the bomb for Harry before Butler and Nield arrived. Then he'd have to drive Harry to Geneva and back after purchasing the motorcycle.

'Tweed has surprised me before,' Newman said, 'but this takes the cake. What can he be up to?'

'I'm trying to work that out myself,' Paula mused. 'Surely he's not going to risk assembling the surviving members of the *Institut* at Ouchy? They'd make the biggest target yet for The Sisterhood organization.'

'I've never heard him sound more determined, more urgent.'

'He must have a plan – the way he's deliberately informed two of those vile women who are key figures in The Sisterhood. He's taking one hell of a chance.'

'I think he knows he's working against a deadline.'

'Let's hope the emphasis isn't on *dead*,' Paula said.

'Well, he did say earlier the job had to be done even if we all ended up dead. I get the impression he thinks the odds are against him.'

'Then he's at his most effective, his most dangerous – to his opponents. Don't forget that. Look, Amos is leaving.'

The strategist had appeared at the exit, run down the steps, flung his bag into the back of his car and, as they watched, driven past them without a glance in their direction. In the rear-view mirror Paula watched him turn on to the road. She heard him ram down his foot on the accelerator and he vanished.

'He's heading back for Geneva,' she told Newman. 'And he seems to be in a great hurry.'

'Perhaps Tweed had a word with him.'

'There's a car creeping into the drive behind us.'

Newman had his .38 Smith & Wesson in his hand almost before she had finished speaking. From the back seat he pressed his left hand on her shoulder to push her down onto the floor.

'It's all right,' she told him. 'Harry and Pete didn't hoof it as Tweed suggested. They've come in the car which originally they drove to the Château d'Avignon.'

'I'll have a word with them,' replied Newman and climbed out.

It was still daylight but Harry had his headlights on. It must have been darker inside the forest than it was when Tweed had driven back. Newman walked over to their car as the two men climbed out. They spoke in little

326

more than whispers and Harry was carrying a satchel over his shoulder. Nield had emerged with his suitcase.

'Tweed phoned us, spoke in coded language,' Nield explained. 'He told me what to do. I told charming Fred I wanted to keep my room and paid in advance for it. Said I had to attend to some business in Geneva, that I'd be back. I won't be.'

'Marler's room number,' Harry said in his terse way.

Newman told him and Harry disappeared inside the hotel. Nield looked at Paula as he asked what was going on.

'We're driving to Ouchy tonight,' Paula informed him. 'After dinner, so you'd better join us. It's going to be a tight squeeze in one car.'

'No, it isn't,' Nield assured her. 'Harry is route marching it back to the Château d'Avignon, after Marler drops him close to the place when they return from Geneva.'

'What about the motorcycle?'

'Harry is insisting on hiding it in the forest on their way back. I'm sure he knows what he's doing. I don't understand the idea of our going to Ouchy.'

'I've just worked it out,' said Paula. 'It's going to turn out to be a battlefield.'

At the reception desk Newman paused to make an enquiry. A well-dressed French girl looked pleased to see him.

'I wanted a word with another guest,' Newman explained. 'Amos Lodge. But I think I saw him just leave.'

'You are quite right, sir. Mr Lodge made a phone call. Then he called down asking me to have his bill ready because he had to check out. Some urgent business had compelled him to leave unexpectedly.'

'Thank you. What about Mr Tweed?'

'He's been on the phone ever since he dashed into the hotel. I think he's off the line now.'

'Your English is perfect.'

'Thank you, sir.' She blushed. 'I spent two years in London with a big hotel. If you're going up to see him perhaps you could tell him a Mr Emilio Vitorelli has arrived. He asked for Mr Tweed. He's out on the terrace having a drink with a man who came with him.'

'I'll tell him.'

Paula left to have a shower, preferably a bath if there was time before dinner. Leaving Nield in the bar, Newman went up to Tweed's room. When the door opened he found Tweed dressing in a dark business suit for dinner.

'The receptionist told me you'd been on the phone,' Newman remarked as Tweed brushed his jacket.

'I have. Time I had a word with Monica. Nothing to report – except Howard is worked up about the hoax bombs planted in the vicinity of key power stations. They haven't picked up anyone who was involved yet. I advised them to concentrate on the East End of London.'

'Why?'

'Because of the character of the staff at the Château d'Avignon. They all come from that part of London, from the way they talk. On my way out I noticed a small slim man who Big Ben called Stan. That type never changes. Wears a permanent sneer on his smooth face. I once arrested someone just like him. He went down for fifteen years for attempted murder with a knife. I think the Englishman has hidden away a powerful reserve of deadly thugs at that chateau.'

'Talking of the Englishman, Amos Lodge received a phone call, according to the receptionist. He reacted by checking out and driving off towards Geneva.'

'Amos is a law unto himself. He's probably gone to

meet one of his secret contacts. And you're having dinner with The Butterfly. The receptionist also told me Emilio Vitorelli has just arrived. He's out on the terrace. Supposing he sees Tina? Anything could happen.'

'I'll go down and see Emilio now. We don't want any more complications in this part of the world . . .'

Tweed found Vitorelli sitting with Mario at a table on the terrace. As soon as Mario saw Tweed approaching he got up and left the terrace, nodding to Tweed as he passed him.

'What brings you to this neck of the woods?' Tweed asked as he sat down facing the rear of the hotel.

'You do, you old bloodhound.'

'I'll take that as a compliment. It doesn't explain why you are here when I'm on the verge of leaving tonight.'

'It would be stupid of me . . .' Vitorelli paused and gave an engaging smile, '. . . to ask where you're off to now?'

'If I said London you wouldn't believe me.'

'I might.' Vitorelli smiled again, ran a hand through his thick hair. 'You're a master of the double bluff.'

'If you say so.'

From where he sat Tweed could see the bedroom windows overlooking the terrace. Tina Langley was peering down at them from a window. She closed the curtain as Tweed spotted her. She now knew that Vitorelli was on the premises. Tweed didn't expect her to have dinner with him.

'I passed this hotel earlier this afternoon,' the Italian said and sipped at the last of his drink. 'I asked for you but they said you were away.'

'I was.'

'If you're leaving there can't be what you're looking for here.'

'If you must know, he has left the hotel.'

'That sounds like either Willie or Amos Lodge. Both

live in Dorset. I gave you a big tip about the courier who travelled there with a case full of money. You owe me.'

'I'll remember that.'

'Sounds as though you really are about to leave. I'm still on the lookout for Tina Langley.'

'You have been for a long time.'

'See you, Tweed. Don't do anything I wouldn't do.'

'There are a lot of things you do I wouldn't dream of doing.'

'Getting chilly out here. I don't think it's the evening air.'

Saying which, Vitorelli gave a little salute and left. On the way out he stopped at reception. He gave the girl behind the desk a great big smile to soften her up.

'I came here hoping to meet my old friend Amos Lodge.'

'Mr Lodge left the hotel suddenly. Do you want to leave me a message in case he comes back?'

'He won't come back.'

Satisfied that Tweed had told him the truth, Vitorelli went outside. If his reference to Amos hadn't worked he'd have asked about Captain Wellesley Carrington. Mario was waiting in the second car they had borrowed from a contact in a distant village earlier in the afternoon.

'Mario,' Vitorelli said quietly. 'Tweed is leaving this hotel soon – or so he says. I'm driving back to Geneva airport to the chopper. You wait here out of sight. Follow Tweed if he does leave.'

'Out of sight? Where?' Mario asked indignantly.

'You'll find somewhere.'

Vitorelli got behind the wheel of his Alfa Romeo, which he had parked behind a large van. He drove off, tyres screaming as he turned the bend from the drive into the road.

He had missed seeing Tweed watching him from behind one of the open doors leading to the terrace. Guessing that the Italian had checked up on him, he felt a wave of relief. The last man he wanted in his vicinity during the next twenty-four hours was Emilio Vitorelli.

Returning from Geneva, Marler had stopped his car a few hundred yards from the Château d'Avignon. He had helped Butler lift the motorcycle from the rack on top of the car. Butler had then wheeled the machine down a narrow track leading into the forest. He had hidden the machine under a dense mass of undergrowth behind a tall fir.

Going back to the car where Marler waited behind the wheel, he climbed in beside him. Marler drove at medium speed past the Château d'Avignon and Butler was relieved to see the gates were still open. He pulled up again beyond a bend and Butler stepped into the road. Marler called out in a low voice.

'Good luck. Don't take any chances. Remember, once you activate the timer the bomb detonates five minutes later.'

'Maybe I'll check my wristwatch,' Butler replied. 'See you.'

He waited for a while so anyone who had heard a car at Château d'Avignon wouldn't associate it with him. Then he shouldered the satchel which contained the bomb and strolled back to the entrance. Big Ben met him as he climbed the steps.

'You've been away a helluva time.'

'I'm a hiker. Like walking.'

'Mug's game. And they're servin' dinner.'

'Wouldn't care to join me, I suppose?'

Butler, who didn't give a damn for the hulking brute, went on upstairs before the other man could reply. He had kept the key to his room in his pocket. Once inside, he relocked the door and went to his suitcase. Bending down he checked for one of his hairs he had inserted when closing the case and before locking it. The hair was gone. His own key didn't work as smoothly as it had before. So there was a man who picked locks on the premises.

Going to the tall heavy and ancient wardrobe where he had stored his clothes, he reached up, ran his finger along the rim. It came away covered with dust. No one had thought to check the top.

From his satchel he extracted the circular bomb about the size of a small dinner plate. It was wrapped in strong blue paper. The timer and certain other small devices were separately and neatly wrapped in tissue. He tugged two hairs from his head, inserted one in each package, then slid the packages well back on top of the wardrobe.

'Don't reckon you'll find those, matey,' he said to himself.

As he got ready for dinner he contemplated what lay before him, a prospect that would have daunted many men. He had to stay in this hotel full of hostile thugs by himself for an unknown period. Until, in fact, Tweed phoned the code word to him.

Being on his own worried Butler not at all. He had the patience of Job. His only regret was he would be missing whatever fireworks Tweed was planning at Ouchy. Knowing Tweed as well as he did, Butler had sensed the time for continuing and mounting action had arrived. Ouchy was going to be an explosion of fireworks.

32

At the Château des Avenières Tina, who had driven there with her luggage and accepted a room overlooking the terrace, had made a phone call soon after arriving. A long way east in Slovakia Hassan answered immediately.

'I have vital news for you,' Tina said.

'I will decide whether it is vital. What is it?'

'Tweed, together with a team of men, is leaving here this evening. He is going to attend a meeting of the surviving members of the *Institut* at Ouchy on Lake Geneva. That should be worth a good fee.'

'You are sure he leaves this evening?'

'I want to know what my fee is,' she demanded.

'You know what happens to people who try to intimidate me?'

'Well, I think it is worth something,' she said in a much more conciliatory tone.

'Answer my question, damn you.'

'Yes,' she said quickly, 'I am certain.'

'Ten thousand dollars.'

Hassan slammed down the phone. He thought for several minutes. Which group was nearest to Ouchy? It was necessary to move very quickly. Then he realized the solution was obvious. He called the Château d'Avignon. Fred Brown came on the line.

'Frederick,' Hassan began in his most persuasive voice, 'I have some urgent and important instructions for you . . .'

When the phone call was finished Fred began to search out certain members of his staff. He took each one aside and spoke to them individually and away from the few guests staying at the hotel. Sitting on the terrace with a drink, Butler noticed some of this activity.

Later, curious, he strolled into the bar, ordered another drink as camouflage, then carried it as he strolled back into the main hall. He was in time to see three cars appear from the side of the chateau where, presumably, they had been parked out of sight.

He sipped his drink, observed that Big Ben was behind the wheel of the leading car. They crawled quietly out of the exit between the open gates and turned in the direction of Geneva. Aware that someone had crept up behind him, he turned and saw Stan standing close to him.

'Feeling restless, Mr Butler?' Stan enquired with a smirk.

'Getting a breath of fresh air.'

'Dinner is being served on the terrace. Don't want to go hungry, do we? Some of the staff are being given a party elsewhere. An expression of appreciation by Mr Brown for their support.'

'You giving me an explanation?'

Stan's smirk vanished. It was replaced by a sneer and he walked away. Butler watched him. Stan had a peculiar walk, reminding him of the slither of a crocodile. Not the sort of chap he'd invite to have a beer with him.

Ignoring the broad hint to go immediately on to the terrace for dinner, Butler went upstairs. Inside his room he called the Château des Avenières and gave a coded message to the receptionist.

'If my friend Pete Nield turns up there for a drink please tell him Harry Butler called. It's gone very quiet here now so I'd appreciate his company. Thank you.'

He put the phone down before the receptionist could say a word. It took him ages to have his dinner that night. There were long gaps between courses because of the shortage of waiters.

Tweed had just joined Paula, Newman and Marler for dinner at the Château des Avenières when the receptionist delivered Harry's message. Nield looked puzzled but Tweed was smiling. He remarked that Harry was not only reliable but also very clever at delivering disguised messages.

'I don't understand,' said Paula.

'That means the receptionist didn't. Harry is good.'

'I thought you were dining with Tina Langley,' Paula said, keeping her voice down.

'She sent me a note, saying she wouldn't be able to join me. She has a headache. I think seeing Vitorelli here scared her.'

'She gives me a headache,' Paula snapped.

'I've been let down too,' said Newman and mocking himself pulled a long face. 'Simone called me, said she was exhausted.'

'So exhausted,' Tweed told them, 'that I spotted her leaving with her bags. I remarked on it to the receptionist and she said the lady received a phone call, then called down to check out.'

'I suppose I'll survive without her,' Newman remarked with a sigh.

'You're more likely to survive without her than with her,' Paula said. 'Remember what she did to poor Pierre Dumont.'

'Tweed, why did you change your instructions and tell me not to mention Ouchy or Vienna to Simone?'

'One is enough.'

They ate their dinner in silence as Tweed was clearly in a hurry. Also, Paula noticed, he had a faraway look as though he was concentrating on his next moves. At the end of the meal she looked at Marler.

'We have to cross the French border to get back into Switzerland. Are you dumping your armoury beforehand?'

'Absolutely not. Everything will be taped under the chassis of my car. The explosive is harmless, of course, separated from the timers. Which brings me to something important I was going to suggest. I think it's safer if Tweed, Nield, Paula and Newman travel in one car. I'll bring up the rear in the other car – just in case I'm caught with the goods.'

'Agreed,' said Tweed.

'Then,' Marler went on, 'in case I lose you in the Geneva traffic I suggest we meet up outside the main rail station.'

'Agreed.'

It was dark on the terrace when they had finished their dinner. Illuminated by lamps, it had an incredible atmosphere of peace and serenity. Paula was trying to forget the attempt on Tweed's life when he stood up, took her by the arm.

'Let's take one last look.'

While the others went up to their rooms to collect their cases Tweed and Paula walked to the edge of the terrace. The moon was hidden behind the only cloud in the sky and France spread out before them. Between the shadowed silhouettes of the hills here and there were tiny islands of light like pockets of diamonds – the hamlets huddled between the ridges. Then the moon came out and bathed the whole landscape in a soft light.

'It's like something out of a dream,' Paula said quietly.

'When I can manage it maybe I'll give you time to come back here,' Tweed suggested.

336

'Maybe you could come with me.'

'It would be my first holiday in twenty years.'

Hassan had second thoughts after calling Fred Brown at d'Avignon. He drank some water to counter the humid air which persisted in Slovakia even after dusk. *Water.* The ultimate weapon of war. He phoned Tina Langley a second time.

'I want you to drive to Ouchy tonight. I'll book you a room at the Beau Rivage – not far from the *Institut* headquarters along the lake front. I think Tweed and the other members will not last tomorrow night.'

'Why tomorrow night?'

'I've heard from Ouchy the meeting takes place tomorrow night. I don't think you'll be needed to do the job.'

'What about my fee, then?' Tina demanded indignantly.

'You'll get some sort of fee.'

Then he was gone. Tina slammed down the phone in a fury. Then she thought about what Hassan had said. With a bit of luck Tweed would survive so she could earn the small fortune he had earlier offered.

Hassan then called Simone Carnot, gave her the same instruction. Unlike Tina, she took the news calmly. In any case, she had saved enough to last her for many years. She was not the type who lived extravagantly – and like Karin Berg, she saved money.

They drove away from the Château des Avenières in convoy, with Paula behind the wheel of the first car and Marler following on her tail. As they came close to the point where they would pass the Château d'Avignon

Marler dropped back. Tweed had said they would not risk being observed by anyone who might be in the drive of that chateau.

'Poor Harry,' Paula said as she drove past the entrance. 'The gates are closed – he must feel he's in prison.'

'Harry is always content to operate on his own,' replied Tweed, sitting beside her.

'He'll have gone to bed,' Nield called out from the back, 'with a chair propped up under the handle of the door. He never takes any chances.'

'Better him than me,' commented Newman, seated next to Nield.

'I think the thugs there have other things on their so-called minds,' Tweed remarked.

'What other things?' Paula asked.

'I like driving at night,' he said. 'It's soothing. Can you see Marler? I can't.'

'No, he's dropped back. I'm sure he'll catch us up. Yes, here he comes . . .'

Marler had a problem, or felt fairly sure he had. A Peugeot had appeared and, although not close, seemed to be keeping pace with him. He would decide later if he was right. Marler never worried about problems which might be a figment of his imagination.

Paula drove at a cautious speed past the summit of Mount Salève. It was late but even at this hour several cars were parked at the viewing point. She presumed some people liked to look down on the dazzle of lights far below which was Geneva. She maintained her careful driving as she descended the spiral of curves leading to the city.

Now well behind her, Marler was convinced he had a problem. The Peugeot had come closer as he also descended. He suspected that it was someone from the Château d'Avignon who was tailing Tweed and himself. He slowed down, as though inviting the other car to overtake. The Peugeot slowed down. Not normal behaviour. The other car was always keeping him in sight as Marler drove round the series of endless bends.

Inside the Peugeot Mario felt pleased with himself. He would get a pat on the back from Vitorelli when he told him where Tweed had headed for. Marler was operating so skilfully that it never occurred to Mario that he had been rumbled. Mario was anxious not to lose sight of the two cars when they entered the complexities of the Swiss city.

He was nervous when they approached the checkpoint on the border. Supposing the car in front of him was waved on and he was stopped? He little knew that Marler had played with the idea of using the checkpoint in some way to lose his tail. He had rejected the idea almost immediately. With what he had taped under the chassis he wanted to pass straight through.

'Marler is acting in a peculiar manner,' Paula commented as they reached level ground and she saw the checkpoint ahead.

'Marler always knows what he's doing,' Tweed reminded her.

She slowed down, prepared to stop as the checkpoint loomed in front of her. The officer on duty waved her on. Marler gave a sigh of relief as the officer also waved him on. In his rear-view mirror he saw that the Peugeot had received the same wave. Marler really began to concentrate.

In his mind's eye he saw the route ahead, the route he knew that Paula would take. She would drive across the great bridge over the river, the Pont du Rhône, and then she would be in the main and complex part of Geneva. From the bridge it was only a short distance to the rendezvous point, the rail station.

'I've got to mess you up, chum,' he said to himself, thinking of the Peugeot's driver.

He deliberately drove quite slowly. Other cars, emerging from different routes, overtook him. One driver honked his horn. Marler was careful not to look at him. We can do without road rage tonight, he thought. There were traffic lights close to the entrance to the bridge. He drove on very slowly.

He timed it so the lights turned red when he arrived. Behind him a car honked, annoyed that it had missed the lights. Now the Peugeot was one car behind him. Not because Mario had wanted that to happen, but an impatient driver had cut in on him. Paula's car was already halfway across the bridge.

Marler kept stopping and starting his engine, knowing from past experience that the lights would stay red for a while. He then raised the bonnet, got out and pretended to peer inside the engine. The driver of the car behind him climbed out and addressed him in French.

'If you've broken down I'll help you move the blasted thing to the side of the road. I haven't got all night while you fool about.'

'I don't speak the lingo,' Marler lied.

The driver cursed in French, returned to his car. The lights had turned green. Marler, sitting behind the wheel, played with starting and stopping again. He had checked swiftly to make sure there were no patrol cars about. On his right, waiting to enter the bridge when it could, was a juggernaut.

Marler watched the green light, ignoring the chorus of blaring horns behind him. He had created a major traffic jam. The lights changed to red against him. He rammed his foot down, shot forward as the juggernaut rumbled forward, its driver pressing his horn which sounded like a large cruise ship's foghorn. Then

Marler was on the bridge, racing across it. Soon after reaching the far end he turned down a side street, followed a devious route which would take him to the rail station.

In his frustration, Mario hammered his clenched fist down on the horn. The irate French driver in front of him reversed his car, slammed it with not too much force into the front of the Peugeot. It was nobody's night. Except Marler's.

Arriving at the station he found Paula parked and waiting for him. Jumping out, he ran to the window Tweed had lowered.

'Sorry about that. Slight problem with a tail. Lost him.'

'Then on to Ouchy. To the Beau Rivage,' said Tweed.

In only a few minutes Paula was enjoying herself driving along the motorway which ran parallel to Lake Geneva, mostly some distance away to their right. There was very little traffic and she drove fast, keeping just within the speed limit.

'This is relaxing,' she said.

'And Marler is behind us,' called out Newman.

'So all is well,' Paula enthused.

'I suspect all is not well at all,' Tweed interjected.

33

One hour earlier a cavalcade of three black cars had proceeded along the same motorway. The front car was driven by Big Ben, who drove fast, but also kept just inside the speed limit. Beside him sat Jeff, a large man whose body was all muscle. His face wore a permanent menacing expression. His head was almost bald and he had the eyes of a lizard.

Years before, Jeff had built up an enviable reputation in the East End of London as The Extortioner. His methods of persuading reluctant shopkeepers and club owners to pay up were legendary and horrific. He had left behind a number of victims crippled for life. Faced with a murder charge, he had broken out of a police station, badly injuring three policemen in the process.

The two men in the rear of the car, and the four men in each of the following cars, had also fled Britain to avoid the risk of long prison sentences. Several of them had recently taken on the Mafia in Germany. The Mafia was still reeling from the onslaught and at least ten mutilated bodies had been dragged out of the Rhine.

They were, in fact, what Tweed would have termed 'the *crème de la crème* of people better never to have been born'. These were men who were the living proof of another of Tweed's maxims, 'There is such a thing as pure evil.'

'Well, we got the bomb past the bloody *flics*,' Jeff recalled as they continued their drive.

'So how does it feel, sitting on it – when it's gutsy enough to blow Buckingham Palace sky high?' asked Big Ben and he chuckled.

'Comfortable,' replied Jeff. 'Bloody comfortable.'

The car they were travelling in had been skilfully adapted in a French workshop in a remote barn in the countryside. The brilliant mechanic who had done all the work himself had been promised a million francs if he succeeded. He had succeeded, hollowing out part of the chassis, believing it would contain a huge drug consignment. Instead, it was carrying the bomb with a radio-controlled device which would detonate it from a distance.

The French mechanic had never seen his million francs. He was now buried in a deep hole under his own barn. Fred Brown, carrying out the orders Hassan had given him, had arranged with Big Ben to 'dispose of the body once the job is done'.

Originally, Hassan's target had been the French President. Then the bomb would have been driven by remote-controlled car without a driver into the court-yard of the Elysée at the very moment when the gates were open for the Presidential car to leave the building, which was the official residence of the President.

Hassan had changed the plan at the last moment. He had realized he had in his possession the means of totally destroying all the surviving members of the *Institut* when they assembled at their headquarters in Ouchy. His instructions to Fred Brown had been precise and these instructions had been passed on to Big Ben.

'I feel like a fag,' Jeff said, his ugly hand reaching for his pocket.

'Light that and I'll smash your face in,' Big Ben said in a normal voice.

Big Ben abhorred smoking. As a youngster his father had forced him to smoke a large Havana cigar until it was no more than a stub. Big Ben had been ill for days. He considered that his only virtue was a sense of humour. Before the corpse of the French mechanic had disappeared down the deep hole he had pinned a note to the Frenchman's blood-stained chest. *IOU.*

'Don't get this business about a boat on the friggin' lake,' Jeff said, removing his hand reluctantly from his pocket.

'Orders. We hijack a big launch from the 'arbour at Ouchy. One man who swims well takes it out opposite the place where these nutcases are meetin' and punts about. With what we 'as in the car, behind us we make up dummies to look like real men. That's it.'

'Don't get it.'

'You don't get a lot of things. Your job is do as you're told and don't ask too many questions. Got it?'

'I got it.'

Big Ben never missed an opportunity to show who was boss. This was how he had become the top man in one of Hassan's key groups of killers. As he drove on he went over again in his mind the plan Hassan had outlined to him for Ouchy.

Hassan, despite his self-conceit, had a good brain and was a first-rate planner. He would never have admitted it but some of the key ideas had come from the Englishman. Hassan presumed he had picked up some of his more brilliant plans from his travels in the Middle East.

He had not forgotten Karin Berg, who had been placed in the Hôtel des Bergues. He had decided he needed a reserve. Just in case everything went wrong. The fact that Tweed was still alive was worrying him. He had called Berg.

'Karin, there has been a change in the situation.'

'What change?'

'Don't keep asking questions. Pack your bags and leave Geneva by the first flight in the morning.'

'Where the hell am I going now?'

'Watch how you talk to me!'

'And you mind your manners when you're talking to me. So where do I fly to?'

'You board a flight for Zurich. You don't leave the airport. You then catch a flight for Vienna – for Schwechat airport. A car will be waiting to pick you up.'

'To take me back to that boring headquarters?'

'You want a bonus of ten thousand dollars to start with, don't you?'

'Make it thirty thousand.'

'You think I'm made of money?'

'I know your father is. Do I get it?'

'You do—'

Hassan cursed. She had slammed down the phone on him again. He sat back in his chair and imagined strangling her slowly.

The three black cars, with Big Ben still in the lead, passed the marina on their right after they had entered Ouchy. A forest of masts swayed slowly in a light breeze. As arranged before it had left the Château d'Avignon, the rear car parked, then the car behind Big Ben overtook him, drove past the harbour and parked a few hundred yards along the lake front.

'We don't want a crowd of us drawing attention,' Big Ben had explained when he had briefed them at the chateau.

He parked his own car in a side road leading up to the Beau Rivage hotel. Like all his men, he wore a tracksuit. In June there were always joggers running at all hours. Before getting out of the car he stared at the Café Beau Rivage, where well-dressed and beautiful women were dining with their escorts both inside and out on the pavement.

He licked his lips as he studied some of the women. They were class, not the sort of companions he had spent his time with. He was due for a huge bonus when the operation was completed. I'll have to smarten up my wardrobe, he thought. He felt sure some of those women would like something different.

'Shouldn't I check the 'arbour?' Jeff suggested cautiously.

'We'll check it together. You two in the back keep your eyes peeled for patrol cars. Use the horn once to warn us if any local *flics* arrive. Ignore them if they drive past. If they check you you're waiting for friends to join you for a jog. Keep your friggin' eyes peeled.'

He climbed out with Jeff and they strolled down to

345

the small oyster-shaped harbour which was full of sailing craft and powerboats. No one else was about and the lake was not too close to the hotel.

They had nearly reached the end of the rows of boats when Big Ben grabbed Jeff's arm and stopped. A bald-headed man was on the deck of a large launch, painting a door to a cabin. Even his working clothes were fashionable and expensive. There was no sign of anyone else aboard.

'That's just what we need,' Big Ben whispered. 'Guy looks like the owner. You've got your gear.'

Jeff was carrying a cloth bag. Inside were several pots of paint and a number of brushes, together with an instrument for scraping off paint. The Englishman had passed very precise instructions to Hassan who, in his turn, had relayed them to Big Ben.

'Nobody about,' Jeff whispered back.

'Then get on with it . . .'

Jeff went closer to the launch. He noticed several items on the deck – a marlinspike, a loop of chain, a pile of cleaning cloths. It was as though the owner had known what was required. Making no sound with his rubber-soled shoes, Jeff stepped off the pavement onto the deck. His weight caused the bald-headed man to stop painting. When he turned round Jeff had picked up the marlinspike and, holding it behind his back, was close.

'Lost me way,' said Jeff. 'Tryin' to get to Vevey.'

'Really?' The bald-headed man was not happy about the ugly face staring at him. 'Well, you simply—'

He never finished his explanation. Jeff brought the marlinspike down with all his considerable strength on the bald pate. The skull was cracked as he sagged. Jeff had dropped the weapon, had gripped the dead man under the armpits, dragging him along the deck to the prow under the small bridge. The corpse was out of sight as he glanced around. On the pavement Big Ben gave him a thumbs-up sign.

Jeff went up into the wheelhouse. He'd had considerable experience stealing expensive boats on the Hamble in Hampshire back in England. The trouble was that starting up the engine would easily attract attention onshore.

Meanwhile Big Ben had waved his arms, signalling to the car parked outside the Beau Rivage café. One of the men who had been in the rear was waiting behind the wheel. He started up the car, drove slowly past the diners on the pavement, turned down to the harbour and executed a U-turn close to where Big Ben was now standing at the stern of the launch. The boot of the car was now hidden from anyone dining who might glance in their direction.

Big Ben helped the two men haul out large sacks from inside the boot. They heaved the sacks onto the deck of the launch at the stern. They had just completed the job when Jeff had a bit of luck.

A posse of motorcyclists arrived opposite the hotel. To annoy the diners they stopped, revving up their engines. Jeff started up the launch's engine under cover of the racket. Big Ben had slipped the towrope, which was looped round a bollard. Jeff guided the launch slowly out into the darkness of the lake and was gone.

'That's the worst part done,' Big Ben said as he slipped behind the vacated wheel of the car.

'Les,' he said to the man who had driven the car and was now sitting behind him, 'is there someone from the car parked near the marina close by?'

'Gave him the go-ahead, as I drove over.'

Les was a tall wiry man with a broken nose. His speciality was as a knife-thrower. He had learned his trade working for a circus – until in a rage he skewered a poor girl through the throat for not agreeing to his suggestion. He had escaped before the police had arrived and Big Ben had met him holed up in the East End of London.

As they drove slowly along the wide road with the lake beyond a wall on their right the third black car appeared behind them. Big Ben grinned, showing his bad teeth. He had given his gang the impression the plan was his own. You took every chance to build up your authority. As he crawled along he glanced out across the lake. The launch had disappeared.

'A job well done,' he said with evident satisfaction.

'He has to do a lot more,' said Les.

Once well away from the shore, Jeff stopped the launch, let it drift as he did a lot more. First, he stripped the owner naked. Using an axe he found among the launch's tools, he chopped off each hand at the wrist. No finger-prints for swift identification. Then, wearing rubber gloves, he put each hand inside a small bag weighted with lead which he'd extracted from the large cloth bag also containing paint and brushes. What he did with the face to make it unrecognizable is best not described.

After binding up the corpse with the chains and loop of rope he had found on the deck, he then heaved the body inside a large sack. He carefully tied up the neck. Stripping off his rubber gloves, covered with blood, he shoved them inside another small sack.

After washing his hands in the galley he went back to the wheelhouse, looked round carefully, started up the engine and headed into the middle of the lake. He was anxious to finish this part of the job before the moon rose. He stopped the launch briefly in the middle of the lake. He did this three times.

At one point he heaved overboard the sack containing the body. On the second occasion when he stopped he threw over one of the sacks containing a hand. On the third occasion he threw overboard the second hand. He allowed himself a sigh of relief as he started up the engine again.

Later, he stopped again. With the aid of a torch and the paint and brushes he had brought with him he painted a green line round the squat funnel. The moon was rising as he covered up the original name of the vessel with sheets of special paper he extracted from his sack and unrolled. The paper carried the name *Starcrest V*. His next task was easy – he removed the Swiss flag flying from the stern and replaced it with a French flag. It wasn't a perfect transformation but the launch would only lie off Vevey for a day before it played its key role in the destruction of the remaining members of the *Institut*.

Tweed, reaching Ouchy, drove to the Beau Rivage's front entrance, which faced away from the lake. Handing the car keys to a porter he went inside the vast and palatial hotel to reception. Paula was beside him while Newman and Nield followed them.

A few minutes later Marler drove up as though an independent visitor. On Tweed's instructions he had reserved his own room by phone before leaving the Château des Avenières.

'Welcome back, Mr Tweed,' the smartly dressed girl behind the counter greeted him. 'We have again reserved you a room overlooking the lake.'

'Thank you. I'm sure my friends could do with a drink in the bar . . .'

After registration he led the way. Paula stared up at the very high vaulted ceiling decorated in excellent taste. She liked the atmosphere of the whole place.

Instead of being handed one of those horrible computer keys she was carrying a traditional key.

As they walked down the long, wide and deserted corridor she continued to admire the decor. The bar was a large room on the left with comfortable chairs and a spacious feel. A Dutch girl sat behind a grand piano singing romantic songs while the few guests inside the bar listened.

'This is civilization,' Paula commented as she sank into a chair which seemed to wrap itself gently round her.

'What is everyone going to have to drink?' Tweed enquired. 'I expect, Paula, you'd sooner have gone straight up to your room but after the drive I thought a drink would help.'

'A glass of wine. And it will help. At least we can relax here.'

'We can't relax anywhere,' Tweed said sharply. 'Not until we have destroyed our opponents or they have destroyed us.'

He smiled after ordering drinks to take the edge off the grimness of what he had said. Paula thought she had never known him show quite such iron determination and ferocious energy. Tweed had reverted to ordering orange juice for himself. When they were refreshed he made his request.

'Paula, Bob, I'd like us to stroll along the lake front to take a look at the Institut building. We can unpack later.'

'We'll come, too,' said Marler who had joined them, glancing at Nield, who nodded agreement.

'Fair enough, but keep well behind us as though you're strangers.'

Tweed knew a short cut to the lake front. They descended in a lift to the ground floor, walked along a corridor and out onto the pavement where people still sat at tables.

Striding out, Tweed walked down the side road alongside the gates which led to the extensive gardens of the hotel. Then, crossing the road, he headed along the pavement by the lake in the direction of Vevey. The moon was up and Paula gazed across the sheen of the lake to the huge mountains of Haute-Savoie in France on the far side. The sight filled her with awe.

After a walk of several minutes Tweed pointed to a large mansion on their left, standing on an eminence above the road. There was something sinister about the ancient dark pile towering above them. It stood well back with a green lawn sloping down to the road. Double wrought-iron gates were closed, barring off a curving drive. A few yards further along a noticeboard was illuminated in front of the railed wall which preserved its privacy. Paula read the notice, which was in English and French.

A meeting of all members will be held at 22.00 hours tomorrow.

'I presume all surviving members have been informed,' she said.

'What sort of meeting would it be without members?' Tweed asked in the same grim tone he had used in the bar. 'There's a side entrance.'

Walking several yards further, he stopped in front of a small railed gate behind which climbed a flight of stone steps. He tested the padlock, which was closed. Nothing about its appearance told him the lock had recently been expertly picked and opened.

'No lights on inside the mansion,' Paula remarked.

'Why should there be?' Tweed's tone softened. 'I

351

think we'll go back now before the Café Beau Rivage closes. You must be hungry.'

'My tummy is rumbling,' Paula admitted.

They had crossed the deserted road to look at the HQ of the *Institut*. Marler and Nield waited on the opposite side, leaning on the wall, apparently staring at the lake and the view beyond in the distance. Both men had observed the mansion closely.

No one had noticed as they were approaching the mansion the rear of a black car disappearing round a bend towards Vevey. The Englishman who had studied the layout during a visit had given very careful instructions to Hassan. He, in his turn, had passed on the details to Big Ben. The large bomb was now in place.

34

They ate an excellent meal at an isolated table inside the Café Beau Rivage. Paula had decided food was more important than a trip to her room to change. Marler had not joined them, to keep up the appearance that he had nothing to do with them. He sat at a table outside, enjoying the view of a number of very beautiful women.

'Do you think there's anything to choose between the three members of The Sisterhood?' Paula asked Tweed over coffee. 'I mean they are all prepared to murder for money, but are they as bad as each other?'

'My choice for the most evil one would be Tina Langley.'

'Why?'

'From certain enquiries Monica has made it's obvious that Tina has only one god. Money. Human emotions mean nothing to her. She's never had any desire to work for her living. From an early age she's concentrated on exploiting men, then throwing them over when she's drained them of money.'

'Anything else?' Newman asked.

'Yes. At least Simone tried to earn her living running an agency in Paris. Before that she was personal assistant to the managing director of a big company – and good at the job. As for Karin Berg, we all know that for years she worked high up for Swedish counter-espionage. I know how well she operated. It was only later in life that they went bad, tempted by big money.'

'And Tina?' Paula persisted.

'Has never had any job of any kind all her life. Doesn't have the brains – or the inclination – to earn her living like other people. As I said, I can only think of exploiting wealthy men. Pure evil.'

'I'm inclined to agree with you,' said Paula. 'Contemptible is the word I would use. Now I'm looking forward to sleep.'

'I won't get any,' said Tweed. 'I'm not complaining. It goes with the territory, as I believe the Americans say. I have to meet someone in another part of the hotel.'

'I'll come with you,' Newman said quickly.

'No one will come with me.'

'You may just need protection,' Newman insisted.

'I can assure you all that I certainly don't need protection.'

When they left the table Tweed expressed the desire to have some fresh air. He led them out onto the pavement and then up a side street. A cool breeze was now blowing off the lake. Near the top he paused, listening to a weather forecast in French coming through an open window.

'You heard that?' asked Paula. 'They expect major thunderstorms tomorrow night.'

'Tonight,' said Tweed, 'it's just after midnight.'

Turning right at the top of the road led them to the

main entrance to their hotel. They were standing waiting for the lift when Paula glanced up. The hall had an immensely high ceiling and it was possible for someone on any floor to gaze over a rail down into the hall. She nudged Tweed and he looked up.

Leaning over the rail on the second floor, gazing down at him, was the auburn-haired Tina Langley.

The three black cars drove slowly into Vevey, the next important town on the edge of the lake from Ouchy. Big Ben knew Vevey well. He had once worked as a packer in a pharmaceutical plant there. His main income had come from drugs he stole and then sold elsewhere. He never took drugs himself, just as he never smoked. His main indulgences were drink and ladies of the night. Since he had a large capacity for alcohol he'd found the two went together rather well.

'Signal to that hotel,' he ordered Les, seated next to him.

The knife-thrower waved a hand out of the window he had opened. The car behind them parked outside the hotel. This technique was repeated a few minutes later and the third car parked outside another small hotel. Big Ben sighed with satisfaction.

'It's goin' good,' he said.

'What's the idea?' asked Les.

The tall thin man with the broken nose stretched his legs, which were becoming cramped. He was always the one who asked questions, and Big Ben would have got rid of him but he was too good at his work to lose. He decided to humour his awkward associate.

'There are twelve of us. Use that thing in the top of your 'ead. It's the tourist season – but twelve of us shacking up in one 'otel could make people talk. Stuck in three different 'otels we won't be noticed. They're all booked in for three nights. So, with it paid for in advance, no manager is goin' to worry when they stay in their rooms all day.'

'And,' Les said brightly, 'we all then meets up at the agreed place outside this Vevey after dark tonight. We 'as the guns and we gives the others theirs when we meet up. Then we drives back in the dark to that big 'ouse in Ouchy. Any guys who gets out after the bomb goes off we shoots down.'

'Les, if you goes on like that you'll be an Einstein.'

'Who's he? Another helper?'

'You're slippin' again.'

'What about Jeff? Be bloody cold out on the lake.'

'Jeff's a wiz with a watch. Timin' to you. He stays with the launch off the 'arbour 'ere. When it gets dark he fixes it up. At the right time he takes it back opposite that big 'ouse at Ouchy. Part of the plan, matey. There's our 'otel . . .'

In his room half an hour later Tweed had had a bath and dressed again, this time in casual clothes – a polo-necked sweater and slacks. The room, almost a suite, was spacious and comfortable. He was just settling himself down at a desk and reaching for the phone when he heard someone tapping on his door.

Going to the door, he stood against the wall opposite the hinge side, opened it. Paula stood outside. She had changed her clothes and was dressed in a smart blue suit. She nodded approval when she saw he was holding a canister of hairspray.

'I can't sleep. Do you mind if I stay with you for a while?' He noticed she was carrying her shoulder bag and smiled as he ushered her inside, relocking the door.

'You've appointed yourself my personal guard.'

'Well, I was worried all the time in the bath. I was remembering Tina peering down at us from a balcony.'

'There's a fresh pot of coffee just delivered by room service. They must have assumed I wouldn't be alone – hence the two cups.'

'I'll pour. I'm not in the way, am I?'

'Not at all. You're company in the wee small hours. I have to make some phone calls. It's all right, you can hear what I say. That couch over there is comfortable. My first call is to the Baur au Lac.'

He returned to the desk, sat down and pressed numbers.

'Baur au Lac. Could I speak to the concierge? Tweed speaking. Is that the concierge? I'm trying to contact my old friend, Amos Lodge.'

'He's not in the hotel, sir,' the concierge informed him. 'He left earlier. He has kept his room on hold. Said he expected to be back in a few days.'

'Did he leave a number where he could be contacted?'

'No, sir . . .'

'Amos has disappeared,' Tweed told Paula after putting down the phone.

'Did you expect that?'

'I rather did. Interesting.'

He had just spoken when there was a light tapping on the door. Before Tweed could move Paula was on her feet. She had extracted the Browning from her shoulder bag and held it openly by her side. Unlocking the door she found Tina Langley standing outside.

Tina was wearing a nightgown, low-cut, exposing cleavage. She was carrying a large canvas bag out of which the neck of a wine bottle protruded. The two women stared at each other. Paula thought their visitor had eyes like slate.

356

'I had some information for Mr Tweed,' Tina said stiffly. 'I didn't realize he'd have company. I expect it will be like that all night long.'

'Like what?' snapped Paula.

'Isn't that a gun you're holding?'

'You should be able to recognize a gun by now.'

'Horrid things. I didn't expect to be interrupting Mr Tweed's tête-à-tête,' she said with a suggestive smile.

'I'd say you're an interruption, an unwanted one, wherever you turn up.'

Paula closed the door in Tina's face, her lips tight. Tweed was still sitting at the desk when she turned round. He looked amused.

'I'd like to have put a bullet through her,' Paula said viciously. 'You got a good look. Would you have been tempted?'

'Silly question. She's rubbish. Thank you for seeing her off. Drink some coffee – you look furious. I'm calling the Dolder Grand now to have a word with Willie.'

After a brief conversation he again put down the phone. Drinking some of the coffee Paula had poured, he turned round.

'Willie has also gone missing. He checked out of the Dolder Grand earlier today – or yesterday. Left no forwarding address. Gave no indication he'd be returning. Interesting, very interesting, what I've learned from two phone calls.'

Paula knew better than to ask him what he found so interesting. If he wanted to tell her he would do so. He turned back to the phone after checking his watch.

'Now I have to call someone inside this hotel.' He pressed numbers, waited for only a short time. 'You know who this is,' he began. 'We're all here – except for Butler. I left him behind in France to do a job when the time comes. How is everything going? Too early to say?

357

They've got a very tough job. Can I come along to see you now? Good.'

After completing the call, Tweed drank more coffee from the cup Paula had again refilled. Then he stood up, glanced at a large map he had spread out on the bed.

'As I told you, I have to visit someone in the hotel. I'm afraid it's highly confidential.'

'You're not wandering round by yourself. Not with *that* woman in the place.' Paula spoke firmly, standing up. 'I'll accompany you, then leave you once you reach wherever you're going. No argument.'

'Then I'd better not argue. Why not go to bed, get some sleep?'

'Because I'll be coming back here if you loan me the key again. Then you call me when you're ready to come back. I'll collect you. Call me fussy, but I'm sure Tina stands to earn a load of money for shooting you in the back. And you once told me that in the case of all the murders no one had heard a shot fired.'

'That's true. They have obviously designed an effective silencer for the Luger. So let's stroll along where I have to go together . . .'

Tweed would have preferred to go on his own, confident of his ability to deal with any situation. But he would not risk disappointing Paula – such loyalty was very rare. They started a long walk through the wide corridors. They met no one on the way. Nowhere is as silent as a great and ancient hotel in the middle of the night.

'Don't forget to call me when you're finished,' said Paula as they stopped in front of a certain door. 'Wait until you hear me tap out our tattoo before you come out.'

She waited while Tweed knocked on the door. He had one finger to his lips as someone opened the door and he vanished inside. Paula was walking back, well away from where she had left Tweed, when she encountered Tina coming towards her.

No longer in her night things, Tina wore a pale blue dress and had clearly spent time perfecting her make-up to match her outfit. Paula smiled as they came close before passing each other.

'All tarted up?' she said. 'Hunting for fresh prey, are we?'

Tina gave her a venomous look, walked past without a single word. She was even more infuriated because Paula had hit the nail on the head. Tina was hoping to bump into a man who had returned late to the hotel by himself. A brief episode might earn her some pin money.

Tweed was absent for an hour. Paula kept wondering what could have kept him so long. Where was Amos? Where was Willie? What could they be doing? Questions without answers. She was greatly relieved when Tweed called, said he was ready to come back.

'Another phone call to make,' he said as Paula relocked the door to his room. 'This one will surprise you. I'm calling Chief Inspector Roy Buchanan of the CID back home.'

'At this hour?'

'I hope you weren't bored while I was away. There are plenty of magazines you could have looked at.'

'I'm not Tina. I've been reading a serious novel I brought with me.'

Tweed didn't hear her answer. He was too busy calling his old sparring partner. He was surprised how quickly Buchanan, at his home number, reacted.

'Who is it now?'

'Roy, this is Tweed. Calling from Switzerland. Sorry if I have woken you up.'

'Of course you've woken me up. I'm in bed at this

hour. It has to be important, I hope. I'll send you some sleeping pills.'

'There's a village in Dorset called Shrimpton. North-west of Dorchester. It's a weird place. Apparently most of the ancient cottages are rented out. No idea who owns them. They may house some dangerous criminals. Can I suggest you go down there, find out who does own them, who does occupy them? There's a pub at one end of the village. You might find something out from local gossip. This is very urgent. Concerns an inter-national menace which could threaten Britain in the near future.'

'Sounds serious, but I'm in a dilemma. The Commissioner needs my advice tomorrow.'

'I've just had an idea. Send Sergeant Warden. He'll fit into the local landscape better than you would.'

'Why, may I ask?'

'I can only put it one way. You come over as a bit of a toff. I think the locals might clam up. Warden has the sort of wooden personality they'd chat to.'

'I'll tell Warden that.'

'You can phrase it more diplomatically. There's something very strange going on at Shrimpton.'

'I could call Warden in the morning . . .'

'I'd feel happier if you called him now. Then he can drive down and put up at a hotel in Dorchester. That would give him time to take a look at Shrimpton in daylight. I suggest he pretends to be a property sales-man – after buying local properties.'

'That's a clever idea. I just need convincing this is serious enough to avoid the Commissioner's request.'

'I don't want to sound pompous, Roy, but this involves the Defence of the Realm. I'm talking about the biggest menace since Adolf Hitler.'

'You can be so blasted persuasive, Tweed. I may go myself with Warden.'

'While you're there check discreetly whether two bigwigs have arrived back suddenly. They both live on the outskirts of the village. One is Amos Lodge, the other Captain William Wellesley Carrington.'

'How high up does this go?'

'To the PM. That's between the two of us.'

'All right, Tweed. I'll do my best. Where do I contact you?'

'At the Hotel Beau Rivage, Ouchy. Here is the number . . . If I move on I'll inform your assistant at the Yard where I am.'

'One question. Do you ever sleep?'

'Only when I can. A thousand thanks, Roy.'

'Jump off a cliff . . .'

'More coffee?' Paula offered when Tweed had dropped the receiver.

'Not now. My head is beginning to buzz.'

'You're really spreading a vast net this time.' Paula walked over to the map spread over the double bed. 'All the way from Dorset to Slovakia. I see you've marked the Château d'Avignon with a cross. Then another cross at that strange house way east in Slovakia. I presume they indicate the main communications centres.'

'They do.'

'Does this business really go up to the Prime Minister?'

'No comment.'

The phone rang as Tweed pulled down the top of his polo-neck, which felt too tight round his throat. He went back to the desk from where he had been studying the map with Paula. A familiar upper-crust voice spoke.

'That you, Tweed? Keith Kent here. I had the devil of a job persuading Monica to tell me where you were. You needed to know who owns the village of Shrimpton

361

in Dorset and surrounding land. It wasn't easy – hence the delay.'

'You mean you've found out?' Tweed asked calmly.

'A man called Conway.'

'Conway?'

'You sound puzzled. I can understand it. He owns a company in the Channel Islands. But it gets complex.'

'I thought it might.'

'The Channel Islands company, which is difficult to penetrate, has a connection with the Cayman Islands. I suspect money – large sums – sent to the Channel Islands is then routed on to the Cayman Islands in the Caribbean. Infiltrating a bank account in the Caymans is next to impossible.'

'You've achieved the impossible before.'

'I think I can do it. I have a very good contact out there – but it will take time.'

'I haven't got time,' Tweed commented.

'I knew you were going to say that.'

'Keith, I need a photocopy of Conway's balance sheet because it will give his real name. I need it tomorrow. No – today.'

'You're a hard taskmaster. I'll drop everything to get you what you want.'

'It's appreciated, Keith.'

'My fee for this won't be appreciated.'

Tweed gave him the same message he had given to Buchanan. He would leave at the Beau Rivage a number where he could be found if he left Ouchy.

'You'll move on from Ouchy. I know you . . .'

'Who is Conway?' asked Paula as Tweed stood up from the desk. 'I'd forgotten that you'd asked Keith Kent to find out who owned Shrimpton. It was a while ago,' she said.

'One of those two Dorset men – Amos or Willie – once mentioned they'd visited the Cayman Islands. The trouble is I can't recall which one. It was a long time ago. When we know who Conway is we'll know who is masterminding this vast operation.'

35

The events which took place on that June night became known as the Battle of Ouchy.

The day started quietly on the surface. Despite being up for the whole night Tweed appeared for breakfast fresh and spruce. He had an almost jaunty air as his team settled down in the Café Beau Rivage for their meal. He had arranged for a table at the end of the restaurant in a corner where they would not be overheard. In any case, the only other occupants while the other tables were being prepared for lunch were the early drinkers at the bar at the far end.

'You look optimistic,' remarked Newman before he tackled a plate of bacon and eggs.

'Let it be clear to everyone,' Tweed replied, 'that complacency is our main enemy. Our opponents are powerful, resourceful, cunning and ruthless.'

'Then we'll have to fight dirty,' responded Nield.

'Any method will be used,' Tweed agreed. 'You'll all have seen that Marler is absent. He had an early breakfast and is now in his room. He is, shall I say, cleaning his equipment. Some of that will be distributed to you late in the day.'

'I can guess where the war will take place,' Paula said. 'At that big mansion along the lake front which we visited last night.'

'In that area, yes. Also a number of red berets were handed to me in a case. You will all wear one when the time comes. That red beret may save your lives.'

'That's right, be mysterious up to the last moment,' Nield commented.

'I suggest,' Tweed went on, 'that after breakfast we separate. Each of us at intervals will take a stroll along the lakeside promenade. This will enable you to study by daylight the HQ of the *Institut* and its surroundings.'

'Don't forget the lake,' Paula warned. 'Remember what happened at the Ermitage on Lake Zurich when you came under attack.'

There were brief pauses in their conversation when a waitress came to serve more coffee. Paula waited for her opportunity to issue her edict.

'This business of walking individually along the front does not apply to Tweed. I will accompany him. Not long ago I saw Tina Langley in the bar knocking back drinks. She had a bottle on the table so I think she must have ordered a generous supply to be sent to her room last night.'

'Reluctantly Tweed agrees,' said Tweed. 'Otherwise he knows that Paula will simply trail close behind him, even if I said no.'

'Well, that saves an argument you wouldn't win,' Paula told him.

Tweed told his fellow diners about phoning Willie and Amos and finding they had disappeared. He didn't mention his hour-long night visit to someone inside the hotel. Nor did he tell them about the unknown Conway. He always keeps something up his sleeve, Paula mused. I wonder what he's kept up his sleeve that he hasn't told me?

'Exercise this morning,' Tweed went on. 'Then use the afternoon to rest inside the hotel. You will need all your wits about you this evening. At 9 p.m. everyone assembles in my room and all will be revealed. Also, I will hand out your red berets. That includes you, Paula.'

'I always fancied myself in a red beret,' she joked,

trying to introduce a lighter note into the conversation. 'And isn't it a lovely day?'

The tall glass doors leading to the pavement tables had been opened and they had a view over a small park to the harbour beyond. Out on the lake, reflecting a duck-egg blue sky, small white triangles moved slowly towards France. They were yachts which sailing enthusiasts had taken out earlier. It was like a vision of paradise, Paula thought. A few miles across the lake the massive giants of the French mountains provided a dramatic background. There was no snow on the summits. The long heatwave had melted the last remnants which had clung to the savage peaks.

'A day to remember,' Tweed observed.

'I'm going to enjoy our stroll along the lakeside.'

'But,' Tweed warned, 'I predict it will also be a night to remember.'

Vitorelli picked up the phone in his room at the Baur au Lac. He was in a bad temper.

'Who is it?'

'Mario. You told me you were returning to Zurich. You flew the chopper there?'

'Of course. It's waiting at Kloten here. Where the hell are you calling from?'

'Geneva.' Mario took a deep breath. 'When I called you on the mobile I was following them down Mount Salève . . .'

'Don't tell me you lost them. I've been waiting all night for you to call.'

'It was the traffic in Geneva. Terrible. I've spent all night touring the city, looking for their parked cars.'

'You could have saved yourself the trouble by reading a newspaper.'

'I could?'

'Yes, dumbhead. The Swiss papers are making it a lead story. I will read the headlines in the one I have here. "Survivors of Mass Murders Risk Assassination. Meeting tonight at Ouchy."'

Vitorelli went on to read the details. They even gave the time of the meeting at the Ouchy headquarters at the mansion on the lakeside: 10 p.m. Mario was sweating as he listened in a café and his eyes wandered to a copy of the *Journal de Genève* a man was reading at a nearby table. A similar headline glared at him.

'I haven't seen a paper,' Mario lied as Vitorelli finished reading the report to him.

'I thought you were grown up,' Vitorelli thundered down the phone. 'Get yourself back into the car. If you haven't had breakfast you'll have to go hungry. Might sharpen up your wits. Drive now to Ouchy, put yourself up in a small hotel, then report to me this evening what happens at 10 p.m. in Ouchy. Shall I spell it out more slowly?' he asked as though dealing with a ten-year-old.

'No. I heard you. I will leave now.'

Mario had not had breakfast. He had been going to order a large meal at the café. Instead he ran to his car. Why, he was wondering, had his boss returned to Zurich and left the chopper at the airport?

In Slovakia Hassan was talking to the Englishman, who had called him. Their conversation was not warm.

'You've heard about the Ouchy meeting?' the voice snapped with military precision.

'Yes. A contact – it was Tina Langley – called me yesterday from the Château des Avenières. It gave me time to make certain arrangements. No one will survive.'

'Including Tweed?'

Tweed, Hassan thought. Always it was Tweed. He

seemed to live a charmed life. And he was everywhere. It was difficult to keep up with his swift movements. Always to – or near – sensitive places. He was developing a hatred of this strange man, who seemed invincible.

'Yes, including Tweed,' he replied. 'Tina said he would attend the meeting.'

'You have time then to fly there.'

'You can't fly to Ouchy—'

'Heaven give me strength. You leave immediately. Catch a plane to Zurich, then another to Geneva. I will have a Daimler with a chauffeur waiting at Geneva's airport. Call me back at this number with the ETA of the Geneva flight.'

'The Daimler—' Hassan began, puzzled.

'Bang your head against a wall. Wake up! The Daimler will drive you to Ouchy.'

The rasping voice of the Englishman sounded like a sergeant major addressing a particularly stupid recruit.

'I see . . .'

'Do you? Wonderful! I need a witness to tell me Tweed is dead. You're the bloody witness. Afterwards the Daimler drives you back to Geneva where you board the first flight for Zurich and, when you can, another flight to Schwechat Airport.'

'I'll have to dress the part . . .'

'He's catching on! The Daimler will be noticed – but it will be assumed it's carrying an important man.'

'It will be.'

'Look in the mirror sometime. Now, get *moving*!'

Strolling along the lakeside with Tweed after breakfast Paula studied the large mansion where the *Institut* held its meetings. A lot of details she had missed in the dark became clear. The first danger point struck her immediately.

367

'When those large gates are opened,' she said, 'anyone going up to that place, even by car, is terribly exposed.'

'Not if they're concealed behind that railed wall protecting the mansion from the road.'

'But they won't be able to attend the meeting then,' Paula objected.

'Wait until I give everyone my briefing in my room tonight.'

'It would be much safer,' she persisted, 'if they entered by that side gate where you checked the pad-lock. The stone steps leading up are shielded by a solid wall about man-high.'

'You are reading my mind.'

'I can't see anywhere else safe.'

'Look to your right at the gap in the lake wall. Steps lead down to a landing stage,' Tweed pointed out.

'You don't miss a thing. I read in the paper this morning before I came down that TV crews are expected to film the event. That could be dangerous – with all their lighting.'

'I have thought of that.'

'You're going quiet on me. All right, I'll change the subject. It occurred to me when I couldn't sleep last night that you've had no contact with Christopher Kane recently.'

'I tried to phone him after you'd gone back to your room. No answer,' Tweed told her.

'So three key men have vanished off the face of the earth.'

'Interesting, isn't it?' Tweed said with a smile.

'You are the most exasperating man I've ever known at times. I wonder why I work for you.'

'Because you like the work. A City job behind a desk would drive you round the bend.'

'That's true. At least you said interesting, instead of significant . . .'

In the evening Paula watched the brilliant red sun sinking in the west like a blood-red coin. Fatalistically, she was wondering how many of them would be alive in the morning. From Tweed's mood which she had sensed during their morning stroll she knew he felt he was carrying a heavy responsibility. He was a man who cared.

As instructed, she had dressed herself in a trouser suit for ease of swift movement. Her Browning fitted invisibly behind the elasticized top of her trousers. She could reach it in a second and her shoulder bag would have restricted her. She sat down and read a book until 9 p.m. arrived. Everyone had had a quick light meal sent up to their rooms. Marler had not been seen for most of the day and she was curious where he had been.

Promptly at 9 p.m. she knocked on the door of Tweed's room. When she was admitted she saw the others had already arrived. Nield, Newman and Marler were seated in chairs. She noticed Marler had a number of large cloth bags perched against the side of his chair.

Tweed sat behind the desk, having removed the chair to the far side so he faced everyone. It was the fifth man who startled her. Arthur Beck, Chief of Federal Police, was seated on a wide couch. He stood when Tweed ushered her inside, came forward and gave her a hug.

'Welcome to the war conference.'

'You were the man Tweed visited secretly in a room here,' she whispered.

369

'He was,' said Tweed, who had overheard her.

'Come and sit with me,' the handsome greying police chief invited Paula.

Each man in the room had a sheet of paper on which was drawn a plan. Tweed handed her an identical sheet. One glance told her it was a plan of the mansion. She studied it quickly as she joined Beck on the couch.

'Marler has worked out the main tactics,' Tweed announced, seated behind his desk. 'In conjunction with myself and with the full agreement of Arthur Beck, who suggested some changes. I won't beat about the bush. No, I think Arthur might like to open the proceedings.'

'Tweed suspected that a large bomb had been planted under the mansion,' Beck said, standing. 'He was right. I had the Bomb Squad brought here. Some brave men worked in the night, checking the mansion. They discovered a huge bomb hidden in the cleaning store under the building. We are sure from certain aspects of it that it was to be detonated by remote radio control. It has been made harmless but we dare not remove it from the building in case the mansion was under surveillance.'

'Could it still detonate?' Paula asked quietly.

'Our top man in charge of the Bomb Squad would give you a reply which differs from mine. He would say that with high-explosive you never can be certain. I say no – in its present state, it is safe. When we can, we will put it aboard a dredger, take it out into the middle of the lake, lower it to the bed of the lake and detonate it there. The top man will not risk transporting a bomb of that size through the streets. Now, the main objective. Tweed will explain . . .'

Taking up the position he had handed over to Beck, Tweed stood behind the desk. He polished his glasses with his handkerchief before speaking. The brief interval was to make sure his audience gave maximum concentration to what he had to say.

'Chief Inspector Beck has given us full cooperation. Just before we left the Château des Avenières Nield received a second brief call from Butler at the other chateau. Butler said, I quote, "I'll take you on with that horse race bet. Odds twelve to one."'

'What did that mean?' Newman enquired.

'It was a coded message telling Nield that twelve of the so-called staff, twelve of the toughest thugs in the world, were on their way somewhere. I guessed it was to here. One of Beck's men, dressed like a tourist, counted twelve men passing along the lake-front road in three black cars. Twelve of the most dangerous men in the world.'

'It takes twelve men to plant a bomb?' Marler called out sceptically.

'No. They're back-up. Partly, I suspect, in case the bomb doesn't work. Partly to gun down any member of the *Institut* who escaped. When the bomb doesn't detonate they'll move in.'

'What is *your* real objective?' asked Paula.

'Paula knows me too well.' Tweed smiled briefly. 'This has to be one of the core groups in the main operation which even Washington now suspects will be launched from the East.'

'How do you know that?' persisted Paula.

'Because I have been in touch with Cord Dillon, Deputy Director of the CIA.'

'The West is then, at long last, waking up?'

'Let's say it's stirring from its long slumber. Can't reveal any details. Marler, hand out those red berets Beck provided us with.'

'It's a fancy dress ball,' Nield said, notorious for joking at moments of high tension.'

371

'It's to save your lives,' snapped Beck. 'A lot of my men are in position, some in plain clothes, some in uniform. When the shooting starts they'll know anyone wearing a red beret is a friend.'

'If it's a shoot-out the public could be in danger,' warned Marler.

'They will be,' Beck said grimly. 'Which is why I've had the lakeside road closed at either end. Not a lot of traffic at zero hours, fortunately. If the three black cars appear—'

'*When* they appear,' Tweed interjected.

'The easily moveable barriers will disappear to let them through,' Beck continued. 'From Tweed's description of the type of thug we'll be up against it would be best to exterminate the lot. That's off the record.'

'Are you risking the *Institut* members arriving?' asked Paula.

'No!' Beck shook his head. 'I am providing plain-clothes men to impersonate them. We're sure they will be observed – probably from the lake. And that's where the main attack may come from.'

'I don't think so,' Tweed contradicted. 'Arthur Beck and I disagree on that . . .'

Beck then took Tweed's place and outlined in detail the plan the two men had worked out together in the early hours. It involved close cooperation between Tweed's team and Beck's large force. At one stage Beck handed out certificates to Tweed's group, permitting the use of firearms. Marler had earlier handed more weapons to Newman, Paula and Nield. In addition to her Browning Paula was equipped with stun and shrapnel grenades and a small pair of high-powered binoculars. Her shoulder bag was bulging, despite her removing all her personal effects.

'You all know the positions you have to occupy,' Beck concluded. 'It's getting close to zero hour.'

372

36

Three black cars drove slowly along the lakeside road from the direction of Vevey. They were well spaced out. Inside the boot of the rearmost car was a motorcycle and the lid of the boot was partly raised to accommodate the machine inside. Big Ben sat in the front passenger seat of the third car beside the driver, Les.

Ever observant, Big Ben had caught a glimpse of the barrier across the road being wheeled out of sight. His thick lips twisted into a smile as Les kept his distance from the car in front.

'They had a checkpoint. Kinda nice of them to move it out of our way.'

'Means they know we're comin'. That ain't too good,' Les replied.

'If it's across the road when we're comin' back we smash it to bits, gun down anyone who gets in our way.'

'What's the motorbike for?'

'Me.' Big Ben grinned. 'I go ahead when we leave to check out what's goin' on.'

In his lap Big Ben was holding a dark box with an aerial he could extend at the press of a switch. There was another switch – the one which, when pressed, would detonate the bomb. His plan was simple. The men in the cars ahead would lay down a field of fire if there was any opposition. Every man was armed with a machine-pistol. The combined fusillade could annihilate an army platoon.

'I see Jeff's launch out on the water,' Les remarked. 'What's his job? You don't tell us nothin' about that big launch.'

'You'll see, you'll see. We're gettin' close to where

we blow that mansion to a thousand pieces. All I needs is a signal from the front car that the big heads of the Institute have arrived. Then – *boom!*'

Tweed and Paula were crouched down on the steps in the gap in the wall leading down to a landing stage. Like everyone else they were holding specially designed scrambler mobile phones. It would be impossible for anyone to overhear their conversations. Beck, holding his own mobile, was crouched beside them.

'A man is entering the drive to the mansion,' Paula commented. 'Now another man has appeared – he's also going up the drive.'

She had pushed up her red beret slightly to give her a clear view. The two large wrought-iron gates had earlier been opened. More men arrived, turned up the drive. She counted seven entering the mansion which was a blaze of lights behind the tall windows, the lights of chandeliers. Beck was listening on his mobile. He replied, '*Bon.*'

'Three black cars have passed the checkpoint,' he told them. 'They are well spaced out. Coming from the direction of Vevey. Just a minute – look out on the lake. That big launch some distance out. It's moving in this way.'

'Ignore it,' said Tweed.

'I can't do that. I have powerful patrol boats coming in from the French side.'

He began to speak rapidly in French over the mobile. Paula was able to catch the drift of his orders. He was warning everyone the main attack could be launched from the lake, that the three black cars could be a diversion.'

'Ignore the damned launch,' snapped Tweed, who

had also understood his orders. 'The launch is the diversion. This was organized, I am sure, by the Englishman with military precision. He's trying to fool us. Make it look like a repeat performance of the attack on me at the Ermitage on Lake Zurich. That's why you are looking in the wrong direction.'

'And you think the right direction is?'

'Those three black cars approaching from Vevey. Arthur, I'll stake my reputation I'm telling you the truth.'

'Never heard you say that before.' Beck paused, then began issuing quite different instructions over the mobile which, Paula realized, were being relayed also to Beck's men surrounding the mansion – and to the whole of Tweed's team. Beck had just countermanded his previous orders, warning his men to concentrate on three black cars approaching along the lakeside road. That was when she heard the first clap of thunder.

She had been aware that the atmosphere had changed suddenly – the temperature had dropped and a strong wind was shaking the trees lining the promenade. The first clap was a mere overture. It was followed by giant rolls of thunder which continued nonstop. Forked lightning slashed down over the mountains of France and then spread over the lake itself. This was going to be a storm to remember.

'Thank the Lord we're dressed for it,' she said to Tweed.

'Let's hope so. This is going to complicate matters.'

Like the police and the other members of Tweed's team they were all wearing waterproof windcheaters. Paula buttoned hers up to the neck as large drops splashed down, then the heavens opened up. A Niagara-like cascade of rain hammered down, bouncing back off the road. The thunder increased in intensity. The forked lightning was so brilliant it illuminated the mansion like a stage set, dulling the lights inside the building.

'This is going to be a night out of hell,' said Tweed.

Just before the storm broke Les saw the driver of the first car, now in sight of the mansion, wave a hand out of his window up and down twice. He had seen seven men in business suits enter the mansion and had stopped his car.

'This is it,' said Big Ben.

He pressed down one switch, the aerial elevated. He pressed down the master switch, waited for the sound of a tremendous explosion. Nothing. No explosion. Nothing. Frantically he pressed the switch down several times. Nothing. He swore foully.

'Signal to the two cars to launch a total attack,' he yelled. 'I'm going to get on the motorbike. I can see what's happening better from it. Soon as I get it out drive forward, join the attack.'

Leaving the car, he flung open the boot, heaved out the motorcycle. Big Ben had also listened to the weather forecast and was clad in an oilskin. Dragging the machine onto the pavement, he sat astride the saddle and, for the sake of appearances, started it and rode on the pavement alongside the car, which was already moving.

The storm was now blasting down on Ouchy. As his men jumped out of the cars a stun grenade landed in front of each of the front two cars, smashing their headlights. Big Ben slowed down, stopped. There were too many figures who were not his men darting about. The men from the front car opened up with their automatic weapons. A hail of return fire flailed both cars. They had walked into a massive ambush.

Big Ben turned his machine round, sped back along

the pavement the way they had come. Both hands gripped the machine but in his left hand he held a live shrapnel grenade. Ahead of him he saw the barrier had been re-erected across the road, but it did not extend over the pavement.

His machine flew along. For a fraction of a second his left hand released his grip on the machine and he hurled the grenade at uniformed police. In the driving rain he saw figures collapsing as the grenade exploded. Then he had driven past the barrier and was heading at top speed for Vevey.

Many of Beck's men were crouched behind the wall at the side entrance to the mansion. They laid down a fusillade from their own automatic weapons at the figures which had emerged from the cars and were firing at random. Marler, always going his own way, had earlier climbed a tree lining the pavement, gripping his Armalite. He remembered the incident in France when Monceau had chosen a tree as his firing point.

'The launch is closing in on us,' shouted Beck. 'It has a lot of men on board with weapons!'

'They're all dummies,' Paula yelled back at him. She had seen the launch coming in fast. Through her binoculars, the lenses streaked with water, she had seen that none of the 'men' aboard moved, that they held their weapons in the same position, like waxwork figures.

'Look out,' roared Tweed.

One of the gang had slithered along the other side of the wall on his stomach. He had spotted the group on the steps above the landing stage. He had reached the gap, had half-stood up, was aiming his machine-pistol at them. Paula swung round, hurled her binoculars. They caught the thug on the bridge of his nose. He staggered, shook his head, then raised the machine-pistol, which had drooped. Paula shot him twice with her Browning. His hair, soaked with rain, was plastered to his skull. He reeled backwards, fell into the gutter which was a river of running water.

The crash of the thunder, never-ending, drowned the sound of continuous gunfire, so to Paula the weird scene resembled some wild chaotic ballet of men running, aiming, falling as Beck's men on the steps of the side entrance went on firing.

Perched high up in his tree, Marler was watching a cunning thug who was making his way up the opposite side of the wall, separating him from Beck's men on the other side. He saw him reach the top, reaching a high point above all Beck's concealed men. The thug stood up, gripping his machine-pistol, aiming it down at the men below him, entirely unaware of his presence. Marler already had his Armalite aimed; in the crosshairs loomed the man's chest. He pressed the trigger. The thug, about to massacre Beck's men, jerked. His machine-pistol elevated skywards for a second, then he dropped in a lifeless heap on his side of the wall.

The front black car burst into flames. The driver had forgotten to switch off his engine. By the glare of the flames Paula realized there was now no movement anywhere. The rain thrashed down on bodies lying in the road. Beck's men were moving out of the side entrance, running along the road as they checked each corpse. The Battle of Ouchy was over.

Wearily, with Tweed holding her arm, Paula trudged back to the hotel. As they passed under a street lamp a Daimler, driven by a chauffeur with a man dressed in a business suit beside him, slowly moved away in the direction of Geneva. Hassan saw Tweed and Paula, closed his eyes.

The Daimler drove at a stately pace towards the checkpoint by the marina. It was allowed to proceed as Hassan shook his head to express his horror. Paula squeezed Tweed's arm when she saw the Daimler begin to move away.

'Some bigwig has decided he doesn't like Ouchy any more . . .'

Another car, a Peugeot, had quietly driven up the side street leading to the Beau Rivage. Mario, seated behind the wheel as the rain hammered his roof, had also seen Tweed and Paula pass under the street lamp. He had been deafened by the crescendo of the storm, had been shaken by the number of bodies he had seen on the lake front. Earlier, he had passed through the marina checkpoint by saying he had a reservation at the Beau Rivage. The police had confirmed this by phoning the hotel's reservation desk. From Geneva he had called the hotel for a reservation, as had Ashley Wingfield, also known as Hassan.

'I'm soaked,' said Paula. 'All I want is a hot shower. I'll not sleep tonight.'

Over an hour later she emerged from the shower in her room, and dressed herself in day clothes after ordering coffee from room service. Looking out of her window, she saw a large dredger moving out towards the centre of the lake. She recalled that Beck had said they would remove the huge bomb by this means. She heard a familiar tapping on her door. It was Tweed, also fully dressed in day clothes after taking a long hot bath. She poured him coffee.

'Come and look out of the window,' she suggested. 'I'll turn off the lights and then we can see more clearly.'

They had stood by the window for a while, neither

379

of them saying anything, both of them surprisingly alert. The dredger, with its dreadful cargo, had moved further away until it was in the middle of the lake.

They had watched through Tweed's binoculars until it got well clear. The historic thunderstorm had abated and it was strangely quiet in the early hours of the morning. Paula poured more coffee and they both drank in silence.

'I won't expect you up very early in the morning – this morning,' said Tweed.

'I think I'll suddenly cave in. What's happening?'

'I expect Beck's explosives expert has rigged up his own radio-control device to explode the bomb. You realize they have lowered it into the lake.'

'No. It must have been while I was pouring more coffee.'

She had hardly spoken when there was a tremendous eruption in the lake. They heard a muffled thump. This was followed by a gigantic upheaval. A portion of the lake climbed vertically into the night, a huge billowing fountain which, by Tweed's estimate, far exceeded the famous sixty-foot-high fountain off the shore of Geneva. It mounted higher and higher as tons of water were lifted to an incredible height. Then the elevated man-made fountain, like a colossal geyser, began to fall. They stood still as it generated giant waves which rolled majestically towards the shore and then crashed against the lake wall, hurling more water into the road.

'That was some bomb,' said Tweed.

37

'Tina Langley is in this hotel at this moment.'

Beck gave the news to Tweed after knocking on his door the day after the carnage. It was eight o'clock in the morning and when Tweed opened the door to the police chief he was fully dressed and his eyes behind his horn-rims gleamed with alertness and energy. A couple of minutes earlier Paula had arrived.

'How do you know?' Tweed asked in an off-hand manner.

'Because one of my men carrying her photo saw her hurrying back to her room. Presumably her curiosity had overcome her caution since she appeared to have returned from a walk along the lake front. I propose to arrest her and interrogate her until she breaks.'

'*Don't do that, Arthur.*' Tweed's tone had changed, had become determined. 'Instead, if she leaves here have her followed by some of your best men.'

'Sorry, Paula.' Beck remembered his manners, turning to talk to her. 'I hope you are recovering from last night.'

'This morning's experience? My brain won't settle, is racing at top speed. Thank you for the enquiry.'

'I don't like it,' Beck snapped, swinging on his heel to face Tweed. 'She's a murderess.'

'She's also a key player in the worldwide drama which is unfolding. She may well lead me to the heart of this enormous conspiracy which threatens the West.' Tweed's voice rose as he hammered at the police chief. 'You've had elite men in our civilization assassinated in Switzerland. You've had an orgy of violence not a quarter of a mile from where you're standing. Don't spoil a major victory.'

'Victory?' queried Beck in a puzzled tone.

'You wiped out one of the hardest cores of the opposition. Those men in the black cars were, I am certain, intended to take part in a much more dangerous operation. So leave Tina Langley alone, but don't let her out of your sight when she moves on, as I know she will. They don't call her The Butterfly for nothing.'

'Reluctantly I'll agree. Now, do you want the bad news?'

'You're so reassuring,' Paula half-joked. 'I think I'm going to need more strong coffee for breakfast.'

'Tell me,' Tweed said quietly.

'Pete Nield gave me a clear description of Big Ben. You told me, Tweed, that he was likely to be the top man.'

'What about him?'

'We have examined all the corpses – now in the morgue – and not one of them bears the slightest resemblance to him. Big Ben somehow escaped last night.'

'The worst of the lot. Well, I suppose at some later stage we will meet the gentleman in question again.'

'I've thought about Tina Langley,' Beck said slowly. 'You are usually right in your decisions. I will put my best trackers on her. If she moves on I'll call you. We need a code word for her. I suggest Jungfrau, which in German means young lady.'

'I know it does.'

'Hardly appropriate,' said Beck with a dry smile. 'Now I must get back to work . . .'

'At least he showed a certain sense of humour,' Paula commented when he'd gone. 'Jungfrau indeed.'

Marler, never a man to indulge in wastefulness, had spent half the night carrying a satchel he had fetched from his room. He wore his red beret as he had quietly mixed with the police who were collecting bodies. When unobserved he had picked up some of the weapons lying everywhere, especially automatic weapons which he had secreted in his satchel.

The fact that a number of the weapons would be marked with fingerprints normally used in evidence bothered him not at all. Who would need evidence when Big Ben's gang were all corpses soon to be on their way to the morgue?

His task was made easier because many of the police realized he had saved their lives by shooting the member of the gang who had made his way to the top of the wall enclosing the entrance at the side. His last trip was to follow the route the thug had taken up the side of the wall. The body had been taken away and there were no police about as he shielded the beam of a small torch to search the ground. Behind a rock he found a collection of magazines which the thug had dropped ready to reload his weapon. Marler scooped them up, added them to the collection inside his satchel.

He walked back to the hotel with an unlit king-size between his lips. Once inside his room he repacked his new armoury. He then took a long hot shower after casting off his sodden clothes.

'There'll be another time, another place, another gang,' he'd said to himself.

Paula, after eating a much larger breakfast than she'd thought she could manage, had told Tweed she was going to sit in the hotel gardens by herself reading her book. She didn't tell him she was suffering from a reaction to what had happened or that she felt a desperate need for sleep.

She found it soothing to wander in the grounds,

which resembled a vast park with many different levels of lawns and flower beds. She had deliberately left behind in the lobby the newspaper which carried banner headlines.

Sitting on a secluded seat, she ran her fingers through her hair, stifled a yawn. She was dozing off, the book in her lap, when a gentle hand grasped her shoulder. She knew it was Tweed before she opened her eyes. He sat down beside her.

'I imagine your bag is packed for instant departure? I told everyone else to be ready to leave at a moment's notice.'

'My case is packed. Except for toilet things. I imagine that nothing is going to happen today.'

'I'm afraid it has happened already. Are you very short of sleep?'

'I was. Now I've had a snooze in the sun I feel much better. So what has happened?'

'Beck called me. He said Jungfrau has left the hotel. While she was having breakfast in the main dining room Beck sent a man to her room to tap her phone. He thought the management wouldn't appreciate anyone listening in on a guest's calls.'

'So she did call someone?'

'She has ordered a hotel limo to drive her to Cointrin Airport in Geneva. She has booked a Business Class ticket on a flight to Zurich. A man who gave no name phoned her, told her to reach Zurich as soon as she could. Then she had to phone him again from Zurich airport. His English was just a little too upper crust. He was obviously disguising his voice.'

'We're moving on, then?'

'Yes. But we'll be travelling in the hired cars to Zurich. Marler apparently is carrying enough weapons to start a small war. So he drives there alone in the other

384

car. I will drive with you, Bob and Nield as passengers. Are you sure you're all right?'

'Quite sure. I told you – I had a snooze. You know if I have a nap I can keep going for hours. Stop worrying about me,' she said with a hint of irritation.

'We'll leave by the front entrance thirty minutes from now. I tried to get Amos and Willie on the phone, thinking maybe Willie'd returned to the Dolder Grand. Neither of them appear to be in Zurich.'

'Just don't say it's significant. I keep thinking about Christopher Kane.'

'So do I. He didn't answer my call either.'

'It's strange that all three men have vanished into the blue at the same time.'

'It's very strange . . .'

It was another gloriously sunny day as Tweed drove his three companions to Zurich. There was little conversation because they realized that Tweed was deep in thought as he handled the car expertly. Beside him, Paula had closed her eyes again but she was still awake. She was marvelling at Tweed's stamina; she had lost track of how little sleep he had enjoyed. It did not surprise her. On other occasions she had known Tweed summon up endless reserves of energy in an emergency. And it told her that there was a grave emergency facing them.

'I had a phone call from Harry this morning,' Nield whispered to Newman. 'Again he coded his message, which was brief. The gist was that most of the remaining staff at the Château d'Avignon had disappeared early this morning. Just enough left to keep the place barely going, I gathered.'

'Big Ben is assembling a second hard core of thugs,' called out Tweed, who had heard every word. 'I'd very much like to know where Big Ben is now.'

385

'Probably scuttering off back to Britain,' Nield suggested.

'I don't think so,' Tweed replied.

'We're staying at the Baur au Lac again, I presume,' said Newman.

'You presume wrong. I want to lie low, out of sight this time. We'll be staying at the Zum Storchen, a good hotel in the Old Town on the banks of the River Limmat.'

He then lapsed into silence and no one else spoke. Paula had taken in this information and wondered what Tweed was up to now. She had no doubt he had a clear plan for the next move but she couldn't work out what it might be. She sagged against the headrest and suddenly fell fast asleep.

At the Château d'Avignon Harry Butler was again displaying the patience of Job. He had no one to talk to – the few remaining guests were all French. Harry could understand what was being said but his command of the language was not sufficient for him to carry on a proper conversation.

He spent part of his time in his room reading a new manual on high explosives and how to handle the latest inventions. At breakfast he had noticed how few staff were left, but he had already covered this development by his brief call to Pete Nield at des Avenières the previous evening.

After lunch he went for a brisk walk. As he passed reception Fred Brown leaned over the counter. He gave Butler his oily smile.

'Taking the exercise, are we?'

'Stretching the legs. I had an accident I'm recovering from,' Butler lied.

It gave a reason for staying on by himself, he thought, as he checked his watch and walked along the deserted road in the direction of Geneva. It was cooler under the tunnel of trees overhead. When he reached his objective – the track leading into the forest where he had concealed a motorcycle – he walked straight past, but checked his watch.

Five minutes from the d'Avignon. Running, he reckoned he could cut that down to two minutes. Harry had not spun a yarn when he'd told Oily Fred he was stretching his legs. He was also keeping in trim for the mad dash he foresaw when he had planted Marler's bomb.

Returning to the hotel, he slowed to a walk before passing between the open gates. He had run all the way back, again checking his watch as he ran past the track from the opposite direction. He glanced at the watch as he sat down by himself on the terrace. Just over two minutes.

One thing Harry was careful not to do during all the time he spent on the terrace was so much as glance up at the turret containing the communications equipment.

Tina Langley disembarked from her flight which had taken her from Geneva to Kloten Airport, Zurich. She now had to find a phone to call Hassan at the Dolder Grand. She had no idea that Hassan had arrived in Zurich on the flight before the one she had taken.

Wearing a rather daring Versace number she put down her Louis Vuitton case, took out a mirror from her handbag and started to apply lipstick. Her eyes were scanning the airport concourse and she noticed a well-dressed man looking at her. He'd had something in his hand which she felt sure was a photograph.

Helmut Keller was one of Beck's senior detectives assigned to check passengers coming off this flight. He had made the mistake of glancing at the photo because

Tina also wore a stylish hat with a turned-down brim. Keller had also been momentarily distracted by her good figure. The expensive suit had been loaned to him by Beck to perfect his cover.

Saucily, Tina walked up to him, carrying her case. She passed close enough to him so he caught a faint whiff of her perfume. The photo was held in the hand behind his back. She snatched it from him, stared at it. Startled, he swung round. She gave him a seductive smile.

'Have you seen this woman?' she asked. 'It's my twin sister and she phoned me to say she was having a problem.'

'Twin sister?'

Keller was confused. He was dazzled by her. This was the last development he had expected. Had there been some frightful mistake?

'Twin sister, I said,' Tina continued, pursuing her advantage as she sensed his confused state. 'Rosemary.'

'Rosemarie?'

'She's English. What are you doing with her photograph? Now you have *me* worried.'

'We wish to interview her.'

'So who is "we"?'

'A private investigation agency,' said Keller, recovering his wits.

'Oh, my Lord. She hasn't passed another dud cheque, has she?'

'Dud cheque?'

'Maybe that's why she ran out on me from the Hôtel des Bergues in Geneva. I knew she was up to something. Poor Rosemary. She sometimes uses the name Tina. Now I'm really worried. And I have an appointment with a director at the Zurcher Kredit Bank.'

'Your sister is still in Geneva?'

'She must be. On top of that she's having an affair with a Swiss banker. You can keep the photo. I must run.'

Keller's head was reeling. He had been so struck by this woman he'd been wondering whether he dare ask her out to dinner. Then duty asserted itself. He decided he'd better call Beck who had arrived in Zurich by car.

Out of sight of Keller, Tina had got into a taxi and told the driver to take her to the Eden au Lac, the only other good hotel she could think of on the spur of the moment. She must avoid the Baur au Lac at all costs.

Tina was a little disappointed. Keller had been a handsome man and his clothes suggested money. She had read his mind and guessed he had been wondering whether to invite her out. Bloody Hassan could have waited if she'd found she had hooked a big fish. But now she knew they were looking for her all over Switzerland. She had not forgotten the tail in Geneva she had recently lured aboard an express train.

'Mario, now you've had some sleep tell me again in full detail about this outrage in Ouchy.'

In his room at the Baur au Lac Emilio Vitorelli was sipping a drink while his subordinate sat down and reached for the bottle on the table. Vitorelli shook his head.

'No alcohol until you have given me the full story. There is a long report in a late edition of the newspaper. But you were there. Tell me about the bomb.'

'Bomb? I don't know anything about a bomb. When the shooting stopped I went straight to my room at the Beau Rivage—'

'Your windows faced the lake?'

'No, the front of the hotel where you arrive.'

'Pity. I am very interested in that bomb.'

'And then I left the hotel in the early morning when you called me, told me to come here.'

'Just tell me what you did see.'

Mario repeated in greater detail what he had seen. When, dog-tired, he had arrived at the Baur au Lac he had given his boss a briefer version of the night's events. Vitorelli had then told him to get some sleep and they would talk later. Mario eventually came to the point where he had seen Tweed passing under a lamp with an attractive woman.

'*Stop!*' Vitorelli stroked his shaggy hair, leaned forward to listen more intently. 'You're sure it was Tweed?'

'Yes, you pointed him out to me when I was last at this hotel.'

'Tweed. I see everything now. In the paper it reports that a huge bomb placed under the mansion where the *Institut* meets was immobilized. After the killing was over – doubtless the attack was the work of The Sisterhood – they transported the bomb aboard a dredger into the middle of the lake. There it was lowered to a great depth, then detonated. A police photographer has supplied this picture of the bomb exploding.'

He passed to Mario the newspaper. Under the glaring headline was the picture of the immense fountain of water the bomb's detonation had created. Mario lifted his eyebrows.

'That must have been a great bomb.'

'You could create such a bomb?'

'With the right materials – including a radio-control device and plenty of advance warning.'

'And several thermite bombs?'

'Fire bombs would be easier still.'

'Tweed,' said Vitorelli, changing the subject. 'Tweed,' he repeated. 'I understand now. He planned an elaborate trap for The Sisterhood's gang. He worked in cooperation with the police. Doubtless with the top man, Beck. Tell your network to locate Tweed. Then you prepare the bombs.'

'The target? I need to know the target.'

'I have no idea. Yet. Use your imagination.'

'You're not saying you've lost her?'

Beck's voice was steely over the phone as he sat in his office at police headquarters in Zurich. He could hardly believe what Helmut Keller was reporting from the airport.

'She talked about this twin sister. So I thought—'

'No, you didn't think! You were so dazzled by Tina Langley you couldn't do your duty. Twin sister, indeed. How was she dressed?'

Beck's expression became cynical as Keller gave a highly detailed description of the glamorous outfit Tina had been wearing. He realized now how easy it must have been for her to deceive Norbert Engel and then blow off the back of his head in Vienna. This was a siren of sirens.

'All right, Keller. I'm sending two men to replace you. Now. They'll arrive in about fifteen minutes. Hand over the photo to them. Clever of you to get it back from her,' he said with withering sarcasm. 'When the two replacements arrive you go home. Where do you think she went?'

'She probably headed for the taxi rank . . .'

'We can check that, find out where she went. But it will take time. Of course, you didn't ask to see her passport?'

'No. Your instructions were not to intercept her. Just to keep her under surveillance, check her movements.'

'You got one thing right, then. When the replacements arrive you go home, as I said before. You're suspended.'

Beck stood up, crossed to the window, stared down at the River Limmat and the University on the far bank. He was uncertain what to do next. When his phone rang he was relieved to hear Tweed's voice.

'We're back in Zurich. Staying this time at the Zum Storchen. Thank you again for your cooperation in Ouchy.'

'Forget it. Tina Langley is floating round Zurich again. I had a call from the airport.'

He told Tweed about the call from Keller. When he had given him all the details of the incident he exploded. 'What is it with this woman? Does she hypnotize men?'

'Quite often she does exactly that. I'm sure she's had a lot of experience in that field of activity. That was a good idea to send two different men to the airport. If she leaves here I'm sure she'll fly out. She'll probably move further east. That suits me – just so long as she's followed. I suggest one of your two men checks passengers arriving for departure and the other one stays in the background, ready to board the same flight she eventually takes.'

'I'm sure you're still her main target,' Beck warned.

'I'm going monastic – avoiding all attractive women.'

Arriving at the Eden au Lac, The Butterfly booked a suite in the name Lisa Vane. Once she was alone in the suite she called Ashley Wingfield at the Dolder Grand. Hassan came on the line immediately.

'I've arrived in Zurich,' she said quickly. 'Staying at the Eden au Lac. I think they're looking for me at the airport,' she lied. 'I saw a man in a business suit

392

checking a photo. Fortunately I was dressed very differently and I was wearing a floppy hat to conceal my hair.'

'You're sure you were not recognized?'

'Quite sure.' The Butterfly made a suggestion typical of the way her mind worked. 'I think I should move from here.'

'Change your clothes first. Tell reception you've just had an urgent call to return to London . . .'

'That's where I'm going?' she asked eagerly.

'No. You come to the Dolder Grand. Get one taxi to take you to Parade-Platz in the centre of the city. Wait until it has gone. Then get another taxi to bring you here. If you see me in a public room ignore me. Sooner or later I'll come to your room. Register as Lisa Vane. If you want food—'

'I need a drink.'

'Get drunk, then, but do it in your room. Now, *move!*'

Hassan, from his suite in the Dolder Grand, shouted the last words down the phone. He slammed the phone down with such force he almost broke it. Jumping up, he began prowling round the room, wishing he could smash some of the ornaments. His face was contorted into an expression of ferocity.

He was known – and feared – back east in his home state for these unpredictable and dangerous outbursts. He had once clubbed to death a colonel who had answered him back. His father, the Head of State, had felt compelled to cover up the murder. He had arranged for the body of the colonel to be taken out into the desert aboard a tank. The colonel's corpse had then been laid out on the sand and the tank's caterpillar tracks had rolled back and forth over it to account for the savagery of the blows the body had endured. The colonel had been a popular man in the military and his death was reported as a tragic accident while on manoeuvres.

It was the huge fiasco in Ouchy which had gradually built up Hassan's inhuman rage. With his own eyes he had seen Tweed walking back to the hotel. Tweed. Always it was Tweed who had upset the Englishman's carefully laid plans transmitted to Hassan.

'May he rot in hell,' he growled as he moved round the suite.

He had ordered Tina to come to the Dolder Grand with the idea that she might be able to locate Tweed, to blow his head to smithereens. A large vase perched on a table grazed his elbow as he continued prowling. With a shriek of rage he grasped the heavy vase, hurled it against a wall where it burst into fragments.

In his imagination he had pictured the giant bomb lifting the mansion into the air, scattering it far and wide, annihilating the remaining members of the *Institut*. Including Tweed. Now he had read in the newspaper that no members of the *Institut* still alive had travelled anywhere near Ouchy. He suspected – and he was right – that Tweed had phoned each member and told them to leave Switzerland immediately.

His large hands clenched and unclenched, as though he was in the act of strangling Tweed with his bare hands. For the moment Hassan had gone berserk – as he had when he clubbed the colonel to death.

At the Zum Storchen Tweed sat on a balcony overlooking the Limmat flowing past below with Paula seated at the same table. At that hour in the scorching afternoon only one other person sat on the balcony at a table at the other end. The ever-watchful Marler.

'You are carrying out a plan, I'm sure,' said Paula.

'Yes, I am. I'm waging psychological warfare. My aim is to demoralize and destabilize the enemy. I want to throw him off balance, to break his nerve by pounding him with blow after blow. Then his judgement and self-control will snap.'

'And we are now succeeding.'

'Yes. To start with he was doing well. Key members of the *Institut* were being assassinated by The Sisterhood. Eight of them were killed. Suddenly the balance swings the other way. The Sisterhood is on the run, which is what I intended. Then a hard core of what, I'm sure, were his top thugs was sent to Ouchy. With the exception of Big Ben all of them are now dead. And his attempt to destroy the rest of the *Institut* with the bomb has failed.'

'What is our next move?'

'We are systematically driving surviving members of The Sisterhood further east. It would not surprise me if Karin Berg and Simone Carnot were now in Vienna. It may be more tricky to break the Englishman's nerve – the key figure in all their planning, I am sure.'

'Which means Amos or Willie. Or possibly Christopher.'

'Or someone we know nothing about yet, but someone who lives in Dorset,' Tweed replied.

'Well, Christopher doesn't.'

'Christopher rents a small cottage north of Dorchester. I heard this from Monica when I spoke to her while we were in France.'

'You have a good idea who it is?' she suggested.

'The field remains wide open.'

'So what do we do now? Apart from enjoying a wonderful rest in this super hotel?'

'It has the great advantage of being tucked away in the Altstadt. The Old City is a maze of streets.'

'But I think you are waiting for something to happen.'

'I am waiting for The Butterfly to take wing again.'

38

In her suite at the Eden au Lac Tina changed into a less glamorous outfit. For once she didn't want to be noticed. Checking her appearance in the bathroom, she swallowed the contents of a miniature cognac, drinking from the bottle. She had pinched it from the minibar in her room at the Hôtel des Bergues in Geneva. She had told reception at that hotel that she hadn't used the minibar. Always prepared to spend a small fortune on a couturier dress, she was mean when it came to paying for something she could have for nothing.

'I'm sorry, but I've had an urgent message to return to London,' she told reception over the phone.

'We understand. There will be no charge for the suite.'

'Most kind of you. Could you call me a taxi?'

As she was leaving she failed to notice a small plump man who sat reading a newspaper. Detective Windlin casually followed her out as she climbed into a waiting taxi. An unmarked police car pulled in at the kerb and Windlin jumped in beside the driver.

'Don't lose that taxi. Beck would not be pleased . . .'

Beck had moved with great speed after hearing of the arrival of Tina Langley. With her photograph in front of him he phoned in quick succession the Baur au Lac, the Baur en Ville, the Dolder Grand, the Eden au

Lac. In each case he gave the concierge a brief description of Tina, emphasizing she would have arrived within the hour if she was staying there. He struck gold at the Eden au Lac.

'Yes, sir,' the concierge informed him in a low voice, 'a lady of that description has just arrived. She has gone up to her suite.'

Beck instantly dispatched Detective Windlin to the hotel. Like many plump men Windlin was surprisingly swift on his feet. When the taxi they were following reached Parade-Platz and Tina paid it off he was out of his car in seconds. He stood at a tram stop, watching Tina, who bought a magazine off a bookstall until her taxi had disappeared. She then hailed another and as she climbed inside Windlin was already seated again next to his driver.

'Tricky, this one,' Windlin commented. 'Beck is clever. You know who we are following?'

'No idea.'

'Tina Langley. I have her photo in my pocket. Half the force in Switzerland is looking for her.'

'We arrest the lady?'

'We do nothing of the sort. We track her, then report back to Beck over the radio.'

In his room at Zum Storchen Tweed hurried to answer the phone. He liked the hotel – it had a certain atmosphere remote from the powerhouse of Zurich with its crowds, its rumbling trams and dense traffic.

'Yes?'

'Beck here. The Butterfly had just moved from the Eden au Lac and has arrived at the Dolder Grand.'

'So she obviously feels she still has unfinished business here.'

397

'You, would be my guess,' Beck said grimly.

'I think I rather fancy a visit to the Dolder Grand. It's a unique hotel. Where all the bankers dine.'

'I suppose if I asked you not to go I'd be wasting my breath.'

'Politely put, yes you would. I'll be going there shortly. And thank you for the information.'

'I should never have told you . . .'

Tweed was just about to leave his room when Paula arrived. As he opened the door to her she stared hard at him. When she was inside she folded her arms and tackled him.

'I know that expression. You're up to something.'

'Beck has just phoned to tell me Tina has moved into the Dolder Grand. I'm going up there to have a chat with her. I want to get her moving again.'

'You don't think you're going by yourself? Promise me you'll wait here until I get back. I'm just going to my room.'

'You do bully me.'

'Only way to make you see sense.'

When she reappeared she was not alone. Both Newman and Marler were with her. Tweed frowned and lifted his hands in protest.

'I don't need a delegation.'

'You're getting one,' Paula told him. 'Marler will be acting as chauffeur. You had enough driving getting us here from Ouchy. Bob has never seen the Dolder Grand. He's just coming along for the ride.'

'If I believed that I'd believe anything!'

As they left the hotel Paula looked round, appreciating the character of the Old Town. The buildings were ancient, built of stone quarried hundreds of years ago. The streets, narrow and twisting, were paved with worn cobbles. To her right the River Limmat flowed between the banks of the two Old Towns of Zurich, the other being across the water. It was a scene of stability and history with hardly anyone about. Beneath the hotel was a covered walk alongside the river. I must explore that, she thought, as Marler drove up with the car. She was very quiet as she got into the back with Tweed.

As Marler drove them away she had a weird feeling that something extraordinary was about to happen. She had no idea what it might be, but the feeling persisted after they had crossed the Limmat and started to climb up the lower slopes of the Zurichberg, the high and dominating hill which overlooks Zurich. Soon the houses were spread out further from each other, had become massive old villas behind railed walls. Then they were travelling through a fir forest with here and there an exceptionally large villa perched higher and well back from the curving, climbing road.

Below she began to get glimpses of the aged buildings and church spires of Zurich, all jammed together. There were other glimpses – of the lake, a sparkling blue under the sun searing down. Tweed nudged her.

'We're coming to the bottom of the funicular. You can use that to get up to the Dolder Grand.'

'What's the point? Coming down you'd find yourself halfway up the Zurichberg.'

'I've often thought of that myself . . .'

They climbed higher and the white stone palace of the Dolder Grand came into view. It had turrets with strange stiletto-shaped spires. Paula's feeling that they were approaching something ominous intensified.

Tweed led the way into a huge lounge furnished with antiques and deep-pile carpet. Several chairs and couches were occupied by distinguished-looking men and women. When they spoke their voices were little more than whispers.

399

A man had entered the lounge at the same moment as Tweed. Of medium height, his clean-shaven complexion was very brown and smooth. He was wearing an Armani suit and suddenly he saw Tweed. He stood stock-still and gazed across the room as though he could hardly believe what he was looking at. Tweed kept his voice low as he spoke to a middle-aged waiter.

'I think I know that gentleman over there. His name escapes me for the moment.'

'Mr Ashley Wingfield. He stays with us occasionally. A most courteous man.'

Tweed was also standing stock-still, hands inside his jacket pockets. His eyes never left the strange pallid eyes staring back at him like a man hypnotized. There was expression in those eyes – disbelief, then hatred, then blankness. The man called Ashley Wingfield had a plumpish face but there was a hint of strong cheekbones which suggested to Tweed the Middle East. Years before at Scotland Yard Tweed had been known for his flashes of insight. He was experiencing just such a flash now. This was the barbaric man behind The Sisterhood. Tweed went forward.

Paula was so disturbed she moved to one side, her right hand inside her shoulder bag, gripping the Browning. Newman moved in the other direction, so at a distance they flanked the two men. Marler leant against a wall, an unlit king-size between his lips.

'Mr Ashley Wingfield, I believe,' said Tweed. 'I am Tweed.'

Hassan, still recovering from the episode in his room when he had gone berserk, smashing the vase against a wall, could hardly speak. Their eyes were still locked.

'I am pleased to meet you, sir,' said Hassan in a choked voice. 'You strike me as an important man, but I regret I have so far not heard of you.'

'Or of what I do?'

'Please tell me.'

It can't be, Paula was thinking. He looks so dapper in his smart suit. She noticed the man had thrust his very dark brown hands inside his jacket pockets. Tweed, she thought, looks so poised, so in command of himself. Wingfield looked as though he might recently have had a fit. The hands which were now out of sight had been trembling. With rage. Why do I think that?

'I don't like any kind of dramatic language,' Tweed went on. 'But perhaps you should call me Nemesis. That is what I do – I destroy evil men.'

'You . . . what?'

Hassan's eyes were blinking as though he had a nervous twitch. He was struggling to control his manic fury. Something about Tweed's personality made him feel at a disadvantage, a unique experience for a man accustomed to unquestioning obedience and servility from all those around him. He had an overwhelming desire to dominate this man, but he felt incapable of exerting the necessary force of will. He controlled the blinking but he was growing more and more nervous of the expression in the eyes staring into his.

'You expect to stay in Zurich long?' he managed to say.

'Further and further east,' Tweed told him softly.

'I beg your pardon, sir?'

'You will retreat – further and further east. Massive forces in the West are stirring. You are too late.'

'I do not understand.'

'I think you do.'

Tweed turned on his heel, walked slowly towards the exit from the lounge. Hassan remained like a man carved out of stone, still standing quite still, the blankness remaining on his incredibly smooth face. Paula remained where she was, as did Newman and Marler. They were guarding Tweed's back.

401

The guests in the lounge had stopped talking. Like Hassan they were like figures carved out of stone. They had not heard a word of the confrontation, but the large room was full of an electric tension which everyone could sense. It was like the moment when people see a bomb falling from a plane and freeze.

Hassan suddenly came to life, left the lounge by the distant door he had entered by. Newman nodded to Paula to follow Tweed, which she did quickly. He walked slowly after her as Marler lit his cigarette, bowed to the guests, then made his way to the car.

39

Leaving the lounge, Hassan hurried to Tina Langley's room. He was on the verge of hammering his clenched fist against the door when he paused. He had to get control of himself. Taking a deep breath, he tapped lightly.

'Oh, it's you . . .'

He pushed her aside without ceremony, slammed the door shut behind him. He took another deep breath and rushed round the room. His expression was vicious. He had his back to her and forced himself to look calm.

'You're shaking,' Tina said. 'What's wrong?'

'Where is the Luger I gave you? Tweed is downstairs. He is just leaving the hotel. Where is the bloody Luger?'

'In that drawer you are leaning against. Beneath some of my underclothes.'

She stopped speaking. Hassan had hauled open the drawer. He was hauling out her underclothes, hurling them onto the floor. She opened her mouth to protest, then decided against saying a word. Hassan had found the Luger, checked quickly to make sure it was loaded.

He had wrapped a silk vest round his hand to hold the gun. He ran over to her, shoved the Luger at her.

'Take it! Tweed will be getting into his car. He must have come by car. Go down now and shoot him. What's the matter with you?'

Tina had stepped backwards away from him. She leant against the bathroom door. She was on the verge of hysteria. Her expression was a mixture of fear and anger.

'You've gone over the top. The hotel is full of staff and guests. How the hell could I get away if I did manage to shoot him? Don't you realize you would be involved? The police would question everybody in the hotel. Look at my hand. It's trembling. I couldn't even aim the gun, quite apart from pull the trigger. You always take care to be nowhere near an assassination.'

Hassan's mood changed. She had experienced this before. At one moment he was in a titanic rage, then he was calm and so cool. He smiled at her, then he grinned and went on grinning.

'It was a good joke, was it not?'

'Joke?' Her saucy nature asserted itself. 'One thing is for sure. You would never earn your living as a comic.'

'You think I am comic?' he asked indignantly.

'Sometimes you are. Hassan—'

'Ashley.'

'OK. Ashley, you are a man of many talents. You have such a powerful personality.' She smiled seductively. 'That is why you are who you are. A great man.'

'I hope to be. Now, let us be practical. You must unload the Luger, then get rid of the gun and the bullets.'

'I put them in the rubbish bin?' she asked with mock innocence, knowing she now had the upper hand.

'There is forest all around us. Take them for a walk. Dump them under some bushes. Just get rid of them.'

'Thank you so much. I'll do what I can.'

'Tweed has been here,' he said seriously. 'Zurich is no longer safe. It is time you left this city.'

'I can't wait to get out of the place. And you have spoilt my best underclothes. They cost a lot of money.'

She began gathering up the clothes he had hurled onto the floor. Folding them neatly, she put them back into the drawer. He watched her and then realized perspiration was pouring off his forehead and into his eyes. Taking out a large embroidered silk handkerchief, he mopped his forehead and face.

'You did say it was time I left Zurich,' she prodded him.

'I think you should leave as soon as possible. Today would be best. Yes, today. I will book you a seat on the next flight.'

'Where to?'

'Vienna. You will be met by a driver and car at Schwechat airport. A room will be reserved for you at the Sacher.'

'Vienna?' she repeated nervously. 'That's where Norbert Engel died . . .'

'Where you killed him,' Hassan said viciously. 'You will not stay in Vienna for long. You will be moved to a safer place. Now, get on with your packing. I will contact you again very shortly.'

'That was one of the most gripping experiences of my life,' said Paula as Marler began driving back down to Zurich. 'The way you looked at that man. He was terrified.'

'That man,' Tweed said slowly, 'is the enemy. I recognized him from photographs I've seen in our files. His name is Hassan, the eldest son of the Head of

404

State of one of the most dangerous powers in the world now.'

'I heard you say "further and further east",' commented Newman. 'You repeated the phrase. What are you planning?'

'A double trap. I think I unnerved him sufficiently for him to leave Zurich and fly east. That is exactly what I want him to do. He knows I will come after him so, when he thinks it over, he will believe he has a chance to lure me into *his* trap. East is where he feels at home, has Heaven knows how many men at his disposal who will kill at a word from him. Also he'll become nervous at the presence of Tina Langley in the same hotel. I expect him to send her east. When we reach police headquarters . . .'

'Now I know where I'm going,' Marler called out cynically.

'I was about to tell you. When we reach our destination I'll ask Beck to have his men at the airport check on any flight reservations made from the Dolder Grand. Also they must keep a close lookout for Tina Langley. And I'll give Beck a description of Ashley Wingfield, also known as Hassan.'

'Why not have him arrested and interrogated?' Paula wanted to know.

'Because we have no evidence against him. Also, arresting him would cause a diplomatic incident. But the main reason is I need him on the loose to see what he's up to.'

'That scene in the lounge at the Dolder Grand was very tense,' Paula recalled. 'The guests couldn't hear what was said but they were affected by the atmosphere. They all fell silent.'

'So let us hope Hassan was equally affected . . .'

* * *

Big Ben had to make an effort to phone the Englishman at the telephone and room numbers he had been given. The intention had been for him to report his success at Ouchy.

'Yes,' the Englishman replied to his call. 'I recognize your voice. Where are you?'

'I've taken a room at the Bellevue Palace in Berne. I had to get here during the night on a motorcycle. It didn't go well . . .'

'It did not. I read the newspapers. Who survived?'

'Well, I did. And Les, the knife-thrower, is here in another room. He hijacked a—'

'Shut up! You seem to have kept your nerve. What about Les?'

'He's OK.'

'This is what you do. Later you will take charge of another unit. Buy some good clothes, a decent suitcase. You have plenty of money?'

'I raided the safe at d'Avignon before we left to—'

'Stop gabbling. When you both have bought clothes you board an express from Berne station, a nonstop to Zurich. Come out of the main station, cross the road and book rooms at the Schweizerhof Hotel opposite. I'll contact you there.'

'Everything here is Switzer . . .'

'Schweizerhof, idiot. I'll spell it.'

Big Ben put down the phone and drank some more beer from a bottle he had taken from the minibar. He had a room which had windows overlooking the river Aare below. In the distance a panorama only seen in the best of weather stretched west and east – the majestic peaks of the Bernese Oberland, one of the great sights of Europe.

Big Ben hadn't even noticed it. Views were not his cup of tea, unless they were of ladies' legs. His talents lay in running a gang of killers. He burped, and went along to another room to give Les his orders.

Simone Carnot had disobeyed the order she had received over the phone from Hassan while at the Château des Avenières. When he had instructed her to move to the Beau Rivage at Ouchy she had had her doubts.

Unlike The Butterfly she disliked always being on the move and she was anxious to get out of France. She could never forget that in Paris she had left behind an unsolved murder – the murder of her married lover. Without informing Hassan she drove her hired car to Geneva's airport. There she handed in the car and flew to Zurich.

She had phoned the Baur au Lac from the airport and a room was waiting for her when she arrived at the hotel. She was brushing her flame of red hair, which so attracted men, when she decided to risk trying to contact Hassan. After all, he didn't own her. She had simply carried out 'assignments' for him – successfully killing two members of the *Institut*. He had paid her the large sums owing to her and this gave her a feeling of independence. On the off-chance she called the Dolder Grand.

She was checking her appearance in the dressing-table mirror when, to her surprise, Hassan came on the line when she asked for Mr Ashley Wingfield.

'Simone, where have you been?' he snapped.

She didn't know she was contacting him only an hour or so after his confrontation with Tweed, followed by the argument with Tina. His emotions were still a mixture of rage and doubt.

'I'm at the Baur au Lac . . .'

'What?'

'If you're in a bad mood I'll call you back,' she said quietly.

'Stay on the line!' Hassan forced himself to calm down. 'I've been up all night. Tell me what has happened.'

'I've only been here a short while. Reading the papers, it's a good job I didn't go to Ouchy. It sounds horrific.'

'We won't talk about that,' he said persuasively. 'Thank you for calling me. I was worried about you. Give me a moment to think.'

A jumble of thoughts passed through Hassan's disturbed mind and then he began to think clearly. The news that another member of The Sisterhood was in Zurich – at the same time as Tweed – was dangerous. His mind cleared and he took a decision.

'Simone, it is going to be safer for you if you do not spend too much time in Zurich. I have my reasons for saying that. I want you to fly to Vienna. I will send you your ticket and flight details by courier. A car will be waiting for you at the other end. A room will be booked for you at the Sacher.'

'You have another assignment for me?' she asked.

'I may have, but it will be up to you whether you accept it or not. In any case you will receive a generous fee.'

He had to wait for her to reply. Simone had once visited Vienna on a business trip. It had struck her as a city where you could easily get lost from the world. And Hassan had given her the option as to whether she undertook another assignment or not. She applied lipstick while she decided whether leaving Zurich would be sensible. At the other end of the line Hassan was forcing himself to control his natural impatience. Instinctively he felt it would be unwise to upset her.

'I'll fly to Vienna,' she said eventually. 'So send me the ticket.'

'In the meantime may I suggest you stay in your room? You can use room service for meals.'

'I'll do that,' she agreed, having no intention of carrying out his suggestion.

In his suite at the Dolder Grand Hassan mopped his forehead after ending the conversation. He was sweating a lot there days, despite the fact he was accustomed to far higher temperatures in his own country.

He left his suite and met Tina coming up the stairs, carrying a large expensive bag. She did not look in the best of tempers. Ignoring him, she walked to her room while he followed her. Once inside she continued to ignore him as he sat down on a couch. She flung the bag on the floor.

'What is it?' he enquired gently.

'I've got rid of the bloody Luger – and the bullets. And for your information it wasn't easy. The garden was full of geriatric guests and I had to find a path where no one was about before I could dump the stuff. You never do your own dirty work.'

She was working herself up into a rage. Standing with her hands on her hips she glared down at him. He would have liked to hit her but he knew that would be a very bad mistake. He congratulated her but that only seemed to fire her up. She picked up an envelope, waved it under his nose.

'The air ticket arrived. I always travel First – or Business if First isn't on the flight. This ticket is Economy. I don't like travelling with the peasants who travel Economy.'

'We are on the same flight,' he said quietly. 'It would not be wise if we were seen together.'

'Oh, I see. There are only two seats in Business, are there?'

'Tweed has turned up. He was in this hotel not very long ago. He had members of his team with him. If you had stayed he might have decided to have you arrested. I look after my own.'

'I see.' She calmed down suddenly. 'I'll just have to put up with the indignity, then.'

'You will have a suite at the Sacher.'

'I should damn well hope so.'

Hassan got up and left the room. He heard her slam the door shut before she locked it. Hurrying back to his suite where he had his bags packed he had no idea that he was doing just what Tweed had hoped he would do. He was moving further east.

In the outskirts of a Midlands city in Britain Willie was standing inside what the company called the laboratory. The factory was hidden in a large underground complex. Admission could only be obtained through steel doors with combination locks rather like those on a bank vault.

'Those containers will immediately dissolve on contact with cold water?' Willie asked.

'That is what we have perfected and produced on a huge scale,' Joseph Harbin, the dwarflike director, explained. 'Bacteria inside one of those containers are quite safe. You have to add a few drops of the substance inside one of these bottles, which are made of armoured glass. You note that the nozzle on each of the containers is divided into compartments. When the substance in the bottles contacts the liquid in the compartment nearest the water in the container the bacteria are released. A further turn of the plastic screw on the nozzle makes the water active.'

'How long from pouring the substance from the bottle into the nozzle and turning the nozzle does it take for the water inside the container to become active bacteria?'

'Ten seconds.'

'How can you demonstrate that this works?'

'I was expecting you to ask that. Come with me to the tank of water over here.'

Willie tried to guess the age of the chemist and found it impossible. The dwarf's face, long and pinched, was lined. He could have been anything between forty and eighty. Walking with a shuffle to the tank, he carried one of the ellipsoid containers made of a special plastic.

The huge laboratory with its tunnel-shaped ceiling had tables everywhere, each with an enamel surface, each supporting a fantastic collection of weird chemical apparatus. To Willie it looked like something out of a horror film where Frankenstein worked on creating his monster.

'Now watch carefully,' Harbin cautioned. 'This is a bottle of blue ink. I am going to put a few drops of this highly concentrated ink into the nozzle of a container.'

It was silent inside the underground laboratory, due to its depth below the surface of the dummy factory above them. Harbin added a few drops of ink into the nozzle of a container, then took off his watch, pointed to it, turned the nozzle three times. The ink dropped to the lowest level and Harbin turned it once more. Inside the container full of tap water the liquid turned a strong blue. Harbin handed the container to Willie.

'You do it. Throw it into the tank.'

Holding the container in both hands, Willie dropped it gently into the large tank of tap water. The entire contents of the tank turned a wild blue as the container immediately dissolved and disappeared. Harbin opened both hands in a gesture of satisfaction. Then he shrugged and shuffled back to his desk in a distant corner as Willie followed.

'I noticed the container had a glutinous substance inside,' Willie said sharply. 'Have all the containers been filled with the substance I supplied?'

'Look at them on the rows of shelves all around you. Every container has been treated with that substance. I don't understand why we need that or what it is.'

'Another chemist produced it. That substance strengthens the containers until they are immersed in water. You saw for yourself how quickly the container dissolved into nothing, releasing its contents immediately. You have on that sheet I gave you the different addresses a specific supply of containers and bottles must be delivered to when I phone you the code word. You are quite clear on that instruction?'

'I am a precise man, like yourself.'

Harbin chuckled and his strange face twisted into an expression which reminded Willie of a devil's mask. Obviously he had at some time in his life suffered a severe accident. He spread out a document on the large desk, produced a pen.

'I need you to sign this as a form of insurance for myself.'

Willie read every word quickly. Its main theme was that he had acted under the instructions of Captain William Wellesley Carrington and took no responsibility. Willie took out his own pen and scrawled his signature. He stared hard at Harbin.

'This is a waste of time. Everyone will be dead.'

'I like to take precautions.'

'The only precaution you have to take is to leave the country as soon as you have displatched the consignments. Someone suggested the Cayman Islands. And don't drink any water before you leave. You will also, I

412

assume, make delivery to the cargo planes flying abroad with their consignments?'

By 'abroad' Willie meant to certain obscure airfields inside France and Germany. At each delivery point in Britain and the other three key countries trained men would be waiting to distribute the containers to reservoirs. The deposit of the containers into the reservoirs of the three countries would all take place at exactly the same time.

'I presume you have brought my cheque,' Harbin said and chuckled again.

'Here is a certified cheque for you to present to your bank in this city. You hand it to a man called Arnold. He will then wire it to your personal bank account abroad within minutes.'

'Thank you.' Harbin frowned. 'It is dated today but the date has brackets round it.'

'That is because it only becomes viable when I have heard from you that you have made all the dispatches.'

'I expected more.'

'Can't you count the zeroes? When you do you will be happy. Now give me the active container.'

'You must be very careful. So very careful. It has a special protective wrapping to make it safe. It is active. Let us hope your plane doesn't crash.'

'I've taken care of that.'

Willie had indeed taken care of that. It was quite understandable that Hassan had asked for a sample to test in his own country.

40

Big Ben was a man who moved fast. As soon as they had paid the bill at the Bellevue Place in Berne they had caught a taxi to the station. After buying tickets they were lucky. Running, they were just in time to board an express for Zurich. Arriving at the main station, they were soon installed in rooms at the Hotel Schweizerhof facing the station. Big Ben called Hassan immediately.

'We're here,' he informed his boss.

'Are you equipped?'

'We're always armed.'

'Be careful what you say. Tweed is your objective. He is in town. I have a feeling he may soon leave for Vienna. Both of you go to the airport.'

'We need to buy more clothes.'

'Be quick then. Hire a car. Les drives. He stays in the car while you check the airport.'

'We're on our way.'

Big Ben knew he was noticeable. He favoured black – for a suit, for jogging gear, for a polo-necked sweater in cold weather. Collecting Les from his room, he left the hotel, avoided the expensive shops in Bahnhof-strasse, found what he wanted in the big department store Globus.

He changed inside a locked cubicle in the toilet. Emerging, he wore a grey business suit, a wide-brimmed black hat. Les came out of another cubicle, wearing a smart suit. He stared at Big Ben, startled by the transformation. From the chemist's section at Globus Big Ben had bought a white surgical collar which was now supporting his neck. In his left hand he carried a prayer book he had also bought at Globus. Big Ben now looked like a clergyman.

'Wouldn't 'ave known it was you,' Les whispered.

'Let's get crackin' – the airport!'

The only other item they had to deal with was a hired car. They quickly found a firm in Bahnhofstrasse. Les used a credit card in another name, but which was backed by substantial credit. He had the other documents required in the same name. A Citroën was placed at their disposal within five minutes.

'I'll guide you to the airport,' Big Ben told Les as they drove off. 'I've worked this city before. Crawls with the filthy rich. You go over the bridge here, then turn left. Twenty minutes and we're at the airport. Watch your speed – the Swiss are fussy old women.'

Tweed sat in the car outside police headquarters where he had spent fifteen minutes talking to Beck alone in his office. Marler sat behind the wheel, patiently awaiting instructions, while Newman, beside him, discreetly checked his .38 Smith & Wesson.

'Expecting to use that piece of old iron?' Marler enquired.

'At any time, the situation being what it is. Zurich is a time bomb. We have Hassan here and Tina Langley.'

'I think one of them at least is due to depart for Vienna,' said Tweed from the rear seat, speaking suddenly.

'How can you be sure of that?' asked Paula seated next to him.

'First, because of the confrontation at the Dolder Grand. But don't forget, at des Avenières I casually mentioned to Tina that we were moving on to Ouchy – and Vienna.'

'The further east we go the more hostile the territory,' warned Newman. 'Remember what happened to Paula when she flew to Austria and Roka – wasn't that his name – drove her into Slovakia? Then Butler and Nield had to cope with the excavator driver. That's Hassan's home ground.'

'Where, sooner or later, we must take him on,' Tweed told him.

'It's Hassan's familiar territory,' Newman insisted. 'So he holds all the cards. Even Vienna could be dangerous. Again, Paula was in great danger – damnit, she was almost kidnapped in broad daylight.'

'Paula can look after herself,' said Paula, annoyed.

'If you two would keep quiet for a moment maybe I could think,' said Tweed. 'We are at a crossroads. Which route we take may decide everything. And I have decided. Marler, drive us to the airport. I want to see whether Tina does board a flight for Vienna. Beck told me his detective – name of Windlin, I believe – reported seeing Tina leave the Dolder Grand. As she was getting into a taxi she was stuffing an air ticket into her handbag. Get us there as fast as you can, Marler.'

Willie had reached Folkestone in his car and traffic was boarding the Shuttle ready to cross the Channel by the tunnel to Calais. There was a queue of cars and he had purposely not joined it as he watched what was happening.

He parked the car in a waiting area, made sure it was locked before he went in search of a phone. He was not sure where Hassan would be by now but he first called the Dolder Grand. He had guessed right but he soon realized the volatile Hassan was in a furious temper.

'Where are you now?' Hassan demanded. 'Why waste time calling me?'

'I won't bother if you talk to me like that. Instead I will return to London. There are other deals I can be attending to.'

'London?' Hassan sounded taken aback. 'I thought you would be on the Continent with the sample. So, if you please, I would appreciate it if you tell me what is happening.'

'I am waiting at Folkestone.'

'May I ask why you are waiting?' Hassan enquired politely.

'Because there is a hold-up.' Willie phrased his next words carefully. 'There is a long delay in getting on to the Shuttle. I have heard that Customs are searching for a large drug consignment.'

'I understand. It will not delay your arrival in Vienna, I hope?'

'Not for very long, I would say.'

'Please keep me informed of your progress. Timing is so very important. If you can't get me here try the Hotel Sacher in Vienna.'

'I'll do that. I have decided to drive via Switzerland.'

'You are going to come here across Germany. It would be much quicker.'

'I just told you. Via Switzerland. Think for a moment. I've heard rumours from secret contacts on the Continent. I will not repeat them over the phone. Goodbye.'

Willie put down the phone inside the public booth before Hassan could ask him about the rumours. Then he returned to his car and sat inside it calmly, watching the progress of the cars boarding the Shuttle at a snail's pace.

* * *

417

Marler pulled in to the airport at a place where he could park. Tweed jumped out of the car and hurried into the concourse, followed by Paula and Newman. There were more passengers waiting to board flights than he had expected. After checking in, they were patronizing cafés and food stalls.

Paula was close to him as he stood scanning the crowd. Then his head stopped and she looked in the same direction. Tina was seated at a table, sipping coffee, her boarding pass clutched in one hand.

She was chatting to a well-dressed man in his forties. From his expression he was entranced by Tina. She is dressed to kill – an unfortunate phrase Paula thought. And even here she is plying her wares in the hope that she had found a minor gold mine. Paula was not worried that she might be recognized by Tina. During the swift journey to the airport in the car she had tied back her glossy hair and was wearing a fake pair of horn-rimmed glasses she always carried. These two changes had transformed her appearance into that of a schoolmistress.

Beck appeared at Tweed's side out of nowhere. He stood as though waiting for a passenger off a flight. When he spoke he was rubbing his hand slowly over his mouth. Paula heard clearly what he said to Tweed.

'Tina Langley is boarding the next flight to Vienna. I waited until she had left the check-in counter and then questioned the girl who had dealt with her. She's definitely off to Vienna.'

'Where we may lose her,' Tweed replied.

'No, we won't. I foresaw this might happen after what you told me at headquarters. One of my men will be aboard the same flight. I have already spoken to the Chief of Police in Vienna. He will have two men there to contact my man. They will have strict instructions to follow her unseen.'

'That was a good bit of organization.'

'I'll leave you now . . .'

Paula's eyes travelled round the concourse. Near the exit, but only yards away from them, stood a very tall clergyman. He appeared to be reading to himself from something he held in his hand, which she guessed was a prayer book. His lips were moving as he read.

'We'll just wait until we actually see Tina heading for the final departure lounge,' said Tweed. 'She's very tricky and might just not board her plane at the last moment. The Butterfly takes various forms of flight.'

'It doesn't look as though Hassan is taking off for Vienna,' she said.

'That's another reason for waiting here. He could turn up at the last moment. He's another very tricky character and I'm sure I put the wind up him. People are starting to move.'

Paula's eyes were still scanning the concourse. She wasn't sure why. Before they had been part of the crowd. Now they stood as an isolated group. Tweed was checking every person as they disappeared from sight. He didn't expect Hassan to adopt a disguise – he was too arrogant for that – but he wasn't taking any chances.

Paula glanced across at the clergyman again. He was putting the prayer book inside a pocket. Perhaps the passenger he had come to meet hadn't turned up, but there had been no new arrivals coming out. She was about to look somewhere else when she saw his hand come out of the pocket – holding a Colt automatic. He gripped it in both hands and aimed it point-blank at Tweed. She had no time to reach for her Browning. With her left hand she gave Tweed a great shove. The Colt had been aimed at his back. Tweed stumbled sideways. The bullet passed over his shoulder and the report echoed through the concourse. The bullet hit a partition, shattering the glass. Several women started to scream.

Her shove had been so forceful Tweed nearly fell over, but his great agility saved him. He stood upright, swung round. Newman had his Smith & Wesson in his hand but the clergyman was disappearing out of the exit. Beck again appeared from nowhere, shouting orders to men who, like their chief, came out of nowhere.

'Stop that man! Shoot him if you have to!' Beck shouted.

Newman was running to the exit, followed by Tweed and Paula. Beck reached the exit first. Outside Big Ben had dived into the waiting car. Les had thrown open the door for him. He drove off at speed, heading back for Zurich. Beck waved to a patrol car to follow the fleeing vehicle. The patrol car was held up by a taxi just pulling out. With siren screaming and lights flashing it manoeuvred round the now stationary taxi.

Les, who had been chosen for his driving skills, overtook one car after another, going well over the speed limit. He made good progress but the patrol car was gaining on him. After a few minutes he entered the curving tunnel which leads into the city. He pressed his horn, warning cars ahead to keep out of his way. The tunnel seemed to go on for ever. Behind him the patrol car had to brake to an emergency stop to avoid a collision. Les was now well ahead. Beside him Big Ben kept glancing back to see how much leeway they had. He gave the order before they reached the end of the tunnel.

'Slow down now. Keep up the maximum speed permitted but when we leave the tunnel we soon pass the Europa Hotel. Turn in there.'

After the tunnel, emerging into the blazing sun was a shock. Les was moving at the speed of other cars now. Big Ben pointed to the Europa. Les slowed a little more, moving at a reasonable speed. The traffic in front and behind him had no idea there was anything wrong. Sedately, he turned and parked in a slot among other cars. They sat and said nothing.

They heard the siren of the patrol car approaching. Traffic was getting out of its way. The patrol car flashed past and descended into Zurich. Very soon it had to crawl despite its siren and flashing lights.

On the pavement outside the airport Beck was listening on his mobile. Paula saw him purse his lips, then speak rapidly. He shrugged as he tucked away the mobile.

'They lost him. He's somewhere in the city traffic. At this time of the year you can hardly move with all the tourists about. Are you all right, Tweed? I should have asked before now.'

'Alive and kicking, thanks to Paula.'

'I should have seen him,' said Newman.

'So should I,' agreed Marler.

'It was a clever disguise,' Paula commented. 'He looked just like a clergyman.'

'It's a reminder that the enemy is formidable,' Tweed replied. 'You'll track him down, Arthur.'

'I'm not so sure about that,' Beck said grimly. 'There are so many ways he could have gone. We'll do our best. Where are you off to now?'

'The Zum Storchen. I want to phone someone. Well, at least you will pick up Tina again at Vienna airport.'

'You can take that as already dealt with. I must get back to headquarters now. Call me at once when you need me . . .'

Inside the car on their way back, sitting next to Tweed, Paula clenched her hands against her thighs. The bullet had passed so close to Tweed. Her emotions were a mixture of relief and fear for the future. He sensed her reaction and squeezed her arm. She smiled wanly.

'The trouble is we won't recognize that bastard if we see him again. He won't be dressed as a clergyman.'

'He was stooped and hobbled a little on his right foot as he ran,' said Marler.

'Part of the disguise,' Newman snapped. 'He was at least six foot tall, thin build and the hobble was probably a fake.'

'Who are you going to call?' Paula asked. 'Or maybe it's a secret. I'm talking too much.'

'No, you're not. I'm going to try and contact Amos. He may have returned to the Baur au Lac.'

When he reached his room Tweed was not able to put in his call immediately. The phone was ringing. He grabbed it.

'Tweed speaking.'

'Monica here. I've been trying to contact you for over an hour. Have you been busy?'

'You could say that. What is it?'

'I'm getting rumours from contacts abroad. Something is up. First it was our man in Singapore. Rumours that the US Fifth Fleet has entered the Indian Ocean. Then Delhi reported the same thing. Nothing in the newspapers. The contacts said what they told me was highly confidential. Should I check with Cord Dillon at Langley?'

'No, don't do anything. Just keep me fully informed. I'll always let you know where I am.'

'It would help if you did. You've been flitting about all over the Continent.'

'Like The Butterfly.'

'Pardon?'

'Just a bad joke. It might be wise if you slept at the office from now on.'

'Slept at the office?' Monica's tone expressed great

indignation. 'What do you think I've been doing for the past week? I brought my own sheets and blankets and used your camp bed.'

'Sorry. Knowing you I should have guessed. I'm grateful.'

'You're forgiven.'

Paula had been sitting in a chair in his room. As the call ended she looked at him with a smile.

'You haven't been upsetting Monica, I hope?'

'I'm afraid so. She's a brick. I must increase her salary when we get back – if we get back. Now I want to try and get Amos.'

Calling the Baur au Lac, he was put straight through to Amos. His voice sounded more like gravel going down a metal chute than usual.

'Who is this calling, may I ask?'

'You may. Tweed here. Have you heard any rumours?'

'No. What kind of rumours?'

'The US Fifth Fleet is heading into the Indian Ocean. That's a big fleet. At least one aircraft carrier, could be more. And they'll be armed with nuclear weapons. I'm telling you because you're a strategist on a global scale.'

'Changes the whole picture. I'll have to rethink my forecast. Thanks for letting me know.'

'Who gets your forecasts? Or shouldn't I ask?'

'One favour deserves another,' said Amos, his tone now amiable. 'Washington, London, Paris and Bonn get my forecasts. They pay well, especially Washington. Just as well. I need the money. Switzerland is expensive.'

'Let's keep in touch.'

'Where are you, then?'

'Just about to move on. I'll call you from my new destination.'

'Amos is good, isn't he?' asked Paula when Tweed left the phone.

'First rate. One of the best strategists in the world. Let's go for a walk along the riverside.'

'Don't you think you ought to stay indoors, particularly after what happened at the airport?'

'No one is going to keep me locked up like a fugitive.'

I'll just freshen up. I'll be exactly five minutes. Time me.'

Alone, Tweed stood to one side of his window overlooking the Limmat. At the far end of the covered walk below him he saw a man coming down the steps leading to the walkway. He watched as the man glanced up at the windows of the hotel, pausing as he did so. Then he disappeared along the walkway.

Tweed frowned. Hassan, he felt sure, had a vast organization. It was possible he had men out checking the hotels. Tweed picked up the phone, told the concierge that if anyone asked if he was staying there he should say no one of that name was a guest. The concierge replied that he wouldn't even say that – he'd just send any noseyparker packing.

Paula returned in exactly the five minutes she had promised, ready for her walk. The phone rang and she cast her eyes upwards.

'Keith Kent is on the line,' he told her.

'I spoke to Beck,' said Kent. 'I gather you'd told him to give me your number if I called.'

'I did. Have you dug up something else?' he asked Kent.

'Yes. Within the past five minutes. A contact I have in the Channel Islands has told me Conway, whoever he is, has instructed his bank out there to move all his assets to the Cayman Islands by electronic means. Before you ask me, I'm no closer to identifying Conway. For the moment, that's it . . .'

Tweed then told Paula what Keith Kent had said. She stared at him with a puzzled look.

'Is that significant?'

'Yes.'

He had to pick up the phone again as it started ringing. Paula sat down, convinced their walk was off.

'Tweed? Beck here. Ashley Wingfield has just phoned the airport and booked a seat, Business Class, on the next flight to Vienna. You'll have to hurry if you want to catch it. I can book seats. You want me to, then? How many?'

'Five in Economy. Me, Paula, Newman, Marler and Nield.'

'Consider it done.'

'We're off to Vienna,' Tweed informed Paula. 'I hope everyone has kept their bags packed, as I asked.'

'They have.' Paula was on her feet. 'Hadn't you better inform Monica?'

'I'll do that while you let the rest know. The cars can be handed in at the airport.'

'What's happening?' she asked, on the verge of leaving.

'The battlefield is moving further east.'

41

Aboard her flight to Vienna Tina sat fuming in her Economy seat. The flight was midway between Zurich and Vienna. Once it was airborne she had left her seat and walked down the aisle to peer through at the Business section.

There were very few passengers in Business although Economy was full. She saw that Hassan was not on the plane. She swore foully to herself and returned to her seat, squeezing past the man sitting next to her. She could have killed Hassan.

'Here I am stuck with the rabble,' she said to herself. 'And Hassan is not on board. Plus the fact there are plenty of seats available in Business. What does he think I am? A peasant?'

She debated whether to call the stewardess, to insist that she was transferred to Business. Reluctantly she decided against taking any action. It would draw attention to herself. He'll pay for this, she raged inwardly – in more cash. Then she was irritated by the man next to her who tried to strike up a conversation with her. One glance at his suit told her he was not in the money. And he was travelling Economy.

'You get a marvellous view of the Austrian mountains on a day like this,' he had said.

'I'm not interested. I don't want to talk. I have a migraine.'

'I have some tablets.'

'Keep them.'

She turned her head away and stared out of the window. The mountains were to be seen on the starboard side as the plane curved, beginning its long descent to the airport.

Two rows behind her Detective Windlin, wearing a civilian suit, had been amused as he had watched her peering into Business Class. The Butterfly was becoming notorious among the Swiss police force. Her liking for wealthy men had percolated through to them.

She pushed past other passengers after the flight had landed.

Back in Geneva she had purchased a small suitcase, one she could carry aboard a plane and stow in the luggage compartment above the seats. It saved time waiting at the carousel. Behind her Detective Windlin saw an Austrian plain-clothes man he had cooperated with in the past. Windlin nodded towards Tina's back.

The Austrian hurried over to a man clad as a motorcyclist who was holding his crash helmet in his hands. The Austrian had a brief word with his colleague who was walking towards Tina as he put on his helmet. Tina noticed nothing – she was scanning the waiting drivers. One held a board with the name *L. Vane.*

'I'm in a hurry to get to the Sacher,' she said with a smile.

'Consider we are at the Sacher.'

Tina was pleased when he opened the rear door of a de luxe limo. It was the only way to travel. They had left the airport, were travelling over flatlands with fields on either side which she found boring. But she thought the driver was rather handsome and in tune with the car.

'What is your name?' she called out. 'You are from the Sacher? I may need a car while I'm in Vienna.'

'After we reach Sacher I go off duty,' the driver said quickly.

The motorcyclist drew alongside them after they had covered a certain distance. He stared at her through his goggles, waved his hand at her, then made a gesture as though drinking. She looked away.

'Bloody sauce,' she said to herself. 'A motorcyclist.'

The man in the crash helmet zoomed ahead and out of sight. As he swept round a bend he raised one hand. The signal was picked up by two plain-clothes men waiting in a Volvo hidden in a side road. They began to follow the limo as it entered the outer suburbs of Vienna.

At Zurich's airport Tweed and his companions appeared scattered. In fact Paula and the four men with her were waiting in tactical positions chosen by Marler. They were covering Tweed from every angle. Beck stood next to Tweed.

'Hassan has passed through Security and is waiting in the final departure lounge,' Beck remarked.

'Could you arrange it so we go aboard at the last moment? They usually let Business Class on to the plane after Economy.'

'Already arranged. No danger of him seeing you.'

'Marler won't be coming with us. He has a job to do for me in Zurich. He insisted on coming with me as protection.'

'Understood.'

What Beck did not understand was that Marler had decided he had to drive to Vienna – to take his armoury across the border into Austria at a remote point, as he had done when he had driven from Vienna after Paula's grim experiences near Slovakia. Marler had also given Newman a note for and the name and address of an arms dealer in Vienna he had dealt with on his earlier trip. As though reading his mind, Beck suddenly said: 'None of your people have weapons, I hope? The metal detector.'

'Dumped them in the Limmat,' said Tweed.

When, at the last moment, they boarded the flight they had seats near the front of Economy. One passenger at the back had a shock when he saw Tweed. Big Ben, slumped in his seat, appeared to be a man of medium height. He was clad in a jogging outfit and his cadaverous face was changed by the large-lensed *pince-nez* perched on the bridge of his nose. He had in his lap a scientific magazine of which he didn't understand a word. But he now had the appearance of a professor, and there were plenty of them in Austria.

He glanced across at Les, occupying the aisle seat opposite. From Les's expression he could tell he had also observed Tweed's arrival. Big Ben wished he had his Colt automatic. At Vienna's airport there was bound to be crowds and confusion. He could have hit Tweed. But Big Ben *had* dumped his Colt in the Limmat.

Paula, seated next to Tweed, who had the window seat, glanced round at the other passengers. The professorial-looking type pretending to read his magazine as the aircraft took off meant nothing to her.

'Look at those mountains,' Tweed said to her later. 'Really you should have had the window seat.'

'You always give it to me. I can see anyway,' she replied, leaning over him.

In the glaring sunlight sabre-toothed peaks seemed to pass just under the plane's fuselage. She stared down, fascinated by the grimness of the view.

'I wouldn't like to be climbing one of those,' she remarked.

'People do. They must have different minds from us.'

Newman and Nield, seated immediately behind Tweed and Paula, were also gazing down at the awe-inspiring view. Therefore they did not see the curtains closing them off from Business Class part. Hassan gazed at the passengers, nervously checking on who else was aboard. Suddenly his eyes met those of Tweed, who had caught the curtain's movement. For seconds their eyes were again locked, then Hassan closed the curtain.

Returning to his set, Hassan thought rapidly. It was a situation he had not foreseen. He checked his watch. In just over half an hour they would be landing. He bit his fingernails, not seeing the view below him. Eventually, he took out a pad and wrote a message addressed to a man called Vogel. Summoning a stewardess he gave her the sheet he had torn off the pad.

Bring a party to meet me at Schwechat Airport. Some of our best friends. Ashley.

He had been so busy working out what to say he had failed to notice a stewardess from Economy had earlier taken another message to the pilot's cabin. This one also had to be radioed urgently. But whereas Hassan's message was sent to a village halfway between the airport and Vienna, Tweed's had been sent to Zurich. To Arthur Beck.

Expect reception group to await us at Vienna's airport. Can you counter them. Tweed.

Ashley Wingfield, a passenger well known to Austrian Airlines, was the first to leave the plane on landing. He carried no luggage, hurried through Security and Passport Control. Vogel, in his forties, of medium height, built like a boxer, had a bald head and squinted through pouched eyes. He hurried to greet Hassan on the crowded concourse of Schwechat.

A large group of Croats, singing a national song and waving flags, were gathered together. Some were dancing while other compatriots clapped. It appeared to be some kind of celebration. Vogel bowed his head, to show respect, then whispered, 'They are over there – the Croats singing and dancing. Every man has a concealed knife. How many to kill? It will look as though the targets have collapsed from the heat. Knives are silent.'

'I will point them out to you and then hurry to my car. It is waiting outside?'

'Yes. Your limo and your driver.'

Hassan turned round, took a few paces forward to get a better view of the disembarking passengers. It seemed to take for ever as the people off the flight slowly appeared, carrying their luggage. No sign of Tweed and his friends. Hassan began to worry. Surely they must have left the aircraft.

Then he saw Tweed with the girl. They were chatting, walking very slowly. Behind them trailed Newman and Nield. They were moving at such a weary pace all the other passengers off the flight had headed for the exit. Hassan began biting his fingernails at how long it was taking. He heard Vogel's voice behind him.

'Cars are ready to drive off with the Croats once they have down their work.'

'I should hope so.'

Now the first of passengers disembarked from another flight were hurrying forward. They overtook Tweed and his team as the Croats continued singing and dancing, waiting for the signal from Vogel. Hassan fretted some more. Then a dribble of passengers overtook Tweed and once again he was alone with his three companions.

Detective Windlin was now talking to his opposite number from Vienna. Verbally, he identified Tweed. As he watched, the last passenger to leave the plane appeared. A short plump-faced man, he carried a small case. Mario looked around at the concourse. Besides the Croat singers and dancers a number of men were gathered in groups, talking to each other.

'I think it's time now,' Hassan said.

Vogel turned to give the signal for the Croats to attack, about to point out their targets. A man came running up to him, spoke rapidly in German. Vogel froze for a moment, then touched Hassan's arm.

'What is it?'

'Bad news. The concourse is crawling with a heavy detachment of Austrian police in plain clothes. It would be madness to launch an onslaught now.'

'Damn it to hell.'

Hassan almost reeled physically from the report. He clenched both hands, took one last look at Tweed and

431

then stormed out to find his limo. Vogel had already sent his messenger back to the chief of the Croats, ordering them to leave the airport at once.

As he was doing so Nield, who had noticed several Croats looking towards his group, took out a small pocket camera and took three pictures of them in quick succession. There were no flashes as he pressed the button. The camera had been designed by the boffins in the cellars under SIS HQ in Park Crescent. It took perfect pictures even in the dark and there was never a flash of light.

The Croats stopped singing and dancing suddenly. Several of the detectives in groups had their hands inside their jackets, gripping automatics. They watched with grim satisfaction as the Croats hurried towards the exit and silence descended on the concourse.

'What is happening?' Tweed asked as Windlin hurried up to him. 'And who are you?'

'Detective Windlin from Zurich. Chief Inspector Beck told me to fly here.' He produced a folder. 'My identification.'

'So what *is* happening?' Tweed asked after glancing at the folder.

'The concourse is full of plain-clothes men from police headquarters in Vienna. Those Croat singers and dancers you saw were going to assassinate you. Beck apparently contacted the Chief of Police in Vienna.

'I rate him as among the best police chiefs in Europe. Give him my thanks. Now have we cars waiting for us?'

'Yes. Two cars. I will take you to them.'

Mario watched them talking from a distance. Standing by a food stall he sipped orange juice. On Vitorelli's instructions he had waited for a long time at Zurich's airport. He had also booked a seat on every flight leaving for Vienna.

'Why Vienna?' he had asked Vitorelli hours before in the Italian's suite at the Baur au Lac.

'Because Tweed has a sixth sense about where the operational centre of The Sisterhood will be. You remember when we were flying near Slovakia?'

'Yes, you took photographs from every angle of that strange house on top of a hill which is almost a mountain. I see you have them on that table.

'At one moment,' Vitorelli continued, 'I saw a car driving along the road leading to that house. You know how powerful my field glasses are. I focused on that vehicle. In the front was a Balkan-looking driver. His passenger in the back was Tweed's assistant and confidante, Paula Grey. So Tweed knows about that house. I think Tina will end up there.'

'Why should she?'

'From the newspapers I know The Sisterhood organization made an attempt to destroy all surviving members of the *Institut* with a huge bomb. The Sisterhood is no longer being used to carry out assassinations. Tina knows too much for the man running that organization for him to risk her being picked up and making a deal with the police. I am sure she will be taken to that house in Slovakia,' Vitorelli had said confidently.

'I'd better get to the airport here,' Mario said.

'Just before you leave. Is the equipment aboard my helicopter at the airport?'

'Yes,' Mario replied and rubbed his hands as though drying perspiration off them. 'It was a job. I spent hours inside the basement of that secret flat you rent off Rennweg . . .'

He recalled this conversation as he discreetly followed Tweed's party. He made a careful note of the registration numbers of the two hire cars which were waiting for them. Then he settled down to wait after buying two litre bottles of mineral water.

433

Vitorelli's chopper would take some time to reach Schwechat as it had taken off just ahead of Tweed's flight. Mario had used his mobile to report that Tweed *was* leaving for Vienna.

42

At the Château d'Avignon Butler, who had gone for a walk, hobbled back, dragging his right leg painfully. Fred Brown, who had helped himself to a few drinks, peered over the counter.

'What's the matter with your bloody leg?'

'Fell down the stairs, didn't I.'

'Drunk again,' Brown responded unsympathetically.

'Means I've got to stay on a bit longer. Don't know how long it will take to heal.'

'That's more money in the till,' Brown said gleefully.

'Don't you ever think of anything except lolly?'

'Yes, women. They go together. Women and lolly. Haven't you found that out yet?'

'I'll know where to come if I'm feeling depressed.'

'Go break a leg,' said Brown and chortled.

As Butler made his way slowly up the stairs to his room, holding on to the banister rail for support, Brown reached for the cognac bottle hidden under the counter, upended it and swallowed another large drink. His head began to swim. He didn't worry. He was used to cognac – he knew his head would clear within the hour.

Once inside his room, Butler removed the large bandage wrapped round his right leg which helped to make the hobble look convincing. He had needed a plausible reason for staying on longer without arousing suspicion that a single man should remain so long.

He was just about to take a shower when the phone started to ring. He lifted it cautiously.

'Yes? Harry here.'

'You know me,' said Tweed's voice. 'Not yet. The code you need for the drug consignment when it arrives is . . .' He gave the number of the Sacher with the code for Austria, adding on his room number. He had reversed all the numbers. 'We're going backwards, I think,' he went on, informing Butler of what he had done. 'Ask for Pete if I'm not here. You're all right? This is Tweed.'

'I'm OK. Understood . . .'

In the deserted lobby Brown was listening in. Befuddled, he still managed to note down the string of numbers and the name. With an effort he found the piece of paper which gave the hotel numbers Hassan had phoned, saying where he could be found if anyone called Butler. He gave the name Ashley Wingfield, a name Brown knew as he had received calls from him before – and a generous supply of banknotes sent by courier. Hassan was always anxious about the key communications centre in the turret, linked to the house in Slovakia.

With a greater effort Brown called the first number, which was the Zum Storchen. The concierge was brief.

'Mr Wingfield is not staying with us. We don't know the name.'

Cursing, Brown called the second number, which was the Sacher. Still befuddled, he noticed no similarity in the number he was calling and the reverse numbers Tweed had given him.

'Mr Wingfield? Brown here at d'Avignon. Guest staying here had a call from man called Tweed. . .'

'Tweed? Did you say Tweed?'

'Sounded like it. Said things were going backwards.'

'Going wrong, you mean?'

'Suppose he meant that. Things going wrong. That's what it sounded like.'

'Excellent. Who is the guest he called?'

'Man name of Butler.'

The name meant nothing to Hassan. But although he was delighted to hear that it appeared Tweed was in trouble he didn't like the idea of anyone Tweed knew staying at d'Avignon. He pressed for details.

'I should keep an eye on this guest, Butler.'

'He can't do no 'arm. Got a busted leg. That's why 'e's stayin' on a bit longer. Thought you ought to know.'

'Thank you, Brown. Just keep an eye on this Butler.'

Keep an eye on 'im? What the flaming hell for, thought Brown. 'E's as useless as a chicken with one leg. I'm not wastin' me time botherin' about 'im.

Hassan, seated on a couch in his luxurious suite, took a different view. The phone call worried him more the more he thought about it. And the few staff left to keep the Château d'Avignon going were no good. Six of the professional thugs he had ordered to head for Zurich fast were a different proposition. They were killers. Rudge, the leader of the group on its way, had left the East End of London years ago after strangling a girl. Hassan had left a message at the Zum Storchen that when Rudge called they were to give him the phone number of the Sacher. Big Ben would, of course, take command of the group.

When the flight from Zurich landed at Schwechat Big Ben and Les left the aircraft quickly, well ahead of Tweed. Reaching the concourse they collected the car Big Ben had hired before leaving Zurich. Then, with Big Ben behind the wheel, they waited.

On their way out they had passed the chanting Croats. Ben had glanced at them contemptuously. No discipline. Just a mob. He made his remark to Les, the knife-thrower, as they waited for Tweed to appear.

'What a load of trash that lot were.'

Well, you're not exactly Winston Churchill, thought Les. He was careful to keep the thought to himself. The heat was getting to him already. He glanced at Ben.

'Mind if I smoke 'alf a cigarette?'

'Not so long as you get out of the car.'

'It's like a bloody fire out there.'

'Give you a suntan. Keep a lookout for Tweed.'

Les stepped out into the torrid temperature. He took off his jacket, threw it into the car. His knives were concealed inside what appeared to be a money belt. He lit a cigarette as Ben peered into his rear-view mirror.

'Get back. Here they come.'

'I've only just lit my puff!'

'I said get back into the car,' Ben snarled.

He hunched down in his seat. Several other vehicles, mostly taxis picking up passengers, were leaving as Tweed's car drove off towards Vienna. They had left the second car as a reserve for Marler when he arrived. Ben was able to follow Tweed's car without risk of being spotted – other vehicles masked him. He drove all the way to the Sacher, watched while Tweed and his companions alighted and entered the hotel, then drove to a small hotel close by, where Hassan had booked two rooms.

His first action on entering his small room was to phone Hassan to report his arrival. Hassan put down the phone and rubbed his damp hands with satisfaction. Tweed had made the mistake of following him onto his home ground. Adding the Croats – murderous fighters – to Ben and Les and the six men under Rudge on their way from Zurich, he had a large enough force to wipe out anything Tweed could summon up. Rudge had just called him from Zurich.

'We're at the airport, Chief. Thought you might want us to fly on elsewhere.'

'Clever of you. Board the first flight for Vienna. Cars will be waiting to take you to a small hotel near the Sacher. You report to Big Ben. He's in charge.'

'Right . . .'

Rudge, a man of few words, was very fat. He sported a large bushy moustache, brown like his thick untidy hair. He always smiled and was popular with the ladies because he joked a lot. People noticed Rudge. On the surface he was an amiable man who enjoyed life. Only someone like Newman would have seen the hard look in his eyes.

His five colleagues were less well dressed. Which was why Rudge booked Economy tickets. Personally he would have preferred to travel Business. You met a better class of passenger.

'Are you surviving?' Tweed asked Paula after she had let him inside her room at the Sacher. 'You were very quiet on the way here.'

'Two reasons. One, did you notice the wave of heat that hit us as we left the concourse? I'll get used to it. Two, it seemed weird landing at Schwechat again. I was recalling what happened when Valja, the driver, took me close to Slovakia and I had to ram a nail file into his neck to get him to turn back.'

'We'll see that there isn't a repeat performance of that.'

'When I was in your room I was surprised when you phoned Harry and mentioned your name. Someone could have listened in to your call.'

'I'm sure they did. Then they would report it to Hassan as soon as they could. That will have disturbed him. Which is the way I want Hassan. Disturbed men make mistakes.'

'What is our next move?'

'We wait here until Marler arrives with his armoury. I don't like the idea of Bob visiting that arms dealer here. He may also deal with Hassan. I estimate it gives us twenty-four hours here. Time to recharge our batteries, to coin a cliché.'

'We stay in the hotel meantime?'

'Definitely. I've given orders to that effect to Newman and Nield. Meanwhile Hassan will be assembling his forces to deal with us. He'll probably have more troops than we can muster, so we'll outmanoeuvre him. I had a call from Marler – he's well on his way. Should arrive in the morning. Only then do we walk into Hassan's trap, which will close on him.'

'Let's go downstairs. I could do with a drink,' said Paula, a rare remark for her.

With Tweed behind her, she stepped out of the lift on the ground floor and bumped into a glamorous woman with auburn hair. Tina turned round, stood stock-still, staring at Paula.

'I'm not used to people following me,' she snapped.

'Unless they're men,' Paula said pleasantly.

'You want to mind your manners.'

'Then I won't copy you,' Paula replied, again pleasantly.

Tina's eyes glared with a ferocity which startled Tweed. She walked away into the bar, her body language expressing fury. Tweed whispered to Paula.

'Keep it up. Go after her into the bar.'

As they entered the well-appointed and spacious bar Paula saw Tina sitting down at an empty corner table with her elegant legs crossed. Paula led the way to the next table and sat so she was facing Tina. Tweed joined her. The tables were close and he gave Tina a little wave. She had just ordered a large Martini and she focused her attention on Tweed.

'At least it's nice to see *you* here. Staying long? I'm on my own.'

'We can't have that,' Tweed replied, smiling. 'Maybe you'd like to join us for dinner.'

'Both of you?'

'I can hardly leave Paula out in the cold. I'm sure you would not want me to do that.'

'In that case I think maybe I would prefer to dine on my own. Nothing personal. I feel I have been flying all over Europe nonstop.'

'Perhaps you have,' Tweed said with a smile.

Tina stared at him, confused. She finished her drink, ordered a second large Martini. Inwardly, she felt rage building up. Paula kept gazing at her as though she was some strange specimen. Tweed had relaxed in his chair, holding a glass of orange juice as he looked slowly round the room, studying the extraordinary variety of guests. He reckoned there must be at least eight different nationalities in the room, some probably from the Balkans. This was Vienna.

Paula, with a glass of wine she sipped at occasionally, continued to gaze at Tina. Drinking half the fresh glass which had been put before her, Tina had an almost overwhelming desire to get out a mirror to check her appearance. Had she a smut on her nose? She resisted the impulse, signalled to the waiter again.

'Please book me a table for dinner in the Rote Bar.'

She gave him her room number. Tweed was bound to pick up that item of information but she had reached the stage where she didn't give a damn. She sat back, giving the impression she hadn't a care in the world. Then she couldn't stand it any longer. Signing the bill, she omitted to leave a tip in her haste to get away from Paula. The moment she was gone Tweed summoned the waiter.

'Could you book us a table for dinner in the Rote Bar? Place us at a table next to the one our friend – the lady who was sitting over there.'

'You're getting on her nerves,' Paula whispered.

'Which, as you may have guessed, is the idea.'

They got up and walked along the corridor to the Rote Bar, which was a restaurant. The head waiter escorted them to a table by the window and next to where Tina sat alone. Paula chose a chair where she would be directly facing her. As she sat down she smiled at Tina.

'This is a wonderful hotel, don't you think? So luxurious.'

'Is there any other way to live?' Tina responded in a tight voice.

'Some people have to struggle to exist,' Paula said.

'That's their problem.'

'Yours, of course, is where the next twenty thousand pounds is coming from. Maybe you could go in for some more target practice.'

For a moment Tweed thought Tina was going to pick up something from the table to hurl it. Paula still sat very still, her expression bleak as she stared down Tina.

After eating only half her main course, Tina stood up, gazed round to see if people at other tables could have heard, but the exchange between the two women had been in low voices. Before she left Tina gave Tweed an inviting smile, bent down and brushed her lips across his face. She glanced at Paula, whose expression was now one of amusement. With exaggerated elegance she strolled out. Several men watched her with longing.

'Bit of a hellcat, isn't she,' Paula commented.

'You handled that beautifully. She's in a towering

441

fury. She'll probably go to Hassan – Nield found out he's in the hotel under the name Ashley Wingfield. Pressure. That's what I want – more and more pressure imposed on the enemy. I'm going all out to destabilize Mr Hassan.'

'I won't stay in this place another night!' Tina shouted.

'Keep your voice down,' Hassan snapped. 'They'll hear you in Salzburg.'

Tina had hammered on his door a minute earlier. The moment she entered Hassan realized he had a female thunderstorm on his hands. She was out of control.

'I don't care if they do. I want out.'

'May I ask what has caused this outbreak of annoyance?'

'Tweed and Paula Grey. First in the bar, then they sit close to me at dinner in the Rote Bar.'

'Well,' he said genially, 'Rote is the German for red. You make it sound as though there was blood.'

'I'd like to blow off the back of Paula Grey's head.'

'I'd prefer you to do that to Tweed. Calm down.'

'I'm not calming down. I want to get out of this place tonight.'

'Sit down. Have a drink.' Hassan poured wine in a glass almost to the brim. 'We have to stay here tonight. A car will take you out of Vienna in the morning.'

'Thank God for that.'

Tina had sat down. She lifted the glass without spilling a drop, took a long drink. Hassan was clever enough to say nothing for the moment. Tina took another long drink, put the glass down. He refilled it.

'I need money,' she said aggressively.

'I haven't any at the moment. I'll give you some

when you're in the car in the morning. Order what you want from room service and put it on my bill.'

'How very generous.'

'I can be generous in the morning.'

'I'm going back to my room. I've had enough of people tonight.'

'Make sure you're packed and ready to leave early.'

'It can't be early enough for me . . .'

When she had gone Hassan sat thinking for a moment. Then he picked up the phone and called another room in the hotel. His tone was brusque.

'Carl, you know Tina Langley's room number. Keep an eye on her. Don't let her leave tonight. Your head's on the block.'

Hassan kept tapping his thick fingers on the glass table top. He was very disturbed. If Tina went over the top she might take it into her head to contact the police, the mood she was in. At least Carl would keep her under his thumb until the morning. He needed the time to contact Big Ben, to explain to him the large force he was placing under his control, details of the trap he was planning for Tweed.

Hassan cursed aloud. Tweed. It was always Tweed who got in his way. Tweed was becoming an obsession with him, upsetting his judgement. He picked up the phone again, this time to call Big Ben in the small hotel nearby.

Hassan was not the only one to worry about Tina. In the Rote Bar several tables had emptied near Paula and Tweed, so they had privacy. Paula finished her first and only glass of wine before she spoke.

'I think Tina could walk out of the Sacher tonight.'

'If she does she'll be followed. Nield is waiting outside in a car. He has her photo. Newman is sharing shifts with him throughout the night.'

'I'm worrying about nothing.'

'Don't agree. Tomorrow could bring anything – and probably will. We must all be ready to leave at dawn.'

43

A few hours before, Vitorelli had landed in his chopper at a remote part of Schwechat. Mario had paid a big tip to the driver of a buggy which carried him out to the helicopter. Despite his long flight, Vitorelli was in a cheerful mood and very fresh.

'Tell me the news, friend,' he said after Mario had asked the buggy driver to wait a distance away.

'They're all at the Sacher. Why is the Sacher the hotel they so often choose?'

'Because it is the finest hotel. Also it is strategically located in the centre of Vienna. Now, the news.'

'I phoned my contact there. Tina Langley is staying there. So is Tweed and his assistant, Paula Grey. There was a scene at the airport . . .'

Mario described the presence of the Croats, their rush to leave, the fact that the concourse appeared to be flooded with plain-clothes police. Standing by the chopper, his helmet in his hand, Vitorelli listened. He smiled grimly when Mario repeated the details of the arrival and departure of Tina by car.

'You have transport, Mario?'

'Yes. I hired a car. The equipment travelled safely aboard your chopper?'

'Yes, thanks to you. We leave it where it is. Now, drive us to the Sacher. When we arrive you go in first. Make sure Tina is not about, then I will come in with you. I need food, and I'm sure you do. I prefer the main restaurant to the Rote Bar. Check it out for me. Let's go now . . .'

They had just sat down in the restaurant when Tweed peered in to see who was inside. Vitorelli saw him, beckoned for him to join them. Paula followed Tweed and Vitorelli greeted her courteously, even enthusiastically.

'I feel the need of some intelligent female company. Talking with you is always a pleasure.'

'Thank you. What are you doing in Vienna?' Paula asked.

'Business. You both know Mario. Please join us.'

'I know Mario,' said Tweed. 'I saw him travelling on the same flight as we did. If you'll excuse us, we've had a long day.'

'And maybe tomorrow will be the longest day,' Vitorelli replied with a quizzical smile.

'If you say so,' Tweed agreed. 'Good night to both of you.'

'What did he mean by that last remark?' Paula asked in the lift.

'We'll find out tomorrow. Now, go and get as much sleep as you can.'

Tweed was woken before dawn by a gentle tapping on his door. Putting on a dressing gown he approached the door cautiously. He stood to one side before he spoke.

'Who is it?'

'This is your favourite aide-de-camp. Would you like tea, sir?' a familiar voice replied.

'Marler!' Tweed greeted him after unlocking the door. 'How on earth did you get here so quickly?'

'I made use of the autobahn from Munich to Salzburg. No speed limit. I'd better wake everyone else up and distribute the goodies,' Marler drawled.

'You'll be popular, but I think that is a good precaution. I have a feeling we may have to leave early. You must need some sleep.'

'Waste of time. Saw Newman outside slacking in a car. He gave me news. When he relieved Nield, Pete told him he'd seen Big Ben coming out of a small hotel to meet Hassan. They went for a walk in the middle of the night. Nield told Bob that Big Ben was a formidable thug he last saw at the Château d'Avignon. Hassan appeared to be giving Ben instructions. Looks as though I've got here in time for bit of a blow-up.'

'I'll order you coffee.'

'Tea would be better. Meantime I'll act as a human alarm clock. Tell me where everyone is.'

Tweed sat down at a desk, scribbled names and room numbers. He handed it to Marler. When he had entered the room Marler had been carrying a bulging satchel which was now propped against a wall. Tweed nodded towards it.

'What have you got inside there?'

'Machine-pistols, stun and shrapnel grenades, smoke bombs, handguns and ammo. We'll be well equipped to deal with Big Ben and the mob I'm sure he'll be commanding.'

'Sounds like you're ready for a small replay of the Gulf War.'

'We'll be well dressed. Incidentally, Newman had some really interesting news. Before he went to bed prior to relieving Nield in the middle of the night he saw two taxis arriving separately. He said the scenery was good. First, a luscious blonde who happens to be called Karin Berg. Then a ravishing redhead by the name of Simone Carnot. Bob said he thought Hassan was greedy.'

'That is interesting. We're approaching a real climax.'

'I'll be back for a cuppa tea.'

Wide awake now, Tweed had a shower, and was dressed when Marler returned. His visitor was grinning and the satchel he dropped on the floor no longer bulged. Tweed insisted he drank some tea before saying a word.

'That's better,' Marler said after two cups. 'And I was so popular, waking up people. Except for Paula. She was already up, fresh as a daisy. I tried to persuade her to accept a machine-pistol but all she would take was a .32 Browning.'

'It is her favourite weapon. What about Newman and Nield?'

'Like me, they're walking warriors. When I arrived I booked myself a room. I won't use the bed. I needed somewhere to dump my own equipment. Any more tea left?'

'I ordered a large pot. Help yourself.'

Marler was reaching for the pot when someone tapped on the door. In seconds Marler, a Walther in his hand, was by the door. He called out.

'Identify yourself.'

'It's me. Paula.'

She came in, and after relocking the door Marler poured her tea. She showed no signs of strain, her shoulder bag over her arm and carrying her packed case. Thanking Marler, she looked at Tweed.

'Any news?'

'Yes.'

He told her about the arrival of both Karin Berg and Simone Carnot. Sitting on a couch, she sipped tea with a puzzled frown. She said nothing until she had finished drinking the whole cup, which Marler promptly refilled.

'That's strange. Tina's here. Now they turn up. It sounds to me as though we have the whole Sisterhood under the same roof. Why?'

'I think Hassan is withdrawing them from the reach

447

of Beck,' Tweed told her. 'At this stage he doesn't want to risk any of them breaking down under Beck's interrogation. This fact alone convinces me we are on the verge of a major climax.'

'What are we waiting for, then?'

'For Pete Nield to report that Hassan is leaving.'

Tweed had been right about the arrival of Karin Berg and Simone Carnot. Earlier in the afternoon Hassan had phoned each of them, had told them they were in danger from being arrested. He had told them to take the last flight – the only one available – from Zurich to Vienna. He had advised Berg to travel Economy and Carnot to buy a Business Class ticket. In this way he had kept them separated from each other. Simone had agreed without argument. Karin was a different proposition.

'I'm not sure I want to fly to Vienna,' she had said firmly. 'I think I'd sooner go elsewhere,' she went on, thinking of Rome.

'Beck is closing in,' Hassan had warned her. 'You need to be hidden and protected for a week or two. You have done a good job,' he added persuasively. 'So you are really independent, I propose to hand you thirty thousand pounds. I did say pounds – not dollars.'

Berg had killed three members of the *Institut*. She felt pretty sure she had outgunned, so to speak, the other members of the Sisterhood. Another thirty thousand and she wouldn't have to worry about money for the rest of her life, being prudent in her spending. She had agreed to take the flight to Vienna.

Relieved, Hassan had given two of his special drivers orders to meet the two women at Schwechat. He had described them carefully, had told them to use the name Ashley Wingfield.

That night he had had little sleep. Meeting Big Ben,

he had taken him to an all-night café which was almost empty, had described the plan. With a map of Burgenland open he had drawn a route, had marked a certain village.

'You leave with your men soon,' he had ordered. 'Rudge will be your second-in-command in case you are injured. A woman,' he had continued, thinking of Tina, 'will be the bait leading them to the ambush points. They have to be close to Slovakia so Tweed is not suspicious. Recently, a woman called Paula was near my headquarters. I saw her in a car through powerful field glasses. That means Tweed knows. You meet the Croats here. They may wipe out Tweed and his men on their own. Now, I will go over the plan again.'

Eventually he had returned to the Sacher. On his way in he noticed the same car, parked with a man behind the wheel who appeared to be fast asleep. He smiled wearily to himself. When he returned to his room the phone was ringing. He picked it up cautiously.

'Yes?'

'Mr Ashley Wingfield, I presume?' an upper-crust English voice had said.

'Willie? Where are you now? Time is running short.'

'I'm well east of Paris, old boy. Thought you'd like a progress report.'

'Progress!' Hassan had screeched. 'Why aren't you much closer?'

'Trouble, this time at jolly Calais. The Customs chappies again. Looking for a big drug consignment. Caused one hell of a hold-up.'

'The sample?'

'Intact, of course. I can step on the gas now.'

'You'd better not be late arriving.'

'I'm never late. Sounds as though you need a spot of shut-eye. Bye.'

Hassan started to worry again. He decided not to

report to the Head of State until he reached Slovakia. By then, he hoped, Willie would be close to his head-quarters on the mountain. He looked at his bed long-ingly, checked his watch, decided he'd better just stay up. He ordered more coffee from room service.

When she arrived in her room Simone Carnot decided she was too washed-out to eat. She took a quick shower, got into her night clothes and flopped into bed. She didn't bother to call Hassan. That could wait until morning. She just remembered to switch off the bedside light before falling into a deep sleep.

Karin Berg had more stamina. After taking a shower, she phoned down and ordered an early breakfast to be sent up at once. Spread out on a couch, she considered her present position. She needed to get the thirty thou-sand out of Hassan as soon as possible.

Unlike the other women, while she was being 'trained' at the house in Slovakia she had gone for walks. Starting out from the front entrance, after tell-ing the guard to go to hell, she had wandered to the eastern edge of the hill. Out of sight of the house she had found a sunken path leading down in the direction of Austria.

'I'm not hanging around there for two weeks,' she said to herself. 'If necessary, once I've extracted the money from Hassan, I'll slip away on foot. Once in Austria I should find transport back to Vienna. From there I'll fly to Rome.'

With this comforting thought in mind, she tackled the generous breakfast with enthusiasm when it arrived. Feeling better, she set her mental alarm clock, climbed into bed, closed her eyes, fell fast asleep.

* * *

450

Sitting in the lounge after a large dinner, Vitorelli nursed a drink and gave Mario his instructions.

'I'm going to leave you the car. You have a mobile so you can call me when anything happens I should know about. Because something is going to happen during the next few hours.'

'You are going somewhere, then?' Mario asked.

'I am taking a taxi back to the airport. I'll get a bit of sleep in the chopper. With what it has on board I think it best I watch over it.'

'What do I do after I've reported to you?'

'Main thing to report is if Tweed leaves – that is, *when* Tweed leaves. Then you can drive to join me at the airport. If I'm right the whole operation will get under way early in the morning. The fact that Tweed is here with Paula tells me something major is about to explode.'

'You have a plan, Emilio?'

'A flexible one. What I need is a diversion. I think Tweed and his team will provide exactly that.'

'You are leaving now, then?'

'Just a moment. Let me think.' Vitorelli ran his muscular hand through the back of his shaggy hair. 'We must get this right. Tweed has a car parked near the exit from this hotel. After paying a visit to the cloakroom I wandered outside. I recognized Newman sitting in that car, pretending to be asleep. If that car takes off to follow another one call me on the mobile, then wait. I'm sure Tina will be leaving early by car. You follow her, see what direction she is taking, call me on the mobile, then drive like hell to the airport. I'll wait for you in the chopper. That's it. I'm off now.'

Much later in the night, close to early morning, Tweed had also changed his mind. He had a detailed map of

Burgenland which he had taken from a display case when he was leaving Schwechat Airport on arrival. It was spread out on a large table and, as Paula watched, he had pored over it. When Marler, who had left to go to his room for a few minutes, returned, he began speaking rapidly.

'Marler, Paula has given me a perfect description of what it is like in Burgenland. It's flat, just flat. So it's like a gigantic chessboard and we must move our pieces across it carefully.'

'The trouble will be,' Marler observed, 'that we shall have no cover.'

'Agreed, but that works both ways. The enemy will also have no cover. We have three cars. Newman will drive one with Paula and me inside it. Nield will drive a second car. The third car will be driven by you.'

'In convoy? A perfect target for the enemy to destroy us at one go.'

'No, not in convoy. The three cars will be well spaced out. To start with, Nield, who is outside now, will take the lead. I leave you to judge the right moment, Marler, when you overtake Nield and Nield drops behind my car. That will put me in the centre of the spaced out cars.'

Tweed was using a walking stick someone had left behind in his room, wielding it as a pointer. Paula thought he looked like a general planning the final campaign in a war. The intensity of his concentration created an atmosphere of tension.

'I see you have put a couple of mobile phones on that desk,' Tweed remarked.

'I know you don't like them because messages over mobiles can be intercepted. I think we need them on this expedition.'

'I agree. We will code-name Hassan as Argus.'

'Good,' Marler said with relief. 'We will all have a scrambler mobile.'

'There will be an ambush on the way,' Tweed warned. 'Once we get anywhere near Hassan's headquarters, the strange house on that hill or mountain in Slovakia.'

'There may be more than one ambush.'

'Like any battle, we have to make it up as we go along. The ultimate objective will be that strange house. Is Nield still outside in the car?'

'He is.'

'Ask Newman to take his place for a few minutes and send Pete to me. Then Pete can go back to the car and Bob can come up here.'

Tweed explained his strategy to Nield when he arrived, then he repeated it to Newman when Nield had returned to his watching post in the car. Newman listened before he commented.

'I agreed. The trouble is there are only five of us. Butler would have been a great asset.'

'Oh, I have arranged communication at the right moment with Butler,' Tweed explained. 'Detective Windlin has stayed here in the hotel. I have given him the phone number of the Château d'Avignon and a coded message to pass on to Butler when the time comes. I can reach Windlin by mobile – I wouldn't contact Harry by mobile from Burgenland.'

'You seem to have thought of everything,' said Paula.

'What worries me is that I may have missed something . . .'

Minutes later everyone was in position. Nield was outside the hotel, waiting and watching from his car. Newman and Paula, with Marler, his satchel bulging again, were in Tweed's room. Newman had paid all

453

their bills so they could leave instantly. Tweed decided it was time he rang Monica.

'I was just about to call you,' she said. 'More news from our secret contacts abroad. The US Fifth Fleet, moving steadily north in the Indian Ocean, has been joined by a second aircraft carrier group. We're there too. A British nuclear submarine surfaced in the same area. It fired one dummy missile a huge distance south towards the Antarctic. Enemy aircraft were patrolling and must have seen it.'

'Any of this in the newspaper?'

'Yes. A brief reference to what they call a rumour in the *International Herald Tribune*. The story also reports another rumour – that British aircraft from our base at Akotiri in Cyprus were seen taking off and heading east. I think soon the world press will be splashing the story.'

'That's very interesting. The West is now waking up, at the eleventh hour – as usual. I may be difficult to reach during the next few hours. I'll call you when I can.'

'What *is* happening?' Paula asked when he relayed the news.

'Pressure will be mounting on a certain Head of State.'

'I don't suppose it means anything,' Newman remarked, 'but I saw Vitorelli leaving the hotel. Mario appeared to be staying behind here.'

'No idea where he went, I suppose?' queried Tweed.

'I followed him to the exit. He jumped into a taxi and the cab rocketed off.'

'Vitorelli is a very tough and determined character. I'm sure he has something in mind. Maybe in due course we'll find out what it is.'

He grabbed the phone before it could ring a third time. Nield was on the line.

'Tina and Argus are just leaving. Big limo. Has an escort car with it. They're moving. Just a minute. Another limo's pulled in. Chauffeur opening door for two women. Blonde is getting in front, redhead in back. They're moving, following Argus. I'm off.'

'It has started,' said Tweed.

44

At that hour, before dawn had broken, Vienna was at its most impressive – and oppressive. Newman, taking instructions about the route from Nield on the mobile, had him in view. Behind them Marler followed. Paula, seated in the back with Tweed, gazed out. The massive stone buildings of Vienna loomed up on both sides, relics of the great days of the Austro-Hungarian Empire before the First World War.

'It must have taken a fortune to build this city,' she commented.

'Built on money extracted from the satellites which made up the Empire of long ago,' Tweed explained. 'The Czechs were especially resentful of the money earned by them which found its way here. The Hungarians too.'

They drove on and on through the wide quiet streets. To Paula Vienna seemed to go on and on for ever. A vast monument to something which had not existed for over ninety years. She noticed that on the seat beside him Newman had two machine-pistols. At the last moment before leaving the hotel Marler had persuaded her to accept several grenades.

'These are stun, these shrapnel, these are smoke bombs . . .'

It had been such a rush leaving the Sacher she hadn't

455

refused them. Now they nestled in her shoulder bag, which bulged in the way Marler's satchel had. Newman drove with one hand on the wheel, the other holding his mobile as he kept in constant touch with Nield and Marler. They were leaving behind the palatial buildings when Newman spoke again.

'Pete reports he's just passed a signpost. Burgenland.'

'I thought so,' said Tweed. 'So far, so good.'

Some time later Vienna was only a memory and they were crossing a vast plain which, in the first light of dawn, stretched away into the distance. No sign of life anywhere. For Paula this was familiar territory, recalling her drive from the airport with the thuggish Valja. Newman spoke briefly.

'Pete reports the limos have outdistanced him. They must have supercharged engines. But he can still see their lights.'

'Tell him to keep them in sight as long as he can,' Tweed ordered.

'Marler's on,' Newman reported. 'Says Mario dived into a car as he left the Sacher. Tailed him a distance, then turned off to a road signposted *Flughafen*. The airport.'

'Makes sense,' Tweed replied.

'Why?' asked Paula.

'We may see Vitorelli again. In the sky.'

'He must like me,' said Paula, attempting a joke.

'I'm sure he does. But he dislikes another woman.'

The luminous light of dawn had grown stronger, revealing the incredible endlessness of the flat plain, sprawling away to the east. The road surface was good but nothing fenced it off from the level fields running away to the horizon on both sides. In the fields stumpy foot-high vegetation was growing, arranged in straight rows.

'Vineyards,' said Tweed. 'Imagine how the sun beats down on them during the day.'

'I did bring bottles of mineral water,' Paula told him, 'remembering my last trip this way. We just passed a signpost. *Bruck*.'

'We're heading in the right direction,' Tweed confirmed.

'Look, a village. They're weird. There are only a few of them with a long distance between them.'

They passed along a street with one-storey houses huddled close together. No one about. It was still very early in the morning. Tweed imagined the inhabitants were already inside, getting ready for another hard day's toil in the fields. Without warning, Marler overtook them, raced ahead. Shortly afterwards Pete Nield's car appeared, moving more slowly. Newman overtook him. They were now sandwiched between Nield behind and Marler somewhere ahead of them.

Daylight came suddenly and the vastness of the plain was exposed dramatically. They were in the middle of nowhere, on Tweed's chessboard. They could clearly see Marler's car now. A signpost appeared by the roadside. *Morzach*. Tweed leaned forward, seeing a much larger village ahead of them. He tensed.

It was larger but of the same weird character as the smaller village they had passed through earlier. A single line of one-storey houses, again huddled together, bordered both sides of the long street. The houses had shallow roofs and the plaster walls of each dwelling were painted a pastel colour, one green, another pink, another yellow, another blue. Paula assumed the colours were an attempt to cheer up the bleak surroundings.

'Slow down!' Tweed ordered. 'Then stop in the middle of this village. Recall Marler urgently. Tell Nield to drive like the wind until he reaches us.'

'What on earth—' began Paula.

457

Tweed's sharp eyes had seen the sun glinting off a pile of junk in the road ahead. The junk was a mixture of brutal, star-shaped pieces of iron and glass. It would have ripped their tyres to pieces, marooned them. He threw open his door, told Paula to open hers. Then he got out, looked around, listened.

A dreadful silence descended on him. Not a sound anywhere. It reminded him of the strange village of Shrimpton in Dorset – where he had been similarly struck by silence and the complete absence of people. Like a deserted village, abandoned by the one-time inhabitants. There was something sinister in the heavy silence. Then it was broken by the sound of Marler returning at top speed, followed by the arrival of Nield. Standing close to his car, Tweed waved both hands and arms in an encircling gesture, the signal for danger.

'What's wrong?' Paula asked standing by her open door as ordered.

'It's an ambush!' Tweed shouted, his voice reaching Marler and Nield.

He had hardly spoken when from inside hidden alleys between the houses a crowd of Croats appeared, screaming their guts out and brandishing long knives as they rushed forward. Nield, who had studied the photos taken by his self-developing camera when they had arrived at the airport yelled out.

'It's the Croats from the airport . . .'

One of them, his expression of vicious glee on his high cheekboned face, rushed at Tweed, his knife high above his head to strike. Paula, who had moved to the rear of the car, shot him in the chest. He gurgled, fell over backwards in a tumble of his strange robe-like clothes. As more of the mob came forward cautiously, Marler's voice rang out in a strident shout.

'Get behind the bloody car!'

Tweed dived back into the car, slamming the door

shut behind him, slipped out of the far side where Paula now crouched beside her boss. The Croats, yelling like dervishes, swarmed towards the car. There was a sudden murderous chatter of machine-pistols. The Croats were caught in a triple crossfire. Marler firing from near the front of the car, Newman firing across the bonnet crouched behind the vehicle, Nield firing from the rear. A hail of bullets hit the mob in the massive fusillade. Bodies sagged in the road, followed by more bodies as the second wave of Croats had no time to flee.

Then Morzach was enveloped by the awful silence again. Marler called out to Newman to stay where he was while he checked the houses. Nield joined Marler. The two men disappeared for what was only a short time but which seemed like eternity to Paula. When Marler reappeared, followed by Nield, she thought she had never seen him with such a grave expression.

'They massacred all the villagers to use their houses for the ambush.'

'Oh, my God! How horrible,' Paula said in a subdued voice.

Newman had already hauled out a sheet of canvas from the boot. He used it as a makeshift brush, sweeping the iron stars and the glass to the side of the road. Shaking it, to get rid of any glass, he flung it back into the boot.

'I think we ought to get moving. We have a job to do,' he said.

'Agreed,' replied Tweed. 'We can call the police anonymously later. What's in the road can't just be left here. To say nothing of the poor devils inside the houses. It's barbaric.'

As the cars started moving Paula deliberately avoided looking at the pile of bodies on one side of the road. Tweed put an arm round her and hugged her. He was careful to say nothing, guessing she was in shock.

His determination to finish the job was reinforced. Hassan was a man who would stop at nothing.

They were several miles away from the village and the billiard-table like plain was extending away for ever. At Tweed's order they had resumed their same places. Marler was some distance ahead of them and Nield had dropped back when Newman began contacting both cars on his mobile. He spoke to Nield first, then Marler. He stiffened during the second brief contact.

'Marler says he can see the hill with the long house on its summit,' he reported to Tweed. 'Says we'll see it in a minute.'

Tweed leaned forward, hands gripping the empty seat back in front of him. The sun was now scorching down on them even at this early hour. The temperature inside the cars was rising. Opening the windows, they found torrid heat pouring in, so they closed them again. Then Tweed saw it.

In the distance a long low hill reared up from the level plain. Perched on its summit was the long house which was Hassan's headquarters. It stood out against the glowing azure sky.

'That's it,' said Paula.

Inside the first limo, sitting by herself in the back, Tina had gazed resentfully up at the house before it disappeared from view as the chauffeur drove it across the border, along the track which took them into Slovakia. She had decided she did not want to come here at all. She had been rushed out of the Sacher into the car.

Her resentment increased as the driver negotiated the steep curving road which took them up one side of the mountain. Arriving at the top, the driver swung their limo right and up to the entrance at the front, facing away from Austria. As he pulled up Hassan, seated in front, jumped out to open the rear door for her. They had not exchanged one word during the whole journey. Hassan bowed.

'Welcome home.'

'I hate this bloody place,' she snapped. 'It's like a morgue. I'm not staying here long.'

'Come inside. Have a drink.'

'There should have been drinks on the way. Some limo you have.'

'It cost a fortune.'

'They must have seen you coming.'

He escorted her inside, followed by the chauffeur with her case. She heard the door being closed and locked. The sound did not soothe her temper.

'I'll have my drink on the terrace,' she said.

'First, let me show you your suite.'

Leading the way through the deep-pile carpeted hall, he opened a door to a suite overlooking Austria. It was luxuriously furnished in an Eastern style which Tina detested. Her case was deposited in a dressing room and the chauffeur left as Hassan moved back towards the door.

'These windows don't open,' she fumed after trying to open the French doors to the terrace. 'They did last time.'

'We are air-conditioned,' Hassan replied smoothly.

'How long – how many days – do you expect me to stay in this crazy house?' she demanded.

'Drinks are on the table.'

'I asked you a question. Haven't you any manners at all? If a lady asks a question she expects an answer.'

'We shall do everything possible to make you comfortable.'

'Stuff that. This is like being in Siberia. Answer me or I'm leaving right away.'

Hassan closed the door from the other side and she heard him lock it. She swore foully. Studying the array of bottles she poured herself a glass of red wine, drank, swore again.

It had taken Hassan an effort to retain his composure when Tina had started playing up. He knew that the second limo would soon arrive. When he opened the front door it was just pulling in. He ran to open the front passenger door where Karin Berg sat beside the chauffeur. He glanced at the woman in the back.

'I will be with you in no time. Give me a minute.' He turned his attention to the Swedish woman, opening the door, bowing. 'Very good to have you as a guest again. One of the superior suites is waiting for you.'

'Where is my thirty thousand?' Berg asked over her shoulder as she entered the hall. 'Payment on delivery. I'm delivered.'

'Let me show you the way. Money is such a sordid subject when you have just arrived.'

'I became sordid long ago.'

Her tone was crisp. Hassan led her down a corridor, opened a door to a suite. She walked in as the chauffeur arrived with her case. The room was spacious, the furniture expensive but the arched windows were very small. Karin was tall enough to peer through one without going up on her toes. Outside the wilderness of Slovakia spread away.

'The view is charming,' she said. 'I prefer the other side looking down on Austria.'

She heard a click, looked round. Hassan had gone, had closed the door and she heard it being locked from the outside. She shrugged. She would hammer away at him until he gave her the money. Looking out of the

462

window again she saw to her right a pile of rocks. It was beyond them that the pathway led down the hill until it crossed into Austria.

Hassan had hurried back to the limo. Opening the rear door, he bowed. Simone Carnot stared back at him with an expression of resignation. She was thinking she ought never to have come. She should have taken her chances with the police. Then she recalled the description someone had once given her of Swiss prisons. No brutality, but no comforts of any sort either. Perhaps this prison was preferable – at least for a short time.

'You have the best suite in my headquarters,' he said unctuously.

'If you say so . . .'

Once he had locked Simone in her own suite, Hassan hurried to his office, sat behind his huge desk. He felt relieved. Now he had The Sisterhood under his personal control. The relief gave way to worry as he remembered he hadn't had another progress report from Willie.

Then he realized, knowing Willie, that he would be hurtling across Europe to deliver the bacillus sample. He wouldn't waste any more time phoning. Anxiety returned as he glanced through the copy of the *International Herald Tribune* the concierge had handed him as he had rushed out of the Sacher.

His pallid eyes were riveted to the story about rumours of the US Fifth Fleet entering the Indian Ocean. Hassan reached under his desk, pulled a lever. Above the roof of the house a system of aerials was elevated, the key to an advanced and complex communications device. He had to call the Head of State.

* * *

463

Leaning forward in his car, Tweed stared at the aerials and dishes which had suddenly appeared. He recognized them and their purpose. He spoke sharply.

'Bob, hand me the mobile, quick.'

Dialling Sacher, he asked to be put through to Detective Windlin urgently. Windlin came on the line almost immediately. Tweed told him to call Butler to transmit the coded message to him at the Château d'Avignon.

At the chateau Butler, an early riser, already showered and dressed, simply said one word.

'Understood.'

He limped down the stairs. Fred Brown watched him with amusement from behind his reception desk. He enjoyed other people's troubles. Stan, the thin sneering porter, joined his colleague in the fun. He called out as Butler limped towards the front entrance.

'Got a bunion have we, old boy? Hope it doesn't hurt. Much.'

Butler could have smashed his face in. Instead he forced himself to smile as he replied, close to the entrance.

'Need a bit of fresh air.'

Once out of their sight he moved. He hadn't bothered to put on the bandage – it would hamper his agility. The previous day he had transferred the satchel containing the bomb, timer and a few of his clothes from the top of his wardrobe to behind a thick shrub in the front of the chateau.

Hoisting it onto his shoulder, he began climbing the network of ivy below the turret. This time he climbed much faster, his gloved hands clutching the ivy. Then he was level with the turret. The deep window had been left partly open, presumably to counter the heat which built up inside it. The eight-sided room was empty, a swivel chair placed in front of the communications system which looked like the control panel aboard a Jumbo jet. He stepped over the window ledge and was inside.

It took him two minutes to extract the pancake-shaped bomb, which had metallic clamps attached to one side. He clamped it over the control panel. Setting the timer for five minutes, he linked it to the bomb. Then, without hesitation, he turned the switch which made it active. Now if anyone came in and tried to remove it the bomb would detonate prematurely. He went to the window, looked down, sucked in his breath.

Below in the courtyard, Stan had decided he needed a spot of fresh air. On his way out Butler had noticed a bulge under the sneering thug's armpit. Stan was carrying some kind of gun in a shoulder holster. Butler checked his watch.

Four minutes to detonation.

Stan was smoking a cigarette, had opened the gates, was gazing along the road.

Three minutes to detonation.

Fred Brown had appeared now. He strolled over to Stan. They were chatting. Butler's hands inside his gloves were sweating. He ran to the door, turned the handle. It was locked. He ran back to the window. Stan was stubbing out his cigarette with his foot. He continued chatting with Fred.

Two minutes to detonation.

The phone rang in the reception area. Both men went back inside. Butler climbed out, half-slithered down the ancient wall, a long piece of ivy came loose in his left hand, he held on with his right hand, grasped some more ivy with his left, slithering down and down, never losing his grip. His feet hit the ground. With the satchel over his shoulder he ran for the exit, not caring that his pounding feet made a noise on the gravel.

'Hey, you! Stop! I said stop . . .!'

Stan the Snake's voice. Butler ran out between the open gates, covering the ground along the road like a marathon runner. *Boom!* He heard the detonation. Much louder than he'd expected. The whole turret exploded outwards, hurling chunks of shattered masonry everywhere. Some of it landed in the road behind Butler. He risked a quick look back. Through a gap in the trees he saw relics of stone like jagged teeth where the turret had reared up.

He was nearing the point where the track led off into the forest when bullets hit the road. Rounding a bend, he dived up the track inside the forest. He could hear feet pounding on the road, coming closer. He thought as he ran. There would be no time to drag his motorcycle out of the undergrowth before his pursuers arrived. Breathing heavily, he slipped behind the massive trunk of a tall tree, his hand feeling inside his satchel. He grabbed a shrapnel grenade, released the safety mechanism.

He could hear feet thumping nearer along the crumpled bracken on the path. He waited, timing his movement carefully. When he peered round the trunk Stan, holding a handgun, was near. Immediately behind him Fred was running towards him, holding a machine-pistol which he was handling clumsily. Stan stopped in surprise as he saw Butler's head. Fred bumped into him.

Butler lobbed the grenade. His aim was perfect. It landed at Stan's feet, exploded. Butler stared. Stan jumped off the ground, jerked his arms in the air. Butler had never seen anything like it. Stan's corpse fell face forward on to the path. Behind him Fred's right arm was hanging down, covered in blood. Fred staggered, turned away, stumbled back along the path towards the chateau. He was still on his feet when Butler last saw him, dragging his way back along the road.

Butler used gloves to drag his motorcycle out of the

prickly undergrowth. He wheeled the machine back to the road, over the machine-pistol Fred had dropped. Sitting astride the saddle, Butler was glad as he switched on the engine that no guests had been hurt when the turret had exploded – he had been the only guest left. His fake limping leg had saved him from suspicion.

The vital communications link between Slovakia and certain other transmitting stations in France, Germany and Britain had been destroyed. Butler raced off, headed down the curving road descending from Mount Salève to Geneva. He was making for the airport, following Tweed's instructions.

45

Hassan had reluctantly decided to let his three guests out of their rooms to enjoy drinks on the terrace looking out over Austria. He had been forced to take this decision because he couldn't stand the pressure. Tina had started the upheaval. Picking up a small stone statuette she had used it to hammer nonstop on the locked door, and the noise had echoed along the corridor to the other suites.

'Let me out of this bloody prison or I'll smash every window,' she had screamed at the top of her voice, beside herself with rage.

When Hassan unlocked the door, opened it, she threw the statuette at him. He just caught it before it hit him and smashed to pieces on the wood-block floor which, unlike the entrance hall, had no carpet. He stared at her, appalled.

'Do you know how much this statuette is worth? It was dug up out of the desert and is thousands of years old.'

'I don't give a damn for the silly thing. I'm going out on to the terrace,' she shouted. 'I hate this flaming log cabin you call a house. Get out of my way.'

Picking up a bottle of wine she had perched next to the wall she pushed past him. She was shouting insults at him as she went past the doors to the other suites on her left. Karin Berg heard her and began hammering on her own locked door with her clenched fist. Sighing, Hassan put the statuette on a side table in the corridor and unlocked Karin's door.

'If you'd just waited I was coming to get you,' he said as she came out.

'Well, you've come, so everyone is happy,' she said calmly, 'I'd like to go for a walk – that means letting me out of the front entrance.'

'You can join my other guests on the terrace. You'll have the view I understood you wanted. Josip will bring you a selection of drinks.'

'Is he still here? Last time he couldn't understand one word of any European language. What is he? An Uzbek?'

Without waiting for a reply she followed Tina out onto the terrace. In one respect Hassan had understood his 'guests'. Intending to let them out onto the terrace later, he had had three tables placed well apart. Tina, holding her bottle, grabbed a glass off a tray Josip was bringing and stalked out. She chose a remote table to the left, sat down, poured herself a drink. She took no notice whatsoever of the panoramic view.

Karin, on the contrary, immediately walked down the steps to the narrow lower level. Gazing into Austria, shading her eyes against the blazing sun, she then looked down. She was on the edge of the ancient quarry and its rock wall fell vertically below her three hundred feet. Not suffering from vertigo, she looked at the litter of huge boulders far below.

'It's like a desert,' she said to herself. 'Now how can I persuade Hassan to let me out of the front entrance? To hell with the thirty thousand if he won't pay up.'

Shielding her eyes again, she searched the sky. She had heard the steady beat of a helicopter somewhere. Unable to locate it, she walked back, sat down at the table as far away as possible from Tina.

Hassan had decided he might as well release Simone Carnot. She said nothing when he unlocked her door and invited her to visit the terrace. When she saw the two women already seated outside she took out a mirror from her handbag, used her hand to adjust her flaming red hair. With no other option, she sat down at the centre table, thankful it was well apart from the other two women.

Hassan had gone back to his office. He felt it vital to pass on the reports in the newspaper to the Head of State. He sat before the communications console after placing earphones over his head. His temper was not lessened by his reception.

'The Head of State is in conference with his generals. He is not to be disturbed.'

'This is I, Hassan. I have urgent news. Put me through to my father at once.'

'The Head of State is not to be disturbed—'

'I'll have your head on a plate!'

In a frenzy, Hassan broke the connection. He had recognized the voice of a man who called himself Secretary-General. He fawned over the Head of State at every opportunity, hoping for more power. In desperation Hassan worked at the console, calling up the centre at the Château d'Avignon. There was no reply. The line seemed to be down. Frustrated almost beyond endurance, he returned to his seat behind his desk and crashed down both clenched fists on its surface.

'I think Tweed is in one of those cars,' said Vitorelli while he looked through his field glasses. 'We are at the right place at the right time.'

Inside the helicopter Mario was at the controls while Vitorelli sat beside him, scanning the bleakness of Burgenland through the binoculars. As they came closer he swivelled his focus on to the terrace of the house on the mountain. Mario heard him suck in his breath.

'What is it, Chief?'

'I can—'

Vitorelli broke off what he was saying as though unable to say any more. Mario glanced at him and saw he was sitting rigidly as though made of concrete.

'Is something wrong?' Mario pressed.

'On that terrace I can clearly see Tina sitting with two other women. I do believe The Sisterhood is there – all of them. And after all this time I have tracked Tina.'

His tone was ice-cold. He was still sitting in the same rigid position. Mario thought he had never seen Emilio, always so full of life and restless, stay so still for so long.

'Carry out the plan,' Vitorelli eventually said, so quietly that Mario, listening through his earphones, had to ask Vitorelli to repeat what he'd said into the microphone. Changing course, it was Mario who spotted something odd in an area between Tweed's three cars and the border of Slovakia.

'There is something strange in that field of vineyards. They look like men sprawled flat on the ground between the rows near the road.'

Vitorelli focused his glasses, stared intently through the lenses. Then he lowered the binoculars and sucked in one of his deep breaths.

470

'They *are* men. Lying flat on the soil. And by their sides they have weapons. Tweed has led me to my objective – without realizing it. One good turn deserves another . . .'

He gave Mario a fresh instruction and again the chopper changed course.

The three cars were, at that moment, well spaced out. In the lead car Marler was behind the wheel. Inside Tweed's car Paula was gazing up at the distant chopper which was coming closer now.

'This is a repeat performance of what I experienced when Valja drove me out here,' she said. 'As I told you, there was this helicopter in the sky further south.'

'Vitorelli,' Tweed replied. 'I rather expected he'd put in an appearance.'

'But what is he doing? Look at the machine.'

Some distance ahead of the car Marler was driving, the chopper was hovering over a field. Then it began behaving in an odd manner. The helicopter, staying over the same piece of ground, climbed a hundred or so feet, then dropped again. It repeated the manoeuvre three times. Then it gained greater altitude and flew towards Slovakia.

'What on earth?' exclaimed Paula.

Marler had caught on to what the pilot of the chopper was trying to tell him. He rammed his foot down, raced at high speed past the marked field, glancing to his right. Several of the stumpy vines quivered, yet there was not a hint of a breeze. Rather the sun was beating down on the plain, turning it into a furnace. Marler slowed down, spoke into his mobile.

'Enemy ambush. I'm turning back. Laager! Laager! Laager!'

They had practised this manoeuvre, had used it in

471

the past in action. It was based on the tactics of the Boer War when the enemy had formed its wagons into a circle, creating a small fortress, difficult to attack.

'You heard that, Pete,' Newman said urgently into his mobile.

'I'm coming.' Nield replied.

Marler had performed a swift U-turn, was hurtling back towards them. A few hundred yards away he stopped, slanting his car at an angle. Newman rushed towards him, braked only feet from Marler's car, swivelled his car to form the second side of the laager. Nield came up behind them, positioned his vehicle to close the third side.

Everyone left their cars, crouched down inside the protected triangle created by the three cars. A dozen yards or so from the verge of the road men were rising up out of the field like something out of a legend, holding machine-pistols. Marler shouted the order.

'Use smoke bombs! A lot of them! Here we go!'

As he'd started to speak Paula grabbed a smoke bomb from her shoulder bag, handed it to Tweed. She was grasping another bomb when Tweed stood up, arm and hand over his right shoulder like the bowler in cricket he had once been. His bomb landed just in front of Big Ben, exploded. Acrid, choking dark smoke burst in all directions. Ben couldn't see, couldn't breathe. Paula hurled her bomb. At the same time the others were throwing more bombs. They aimed them in different directions, covering the group of advancing killers.

'We'll take them as they come out of the smoke,' shouted Newman.

He had already left the laager, a knuckleduster over the fingers of his left hand, his right holding the Smith & Wesson. Behind him Tweed rushed across the field at astonishing speed, heading for another edge of the black

472

cloud. Paula and Nield spread out while Marler ran round the far side of the cloud.

A tall stumbling figure emerged from the smoke near Newman. It was Big Ben, his machine-pistol clutched under his arm. Seeing Newman, he managed a croaking bellow.

'Rudge . . . here . . . they are . . .'

Newman hit him on the bridge of the nose with the knuckleduster. Ben, face covered in blood, sagged to the ground. Paula saw Newman bending over the body, checked the neck pulse, realized the man was dead. Paula ran towards Newman, Browning in her hand. She had seen Rudge *crawling* out of the smoke, a handkerchief he had spat into covering his nose. Blinking, he stood up behind Newman, lifting his machine-pistol. Paula hammered the muzzle of her gun down on the back of Rudge's head with such force it bounced off his skull. The large fat man dropped his weapon. He fell forward, hitting the ground hard. Paula felt his pulse. He was dead.

A thug stumbled out of the smoke within feet of Tweed. His eyes were streaming as he fumbled with his weapon, waving it about futilely. Tweed kicked him in the groin. The thug bent forward, choking. Standing behind him, both hands clasped together, Tweed brought them down on the back of his neck. The thug collapsed.

At the far side of the cloud, leaderless, two more men came out of the cloud. One tried to aim his machine-pistol when he saw Marler. Stooping, Marler used the barrel of his Armalite like a club, smashing it against his opponent's kneecaps. The other man moved as though drunk. Marler brought the barrel down on his head. The thug curled up on the ground, lay very still. Swinging round, Marler saw the first thug lying on the soil, trying to aim his weapon. Marler jumped on his hands. Releasing his weapon, the thug yelled with pain, opened his mouth and took in more smoke. He rolled his eyes, closed them, lay lifeless. The last man, a handkerchief tied round his face, walked out, his machine-pistol held steady. He looked to his left. The wrong way. He had almost walked into Nield to his right. Nield hit him hard on the side of the neck with his stiffened hand. It was like striking a man with an iron bar. He fell, his head twisted in a grotesque position.

Stepping back from the smoke cloud, Tweed's team stood and waited. Gradually the smoke settled, became a thin transparent smear. It was obvious they had dealt with the whole gang. Tweed waved for his men to return to the cars. He spoke when they had all come back. Paula, who had accompanied him, stood by his side.

'Not a shot fired. That's very good.'

It was one of Tweed's key maxims, one he had dinned into his team on many previous occasions. 'Don't shoot unless you have to.'

Tweed stood in the road with Paula. He waited until Marler had manoeuvred his car and driven off ahead. At the same time Nield steered his car until it was pointed towards the east, then sat still. Paula pointed, her voice full of anxiety.

'Oh, Lord. Look at the chopper. It's on fire.'

Heading close to Slovakia, the helicopter was trailing smoke from its tail. It wobbled, then disappeared behind and beyond the mountain where the strange house stood like a toy building. Tweed shook his head before getting into the car which had Newman already behind the wheel.

'No, it isn't crashing. We still have a way to go before we're close to our objective. Let's get moving.' He

474

nodded towards the field they had just left. 'That rates another anonymous call to the police.'

46

'What the hell is happening?' Tina demanded. 'Is that field on fire? Not that it matters – just a few mouldy old vines.'

It mattered to Hassan, who stood near the edge of the lower level below the terrace. He had been watching through field glasses for several minutes. He had sprung his trap. Now he was struggling to keep his nerve.

To the naked eye the three cars stationary on the road were like miniatures. Seen through his field glasses they were only too real. In disbelief, he continued watching as the smoke cloud cleared. He had his greatest shock when he saw clearly Tweed standing in the road next to Paula. He lowered the binoculars, hardly able to stop his hands trembling. Tweed was now close to his headquarters.

'Oh, look,' trilled Tina, 'that helicopter is on fire. And it is coming this way. It's not going to crash on this house, is it?'

'No, it's veering away,' Hassan said in a strangled voice.

'Could be exciting if we saw it crash in the fields.'

'Shut your mouth.'

'People don't talk to me like that.'

'I told you to shut your face.'

'I'm leaving here.'

'Sit down before I shove you off the cliff.'

Tina was taken aback. She had never heard Hassan speak with such ferocity. She sat down, watched the helicopter, which was still fairly high up. More smoke billowed out and now it was wobbling. Everyone was silent as the machine flew beyond the house, lost altitude and disappeared behind the ridge of the mountain, diving into Slovakia.

'I'd like another drink,' said Tina, expecting Hassan to refill her glass.

'The bottle is on the table,' Hassan said quietly.

He went back inside the house and summoned the chief of the elite force of eight guards who stayed out of sight. Hassan had had the house built as his headquarters. He had specified it must have the character of a house in Slovakia, so undue attention would not be drawn to it.

'Tell your men to be on the alert,' he ordered. 'If anyone tries to break in, shoot them down without mercy. Take no prisoners. All the guards must remain inside the house in their normal tactical positions.'

Tweed had been right when he said the helicopter was not crashing. Once out of sight of the long house behind a ridge, Mario landed the machine where it was invisible to any watchers. Vitorelli had photographed the landing point when he had last flown over the area on the day when Paula had been driven by Valja.

They left the machine when they had loaded the backpacks they had brought with them. With Vitorelli in the lead, they made their way to the sunken path climbing the mountain near the eastern end of the house. This was the path Karin Berg had discovered on her training visit.

The heat was intense as the sun glared down on the path but they climbed it rapidly. Reaching the top, Vitorelli crouched down behind a boulder. The photographs he had taken earlier from every angle, which he had studied so carefully, had shown him accurately the curious construction of the headquarters.

Due to a backward slope at the top of the mountain the men from the east who had built the house had erected the front on short squat stilts. The necessity to do this had left apertures under the building at the eastern end. Vitorelli studied the apertures quickly through his binoculars.

'We can crawl along the ground on our bellies,' he told Mario. 'In no time we will be under the house. We must work quickly. We must keep our bodies flat on the ground so they seem part of that ground. We must move from boulder to boulder.'

'You have told me this before,' Mario grumbled in a whisper.

'I tell you again. We shall only get one chance. And on the way back we do the same thing. There will be an impulse to hurry. We do not hurry.'

'You repeat yourself again.'

'Because it is so important.'

'I had realized that!'

'Keep your voice down.'

The last remark was a sign of the tension Vitorelli was labouring under. They had carried on the conversation in whispers. Dragging their backpacks alongside them – perched on their backs the packs would have made them more visible – they slithered like snakes over the arid ground. Here and there boulders were scattered. With Mario following, Vitorelli slithered from one boulder to another, forcing himself to move slowly when he was exposed in the open.

The sun scorched them with blowtorch intensity. Accustomed as they were to the heat in Italy neither man had ever experienced such high temperatures. Their bodies were covered with sweat. Their clothes were already sodden. Then it happened when they were halfway from the top of the path to the house.

They heard the heavy, steel-lined front door being unlocked and opened. Vitorelli lay still behind a boulder he had reached. He hoped Mario was not in the open but dared not look back. He felt sure guards were coming out to patrol.

There were guards, carrying machine-pistols. Two of them had opened the door and stood in the entrance surveying the arid desert. A wall of heat flooded over them. The head guard grimaced and shook his head. Despite Hassan's orders he had intended checking the front of the house. He spoke to the other guard.

'It is too hot to go out there. No one is about. It would be pointless to search for nothing.'

Behind his boulder Vitorelli heard the voices clearly but he did not understand a word. The guard had spoken in a strange language. He held himself absolutely still, although he had cramp in his left leg. The pain was agonizing but he refused to move. Then he heard the door close, several locks being turned. He waited for the crunch of feet on the stony ground, then realized they had returned inside. He stretched his left leg several times, reached back and rubbed his calf with his hand. The cramp disappeared.

Mario had watched all this through a slit between two boulders close together. He began to slither forward again as he saw Vitorelli moving. They had to move very slowly because they made a noise passing over the stony ground. It was a nerve-racking progress, so slow while the sun continued to roast them.

Vitorelli was careful not to move any faster when he left the last boulder behind. Now he had to move across open ground between the boulder and the house. He could hardly believe it when he slipped through one of the apertures between stilts supporting this end of the house. Mario joined him sooner than he had expected.

They lay still for a short time, recovering. It was hot under the house but seemed incredibly cool now the sun could no longer get at them. They communicated with mimes and gestures.

'We lay the bombs well apart,' Vitorelli indicated, waving a hand, pointing to one location and then another.

All the bombs, some high explosive, some thermite, were linked together with a thin cable. The first job Vitorelli had to do was to link up one of his bombs to one of Mario's. It was a tricky undertaking and he first took out a comparatively dry handkerchief to wipe his streaming hands dry. It was dark under the house but gradually their eyes became accustomed to being out of the sun and they could see clearly.

Vitorelli worked partly by feel. It took longer than he had expected to complete the connection but then all the bombs were linked up. He sighed, the first time he had expressed any kind of emotion. Then he froze. Footsteps echoed above their heads. People were walking about inside the house, possibly guards.

'We shall have to be very quiet. If we can hear their footsteps down here then they may hear us slithering about on all these loose stones under the house.'

Vitorelli indicated this message by pointing upwards with his two index fingers, then cupping hands to his ears, then spreading his hands to emphasize the rubble they would have to slither across. Mario kept nodding his head to show not only that he understood but also would Vitorelli please shut up so they could get on with the job. His boss grinned, nodded back. They began their work.

Each man, watching the cable carefully, placed a

bomb under a different part of the house. Slimmer than Mario, Vitorelli carried bombs to the other end of the house. It was difficult. The slope which had caused the builders to erect the eastern section on squat stilts ended close to the front door. There was now less space to slither along and the house was pressing down on him. He had placed the last bomb when he realized he couldn't work his way back. The floor was pressing down on his shoulder blades. He waved a hand, hoping Mario would realize he was trapped.

The next thing he knew was Mario's strong hands had grasped each of his ankles, was gently hauling him backwards. Vitorelli expected that at the least he would suffer bruised shoulder blades but Mario had been slow and careful. Reaching the eastern end Vitorelli stretched himself. No damage.

The last – vital – thing he had to do was to place the transmitter linked to the bombs. Holding the square box, he poked his head out, saw no one, placed it at the eastern corner and elevated the aerial which would receive the signal and detonate the bombs. It was no accident that the prominent aerial, extended outside the house, was the same colour as the house's wall.

They now had to return the way they had come. As Vitorelli, taking the lead, emerged into the open the sun's heat hit him like a blow after the apparent coolness under the house. Gritting his teeth, he headed back for the first boulder.

It seemed to take them twice as long to cover the ground as it had coming. Vitorelli had to strain every nerve of his willpower not to hurry. The ground itself was almost too hot to touch and by now both men were close to exhaustion. With Mario behind him Vitorelli forced his aching body to keep moving. His sodden clothes were caked with dust and he had a pounding headache.

Unexpectedly, he found himself on the edge of the sunken path. He rolled down into it, lay still for a few minutes revitalizing himself until Mario arrived. They said nothing to each other for a short time. Then Vitorelli laughed and spoke.

'Come on. Don't go to sleep. Back to the chopper.'

Still aching, they made their way back down the path, reached the bottom, turned left away from the house to where the chopper was standing. Vitorelli opened a door to the control cabin, climbed up, sat in the co-pilot's seat. From beneath the seat he lifted out a black control box and elevated the aerial. When he pressed a switch it would send a signal to the receiver next to the house, a signal which would transmit simultaneously to every bomb and detonate it.

'Take her up high,' he ordered Mario, already seated at the controls.

The main rotor started to turn, whizzed round faster and faster in conjunction with the tail rotor which guided the machine. The Sikorsky began to climb, climb, climb.

47

The three cars moved steadily along the road, drawing closer and closer to Slovakia. In the middle car Tweed sat next to Paula, who was now driving. In a rear seat Newman, Smith & Wesson in his hand, kept gazing at the fields on either side for any sign of a fresh attack.

'I don't think anything else will happen, Bob,' Tweed called back, guessing what was in Newman's mind. 'Hassan has shot his bolt.'

'Be prepared. The Boy Scout's motto,' Newman

retorted. 'It's always dangerous to make assumptions where safety is concerned.'

'You are right,' Tweed admitted.

Looking ahead, seeing Marler's car in the distance, Paula was blinking at the shimmering heat haze sizzling over the plain in the far distance. She had the car's visor pulled down to shield her eyes against the dazzling light.

'I think it's hotter than when I was last here,' she said. 'And it's incredible the way this plain goes on for ever.'

'Well, this is one of the areas Genghis Khan and his hordes of men on small shaggy horses swept across towards Europe,' Tweed commented. 'Or rather, it was his successor, Ogdai, who reached Liegnitz in Germany, only two hundred and fifty miles from the Channel. There he was at long last defeated by a mixed European army. What happened before could happen again – and this time succeed.'

'You give me the shivers,' Paula told him. 'I wonder what Hassan is doing at this moment?'

As she spoke Hassan was inside his office desperately trying to communicate the news he had heard to the Head of State. And again the Secretary-General was blocking him off.

'The Head of State cannot be disturbed. He is in a meeting with his generals.'

Hassan called him a filthy name and broke the connection. He need not have worried. Enemy aircraft patrolling in the sky above the Indian Ocean had seen the vast array of the US Fifth Fleet, now backed by a second massive aircraft carrier group, moving north at top speed. They had seen a British nuclear submarine surface and fire a trial missile without a warhead to the south. They had reported this menacing development to

482

their home base. Which was why the Head of State was conferring with his nervous generals endlessly.

Frustrated, in a ferocious rage, Hassan had stormed out of his office. To calm down, he had walked slowly along the corridor and out onto the terrace. The three members of The Sisterhood were still sitting at separate tables, hardly exchanging a word with each other.

'There are three cars coming towards us,' said Tina.

Hassan snatched up a drink which she had just poured for herself and swallowed it. Then he grabbed a pair of field glasses off her table.

'For your information,' she protested, 'that was my drink – and I was just going to use those binoculars.'

Hassan ignored her. He screwed the glasses to his eyes and scanned each car. The vehicles were close enough now for him to see who was inside each of them. He slammed the binoculars down on Tina's table. For a moment he couldn't get the words out.

'Tweed is in that middle car. He's coming to attack the house. He will end up stone cold dead.'

'Can I watch it happen, then?' Tina enquired.

'Don't be so grisly, dear,' said Karin, speaking for the first time.

'I was talking to Hassan, not you,' Tina snapped.

'We're all guilty,' Simone said quietly.

'Speak for yourself,' Tina snapped back.

'I'm speaking for all of us,' Simone replied in the same quiet tone.

'You'd do better to keep your mouth shut,' Tina retorted.

She stood up and walked down to the lower level to get away from the other women. Hassan followed her, passed her, stood close to the edge, raised his glasses again. He was hypnotized by the fact that Tweed was still alive.

What had happened to the Croats in Morzach? he wondered. What had happened to Big Ben and his experienced killers? The Sisterhood on the terrace had seen the smoke cloud but it had been so far away they hadn't been able to make out what was going on. As he stood, glaring through his glasses, Hassan suddenly felt movement under his feet. He stepped back quickly as a small part of the cliff gave way. Frightened, he returned to the terrace where Tina, seeing what had occurred, had run to.

'What's that noise?' she said. Turning to the east she giggled. 'Look, that helicopter didn't crash. It's coming back.'

'Probably tourists,' Hassan said in a bored tone. 'We get a few occasionally. A travel outfit in Vienna charges a fortune for the trip.'

'When do I get my binoculars back?' Tina demanded. 'Now!'

He shoved them at her. He was angry, confused, indecisive. He planned to make sure the Secretary-General had an accident – a fatal one – when he got back home. The arrival of Tweed, even though still a distance away, seemed a bad omen. The rock fall from the cliff edge worried him.

When he had had his headquarters built, disguising it as typical Slovakian architecture, he had flown in builders from his home state. They had worked much faster than Europeans would have done. But he had also brought the surveyors who had checked the site from home and now he had the vague fear they had not known their job.

Tina remained standing at the edge of the terrace, close to the lower level. She wanted to be away from the women, away from Hassan who had no manners at all. She was furious that he had taken her drink – and then her binoculars – without asking her permission.

Something was happening to the three spaced-out cars. Puzzled, she watched them, wishing she had picked up the binoculars from her table. Glancing back, she saw Hassan standing near to her. She had no intention of asking him for the binoculars. She did not even want to go near him.

Inside the middle car Tweed was staring upward into the sky. He was about to ask for the mobile when Paula spoke, her tone one of surprise and disbelief.

'That helicopter's reappeared. It must have been all right. And it's climbing to quite a height.'

'Hand me the mobile, please,' said Tweed. He called Marler first. 'I'm waiting here. Come back quickly.' He then called Nield. 'Close up on me. Now!' He then spoke to Paula. 'Stop here.'

As soon as the car was stationary he got out. Standing in the road, a pair of binoculars looped round his neck, he waited as Marler returned, got out of his car, followed by Nield from behind them. Paula had run round the front to join him.

'What's wrong?' she asked.

'Something dreadful is about to occur.'

'What do you mean?'

Without replying he raised the binoculars and focused them on the house at the top of the mountain. Newman, who also had binoculars, followed suit.

'Will someone tell me what is going on?' demanded Paula, exasperated.

'You will see,' Tweed replied in a blank voice.

She stared at the house. Then she switched her gaze to the helicopter which had started to fly away. Aboard the machine Vitorelli was staring down at the house. Without looking, he pressed down the switch which transmitted the radio signal. The result was instantaneous. All the high-explosive bombs and the thermite bombs detonated together.

485

There was a deafening roar which echoed across the plain. A wall of flame enveloped the rear of the house. The high explosive lifted the roof which fell forward. The entire house from one end to the other toppled like a stage set towards the terrace. The unstable ground was shifted by the force of the explosion. It began to give way, a gigantic slab of rock carried the terrace to the edge of the quarry face. Through his glasses Tweed caught sight of The Sisterhood and Hassan, still on the terrace, caught up in the massive landslide. Several men carrying weapons had run out onto the terrace. Guards, Tweed presumed. In the chaos of flames and terrifying movement of the ground The Sisterhood and Hassan vanished.

Then they witnessed an awesome sight. A portion of the mountain a hundred yards wide, which had supported house and terrace, slid forward like a moving platform. It crashed down the three-hundred-foot drop, hit the base of the quarry like an immense clap of thunder. A vast cloud of dust rose into the air as huge chunks of rock were hurled in all directions. For the third time Paula asked Tweed to give her the binoculars.

'No!'

He thought he had seen one of the women, clothes on fire, flailing her arms as she dropped like a marionette when the slab had plunged downwards. It was so terrible he didn't want Paula to see it. Newman, like Tweed, still stood with his glasses glued to his eyes.

They all stood watching it, not moving. It took some time for the dense cloud of dust to settle, to expose what had been hidden behind it. Only then did Tweed hand the glasses to Paula. At the base of the quarry an incredibly high mass of debris had appeared. Tweed was sure all the bodies would be deep under the pile. The whole shape of the quarry wall had been altered. A great curve of rock face was now indented into what had been a sheer straight face. There was no trace of the house left, the terrace had vanished. It was as though there had never been a long strange building perched at the summit.

'I don't believe it,' said Paula. 'It's all gone.'

'And now we must go,' Tweed told everyone. He had glanced to the south and the helicopter was no more than a diminishing dot in the sky. 'Get back into the cars, everyone.'

'Where are we going to?' asked Paula.

'I had a call from Monica just before I left the Sacher. We fly to London, then we drive straight down to Dorset.'

'Dorset?'

'There are two men near Shrimpton I want to interview.'

48

In the late afternoon Newman was driving Tweed and Paula down to Dorset. After returning from the collapsed cliff in Slovakia they had avoided Vienna, motoring direct to Schwechat Airport. From there they had caught a flight to Zurich where they had changed planes and flown on to Heathrow.

Tweed had spent a short time with the Director, Howard, then he had left for Dorset. Butler had earlier arrived at Park Crescent, as instructed by Tweed after destroying the communications turret at the Château d'Avignon. Marler and Newman, who had flown back with Tweed, had gone home to get some sleep.

'How do you know both Willie and Amos are back in Dorset?' asked Paula.

'Because at Park Crescent I called Chief Inspector

Buchanan. You may remember I arranged for Roy to go down with his side-kick, Sergeant Warden, to investigate the strange village of Shrimpton.'

'I do remember. Seems ages ago. Did they find anything?'

'Yes. Patrol cars had to be called in urgently from all over the county – many with armed men inside them. Buchanan had discovered those silent houses in the village were the hiding place of saboteurs – trained thugs from London and the North. They were waiting to travel to a certain Midlands town where they'd have collected containers of deadly bacillus to distribute to reservoirs all over Britain.'

'Bacillus!' Paula exclaimed. 'How horrific.'

'Roy Buchanan had them all rounded up in Shrimpton and carted off for intensive questioning. Some of them broke. Their controller was a man called Conway.'

'Who *is* Conway?'

'That's what we're going to Dorset to find out. Both Amos and Willie are back in their homes. Roy checked that out.'

'Is Conway that important?'

'I think,' Tweed said grimly, 'he is the mastermind behind the whole vast operation which was planned to be launched from the East.'

'I can't see either Amos or Willie being Conway,' Paula replied.

'It could be a third party,' said Tweed. 'Not something I want to speculate on any more.'

Well, it is a glorious day, Paula thought. The sun was shining in a clear blue sky. It was very warm for Britain, but the heat was nothing like what they had endured on the plain on their way to Slovakia.

'You are both armed?' Tweed asked suddenly.

'A Smith & Wesson in my hip holster,' Newman assured him.

'And I picked up a Browning while we were at Park Crescent,' said Paula.

'Good.'

Sitting in the back next to Tweed, Paula was as surprised as Newman. It was rare for Tweed to put such a question when they were on what they both assumed would be a peaceful visit.

'It could be very dangerous,' Tweed remarked.

'Well, we've experienced plenty of danger already abroad,' Paula pointed out.

'So,' Tweed hammered home, 'it would be easy to be complacent on home ground.'

'I'm so glad to be on home ground. Dorset is a beautiful county. It's such a relief to be back among gently rolling hills with here and there a clump of trees. I'm feeling less tense already.'

Tweed grunted, gave her a look. She decided she'd better be more careful what she said. It was early evening as they entered the old town of Dorchester, driving through the narrow main street lined with buildings which had been built centuries before. As he reached the far outskirts Newman turned north on the road to Yeovil. Soon he was looking for the turning on his left. He had passed the road to Evershot and later he saw the signpost. *Shrimpton.*

Tweed's warning remarks had gradually sunk in to both Newman and Paula. There was an edgy silence inside the car as he drove down the tree-lined lane. There was no other traffic and Paula had the odd sense of entering a secret world. They could see the first houses in the distance, the beginning of High Lane, the main street Tweed and Newman had walked down during their earlier visit before heading into Europe. Tweed leaned forward.

'Bob, can you pull into that field as you did before? I'd like to walk down the street, again as we did before. We'll call in at that pub, the Dog and Whistle.'

When Newman had backed his Mercedes into the field they all got out. The cobbled street was so narrow the sun no longer shone on them. It was close to dusk. Paula was struck by the heavy silence of the atmosphere as she walked alongside Tweed. He glanced at her, seemed to read her mind.

'Just like the silence of Morzach before the Croats attacked us.'

'There's no one about. It's eerie. And look at the cottages. They don't look occupied.'

'They are empty now. Buchanan cleared out the saboteurs. It seemed like this when we last here. Remember, Bob?'

'Yes, I certainly do. And to think these places were full of saboteurs. They must have kept very quiet.'

'Look at the frayed net curtains,' Paula commented in a quiet voice. It was a place where you naturally whispered. 'I'd have said no one had lived here for years.'

'Which was the impression we were supposed to get,' said Tweed. 'Mr Conway thought of almost everything. Here's the pub.'

They went inside and the men sitting behind benches were again farm-workers, chatting in subdued tones. The same barman was behind the counter.

'Back again, sir,' he said cheerfully. 'I never forget a face.'

'I'll have a mild and bitter,' said Tweed to merge into the atmosphere. 'What about you two?'

Paula ordered an orange juice while Newman plumped for a Scotch. Tweed stayed by the bar after paying, continued talking to the barman as he sipped the drink.

'I believe my friends are back. Wellesley Carrington for one.'

'The Cap'n. Yes, he's at home again in Dovecote

Manor. Funny thing is he hasn't been in here. Usually comes here when he gets back from abroad.'

'I seem to recall you said he was a bit of a one for the ladies,' Newman reminded him. 'Probably got a girl-friend or two he's entertaining.'

'Don't think so.' The barman was polishing a glass. 'The postman was in here when he came off duty. He'd delivered one of those registered envelopes, a thick one. Said the Cap'n was on his own. In a bit of a mood, the postman said.'

'Then there's my other friend, Amos Lodge,' Tweed remarked.

'Oh, he's back, too. Got back after the Cap'n. Imagine he'd been abroad too. Brown as a berry. Haven't seen him since he returned to The Minotaur.'

'It struck me the names ought to be reversed,' Tweed said casually. 'The Minotaur would be a better name for Dovecote Manor with all that weird statuary and lakes Carrington has in his large garden.'

'Funny you should say that.' The barman leaned on the counter, lowered his voice. 'You remember Jed, who was here last time you were here? He used to do the garden for Amos. He tried to get the Cap'n to give him some work, saw round the crazy garden. The Cap'n wouldn't take him on, said he preferred to look after the place himself. Likes his privacy.'

'Well, I think we'd better be going,' said Tweed after checking his watch. 'Sorry to leave the drink, but I had one in another pub and I'm driving.'

'You're wise. We hadn't see the police for years. Then recently in the middle of the night they raided all the cottages. No idea why.'

'Oh, there was one more thing,' Tweed added. 'Last time you said the whole village was owned by a man called Shafto, that he rented out the cottages. Ever heard the name Conway?'

'Never. Drive carefully.'

Keeping up with Paula, who was striding out, they hurried back up High Lane. To Paula, watching her footing on the cobbles, High Lane seemed to go on for ever. The only sound was that of their footfalls.

'You're stepping it out,' Newman remarked.

'I don't like this place,' said Paula. 'Gives me the creeps.'

'Ghosts from long ago,' suggested Tweed.

'I can do without any more remarks like that,' she retorted. 'I have the feeling something awful happened here long ago.'

'Shafto. Conway,' mused Newman. 'Why the different names?'

'Because Mr Conway is a devious and secretive man,' Tweed told them. 'Here's the car. Do you want to drive, Paula?'

'I'd sooner Bob went on driving.'

'We'll go and see Willie first. While he's still here,' said Tweed as he settled himself in the back with Paula.

Newman drove through the village and past the pub at a moderate speed. He remembered the way to Dovecote Manor and they had left the village behind as he approached the entrance. Again the gold-painted wrought-iron gates were open and beyond them the curving drive led up to the Georgian house.

Glare lights attached to the whole of the front of the house were on. Tweed couldn't remember seeing them when he had last visited Willie so they must have been installed recently. He wondered why. Again a new red Porsche was parked on the tarred turn-round close to the entrance. There were lights on inside the house.

'So, we come full circle,' Newman commented as he parked behind the Porsche. 'This is where it all started.'

'No, it isn't,' contradicted Paula. 'It started when I was in Vienna, standing in a courtyard in Annagasse, watching the woman in a black robe and veil entering and leaving Norbert Engel's building.'

As the three of them got out of the car Tweed issued a fresh warning.

'Be ready for anything.'

49

History does repeat itself, Tweed thought. He pressed the bell, waited and when the door was opened Willie stood framed in the entrance, wearing a navy blue tracksuit. He smiled warmly at his visitors and ushered them inside.

'Welcome to my humble home.'

'I don't think I have to make introductions,' replied Tweed.

'Of course not. I do have someone with me but you are still most welcome.

He *has* got a girlfriend with him, Newman thought. He was wrong. Willie closed the door to the panelled hall, led Paula to an open door and into the spacious drawing room. As she entered Amos Lodge stood up from a large couch and began plumping up a cushion in one corner.

'A long way from Zurich,' Amos said in his gravelly voice. 'I expect, like me, you are all glad to be back in England.'

'When did you fly back?' Tweed asked, sitting in a carver chair.

'Yesterday.' Amos beckoned to Paula. 'Please do come and join me. You really are a most attractive lady.'

'Thank you.'

Paula thought it would be more comfortable to sit in the opposite corner of the couch. Like Amos, she shifted a cushion so she could relax. Newman occupied another carver chair close to Tweed. From where he sat he could see through the open French windows at the back into the extensive garden as far as the strange stone arch inscribed with peculiar symbols. It was a warm evening and the open French windows freshened up the room.

'Drinks for everyone,' Willie said buoyantly. 'Paula?'

'A glass of dry white wine would go down well.'

Tweed asked for orange juice while Newman, expecting to drive, also requested orange juice. Amos had a drink he didn't recognize. Looking at her companion at the other end of the couch Paula thought he looked more square than ever. His large bulk was held erect and his eyes flashed from behind the square-rimmed glasses.

'Well, you survived,' Willie said jovially as he placed Tweed's drink on a coffee table.

'Yes, no thanks to someone,' Tweed replied.

There was an awkward silence as Willie fetched more drinks and then sprawled in an armchair, long legs stretched out and crossed at his ankles. He raised his glass.

'Here's to survival.'

'Of the good,' Tweed added.

'Odd remark that, old chap,' Willie responded. 'Don't get it.'

'Someone does,' Tweed went on, staring straight at him.

'Things looked pretty grim – maybe still do,' said Amos.

'The international crisis is over,' Tweed told him. 'I don't think the media have got hold of it yet, but I heard at Park Crescent that the Head of State has been removed from power. His generals were so alarmed at the arrival of so much naval power in the Indian Ocean they staged a coup.'

'That didn't come into my strategic calculations. But it is always the unexpected which turns the tide. I understand why the Americans reacted so quickly. What persuaded the British to send a submarine?'

'I did.'

The door bell rang and Willie excused himself. When he came back he escorted Christopher Kane into the room. Paula was astonished. Christopher caught her expression, came forward, bowed and kissed her hand. Straightening up, he looked round, chose an armchair, settled himself in it and adopted the same posture Willie had. He stretched out his long legs and crossed them at the ankles.

'*You* did?' said Amos with almost a growl.

'Did what?' Willie asked in an offhand way.

He poured Christopher a glass of red wine, knowing what his new guest liked. This time Willie sat very erect in a carver chair. He studied Tweed as he sipped his drink.

'I'm going to sound egotistical, but I can't help that,' Tweed began. 'While I was at the Château des Avenières in France I spent a long time on the phone. First, I contacted Christopher and eventually asked him to catch the first flight to London. Then I phoned the Prime Minister and explained certain developments. I had to go on at him, threatening to get in touch with CNN and the press to tell them that I had told him. To give him credit, he agreed to phone first the President in Washington, then the President of France and the Chancellor of Germany. It was fortunate that the US Fifth Fleet was in a position to sail into the Indian Ocean immediately. The PM sent a nuclear submarine to support the Fifth Fleet. It fired a trial missile from the same area. Also, a spoke was put in the wheel of a fiendish operation to poison the reservoirs in the West.'

'Poison?' Willie enquired with obvious interest.

495

'Bacilli.'

'What on earth have bacilli to do with it?' asked Amos.

'That was what the enemy had arranged to be put into our drinking water. The same with France and Germany. The agents who would have laced our reservoirs with bacilli were lodged in Shrimpton. The villain is a local man called Conway.'

'Conway?' queried Willie. 'Never heard of him.'

'Neither has the barman at the Dog and Whistle. Which is very curious. Barmen usually know everything that's going on locally. He doesn't know of any Conway.'

'Not surprised,' Willie said. 'I'd have heard of him.'

'Would you?' Tweed asked with a smile.

'Of course I would. I go into that pub for a drink.'

'But you don't take any of your glamorous girlfriends there.'

'Of course I don't. Hardly the thing to do, old chap.'

'You knew at various times Tina Langley, Karin Berg and Simone Carnot?'

'Over a period of time, yes.'

'And where did each of these three women go when they left here?'

'With Amos. He likes women too.'

'This is nonsense,' growled Amos. 'I've never heard of any of these women.'

'Of course you have,' Willie protested angrily. 'You invited each of them back to The Minotaur to have a drink. What's the matter with you?'

'You made a mistake a few minutes ago, Amos,' Tweed interjected. 'I made a reference to naval power in the Indian Ocean. The American deployment has been widely reported, yet you said, "What persuaded the British to send a submarine?" So how do you know? Incidentally, Hassan was captured and he's trying to

496

save his skin by telling everything. He's implicated you up to the hilt – Mr Conway.'

Amos's right hand disappeared under the cushion he had plumped up. His movement was so quick it was a blur until his hand reappeared holding a Mauser – aimed point-blank at Paula. He stood up.

'I'd hate to shoot a woman . . .'

'Then don't,' rasped Newman.

He was holding his Smith & Wesson, the muzzle pointing at Amos's chest. He remained seated as Paula stared at Amos, her eyes never leaving his. Amos moved slowly back to the open French windows. He began speaking as though orating at the Kongresshaus in Zurich.

'The West is decadent, enfeebled. It has no moral code. It is going down like the Roman Empire did when that organization gave itself over to sexual orgies, and society collapsed, as it has in the West.'

'Pull that trigger and you're a dead man,' Newman warned.

For a large man, Amos moved with great speed, vanishing out of the open French windows into the garden. Newman aimed, then lowered his gun. Amos was a shadow, zigzagging as he ran deeper into the garden, passing under the weird arch. Newman went after him followed by Paula and Tweed. As he left the room Tweed glanced back, saw Willie grab hold of a long thick walking stick.

'That's no use,' he shouted.

He ran after the others. Behind him in the drawing room Willie opened a panel in the wall, pressed down switches. Outside in the maze-like garden lights came on and illuminated the garden islands. Willie followed Tweed, holding his walking stick like a club.

'He's gone under the arch,' Paula shouted back to Tweed.

She ran under it and saw Newman ahead of her. No sign of Amos. They heard the sound of an outboard motor starting up. One of the dinghies was speeding towards the island where a weird statue of a man and woman with a serpent twined round them stood. Newman had stopped, was aiming his gun.

'He's not in the dinghy,' Paula shouted. 'He set it going to fool us!'

Newman started running again, crouching as he ran. Arriving at the second lake, with perched on another island an eight-sided temple, the windows painted black, he paused, stood in a shadow, listened. Paula heard pounding feet running at top speed behind her. It was Willie, holding his stick as though on a hike.

'Amos was out here when I got back!' he shouted. 'I think he concealed weapons.'

He charged past her after Newman, who was again running. To Paula everything seemed bizarre – the statuary, the temple illuminated by spotlights. A nightmare. Ahead of Willie, Newman reached the third lake after passing through the avenue of box hedge. At the end of the avenue he had paused again, gun gripped in both hands. He swivelled it to his left and then his right, suspecting Amos was waiting in ambush. No Amos. He ran on despite a warning shout from Willie.

'You're going into a wilderness!'

Newman slowed down, then began to creep forward through a mass of undergrowth. To his right was the third lake with another island. Perched on it was the squat Assyrian-type building and the stone plaque with the Turkish flag engraved into it. The shore of the lake was bordered by trees with thick trunks. Dense banks of reeds stretched out into the lake, seen by a searchlight projecting from the island.

As he passed one tree Amos, crouching low, appeared behind him holding a machine-pistol. He took aim at Newman's back. Paula opened her mouth to shout a warning she knew would be too late. Willie appeared behind Amos, brought down his clublike stick on Amos's shoulder. Amos dropped his weapon, started to stand up. Willie brought down the stick on his head. The large man staggered back, fell into the lake among the reeds.

Paula saw his arms struggling, waving the reeds. The arms sank. His hands struggled, disappeared below the reeds. Newman, who had turned, seen what had happened, began to strip off his jacket to go in after him. Willie gripped his arm.

'No good. You'd drown too. The reeds strangle you. I had a German shepherd dog. Went in after a swan. Just vanished. Never seen since. Amos has gone for good.'

'We can't do a thing, then?' asked Tweed, who had caught up.

'Not a thing,' said Willie. 'We'll have the lake dragged. It may take weeks to find him, if ever we do. We never found the dog.'

Epilogue

At Tweed's suggestion they were driving back to the country hotel, Summer Lodge, at Evershot, to spend the night. They had left behind Christopher, who was alert and wanted to talk to Willie. Paula felt exhausted, but her mind was still racing as Newman drove through the night.

'Did you always suspect Amos?' she asked Tweed.

'Yes and no. I was bluffing, of course, when I said Hassan was spilling the beans. We had no proof against Amos so I had to provoke him into giving himself away.'

'You didn't suspect him earlier but you did when we arrived at Willie's house?'

'The massive operation which was planned, including the killing of the men from the *Institut* – who might have eventually alerted their governments – was clearly the work of a master strategist. Which was Amos's genius. Also his attitude towards the West – especially his brilliant speech at the Kongresshaus in Zurich – suggested to me he could be the mastermind. Mind you, there are people who would agree with a lot of what he said. It was his solution – being taken over by the East – which was flawed, evil.'

'You showed great perception.'

'I can't take too much credit. Willie is an arms dealer, but also a patriot. When he discovered that bacilli were

500

to be used he reported it to Christoper who in turn reported to me. Fortunately Christopher had discovered the antidote to the bacilli. All the containers produced by a man called Harbin were lined with the antidote on Christopher's instructions. Harbin didn't know what the substance was doing, that it had eliminated the bacilli in the containers. At my suggestion over the phone from Europe, Willie pretended to be driving to Slovakia with the "sample". He called Hassan, telling him where he had reached on his trip. Actually, all the calls were made from Folkestone – in case Hassan had him watched. Customs faked a search for drugs to make Willie's story convincing. Another man, dressed like Willie, eventually drove via Le Shuttle to a place east of Paris. Harbin, by the way, is under arrest by Special Branch. His chemical plant has been sealed off.'

'So we have to thank you, Christoper and Willie.'

'Let's not forget Emilio Vitorelli. He destroyed Hassan – and in doing so also eliminated The Sisterhood.'

'I feel sorry for Vitorelli. I think he's a very unhappy man.'

'And likely to remain so for the rest of his life.'

In Rome it was dark when Mario watched as Vitorelli walked slowly along the edge of the Borghese Gardens. He walked like a man in a dream. Several attractive women looked at him but he did not see them. He continued walking with plodding steps.

Reaching the balcony which overlooks the Pincio Terrace he stopped at the exact place where he had seen his fiancée, Gina, her face bandaged from the horrific acid scars, climb on to the balcony. Too far away, he had called out to her.

She had not turned her head as she sat poised on the

balcony, then plunged to her death on the iron-hard stone of the piazza. Placing both hands on the balcony, he stared down. He was looking at the exact spot where she had hit the stone so far down. There were tears in his eyes.

He had had to identify her body before it was moved. It was a moment he would never forget. Now he had done what he had to do. He had destroyed the woman who had destroyed Gina's face. No amount of plastic surgery would have repaired the damage, a top surgeon had told her.

He gave a deep sigh. Then he began to walk slowly back to where Mario was anxiously waiting. It was the last time he ever went to the balcony. For the rest of his life he would never walk or drive through the piazza again.